Praise for

THE LOST PASSENGER

"Stories of loss and survival on the *Titanic* never cease to fascinate us, and France Quinn's *The Lost Passenger* is no exception. This deftly plotted novel goes far beyond a suspenseful page-turner. It's also a heartfelt immigrant's story, as well as a story of motherhood, reinvention, and a testament to the human spirit. I couldn't put it down."

—RENEE ROSEN, author of *The Social Graces* and *Park Avenue Summer*

"*The Lost Passenger* tells the story of an emotional transformation: a young woman's journey from a stifling, sheltered life to one of risk, impoverishment, and survival. Quinn explores both the gilded realm of London's high society and the desperate underbelly of New York's Lower East Side, allowing her heroine to not merely overcome the odds against her, but to thrive. It's a compelling examination of the cost of dreams, the delusions of the heart, and the unbreakable bond of mother and child."

—SHANA ABÉ, author of *An American Beauty* and *The Second Mrs. Astor*

"An acutely observed account of one woman's struggle to escape the shackles of an aristocratic marriage, and the desperate decisions she has to make after the sinking of the *Titanic*. You'll be rooting for Elinor Coombes all the way in this compelling, heart-warming novel."

—GILL PAUL, author of *Women and Children First* and *The Secret Wife*

"Move over Rose and Jack, because Elinor Coombes has come to tell her story of surviving one of the greatest maritime disasters of all time, and it's a story that readers won't want to miss. From the richly drawn characters to the vivid descriptions of New York in the early twentieth century, Frances Quinn's *The Lost Passenger* stands out as a must-read for 2025."

—MICHELLE MORAN, author of *Maria* and *Nefertiti*

"A juicy story of Dickensian scope, underpinned with serious themes of class and misogyny, and packed with color and characters that leap from the page . . . Quinn deftly leads you from domestic turmoil to heart-stopping adventure, bringing the pre–World War I period to life with just the right amount of historic detail. . . . A delightful tale of female courage against the odds that will keep you pinned to your chair till the last page."

—JENNY LECOAT, author of *The Girl from the Channel Islands*

"*The Lost Passenger* is storytelling at its very finest. Quinn writes a multi-layered novel with absolute ease, bringing her characters wonderfully to life. This spellbinding and evocative tale about Elinor Coombes takes the reader on a journey from the suffocating, cold world of aristocratic pre-war England to the overcrowded maelstrom of Lower East Side New York, and the stark contrast of poverty, hope, and love she finds there. The author perfectly captures the terror and tragedy of the sinking of the *Titanic* without salacious melodrama, and the jeopardy Elinor finds herself in as she makes life-altering choices to protect her son and build a new life is utterly captivating. I cannot recommend this book highly enough!"

—LOUISE FEIN, author of *The Hidden Child* and
Daughter of The Reich

"I'm such a fan of Frances Quinn's writing and her new novel certainly doesn't disappoint. Elinor is such a wonderful heroine and I was rooting for her all the way. It's a thoroughly enjoyable novel about being brave enough to grab hold of a second chance and make the most of it."

—LOUISE HARE, author of *This Lovely City*

Also by Frances Quinn

The Smallest Man
That Bonesetter Woman

THE LOST PASSENGER

THE LOST PASSENGER

a novel

FRANCES QUINN

BALLANTINE BOOKS
NEW YORK

A Ballantine Books Trade Paperback Original

Published in the United States by Ballantine Books,
an imprint of Random House, a division of
Penguin Random House LLC, New York.

BALLANTINE BOOKS & colophon are registered
trademarks of Penguin Random House LLC.

LIBRARY OF CONGRESS CATALOGING-IN-PUBLICATION DATA
Names: Quinn, Frances (Journalist), author.
Title: The lost passenger : a novel / Frances Quinn.
Description: New York : Ballantine Books, 2025.
Identifiers: LCCN 2024057865 (print) | LCCN 2024057866 (ebook) |
ISBN 9780593973035 (trade paperback ; acid-free paper) |
ISBN 9780593973042 (ebook)
Subjects: LCGFT: Historical fiction. | Novels.
Classification: LCC PS3617.U5638 L67 2025 (print) |
LCC PS3617.U5638 (ebook) | DDC 813/.6—dc23/eng/20241203
LC record available at https://lccn.loc.gov/2024057865
LC ebook record available at https://lccn.loc.gov/2024057866

Printed in the United States of America on acid-free paper

randomhousebooks.com

1st Printing

Title-page image by BCFC (life ring buoy)

Book design by Elizabeth A. D. Eno

For my friends Mikael and Lena Westin,
Camilla and Magnus Lif, and Ann Dahlqvist,
with thanks for good times (and Swedish practice)

THE LOST PASSENGER

On the day I stole another woman's life, I saw New York for the first time, against a charcoal-gray sky with rain teeming down in sheets. It wasn't much of a sight, but I didn't care and I don't suppose anyone else standing there on the deck, soaked to the skin, did either. We were all just desperate to see land, though the downpour was so heavy that the buildings looming up ahead were no more than vague shapes.

Suddenly the gray was lit up; a flotilla of tugboats sped toward us, cameras pointing up, flashbulbs exploding, men yelling questions.

"Damn journalists," said someone behind me. "Parasites, the lot of them."

I stepped back quickly, into the shadows. I'd been concentrating so hard on what I was about to do, thinking through how it could work—*if* it could work—and telling myself it was the only way, I'd not given a thought to the fact that we'd be news. But of course we were: over a thousand people had died, on a ship that was claimed to be unsinkable, and we were the ones left to tell the story. Well, I wouldn't be telling them mine.

CHAPTER 1

If I shut my eyes, I can still picture the invitation that started it all. Thick, cream-colored card, embossed with black copperplate.

LORD AND LADY BURNHAM REQUEST
THE PLEASURE OF YOUR COMPANY FOR A
NEW YEAR'S BALL AT CHILVERTON HALL,
12TH JANUARY 1910

I'd been with my father at Star Mill all afternoon, arguing up hill and down dale with him over dye samples for our spring prints. I won the fight for sapphire blue and a beautiful emerald green—the ladies' magazines were going mad about jewel colors—and while he made out the order, I sorted through the post. Mostly invoices, but then this very swish cream envelope.

His eyebrows shot up as he read the words. Our house, Clereston, wasn't far from Lord and Lady Burnham's estate, but we didn't move in those circles at all.

"Why the heck would they invite us?" He held the card

over the wastepaper basket, his eyes twinkling. "We'll say no, won't we?"

He knew perfectly well that I'd be for going. I'd been taken with the idea of going to a ball since my mam told me the story of Cinderella, when I was a little girl, and just lately I'd read all Jane Austen's novels—even *Lady Susan*, which hardly anyone likes—and they're full of them. Of course we'd go.

As we walked in that evening, both a bit nervous though we'd not admitted it, he said, "Think how proud your mam would be."

He was wishing she was with us, and I was too, but then there'd barely been a day in the past five years when I hadn't thought of her and missed her, and him the same. And she'd have loved it, my mam: women in satin and silk, jewels glittering under the chandeliers; men in tailcoats with snow-white waistcoats and ties; a violin quartet playing; and this lovely hum of conversation and laughter over it all. Everything I'd imagined.

Lady Burnham greeted us, very friendly, and promised to introduce us to "some delightful people" once everyone had arrived. After we'd stood and watched the dancing for a while, my father went to refill our glasses and she led him over to the far side of the room, where he was soon caught up in conversation. I had *Pride and Prejudice* and Elizabeth Bennet's humiliation at the Meryton ball fresh in my mind, so I wasn't going to stand about looking desperate for someone to ask me up. I'd tucked myself a bit behind a pillar when a lanky young man, a few years older than me, walked by. He stepped back, and smiled.

"Are you hiding? Wouldn't blame you, there are some dreadful people here."

I was flattered he didn't lump me in with the dreadful people, and that smile, easy and open, made me like him straight away. Doing my best to sound as though I went to balls every night of the week, I said, "Just waiting for my father to stop chatting and bring me a glass of champagne." And then, because he had kind eyes. "But I am hiding, a bit. I don't know anyone here."

"We must remedy that." He put out his hand. "Frederick Coombes."

"I'm Elinor Hayward."

"There, now we know each other. I'd ask for a dance, but I'm a little incapacitated." He tapped his leg. "Riding accident, sprained my ankle."

"That sounds painful. Did you fall off?"

"Rather spectacularly. But it'll mend, and it gives me a good excuse to stay here and talk to you."

When my father came back, I introduced them.

"Of course! Hayward! I should have realized," said Frederick. "You're the cotton king."

My father rolled his eyes. "Just a daft thing the papers say."

He loved it really. They all called him that, and they liked to tell his story. How he'd started out working in a little drapers' shop in Manchester, realized he could run it better than the owner, scrimped and saved to buy it, and built the rest from there: the mills and the printworks, two more shops, and hundreds of people working for him.

"Very impressive," said Frederick, "what you've done with your business. Didn't I read you've electrified one of your mills completely?"

"Star Mill," said my father. "You read about that?"

"I did. Very interesting."

I checked his face for signs of sarcasm, because not everyone found the cotton trade as fascinating as we did. But he seemed properly interested, even asking quite a sensible question about how we'd switched from steam to electricity. I liked him all the more then, because I was proud of my father's achievements, and our business.

Even so, when a bell rang for supper, I expected he'd make his excuses. My father was talking about his new looms by then, and my mam always said that if you let him near the subject of machinery, you'd get the ins and outs of a pig's backside, no detail spared. But Frederick said, "I wonder, Mr. Hayward, may I introduce you to my mother? My father was unable to attend this evening, so it falls to me to take her in to supper, and I was hoping you might allow me to escort Miss Hayward."

My father looked as surprised as I felt, but he said yes. (It was only much, much later that it struck me: neither of them asked me.) We followed him over to the other side of the room.

"Miss Hayward, Mr. Hayward . . . my mother, Lady Storton."

Lady? I wasn't expecting that, and my father's intake of breath said he wasn't either.

She was frighteningly elegant, slender on the verge of bony. The dress was very good silk—my father was pricing it with his eyes—and diamonds glittered at her throat. I'd a diamond necklace on too, but mine was bought that week, and I kept checking it was still there. Hers had the look of a family heirloom and she wore it as though she hardly knew she had it on.

Lady Storton smiled. "I see my son has found better company than mine. May I prevail on you to take me in, Mr. Hayward?"

My father copied the way Frederick held out his arm to me, and we strolled in to supper, the cotton king and the cotton king's daughter, with the wife and son of an earl.

It was stupidly easy to fall in love with Frederick; I got halfway there that very evening. But I'd like to point out, before you decide I must've been soft in the head, that I was nineteen, he was the first man ever to pay attention to me, and he was very, very charming.

As Lady Storton swept my father away, he waited on me as if I were a princess, fetching me a glass of champagne, then dashing off and coming back with a plate of chicken in a creamy sauce speckled with herbs.

"Lady Burnham's cook is famous for her fricassée. I had to distract the Duchess of Bolton to snaffle this portion."

"How did you do that?"

"Told her the Prince of Wales had made a surprise appearance. She'll never speak to me again when she finds out he hasn't, so I hope you wouldn't have preferred the roast beef."

I'd read that a lady never finishes everything on her plate, but it was quite a small portion.

"I should probably warn you," I said, "that I'm hungry and I might have to embarrass you by eating the lot."

He grinned. "Eat away. We'll be pariahs together."

I'd never been flirted with before, but when you've read as many novels as I had, you know what it looks like. What I didn't know was how it makes you feel, when a personable young man ignores everyone else in the room to talk to you, and looks into your eyes as though he's never seen eyes before, and every so often brushes your hand with his, as though by accident but definitely not. And all the while, we chatted like old friends, finding we had all sorts in common. Neither of us thought much of the latest Mary Pickford film; both of us were intrigued by the rumors of a fresh attempt on the South Pole. We'd both read about the new ship being built in Belfast, the biggest ever, with restaurants and squash courts and a swimming bath, and when I said my father planned to book us on its maiden voyage, Frederick was envious.

"How marvelous. I'd love an adventure like that!"

We'd ordered our car for midnight—late for my father, who

liked to be up and getting on with the day before most people had even had breakfast—so all too soon, it was time to go.

Dropping a kiss on my hand that made me blush, Frederick said, "This won't, I hope, be goodbye. I'm staying here at Chilverton a while. Might I call on you both before I go back to Kent?"

Everyone knows what it means when a single man asks to call on a household with an unmarried daughter in it. Even my father, who normally paid very little attention to anything that didn't involve cotton.

"Well," he said in the car, "I wasn't expecting this." He drew himself up and said in a plummy voice, "Lady Elinor, pleased to make your acquaintance."

"Stop it!"

"Any fool could see he likes you. But do you like him? If not, earl or no earl, we'll call a halt to it."

"I do like him."

"Good, because so do I. And I daresay we'll see him at Clereston before the week's out."

We did. He came to tea twice, entertaining us with stories of his time at Eton, where he said he was hopeless at everything except cricket. I had a copy of *Villette* beside me the second time, and he asked if I was fond of reading. My father chuckled.

"Fond of reading? She's read every book you can imagine. I've no patience for stories, me, but she gets through them by the cartload."

He made it sound as though I read nothing but cheap novelettes, so I said quickly, "I've just finished *Under the Greenwood Tree* by Thomas Hardy."

"Ah," said Frederick. "One of my favorite authors."

"Mine too! Which is your favorite of his?"

He thought for a moment, his head on one side. "I think it is *Under the Greenwood Tree*, actually."

"You didn't find the end unconvincing?"

"Long time since I read it, but yes, I seem to recall I did." He held out his cup. "May I trouble you for a little more tea?"

Once I'd poured the tea and offered him more fruit cake, the conversation turned, disappointingly, to the weather, and what sort of summer we seemed likely to have. When that tedious subject was exhausted and I was about to ask what he thought of *The Mayor of Casterbridge*, he stood to leave.

Thanking us for our company, he said to my father, "Might I visit one of your mills while I'm up here? I'd be fascinated to see how it all works."

After he'd gone, my father said, "If he's interested in cotton milling, lass, I'm Harry Houdini. Shall I bring him back here for some dinner after he comes to the mill?"

"I'd like that," I said.

I wore my pale green with the rosebud print and asked my maid Rose to copy a hairstyle from the *Ladies' Gazette*. With her usual antipathy to anything new, she warned gloomily that she doubted she could do it and it might not suit me anyway. But I was pleased with the result, and even more pleased with Frederick's appreciative glance.

It was a raw old evening and, as we sat down, Frederick gestured to our big iron radiators.

"These are marvelous. Winterton's riddled with drafts, colder inside than out. Do you have electricity throughout too?"

"Everywhere," said my father. "You don't, at Winterton Hall?"

"Only the main rooms. Hell of a job—sixteenth-century walls don't lend themselves to wiring."

My father gave a low whistle. "That old? Upkeep must be summat terrible."

"It's never-ending."

"You want to do what we did here," said my father. "Knock the whole thing down and build new. Save you money in the long run."

For a moment, Frederick looked as though my father had suggested he eat a small child for breakfast. I had the impression he was choosing his words carefully when he replied.

"You've done a tremendous job here, no doubt about it. But when the place has been in the family for four centuries, it gives one a certain responsibility to the generations who've gone before and the ones to come."

I should've paid a lot more attention to that remark, and the look, but he quickly smiled and said, "I imagine it's much the same with a business like yours."

"Oh aye," said my father. "Nowt I'd like more than to hand it on to a son, when the time comes, but it wasn't to be. Our Elinor's got a cracking head for business, mind you—it was her idea to go into printed cottons and get the premium ourselves, instead of handing it to the printworks. Just a pity she wasn't a boy."

He threw me a warning glance, but I'd no thought to start that row again. I'd argued it till I was blue in the face, but more from frustration than any real expectation that I could change his mind. Because the truth was, I knew he was right. The trade would never accept a woman at the head of Haywards, and the solution he'd found, bequeathing the company in trust for the workers, with a management committee I could be part of, was the best I could hope for, when the time came.

Anyway, Frederick had obviously heard enough about cotton, because he politely changed the subject, complimenting the apple charlotte and asking if we had our own orchards.

I nearly fell off my chair when, as he was ready to leave, he asked if he could have a word with my father. Surely he couldn't mean . . . I'd known he *might* have intentions, but I'd imagined a lot more snatched glances when my father wasn't looking before things went any further.

I paced the drawing room floor, my stomach jumping and jittering like I'd swallowed a bat. Then the door opened, my father winked at me, and I knew.

Next morning, I was a cat on tacks. He was to come at eleven, and I didn't want to be running downstairs all red and flustered if he was early, so by half past ten I was in the drawing room. Sitting first on one couch, then the other, arranging and rearranging my skirts, jumping up to check my hair in the mirror, and then having to arrange them all over again.

We'd talked, me and my father, about how sudden it all was.

"Imagine you and Mam deciding to marry so quickly."

My father laughed. "It's not as though you've to save to make a home, like we did. But it's up to you—it's a good match, but you've no need to say yes unless you're sure you want to."

But you see, I did want to. I was dreaming of love, as most nineteen-year-old girls are. Frederick was so charming, I was half dizzy with the excitement of it, and the suddenness only made it more romantic—show me a girl who'd choose a sensible long courtship over a man who couldn't wait to make her his wife. And though I was sure my father meant it when he said it was up to me, I wanted to make him proud.

Frederick arrived on time and said, with a sheepish smile, "I think you know why I'm here."

I nodded, my cheeks warm.

"Then I won't witter on about the weather. I'll come straight to the point and ask if you'll do me the honor of becoming my wife."

What?

Wasn't he supposed to say he loved me first? Even the first

time Mr. Darcy proposed to Elizabeth, when he was so be-
grudging, he said that. My surprise must have shown.

"Your father thought you were agreeable, but if he was mistaken—"

The disappointment on his face said what his words hadn't.
Perhaps in real life people didn't say the other thing out loud,
or not yet, anyway.

"My father wasn't mistaken."

"So your answer is yes?" he said, taking my hand and looking into my eyes.

I nodded, suddenly shy at the thought that he was about to
kiss me. But of course he didn't: he wasn't a savage.

"Wonderful!" he said. "Let's tell your father the good news."

They announced our engagement the very next day, in *The
Times*. We might easily have missed it; we never read the society announcements. But that day, there was a piece about that
new ship, the *Titanic*, saying it'd be at least two years before it
was ready.

"Well," said my father, "I dare say you'll be married by then.
How about we see if Frederick fancies a trip across the Atlantic?"

"He will! He said it sounded marvelous."

"And you won't mind your old father being a gooseberry?"

"Of course not."

"Then we'll do it."

I tore the article out to save it, and as I refolded the paper,
there was my name.

Lord and Lady Storton of Winterton Hall are delighted to
announce the engagement of their son, Frederick, to Elinor
Hayward, daughter of Mr. and the late Mrs. Robert Hayward,
of Clereston.

He must've telephoned the newspaper straight away. What girl wouldn't think that romantic, that he was so keen to tell the world? It made up for the actual proposal being, if I was honest, a bit disappointing. But my father frowned.

"That's quick off the mark. There's the settlement to discuss, and I don't want them backing me into a corner."

"Who's ever managed to back you into a corner?"

He smiled. "Don't you fret about it, anyway. You start thinking about wedding dresses."

CHAPTER 2

A week later we motored down to Kent to meet Frederick's family, stopping overnight on the way. As the car wound its way up a gravel drive edged with lime trees, through woodlands and rolling pastures with deer grazing on one side and sheep on the other, we looked at each other, taken aback. We had grounds at Clereston, but they were a pocket handkerchief compared with this. Then we rounded a bend and there was Winterton Hall: huge, in honey-colored stone, with towers at each corner. Not quite a castle, but not far short.

The entrance hall had a vaulted ceiling like a cathedral, and dark wooden paneling hung with portraits in heavy gold frames. A wide stone staircase led to a gallery running round all four sides, like the center of a spider's web, connecting the two wings on either side. Lady Storton was as forbiddingly elegant as she'd been at the ball, in lilac wool crêpe with a long rope of pearls. She introduced us to Frederick's older sister, Kitty—dark like her mother, and pretty in rose pink, but with a pinched look about her face—and Lord Storton. He was

Frederick to a tee, tall and rangy, with the same fair hair and easy smile.

"It's wonderful to meet you both," he said. "Frederick's told me all about your mills, Mr. Hayward, and how clever the whole setup is. You must tell me all about it over luncheon."

We were on the second course, and the conversation had moved on from our mills to the rumors about the King's health, when Kitty, sitting beside me, noticed me looking at one of the portraits on the wall opposite.

She murmured in my ear, "Great-great-grandmother. It's through her we're distantly related to the King."

"I didn't know that."

"Really?" Still speaking softly, she said, "Surely your father's checked the family tree? Doesn't he want to brag to his friends about how far up you're marrying?"

The words were delivered with such an angelic smile that it took me a moment to realize what she'd said. She broke a little piece off her bread roll, buttered it and popped it into her rosebud mouth, as though we'd just been discussing the weather.

By the time I'd picked my chin up off the table, Lady Storton was saying, "Now, the wedding. We were thinking the second of March."

"That's very quick," said my father. "We've a lot to discuss first."

Lord Storton smiled. "You know how women are with weddings, Mr. Hayward. Let's you and I sit down in the library while Frederick shows Elinor the estate, and we'll have a good talk."

"Fair enough," said my father.

Oh heck. He had that glint in his eye, the one that was always there when he was about to strike a deal. He loved bargaining, my father, and he had three golden rules: look them in the eye and smile when you name your price; hold your nerve once the bargaining starts; and don't miss the moment when you've got them where you want them. I hoped he wouldn't try to drive too hard a bargain over me, just for the challenge of it.

We set off down the drive, Frederick driving a dark green two-seater with a canvas roof. The cabin was tiny, the seats close together, and my stomach was doing somersaults; would he take the chance to kiss me?

Raising his voice over the noisy engine, he said, "Is it what you expected, the house?"

"It's very big. How many rooms is it?"

"Around two hundred, I think, if you include storerooms and the servants' quarters. When we were young, Kitty told me there was a secret room where a monster that ate little boys lived."

"That's not very nice."

"I got my own back. I put a dead mouse in her bed."

I hoped it was a big fat one, and not too freshly dead.

"Do you get on well?" I asked, because he was so nice, and she was horrible.

"Well enough, considering."

"Considering?"

"That Kitty's the eldest, and she doesn't think it's fair that I inherit the estate and not her."

"Can't you share it?"

"Crikey, don't let her hear you suggest that. You don't divide an estate like this—it'd get smaller and smaller over the generations and some poor soul would end up Earl of little more than a farm. And you don't want it inherited down the female line, because then you may as well say it's passed into the husband's family. So it's entailed—passes, whole and complete—to the eldest son of the current heir. That way the title goes with the land."

Ah. Well, I'd good reason to understand Kitty's view on that, but it didn't give her cause to be nasty to me.

"What happens if you don't have a son?"

"We don't talk about that! The title fails. Disappears forever. The entail fails too, so the estate could in theory be bequeathed to a daughter, but as I say, practically speaking, it's out of the family line then, so that's a last resort—ideally there's a cousin or someone to step in instead. But it's never happened, not in thirteen generations. Now, close your eyes. I want to show you my favorite place."

When he stopped the car I opened my eyes to a view that was like a painting: green pastures rolling down to a river fringed by willows, a cluster of thatched cottages in the hazy distance.

"It's looked exactly like this for over two centuries. I've been coming up here since I was a boy, and I never get tired of looking at it." He took my hand and looked into my eyes. "It's a responsibility, an estate like this, the title and everything that goes with it. But I know you'll grow to love this place as much as I do. It's my family's history but it's our children's future too. I hope you won't make me wait too long to share it with you."

And that was how they hooked their fish.

CHAPTER 3

That sunny morning in the spring of 1910, I remember smiling when Rose asked me, as she poked the last diamond pin into my veil, if I wasn't nervous about going to live with "titled folk."

"They're just people, same as us, Rose. They've got different ways, but I'll get used to that, and so will you. I'm sure their servants'll be friendly sorts."

Her face said she doubted it, but that was just Rose, who couldn't see a rain cloud without wondering if she should start building an ark. To tell the truth, though, I *was* a bit anxious about going to live with people I hardly knew, whose world was so different from mine. But I squashed down those fears because Frederick would be there. He loved me, and he'd chosen me despite the differences in our backgrounds. Those differences could be overcome, couldn't they? In books, love bridged gaps as wide as ours and quite a lot wider: Elizabeth Bennet and Mr. Darcy, Gabriel and Bathsheba, Jane Eyre and Mr. Rochester. Even Cinderella, if you thought about it—and yes, I did know that was just a fairy tale, but when a story's been around for that long, wouldn't you think there must be some truth at the heart of it?

If I was trembling as the first notes of the Wedding March rang out, well, what bride can say she isn't nervous at all?

My father squeezed my hand. "You look like a princess."

I didn't know about that, but my dress was fit for one: heavy silk crêpe with a high waist and a bodice overlaid with Flanders lace, the long train scattered with tiny seed pearls. The designer Lady Storton recommended went puce with affrontery when my father asked the cost, and I was relieved when he didn't try to bargain her down. He just winked at me and said, "Only the best for you, lass." And then to her, "Don't stint on those pearls, I want them to show."

As we stepped into the body of the church, I couldn't help a glance across to Frederick's side of the aisle: a sea of expensive hats, perfectly cut morning suits and eyes, eyes, eyes. Inspecting my dress, the pearls at my throat and ears, my face.

They're curious, that's all. You knew to expect that.

I made myself look straight ahead, to where Frederick stood at the altar, handsome in a mulberry frock coat and gray trousers, waiting for me to become his wife. At that moment he turned, and it made my heart flip to see that he looked nervous too. Then he smiled, that same easy, charming smile I'd seen when he'd stopped to talk to me at the ball. I smiled back and walked toward the happy ending I'd read about in all the books.

We were a small family, no uncles, aunts, or cousins, so my own wedding was the first I'd been to, and it surprised me how quickly it all happened, how few words we had to say for the knot to be tied. My voice came out small and squeaky for the first "I will," but I spoke up for the next bit, and in no time at all the ring was on my finger and it was done. We signed the register—pride shining out of my father's face as he wrote his name under Lord Storton's—then bells were pealing, and we were walking out, man and wife, to a hail of rice.

A dark gray Rolls-Royce was waiting to take us back to Winterton Hall. Frederick helped me in, scooping up my train and bundling it inside.

"There, that's the first bit done," he said. "You look lovely, by the way."

"Thank you. So do you."

He laughed. "Are you ready to wave?"

He pointed up ahead; there were people standing along both sides of the road.

"Who are they?"

"Estate workers, people from the village."

There were dozens and dozens of them, men, women, and even children, and as the car drew level with them, they peered in at us, waving and clapping. Frederick waved back, and a cheer went up.

"Do you know them all?"

"No, of course not. They're just paying their respects. Best give a wave."

So I did, very awkwardly. It felt daft, as though I was pretending to be the Queen, and I gave a sigh of relief when we left the village behind and turned up the hill toward the hall.

"Comes with the territory, I'm afraid," said Frederick. "But you'll get used to it."

The house was full of faces I didn't know, and as the guests milled around, drinking champagne, I realized I was in need of the facilities. I'd never even been upstairs in the huge house that'd just become my home, and I didn't want to get lost, so I whispered to a maid to show me where to go.

I followed her along the upper landing past more paintings of Coombes ancestors, Frederick's features repeated in a stern-faced elderly woman, a man in military uniform, and a boy with his arm round a dopey-looking spaniel. All, to judge from the clothes, generations back.

"This is to be your room, madam, and the bathroom's there. Shall I wait?"

"No, thank you. I'll find my way back."

I shut the bathroom door and leaned against it, suddenly grateful for a moment to myself. I looked down at the shiny gold ring on my finger and thought of my mam. She used to love telling me about her own wedding day. Long before my father made his fortune, so no satin dress and no champagne: they wore their Sunday best and celebrated at the pub with brown ale and ham sandwiches.

"Yours'll be different," she used to say—she couldn't have guessed how different—"but just make sure you love him, and he loves you. That's the important bit."

Just then I heard voices from the room next door.

"Well, you got there in the end," said a woman.

Where did I know that voice from? The one that answered was Frederick's mother.

"In the end! But, by God, he's not an easy man."

Paper-thin walls, but then they'd have carved that bathroom out of a bedroom built when Shakespeare was a lad.

The other woman laughed. "Let's hope it's not in the blood."

Even then, I didn't fall in. Not until my mother-in-law said, "She's been rather indulged at home, encouraged to think herself clever, unfortunately. It's made her dreadfully bold in her manner. And the way she speaks! A great deal of work to be done there. But she's only nineteen—easy to mold."

Dreadfully bold?

"But the father!" she went on. "Appalling man. Couldn't back out of course, once it was announced, but he haggled all the details. Not a bit grateful."

The other woman laughed. "I imagine that's how he clawed his way up in the first place. But you're pleased with the outcome?"

"It's what we needed, with the taxes this wretched government is threatening," said Lady Storton. "And we couldn't have done it without you. No one else would invite the man anywhere, and we couldn't get her without him."

For a second, I couldn't breathe. Because now I knew who the other woman was.

CHAPTER 4

As I walked downstairs, stepping carefully to keep from tripping on my train, I kept thinking, *Surely I didn't hear right?* Because the woman on the other side of the wall was Lady Burnham. Who'd invited us, out of the blue, to the ball. Where Frederick happened to walk by and stop to talk. Apparently not knowing who I was, not even recognizing our surname until I introduced my father to him.

No one else would invite the man anywhere, and we couldn't get her without him.

Lady Storton had asked for us to be invited, so Frederick and I would meet. They'd picked us—me—out when the only thing they could know about me was that my father was rich. So all along, Frederick knew exactly who I was.

He'd made it seem that he'd met me by chance that night and then fallen in love with me, but the first part wasn't true. So was the rest a lie too? Because it sounded like they'd decided Frederick would marry me before he'd even met me. It sounded like he'd have married me whether he liked me or not, let alone loved me, as long as the price was right.

That day when we came to meet them all, she said they were delighted to be welcoming me to the family. And Lord Storton sat there, pretending to admire my father's achievements. But all the time, they were looking down on us.

Encouraged to think herself clever. And the way she speaks!

Was that what Frederick thought of me too?

I wasn't daft; I'd read enough Jane Austen to know that in families like his, marriage and money were glued together, and people like them didn't always marry for love. But I wasn't like them, and I thought I would. I thought we had. He *made* me think we had.

The French windows were open onto the wide front terrace, the drive just there through the trees. What would they do if I ran? Just ran, like a scalded cat? But I couldn't, could I? The knot was tied. I'd said the words, and he'd said the words. So I sipped champagne and smiled until I thought my face would crack with the effort of it. Still hoping that, somehow, I'd got it wrong.

Just after four, we were waved off in Frederick's two-seater for Broadstairs, where we were to spend a few days' honeymoon. The engine was so noisy, I had to raise my voice, but I couldn't put it off.

"I want to ask you something."

"Ask away, Mrs. Coombes."

It should have been wonderful, hearing him say that. But it gave me a stab of panic.

"Why did you pretend not to know me at Lady Burnham's ball?"

He smiled his easy smile, completely unconcerned. "What do you mean?"

"You knew who I was. I overheard your mother say she'd asked Lady Burnham to invite us."

"You must have misheard."

Same breezy tone, as if it didn't matter in the least.

"I didn't mishear. She thanked Lady Burnham for doing it."

The tiniest pause before he said smoothly, eyes straight ahead, "I expect she meant she was grateful to Lady Burnham for bringing us together, that's all."

Did he really think I was that daft? Of course he did. They all did.

Been encouraged to think herself clever.

"That's a nice explanation. She also called my father an appalling man. Is there a nice explanation for that as well?"

"Look, this is all very silly—"

"That's why you put the announcement in *The Times* so quickly, isn't it? So you had my father over a barrel."

"Your father was very happy about the match, as well he might be."

"He didn't know you'd lied to us, and nor did I."

"You are rather exaggerating things."

A red flush crept up his face. He'd been caught out, and he didn't like it. There was a moment's chilly silence and when he spoke again, there was irritation in his voice.

"Would it have been better, then, if I'd said 'Hello, Miss Hayward, jolly good to see you, because I'm in the market for a bride and my parents think you'd be suitable'?"

So there it was.

"It would have been honest. More honest than pretending you loved me."

He sighed. "Oh, Elinor. I pretended nothing of the sort. You're very young, and perhaps you've read too many silly novels. People like us don't marry for love, surely you knew that?"

"People like me do. My mother and father did. I thought that's what I was doing."

"Well, sometimes we see what we want to see. I'm fond of you, of course I am. You're my wife now; I hope that before long you'll be the mother of my children, and if you just drop these romantic notions, we'll rub along perfectly well together. Now, I think perhaps the strain of the day has made you irritable. Why don't you take a nap, and let me concentrate on driving?"

Irritable? I wanted to punch him. And not just him; I couldn't stop thinking of all the people at the wedding. There hadn't been many to invite from our side, so the receiving line was a blur of Frederick's family and their friends. Lady this and Lord that, so lovely to meet you, my dear, congratulations, what a beautiful dress . . .

No one else would invite the man anywhere, and we couldn't get her without him.

How many of that lot had she asked? Which of them had turned their well-bred noses up at my father but stood there swigging the champagne he paid for? No wonder Lady Storton hadn't wanted the wedding at Clereston; if they didn't want my father in their houses, they'd hardly lower themselves to come to his.

I said, "You look down on my father, but you were happy to take his brass, weren't you? Well, just you wait till he finds out you took it under false pretenses."

He looked at me as though I was daft. "You seem to be forgetting what a very advantageous match this is for you. You've married into one of the best families in the country. Your father's grandsons will be gentlemen. One of them will be the Earl of Storton. A lot of men in trade would kill for that."

"My father doesn't care about that! He wanted me to be happy."

"And so do I!"

He slapped the steering wheel, then took a deep breath and spoke more calmly. "Why would I want to make you unhappy?

As I've said, if you stop carrying on like the heroine of a novel, we'll be fine."

"I wouldn't have married you if I'd known."

"Well, I'm sorry to hear that, but here we are. Man and wife. And we'll have to make the best of it, like everyone else does."

I wanted to scream. I wanted to cry. I still wanted to punch him. How had I let myself be fooled into this? And my father too. No one ever pulled the wool over his eyes; he was as shrewd as they come. And yet . . . that morning, before we left the hotel, I'd spotted a list in his handwriting, headed "Topics of conversation." The recent peculiar weather was there, and the new ship being built in Belfast. He'd underlined that but crossed out "the King's illness" and "Albanian uprising." He was nervous about today, and that was a shock to me. Because in his own world—our world—my father was fearless. Whether he was talking to a mill worker or an important customer, he said what he thought, plain and straight. But with all he'd achieved in life, these people still intimidated him, and he'd wanted to show them a good face.

We spent the rest of the journey in silence. The last time we were together in that car, the tiny cabin seemed intimate and exciting. Now it was a trap closing in on me.

The morning after my wedding day, I woke up sore and sticky between my legs, and at the memory of what took place between me and Frederick the night before, a hot wave of embarrassment swept over me.

We'd eaten dinner in the hotel dining room. Being out of season, only a couple of tables were occupied, and our painfully awkward conversation had the other diners' ears out on stalks. Frederick yammered on about Broadstairs and what we might do there, as though the conversation in the motor car had cleared up any misunderstandings, while I barely answered, because a voice in my head was saying—screaming—*What am I going to do?* And each time coming up with the same awful answer:

We'll have to make the best of it, like everyone else does.

As we walked upstairs to the suite, he said, "Look, I think we've got off on the wrong foot, you and I. It's quite a performance, a wedding day, and now it's all over, I'm sure we'll settle down perfectly amicably."

When I didn't answer, he gave an embarrassed cough, and said, "I'll let you get ready for bed before I come in, then."

I think I must have stared at him dumbly, because he said, quite kindly, "You do know what's expected?"

Oh. It came back then—a conversation with Rose the night before, as she combed my hair before bed. She said there were things a girl usually heard from her mam before she married, and had anyone else told me? When I said no, she repeated, blushing furiously, what her married sister had told her, that men had needs, and the thing they needed to do went on "down there."

"Mary says it's disgusting but you get used to it and the best thing is to lie still and think about something else until it's over."

I couldn't imagine what the heck she was describing, and put it down to her usual doom-mongering. But this must be what she meant.

"I'm tired," I said. "I just want to go to sleep."

"Best get it over and done with."

"I don't want to."

He sighed. "Look, I'm not a monster, and I have absolutely no wish to force you. I'll wait till tomorrow if you prefer, but really, it'd be better to get it over with."

I lay there, rigid and terrified, as he lifted my nightdress, parted my legs and fumbled around in my most private place.

Suddenly it hurt so badly that I screamed out in shock and tried to wriggle away, but his weight held me down.

"You're hurting me!"

He put his hand over my mouth and said, "Ssh, it's all right. I'll be gentle, don't worry."

He kept shoving at me and the pain was so awful that I cried, the tears running down the sides of my face and wetting the pillow. Then he grunted and stopped.

As he lifted himself off me, he said, "It won't be so bad next time, I promise. And I'm sure we'll have happy news before long."

He tucked the covers in around me, said, "There, you're nice and cozy. Sleep well," and then the door closed behind him. I lay there, like a chrysalis, the pillow damp from my tears, just staring into the dark. How could this be happening? I'd walked down that aisle a happy bride, but here I was married to a man who only wanted my money, into a family who must all have been in on the plan. And now this last humiliation. Rose said all wives had to suffer it, and I could've borne it if I'd still thought Frederick loved me. But lying there while he did that to me, knowing what I knew, I kept thinking, I'm nothing to these people. Just a means for them to get their hands on my father's money. They had it now, and I just came along with it, like the end scraps on a bale of cotton.

CHAPTER 5

The first time I woke at Winterton Hall, the chink of silver on porcelain as Rose stirred my tea made me think I was back at home. Then I felt the cold. Frederick was honest about the drafts, if nowt else; even with a fire blazing, the air nipped at my face. I wanted to burrow under the covers and never come out—and not only on account of the chill—but I sat up when Rose said, "There's a letter for you, miss . . . madam. Came yesterday."

I tore it open.

> *My dear daughter,*
>
> *Well, here you are, a married woman! It seems like only yesterday your mam used to bring a baby with golden curls and two little teeth to Star Mill of a dinnertime, and perhaps I'm getting old, but I don't know where the time's gone since then.*
>
> *I wanted to clear up something that's been a thorn between us, the matter of passing on the business. There was often more heat than light in our arguments, so I want to*

be sure you understand my position. Ellie, even now, young as you are, you've got more business sense than some of my managers. But a business needs a man at the head—and a woman needs a husband, and a family.

That's why I took the decision I took, to make other arrangements for Haywards, and it eases my mind to know that, with this marriage, I can see you well set up in life regardless. I couldn't give you the opportunities I could give a son, but a good marriage is the best a father can do for a daughter, and this is a better one than I'd ever imagined. Who'd have thought, the little girl who played with bobbins under my desk would end up a countess? Your mam would be proud of you, lass, and so am I. I don't suppose I'll see a lot of you now, with the distance and all, but think of me now and then, and write with all your news.

I slumped back against the pillows, ridiculous disappointment crushing me. His handwriting on the envelope had sparked a half-formed hope that he was saying, "I know it's all been a mistake, come home." But of course he wasn't. Even the cotton king couldn't renegotiate this bargain.

"I'm to tell you breakfast isn't till ten," Rose said. "The housekeeper was very particular about it."

"What do you mean, very particular?"

"She said we don't keep factory hours here."

So that was the thought that accompanied me down the grand stone staircase: even the servants here looked down on me. I was all for complaining about the housekeeper, but Rose begged me not to, saying no one downstairs was friendly and it'd only make it worse.

It was a bit after ten when I walked into the morning room, because at the last minute I'd changed my mind about what to wear, swapping my flannel blouse for a smarter cotton one.

The flannel was cozy but I needed armor. The crisp cotton reminded me of Haywards, giving me courage that made me stand tall and pull my shoulders back.

They were eating already and Lord Storton was frowning at his pocket watch. But they all said good morning, perfectly pleasantly. When we got back from Broadstairs the night before, very late because Frederick's stupid car broke down, only the servants were up, and it looked as though he'd not told anyone, this morning, what I knew. Perhaps he didn't think he needed to: in the three days away he'd never mentioned it again, just carried on as though we'd had a minor disagreement and the matter was settled now. Well, I wasn't going to let them go on smirking behind their hands, thinking I was a fool who didn't know what they thought of us.

My throat was as dry as a three-day-old barm cake; I'd need a drop of tea and something to settle my churning stomach before I said what I had to say. A sideboard was laid out with silver chafing dishes of kedgeree, scrambled eggs, bacon and kidneys, platters of muffins and rolls, and Kitty was helping herself, so I copied her, taking some eggs and a bread roll.

I sliced the roll in half and spread it with butter, and as I bit into it, I glanced up and caught Lady Storton wincing. What was that for? My mam was strict about not talking with your mouth full or putting your elbows on the table, and I'd done neither.

She leaned forward.

"I believe you may need some guidance on etiquette at the table, my dear. When we eat bread, we break off a little, butter it lightly and eat that piece before we take more. We don't bite into it like a starving urchin."

That first luncheon, Kitty popping a morsel of buttered bread into her mouth. I must have eaten mine like I'd just done, and my father the same. And they'd all been looking down their noses at us.

Now I was ready.

"I don't reckon starving urchins get a lot of butter," I said. "So that's not a very good comparison. Perhaps you mean I eat like the daughter of a man who's clawed his way up."

Kitty's mouth dropped open, and Lord Storton stared at me over his newspaper, but Lady Storton didn't turn a hair. So Frederick *had* told her. You'd have thought she'd be embarrassed to be caught out, but no, not a bit of it. She just gave a frosty little smile and said, "It's *butter*, Elinor," pronouncing it the southern way.

Only nineteen, easy to mold.

We'd see about that.

"Where I come from," I said, stressing the U, "it's butter."

"Well, you're not there now, so that will have to change."

"No, it won't."

I looked around at them all. Lord Storton was staring as though he'd never seen me before. Kitty was smirking; Frederick had his eyes fixed on his plate.

"I know you all look down on me, and my father," I said. My voice was annoyingly quavery—so much for my armor—but I pressed on anyway. "But you didn't mind taking his money, did you? If you don't like the rest of the bargain, well, I don't like it much now either. You wanted the cotton king's daughter, and the cotton king's daughter is what you've got. So I won't be changing the way I speak."

"Goodness," said Kitty. "This is going to make life more interesting."

"Shut up, Kitty," snapped Lady Storton. "It's understandable, Elinor, that you're anxious about how you'll fit in here."

"That's not what I—"

She held up a hand. "But there's no need to be defensive. We're all here to help knock off those rough edges."

"My mam taught me table manners."

"And that's to her credit. But we're looking for rather more than simply being able to use a knife and fork."

With that, she stood and said, "If everyone will excuse us, Kitty and I have a meeting of the cottage hospital committee."

I sat there, humiliation and anger burning my face, as Lord Storton said to Frederick, "Will you ride this morning? It's threatening to rain."

As though we'd been having a pleasant chat but the topic had moved on, they started talking about a horse that had something wrong with its fetlock, whatever that was. I picked up my bread, then put it down again. I'd lost my appetite.

That was the start of my new life, and short of taking to my bed permanently or throwing myself in the lake, I'd no choice but to fall in with it. It was like one of those nightmares where you scream but no sound comes out. How could this have happened to me? But it had, and there was nowt I could do about it. Of course, I thought of writing to my father, telling him how we'd been deceived. I started the letter, more than once. But every time, it ended up in the wastepaper bin, because what could he do? And how could I bear for him to know the marriage he'd been so happy and proud about was nothing but a business transaction, and one that we'd got the wrong end of?

All the "delighted to welcome you to the family" nonsense was forgotten. I was there under sufferance, and for my new mother-in-law, I couldn't do a thing right.

"We spoon soup away from us, Elinor."

"Goodness, my dear, have you never used a fish knife?"

"Elinor, must you walk in such a strident manner?"

Even my clothes were wrong. My day clothes were too showy—"That print is rather too flashy for daytime, my dear"—and I didn't have enough evening dresses, only the one that was made for the ball. I'd had no idea I'd be expected to dress up like Cinderella just to eat my dinner, and you'd have thought people who lived in a freezing cold house might avoid the bare shoulder, but no. As for tea dresses, I'd none at all. At home, we never bothered with the meal, never mind the change of clothes. But I used the pin money my father had included in the settlement to order new things, because even the most beautiful dress stops being beautiful if you feel silly and out of place in it. Rose packed the old ones away in a chest so they didn't look at me sadly from the wardrobe.

About all that, I made myself listen and learn, because it'd have been cutting off my nose to spite my face not to. She kept talking about the house parties they threw, and went to, during the summer. There'd be people who'd been at the wedding, and I wasn't going to give them a chance to smirk at me a second time. But I wouldn't change the way I spoke, however much Lord Storton winced at my broad vowels and Kitty rolled her eyes. Frederick, to give him his due, never showed if he noticed, but that hardly mattered when Lady Storton corrected me a dozen times a day. I said "mirror" when I should've said "glass," "serviette" instead of "napkin," "perfume" instead of "scent." I pronounced *book* and *look* wrongly, *bun* and *bath* as well. I'd steel myself to reply, "That's how we say it where I come from" or, "It's a perfectly good word, I've seen it in books." She'd snap back that I'd have to do better "before you're seen in company," then she'd turn and speak to Kitty, or Lord Storton, and put a full stop on the conversation. It's a clever trick, that—carry on the argument and you look like a petulant child, trying to get its mother's attention. So I let her think she'd won, then enjoyed her irritation when I said the "wrong" word again later.

The table manners and the clothes were one thing, but the way I spoke, that came from my mother and my father, and the place where I'd grown up, and changing it was like rubbing out a piece of myself. If they didn't like it, they could go and scratch.

CHAPTER 6

I tried to cling on to being the cotton king's daughter, I really did. When Lady Storton said I should join her charity committees, I thought, all right, at least I'll learn summat here, and my brain won't shrivel up like a currant. At the cottage hospital, I caught sight of the accounts book, and of course I couldn't resist a look. Someone was creaming off a cut from their suppliers—the fiddle was plain as day—but what did I get for pointing it out? A telling-off for embarrassing her by talking about money in front of the other ladies.

I'd already learned by then that you couldn't argue with her, so I didn't rise to that, but then, a few days later, when we were having tea in the drawing room, I ventured a suggestion about their problems with the estate—the place was leaking money, and neither Frederick nor Lord Storton had any business sense at all. Lord Storton, who usually barely spoke to me, gave me a patronizing smile.

"You've no need to concern yourself with estate matters, Elinor."

"But I'd like to be useful. I learned a lot from my father."

He laughed. "A country estate is hardly the same thing as a cotton mill."

"I know, but a business is a business, surely? And a business is meant to make money, not lose it."

"The Winterton estate isn't a *business*." He spat the word out as if he didn't like the taste of it. "We're holding something precious in trust for future generations, not looking to make money for the sake of it. Your father's done well at what he does, but you must see, it's a different thing entirely to what we have here."

What he does.

He all but wrinkled his nose, as though the business that gave people jobs, that manufactured something people could use, and made the money that lot had taken, was something distasteful. I glanced up to see the two footmen by the door exchanging smirks. It was that, as much as Lord Storton's words, that made me see red, and the anger came out in my voice. I couldn't help it.

"I do see that it's a different thing, yes. Because my father's business didn't need me to marry a rich man to shore it up."

"Elinor!" said Lady Storton. "We don't raise our voices in this house."

I was so angry by then, I couldn't stop the words coming out.

"If any of you had half the sense my father's got, you wouldn't have needed his money, and I wouldn't have to live here, where you don't want me and I don't want to be! So don't talk about him as though he's something I should be ashamed of, because I'm not and I won't ever be."

Lord Storton raised an eyebrow at Lady Storton and said stiffly, "I'm sorry to hear you feel unwelcome here, Elinor. That's certainly been no one's intention. But when it comes to estate matters, Frederick and I have everything in hand, and I'm sure Lady Storton has quite enough charitable work to keep you occupied."

No point even answering that. I took a sip of my tea. In the silence that followed my cup rattled in the saucer; I was shaking with anger.

Frederick spoke first, asking his father what he thought of a new Italian sports car he was thinking of buying, and they moved smoothly on, as though the previous conversation had never happened. But it hung in the air like frost, and when Frederick and Lord Storton left, Lady Storton leaned over to me, her face tight.

"You really are the most ungrateful girl. I do not want to witness another outburst like that in this house again. Is that clear?"

"All I was doing was trying to be useful."

"If you want to be useful, then for goodness' sake, try to fit in here! You are the next Lady Storton—Lord help us—and it's time you started behaving accordingly. You might start by making an effort to speak properly and not sound like an illiterate shopgirl."

With that, she stalked out.

"Well," said Kitty. "You really are rattling the cages, aren't you?"

I got up to go; tears were pricking at my eyes, and I didn't want her to see them. I didn't cry easily, back then. But it hurt, what Lady Storton said. Illiterate? My father had paid for a good education for me, and I bet I'd read more books than any of them. Yet every time I opened my mouth, that was what she thought. What they all thought.

Kitty followed me and caught my arm.

"Come on, we'll go for a walk. I want to talk to you."

She usually avoided my company like you'd avoid the chickenpox, and me hers. She laughed at the expression on my face.

"Don't worry, I'm not going to push you over a cliff!"

Curious, I followed her on a path up through the woods.

"Where are we going?" I asked.

"You'll see. Save your breath, it gets steep here."

Before long I was wishing Rose had been a bit more lax with my corsets that morning, and wondering if the remark about pushing me over a cliff was or wasn't a joke. Just when I thought my lungs might burst, we came to a clearing.

"There," she said.

Below us, a river babbled past willow trees. The same view Frederick showed me, just from a different perspective.

"Frederick's favorite place," I said.

"And I expect he told you that it's looked like this for over two hundred years?"

"Yes."

"But you didn't understand what that meant, did you? You didn't understand that that's what this family, and all the families like it, are about. Keeping things the same. Keeping what we've got. Passing it all down to the next man in line, so it stays in the family. Which means women are only required for one thing, and that's to provide the heirs. No future in daughters."

She turned to me.

"What you suggested, about selling off the unproductive areas of the estate—I said the same thing, months ago. But they won't hear of it. So by the time you and my dear brother have a son, they'll need another heiress to bail this place out. And in the meantime, I'll be married off to anyone who'll have me, even though I could run this estate ten times better than Frederick."

"Here's a surprise, then—I reckon you're right to be cross about that, same as I was when my father decided not to hand Haywards on to me. But it's not my fault you won't inherit."

"No, and it's highly unfair of me to dislike you for it, but there we are. I'm already nobody here, and when you have a child, it'll be worse, so I'd have to be a saint to welcome your arrival. And I'm not."

I wasn't going to argue with that.

"But I'm not completely awful," she went on. "And while it's been entertaining to see you butting heads with my mother, it's starting to feel like watching a Christian thrown to the lions."

She sighed. "You can't win this, Elinor. When you speak your mind like that, it frightens them. They don't understand you. They don't understand me either, but I'll be out of their hair soon, so it doesn't matter. But you have to realize that what you think you've got to offer, this family doesn't want. They don't want the cotton king's daughter; they want you to stop fighting and fit in, so they can forget they ever needed money made in trade to keep it all going."

"I don't want to fit in. Because I don't believe you're better than us." I waved a hand at the view. "Frederick told me how you got all this. Someone in the sixteenth century made up to the right person and got his reward, and all your family's done is hung on to it."

"The fifteenth century, actually. The first Lord Storton."

"Good for him. But my father started with nowt much, and he worked and worked to turn it into a lot. I'm proud of that, and I won't kick over the traces and pretend I'm summat I'm not."

She shook her head. "I was rather afraid you'd say that. Well, it's up to you. But don't say I didn't try."

I meant every word I said. But when you've gone from the happiest of homes, where you were useful, to being constantly pecked at and having to think twice every time you open your mouth, it gets hard to hold your head up and keep fighting your corner. So after that, I kept my opinions to myself. Sometimes I barely spoke all day but no one seemed to notice, much less care.

The only person I really talked to was Rose, who wasn't having a much better time of it than me.

"They're a snobby lot, downstairs," she told me. "Carry on like they've got blue blood in their veins as well, just from working here, and I'm a bit of rubbish, because . . ."

She blushed and didn't finish the sentence, but she didn't need to. Had I been her, I'd have up and left, but I prayed she wouldn't, because I couldn't bear to think of how lonely I'd be if she did.

As for my new husband, at first he behaved as though everything was fine between us—chatting about his plans for the day at breakfast, reading out tidbits from the newspaper that he thought would interest me. But before long my curt replies put a stop to that and aside from the humiliating visits to my bedroom every Saturday and Wednesday, we avoided each other as much as possible, and rarely had a conversation even when we had to be in the same room.

I tried not to think about the hopes I'd had. In books, the wedding is a happy ending, isn't it? No one writes stories where, on the last page, the heroine marries a man who's "fond of her." Who'd want to read that? And now, when I tried to lose myself in *Pride and Prejudice*, or *Middlemarch*, or *Jane Eyre*, they just reminded me what a fool I'd been.

Sometimes I wondered, would it have been different had my mam been still alive? She was a very wise woman, my mam, a good judge of character. Maybe she'd have seen through it all, and warned me off. But then my father was a clever man, and he'd been dazzled by them, hadn't he?

I missed him so much. Even though he'd said he didn't expect to see me often, given the distance, I'd thought I might manage to go back to Clereston once a month to see him. But

I couldn't face it. I was afraid I wouldn't be able to pretend everything was fine, and the idea of being there, where I'd been happy, and then having to leave and come back here . . . I couldn't do it. At first I wrote to him once a week, but it was a struggle, pretending I was happy, and after a while my letters dwindled to once every two or three weeks, with whatever news I could scrape up that didn't hint at how things really were. He always replied straight away, and I'd read the letter over and over, hearing his voice as he talked about a big contract he'd signed, or an idea for a new market to look into. Longing to be back there with him, being useful, using my brain. And for the first time in my life, I wished I'd been born a boy.

CHAPTER 7

I met Lissy Harcourt at the first house party of the season. Met her properly, that is—she was at the wedding too, and we barely spoke then, but I remembered noticing her several times. You couldn't not notice Lissy; she caught the eye without even doing anything. Petite with beautiful copper-red hair, at the wedding she was in eau-de-Nil silk and a hat smothered in pink roses, and every time I saw her she was laughing, or saying something that made everyone around her laugh. She looked like the sort of woman everyone wants to be friends with, and by the time I saw her again, I needed a friend very badly.

The house parties had been put off for a while that summer, because of mourning for the King, but all too soon the first one loomed. A "Saturday to Monday," Lady Storton called it; thirty guests, the same bunch who'd been at the wedding, plus a Mr. Bannerman, who they had hopes might be interested in Kitty. The prospect of it woke me with a knot of anxiety in my stomach that day. Hard to believe I was the same girl who'd hosted a Christmas party every year for hundreds of my father's workers, but then, they weren't sniggering behind their hands at me, were they?

The servants had been preparing all week, but that morning the place was completely barmy. Carafes of water and tins of biscuits being carried to every bedroom; a vast luncheon table being laid with what looked like every bit of silver in the house; three footmen raking the gravel smooth outside. And flowers everywhere: corsages of rosebuds on all the lady guests' pillows, barely a flat surface downstairs without a huge urn of lilies and roses. You'd have thought the Queen of Sheba was coming and bringing all her relatives.

At twelve, a procession of motorcars started delivering the guests, and as a dark blue one brought up the rear, Frederick smiled and waved. "George and Lissy, last as usual."

She was in a pure white summer dress that day, with frothy ruffles of lace, carrying a sad-looking Labrador puppy in her arms. Her husband handed a screwed-up tartan blanket to a footman.

"Damn animal puked all the way here. Leave it at home, I said, but she wouldn't listen."

She kissed Frederick lightly on the cheek, then did the same to me. She was wearing a beautiful perfume, like roses in full bloom.

"Elinor, it's so lovely to see you again. We didn't get a chance to chat at the wedding." She lifted up the puppy. "Rollo, my new baby. Couldn't bear to leave him behind when he's so tiny."

He was a sweet little dog. I stroked him, and he licked my fingers with a lolloping wet tongue.

Her husband sighed. "Can a man get a drink around here, or are we going to stand about looking at this wretched puppy all day?"

To my face everyone was polite, but did they think I didn't see the snooty sideways looks? I overheard one chinless wonder mutter, "Father's rich as Croesus but doesn't own a single horse. One wonders what that sort of people even want money for."

A few months earlier, I'd have turned round and told him my father's money had paid for the smoked salmon canapés he was scarfing down, but what would be the point? He wasn't going to reply, "Quite right, I'm sorry I was rude," was he? I'd just confirm what they all thought: that I couldn't behave myself in company.

Lissy happened to be sitting beside me, and she must have heard it too.

"You're finding all this difficult, I should think," she said quietly. "It can't be easy, coming from such a different background."

I wasn't expecting that at all, and you know how it is, when you're upset and angry someone being kind can be the thing that tips you over the edge. To my horror, tears welled up. I honestly wasn't a crier, before, but Winterton was turning me into the weepy heroine in a penny dreadful.

"Oh dear," she said. "Come on, let's go outside for a bit."

The French doors were open, and we walked down to the fountain on the front lawn. She sat on its wide edge, patting the space beside her.

"Tell me all about it. Has it been awful, coming to live here?"

Would it go straight back to Lady Storton? Well, she knew anyway, and it was a relief to say it.

"Yes, it has. I don't fit in here, and I don't even want to. I hate it."

"You know, it's early days. I found it strange going to live with George's family, and we'd known them for years, so it must be hellishly difficult for you. But it'll get easier, I'm sure. One day you'll wake up and feel quite at home."

Hell would freeze over first, but I didn't say so.

She went on: "Freddie's kind to you, I hope?"

"He's not unkind. But that's the best I can say. And you'll think this is daft because people like you don't marry for love, and you all think that's all right, but I don't, and I did think I was marrying for love, and he made me think he was too."

"I see."

She picked at a fleck of moss on the stone, then looked up and said, "I've known Freddie all my life, and he'd never have set out to deceive you. He flirted, I imagine, but you see, no one is blunt about these things. No one stands up in church and says, honor and obey, yes, but I can't promise to love you. We all play the game, but we know the rules. It's just unfortunate no one explained them to you."

"Don't you love your husband?"

"In my way. But not the way you mean, not hearts and roses. If I'd married for love, it wouldn't have been to George."

"Did you want to marry someone else?"

"As it happens, I did." She tapped her nose. "Don't ask me who, because I won't tell."

"Did he want to marry you?"

"Yes. But that's not how things work. I'm one of five sisters, which rather cuts down my ability to swell the coffers. George's family didn't need that, luckily; my mother-in-law was a dollar princess, looking to marry into English society and bringing American money with her, so she'd already saved the estate before I came along."

"So I suppose I'm a cotton princess."

She smiled. "Look, you wanted the romantic dream, and when I was a girl, so did I. But we can't always have what we want, and I have, on the whole, rather a nice life. Freddie's not your fairy-tale prince, but he's a decent man, and I think if you try to rub along with him, you could have a nice life here too." She patted my hand. "Give it some thought. Now, wipe those eyes and let's go back in."

* * *

George and Frederick were chatting by the piano. Lissy put on the gramophone and, with her hands on her hips, said, "Are you two going to dance with your wives, or stand there yakking like a couple of old duffers?"

Frederick looked at me hesitantly. "Would you like to dance, Elinor?"

She gave me an encouraging glance behind his back, and to say no seemed like throwing her kindness back in her face. He was a good dancer, steering me gently, but dancing with him made me think of Lady Burnham's ball. Usually that memory made me angry, but that night, it just made me sad.

After two songs, Lissy leaned over. "Can I borrow yours for a bit? Mine's such a clodhopper."

Taking my hand, George said, "I'll try not to step on your toes, but I can't guarantee it. Not as light on my feet as old Freddie."

Without a good partner, I wasn't as sure of the steps, and when he twirled me around, I tripped. As he caught me his hand squeezed my bottom, but he carried on singing along with the song as though nothing had happened. I couldn't be certain if he was just stopping me falling over, but I didn't like it. As the record ended, I excused myself to sit down. Lissy and Frederick danced the next one, then she picked up her puppy and flopped down beside me.

"Kitty and Mr. Bannerman seem to be hitting it off," she said, fondling the dog's ears. "Perhaps we'll have another wedding this year. I hope Kitty'll have our boys as pages, they were too little for yours."

"You've got children?"

"Twins. Just turned two. Little monsters, though I love them really."

"Didn't they want to come with you?"

She laughed. "No one brings children to a Saturday to Monday. In any case, Henry has the chickenpox, and Nanny says he's dreadfully grouchy with it."

"Poor lad, chickenpox is nasty," I said. "I remember my mam sitting with me for hours, telling me stories to distract me from the itching."

"Did she? How clever. I've rather avoided the nursery, I don't want to catch it." She smiled. "Now, how about you and I plan a little expedition? To London, for shopping."

The party went on well after midnight, and I was dog-tired when I fell into bed. I waited for Frederick's knock on my bedroom door, it being a Saturday night, but it didn't come. Whether he'd just fallen asleep—he'd had a lot of champagne—or it wasn't the thing to visit your wife's bed when the house was full of guests, I didn't know, but I certainly wasn't complaining.

On Monday morning Lissy and George were last to go.

"I'll see you soon," she said to me, then smiled and waved as she got into the car. She had a beautiful smile, Lissy, wide and open—the sort that makes you trust a person. I think now that human beings would be better to take their cue from dogs and distrust a display of teeth, but as they say, hindsight is a marvelous thing.

CHAPTER 8

It turned out that Frederick had already done his duty: two weeks after the house party, I found out I was expecting a child. The very next morning, Lady Storton caught me at the bottom of the stairs.

"So, my dear, it seems we have happy news at last."

I knew how she knew. Rose washed my sanitary napkins and when she told me how I'd know if I was expecting, she confessed she'd been instructed to tell the housekeeper as soon as that service was no longer required. No point asking her not to: the estate paid her wages now, and for both our sakes, I wouldn't risk her being sacked for disobedience.

"Yes, I think so," I said.

"I gather you're quite regular in that respect?"

Was there nowt she hadn't made her business?

I nodded.

"Marvelous! Early days, so we won't discuss it widely, but we'll tell the rest of the family the good news at dinner."

* * *

Let her announce it as though she'd brought the entire thing about, when it was me who had to put up with the horrible business that caused it? No, I wasn't having that. So, just to spite her, I told Frederick myself.

I caught him at the stables when he came in from his afternoon ride. It was rare that I ever began a conversation with him, let alone sought out his company, so he was surprised to see me waiting.

"Elinor—what's wrong?"

"Nowt," I said. "I just wanted to tell you the news. We're to have a child."

To my surprise, he took my hands in his and kissed me on the cheek.

"The best news possible! Mother and father will be so pleased. Shall we tell them this evening?"

"Your mother already knows. She made it her business to find out."

He laughed. "Don't mind Mama, she means well." He squeezed my hand. "I know you've found it difficult, settling in here. But that'll change now. You wait and see."

The announcement got a satisfying frown of surprise from Lady Storton—that woman did hate to be thwarted—and suddenly I was the heroine of the hour. Champagne was fetched from the cellar, and Lord Storton made a toast.

"To Frederick and our marvelous Elinor!"

Our marvelous Elinor? He spoke to me so rarely, usually, I was surprised he remembered my name. Frederick raised his glass to one of the portraits on the wall.

"What do you think of that, Great-Grandfather? The fourteenth Lord Storton!"

They all laughed, except Kitty, who said, "Who's to say it'll be a boy? Awful if you end up as disappointed with your first born as Father was."

"Kitty!" said Lady Storton. "Must you always be the spectre at the feast?"

"I don't have any other role, do I?"

Lord Storton sighed. "No one was disappointed when you were born."

Kitty snorted a laugh. "Of course you were."

"I am, however, disappointed that you can't be happy for your brother, for Elinor, and for the future of this family. It does you no credit."

She shot me a vicious look, then turned away, a flush coloring her cheeks. I'd no love for Kitty, nor she for me, but perhaps because I was enjoying having finally done something right, I felt sorry for her just then. Much as my father would have liked a son, he'd never for a second made me think he was disappointed in me.

Lissy was pleased at the news too. A few weeks after I discovered I was expecting, she'd telephoned to suggest a day trip to London, and she guessed it within minutes of their motorcar picking me up.

"How did you know?" I asked.

She waved a hand airily. "I have a sixth sense for these things."

"I'm not supposed to tell anyone yet . . ."

"I won't say a word, promise. It's wonderful news—Freddie must be delighted."

"He is. They all are. Well, except Kitty."

"Still got that ridiculous bee in her bonnet about inheriting the estate? Honestly, what on earth is she thinking?"

"I've some sympathy with her on that, to tell you the truth. I felt the same about my father not leaving Haywards to me."

"That's rather different, though, isn't it? Your father's mills could still make cotton with someone else at the head of it all. But the estate and the title have been passed down from father to son for—"

"Thirteen generations, yes. It's been mentioned once or twice."

She laughed, then said, "It's important though, that continuity. Families like ours are the backbone of this country, and we've a responsibility to future generations to keep the line going."

If Lady Storton had said that, I'd have snapped back, quick as you like, that if anyone was the backbone of the country, it was people like my father—he might not be able to trace his family back to Henry the Eighth's time, but he'd given jobs to half of Manchester. But I couldn't bring myself to disagree with Lissy and spoil our first outing together. I was so lonely at Winterton, and I badly wanted her to be my friend. And friends didn't always have to have the same opinions on things, did they?

After some shopping in Knightsbridge, we left the car piled high with parcels and went to her dressmaker for a fitting.

"What do you think?" she said, twirling round in a tunic and hobble skirt in a lovely silver-gray damask. "Does it suit me?"

"Everything suits you," I said, and it was true: she was like a doll, perfectly in proportion. "But I think the skirt should be narrower; that fabric can take a bit more structure."

"You have such a good eye! Yes, let's take it in a little."

"Certainly, madam," said the dressmaker, through gritted teeth (that damask would be terrible to unpick; she'd be cursing me when we left).

We went for tea at the Ritz afterward, and as we sipped our Earl Grey, Lissy said, "You'll need a new wardrobe yourself soon. It really is the most wearying thing—I got as fat as a whale with the boys—but you must use it to your advantage. Say you need a nap in the afternoons, and you'll escape all those dreadful charitable endeavors Lady Storton drags you along to."

She nibbled at an éclair, then said quietly, "And, of course, there's what my mother always called the burden of womanhood." She leaned toward me and whispered. "The bedroom. I take it Frederick's stopped bothering you in that area?"

"Yes."

She smiled. "Well, there you see, that's another bonus. Now, go on, have a macaron. They're delicious, and you've no need to watch your figure now."

As I deliberated between the raspberry and the lime, she said, "I know it's been hard to settle in, when everything's so different from what you're used to. But you know, you can always talk to me if you need a friendly ear." She smiled. "And it's been fun, today, hasn't it? Shall we have a little jaunt once a fortnight, you and I? If you can escape now and then, it'll make life a bit cheerier."

After that, every couple of weeks, we'd go off to London for shopping, or explore a pretty town like Tunbridge Wells or Lewes. She was there at the houseparties that summer too, which made them so much less daunting for me, and when my condition began to show and it wasn't the done thing to be out and about, she came over for tea, or I'd visit her at Bellingham Hall. And all the time, she was so thoughtful, asking me how things were with Frederick, and was I feeling happier?

I was, a bit, and it was down to her advice. I'd done as she suggested and claimed to need a nap in the afternoon, and oh, the joy of being able to escape to my room with a book for a couple of hours! That alone made it easier to get through the days. The other piece of advice, about trying to "rub along" with Frederick, was harder to take. It was like admitting that the way he'd deceived me was quite all right, and it wasn't. But at the houseparties, I watched her and George together. They weren't a love match, that was plain, but they got along, and I had to admit that did look more pleasant than the way we were, rarely speaking and avoiding each other's company as much as we could.

I didn't think I could ever forgive him for trapping me the way he did. But I was stuck now, and I didn't have any other way to improve my situation. So I made myself ask him, at tea or dinner, about what he'd done that day, or what he thought about something that was in the news. He seemed pleased to respond, and it did make me feel a bit less lonely, having someone other than Rose I could talk to.

The family doctor advised that I should take some fresh air every day, so I got into the habit of a walk in the gardens just before the dressing gong. One evening, Frederick asked if he could walk with me. We strolled through the rose garden, quite companionably, and I stopped by an arch of blousy pale pink roses to smell the blooms. He stopped too and said, "I wanted to say . . . I underestimated, I think, how difficult it would be for you, adjusting to life here. So I'm glad you seem more settled, since our happy news. I know I'm not the fairy-tale prince you dreamed of, but I think we're a decent match."

I hadn't dreamed of a fairy-tale prince; I'd just dreamed of someone who loved me. But that dream was dead. Rubbing along was the best I could hope for.

"Lissy's helped me a lot," I said. "She's given me some good advice."

"Very wise woman, Lissy. She's given me good advice at times too."

He leaned over, plucked a rose and handed it to me. There was no romance in the gesture at all, but still, it was nice of him.

"She'll be a good friend to you," he said. "Now, shall we go in? I think I heard the gong."

I was in my fifth month when Lady Storton said it was time to find a nanny.

"One has to get in early with Norlands. Their girls are in

such demand, and there's nowhere else one can be sure of for getting the right kind of person."

"I thought we'd just find a nice local lass to help out," I said. "That's what my mam did."

By the time I came along, my parents were living in a big house on a smart street, and my father had hired a full staff for the first time, telling my mother she'd never need to lift a finger again. But when he suggested a nanny, she'd laughed, she told me, and asked him what important thing she was supposed to do with her time, while someone else took care of her daughter.

"Goodness," said Lady Storton. "How odd. But your situation is rather different from your mother's. Now, do you wish to meet the candidates, or would you prefer I made the choice?"

I did meet them, but I might as well not have done. My preference for the only one who seemed kind and smiley, a newly trained lass from Yorkshire, was overruled by Lady Storton in favor of a Miss Cairns, who'd worked for two duchesses and looked like she had a broomstick up her bottom. She only smiled once, when Lady Storton complimented her on her diction and said it was important the baby didn't pick up any "unusual accents." Did I imagine it, or did Miss Cairns glance at me then? In any case, she plainly realized who was doing the choosing, addressing her answers to my mother-in-law, even when I'd asked a question, and ending the interview saying that she hoped "Your Ladyship" would find her references satisfactory. She was duly appointed, to arrive a fortnight before the baby was due.

Well, if they wanted to waste their money on a servant who'd have very little to do, let them. It was my baby, and I was going to look after it, the way my mam looked after me.

CHAPTER 9

I'd been horrified to learn how my baby would emerge, and the reality was every bit as bad as Rose's terrifying warnings made it sound. More than I ever had in the years since she died, I wished my mam was there with me. Holding my hand and telling me I was brave, the way she did after I broke my wrist when I was nine. But when the nurse who'd arrived with the family doctor put our son in my arms, the pain and fear disappeared like a bad dream does in the morning, receding and blurring as I looked at his little face. I'd never seen a newborn baby before, and it seemed a miracle that he was so tiny, and yet a real person already, waving a tight little fist and looking up at me with his midnight-blue eyes. I touched his hand and he closed his fingers around mine. Surely everything would be different now: I'd given them what they wanted, a boy, and I had someone of my own to love and take care of.

It was only seven in the evening, but the curtains had been closed since my pains began the afternoon before, and as the doctor packed his bag, the nurse turned out the wall lights.

"You can leave those on," I said. "I won't sleep yet, I want to look at him."

"First-time mothers often become overexcited," the doctor said, "but for your baby's sake and your own, you require rest, and a complete absence of noise and stimulation."

He nodded at the nurse, who turned out the lamp on my dressing table, leaving just the one beside the bed, so the room was almost in darkness.

"A brief visit from your husband, a very light meal, then sleep," said the doctor. "And for the next seventy-two hours, avoid sitting up for more than a few minutes at a time—you must lie flat for the womb to heal."

When they'd gone, Frederick came in. We'd reached a kind of truce by then, him and me, just rubbing along together like Lissy and George did. And at that moment, I was happy and proud to show him his son.

"Look at him. Isn't he beautiful?"

"Hello," he said, stroking the baby's cheek with a finger. "Hello, my son."

I showed him how to hold his finger for the baby to grab, and he laughed as the tiny fingers closed around his.

"He's got a strong grip!"

Jiggling the finger that was still held tight, he smiled at me. "I was sure we'd have a boy, but it's a relief to know for certain. Mother and Father are delighted; they send their congratulations."

A tap on the door, and Miss Cairns appeared.

"Congratulations," she said, with an ingratiating smile that was largely aimed at Frederick. "I'll take the baby now."

"There's no need," I said. "I'll keep him with me for a while."

"Doctor's orders," she said. "Mother needs her rest."

She leaned forward to take him, but I turned away. "Come and get him later."

She looked at Frederick, and as though I wasn't in the room, said, "Lady Storton gave strict instructions . . ."

"He's not Lady Storton's baby, he's mine, and he's just been born, and I want him to stay with me. Frederick, tell her."

He patted my hand. "Don't be silly, Elinor. If the doctor says rest, you must rest. Let Nanny take him to the nursery."

She reached for my baby again, and I tried to hold on but he whimpered, and I was so afraid of hurting him that I had to let him go. As she took him he wailed, and I couldn't bear it.

"Give him back! You're frightening him!"

Frederick turned to her. "Is he all right?"

"He's perfectly fine, sir. It's quite normal for babies to cry; it helps their lungs develop. I'll take him to the nursery and let madam get some sleep."

As the heavy door closed behind her, it shut out his cries.

"How could you let her take him?"

I was weeping now; I couldn't help it.

Frederick stood to go. "Don't upset yourself, there really is no need. I'm sure you'll feel better after a rest."

I listened for the cries as he opened the door, but the nursery was at the far end of the opposite wing, with its own thick, silencing door. He might be sobbing his little heart out and I wouldn't even know. I lay there in the dark, my face wet with tears. He was so tiny, so defenseless. It was my job to protect him and I'd failed already.

I tried to calm myself down. But I couldn't stop picturing him, lying in his crib, all alone. Was he wondering why I let her take him? I'd no idea if a baby so little could even think proper thoughts, but he'd feel, wouldn't he? He'd feel frightened and lonely, even if he didn't know why.

I couldn't just lie there fretting. I had to see him, to know if he was all right. I waited until the house was dark and completely quiet and then, in bare feet, I crept to the nursery suite, at the far end of the house. The door handle was stiff so I left the door ajar and stood still for a bit, letting my eyes adjust to the darkness until I made out the crib, under the window. What I'd forgotten was that Miss Cairns's bed was beside it.

I hesitated, watching and listening. She was quite still, breathing deeply. She had to be a heavy sleeper, or she'd have heard the door open. And I couldn't go back now without seeing him.

I tiptoed across the room to the crib, and my heart swelled when I looked in and saw him. Asleep on his back, his arms flung out like a starfish, his little face peaceful. Holding my breath, I reached in and picked him up, holding him close to my chest in case he woke and made a noise. But he just settled in my arms, as though he knew he belonged there.

Miss Cairns mumbled in her sleep. I stood stock still.

Don't wake. Please don't wake.

She mumbled again but her eyes stayed closed. I couldn't stay there, but I couldn't bear to leave him. Holding him tight, I crept toward the door. I was nearly there when my foot caught the edge of the rug and I stumbled, banging into a table. A shriek from the bed, and the room was flooded with light from the bedside lamp. Dazzled, I screwed up my eyes as Miss Cairns sat bolt upright and clapped a hand to her heart. The baby woke with a shocked little cry, then began to wail.

"It's just me!" I said, trying both to whisper and be heard over his cries. "I'm sorry, I didn't mean to frighten you."

"Mrs. Coombes! I thought you were an intruder."

I patted the baby's back to try and soothe him, but I think he sensed my panic, crying even louder. "Look, Miss Cairns— Nanny—I just wanted—"

The door crashed open; Frederick, in his nightshirt, his hair all on end.

"What's going on? I heard a scream."

Then he caught sight of me.

"Elinor?" He looked me up and down, his eyes anxious. I was in my bare feet, my eyes sore from crying and squinting against the light, my nightgown soaked where my breasts had leaked milk. Clutching my baby who was screaming as though he was terrified.

"What on earth are you doing?"

"I just came to get him, he's too little to be away from his mam."

"It's the middle of the night!"

"Well, if you hadn't let her take him away from me, I wouldn't have had to come and get him in the middle of the night!"

The baby was screaming his little lungs out now, his face livid red.

Frederick snapped at Nanny, "Can you stop him crying? He'll wake the whole house up!"

She reached to take him but I turned away.

"No! How would you like to be taken from your mother when you're only an hour old?"

"Elinor, this is ridiculous. Nanny is here to look after him."

Her face was all pinched, and she said quietly, "I'd advise calling the doctor in the morning, sir. Sometimes the birth can disturb the mind."

"My mind is not disturbed!"

I was crying again now, tears of anger and frustration. Frederick spoke gently this time.

"You're tired. Let's get you back to bed. I'm sure all this isn't good for the baby, is it, Nanny?"

"Most certainly not, sir."

At a nod from Frederick, she reached over and took my son from me. Frederick took hold of my elbow and I tried to resist but he all but pushed me from the room.

"Back to bed before you wake up the entire house. We'll call the doctor in the morning."

* * *

When the doctor came, Lady Storton was with him. She stood looking out of the window while he conducted an embarrassing examination of my private parts.

When he'd finished, he said, more to her than me, "No signs of infection, so the problem is in the mind, I'm afraid. It's not uncommon for mothers to be overstimulated by the experience of childbirth, and sleepwalking is certainly a sign of an overstressed system."

What?

"I wasn't sleepwalking; I was wide awake. I just wanted to have my son with me."

"Your motherly instincts do you credit," he said, and then, as if to a slightly simple child, "but you must concentrate on your recovery."

What the heck was wrong with them all?

"I'll recover better if I don't have to worry about him being left alone to cry. He's my son, I want him to know his mother loves him, and I don't know why you all find that so peculiar."

My voice came out shrill; they exchanged a look.

"As I mentioned," Lady Storton said quietly, "Elinor has always had a somewhat volatile temperament. I wonder if that might predispose her to this kind of instability?"

"Quite possibly," said the doctor. "But no need to worry unduly. Puerperal mania of this kind only rarely requires treatment in an asylum."

My insides turned to water. Surely you couldn't put someone in a nuthouse for wanting to be with their child?

"It can usually be managed at home," he went on, "providing the patient is compliant. Rest is the remedy, and a sedative will help." He turned to me. "Now, Mrs. Coombes, four weeks in bed, complete peace and quiet, no visitors, no talking, no exciting yourself. After that you may try sitting up in a chair, an hour a day at first, loose clothing only, slowly increasing the time if you feel no ill effects."

"Four weeks? That's daft, I'm not ill!"

He opened his bag and took out a syringe.

"I want to see my baby!"

"I would advise against it, until your mind recovers."

"I can't not see him for a month! He'll think I've abandoned him."

Lady Storton rolled her eyes. "Must you be so dramatic, Elinor? Babies are like puppies, as long as they're fed and watered, they thrive. Isn't that so, doctor?"

"Indeed. And furthermore, heightened emotion around an infant is certainly not to its benefit. If you want to do the best for your son, Mrs. Coombes, you must attend to your own welfare. We don't want your condition to worsen and require more extensive treatment."

He glanced at the nurse, who stepped forward and gripped my arm, while he injected the sedative. "There, now you'll feel calmer, and be able to sleep."

When I woke, dry-mouthed and bleary-eyed, the late afternoon sun was slanting through the window. As the events of the morning came back, I went hot with anger. How dare they suggest I was mad? If they thought they were going to keep my baby from me for a month, they could think again. I went to ring for Rose to help me dress, then hesitated. I was still so dozy that I might fall asleep again by the time she came, and if I didn't get this sorted out now, the poor baby would have another night without his mother. Tying my nightdress tight at the neck, I went downstairs.

Frederick was in the drawing room, alone. He looked me up and down. "Elinor, what on earth are you doing? You're supposed to be in bed."

"I don't need to be in bed; I'm not ill. And I'm certainly not mad."

"No one has said you're mad, but—"

"The doctor was talking about putting me in a nuthouse!"

"No, he wasn't." He was talking to me like the doctor did, like I was a child. "As I understand it, he said—"

"I heard what he said, and it's ridiculous. There's nowt wrong with my mind."

I hadn't heard Lady Storton coming up behind me until she spoke.

"Elinor, you went prowling about in the middle of the night; you frightened Nanny; you were shouting like a fishwife. My dear, that is not normal behavior. And now look at you."

"I was not shouting like a fishwife. And what's not normal is taking a baby away from his mother."

"You really mustn't excite yourself like this while your mind is unsettled by the birth," she said. "If you go back to bed, I will go personally and check on the baby, and come and let you know he's all right. Will that satisfy you?"

It didn't. It didn't at all. But I kept thinking of what the doctor said.

If the patient is compliant.

"Yes," I said. "Thank you."

I wasn't sure if she'd come but she did.

"He's sleeping peacefully. Nanny says he's avid for his bottle and settles easily afterward," she said.

"Thank you."

She sat down on the side of the bed. "You really must rest now. It's for your own good, and for his good too. I know you wouldn't want to risk him coming to harm."

"What do you mean?"

She hesitated, then said, "Dr. Harris says women with a mental disturbance after birth have been known to harm their babies."

"I would never harm him!" She stood to go, and I grabbed at her hand. "Wait! You can't think I'd do anything to hurt him?"

"Elinor, let go of me! I'm sure you wouldn't mean to hurt him, but it's for your own good that we don't take the risk."

As she closed the door behind her, a key turned in the lock.

CHAPTER 10

For a week I took the pills they gave me, because it was better than lying there, locked in, wondering if my baby was crying for me. I drifted in and out of sleep, leaving the meals Rose brought me untouched. I had a terrible thirst whenever I woke up though, and Rose took to putting three sugars and far too much milk in my tea.

"You must get some nourishment from somewhere, madam, or you'll waste away."

It was revolting, but I drank it. Resisting took too much energy.

At night I often woke and lay there in the darkness, straining my ears for my son's cry. But no sound escaped the nursery suite, so far away. It was only because I'd left the heavy door ajar that Frederick had even heard Nanny's scream that night.

The morning when I woke to the clang of bells ringing from the village church, it told me that my son was a week and a day old. The longing to see him and hold him was like a physical pain, and sharper every day. But I couldn't picture his little face anymore. If I saw him with ten other babies, would I even know him? Then it hit me: how would he know me? I'd seen him for less than an hour, on the day he was born. How would he even remember that I was his mother?

I couldn't let them keep me from him for another three weeks. I had to make them see there was nowt wrong with me.

When the doctor came next morning, I was sitting up in bed, reading *Sense and Sensibility*. Or at least I had the pages open. I was so nervous that the words were a blur. I had on a fresh nightdress; Rose had pinned up my hair, and as she showed him in, I laid the book aside and smiled brightly.

"Good morning, doctor."

"You're looking rather perkier, Mrs. Coombes. That's good to see."

"I'm feeling a lot better. You were right, I needed to rest."

"Marvelous. If you continue in this vein, you'll be quite recovered by the end of the month."

"Honestly, I feel so well now that lying in bed seems very lazy. I'm sure I could get up and about again without any problem at all."

He wagged a patronizing finger at me. "Ladies in your position don't always know what's best for them, I'm afraid. We wouldn't want to set your recovery back, would we?"

"Well, then, do you think I could just see my baby for a little while? I'm sure that would help."

"Best not. But I can assure you he's doing well. I checked him over myself this morning, at Lady Storton's request."

Panic darted through me. "Why? Is he ill?"

"Just a slight temperature and a little rash."

I sat bolt upright. "He's got a fever?"

"There's no need for concern—"

"I want to see him." I threw off the blankets and sprang out of bed. "You can't keep him from me if he's ill."

He reached out and grabbed my wrist.

"Let go of me!"

He tightened his grip. "Mrs. Coombes, this is quite unnecessary—"

Without even thinking—I just had to get to the nursery—I
bent down and bit his hand. He yelped and let go. He was quite
a portly man, Dr. Harris, and by the time he'd got to the door,
I was halfway along the corridor, my bare feet pounding on the
boards. His shouts brought servants running, but I made it to
the nursery.

The crib was empty. For a moment, I just stared at it. Then
I remember screaming, "Where's my baby?" over and over,
sinking to my knees beside the crib. Suddenly it made sense: he
was dead and that was why they'd kept him from me.

In the end, they had to let me see him. Dr. Harris tried to inject
me with a sedative, but I fought him off, kicking and scratching
as if my life depended on it, as a gaggle of maids watched open-
mouthed. Making things worse for myself, but I couldn't let
them knock me out and then wake up in my room again, not
knowing what had happened.

"Where is he?" I kept saying. "What have you done with
him?"

Lady Storton appeared in the doorway. She must have been
out; she was in her hat and coat.

"Good grief, what on earth is going on?"

I heard myself shriek at her, "Where's my baby?"

"He's in the walled garden. Nanny took him out in his perambulator, to get some fresh air."

"He's alive?"

"Of course he's alive." She looked at the doctor. "What's
happened here?"

He glanced at his hand, where I'd bitten him.

"Perhaps we should discuss it in private, Lady Storton."

I'd proved them right, hadn't I? I'd behaved like a madwoman. And now they were going to take me back to that room and lock me in for three weeks. Or worse. I darted to the window, climbed onto the sill and opened the casement.

"If you let me see him, I'll go back to my room and I'll take the sedative and I'll stay in bed for as long as you want me to," I said. "But if you don't go and get him, right now, I'll jump."

Did I mean it? I don't know. But it was all I could think of to do. I couldn't survive being shut up in that room again without knowing for certain that he was all right.

She looked at the doctor, and when he nodded, said to one of the maids, "Go and find Nanny, and tell her to come back here with the baby."

I had ten minutes with him, Nanny sitting there with a face like a lemon, and the doctor standing between me and the window. As soon as she put him in my arms, my breasts spurted milk, and he nuzzled in, but I didn't dare try to feed him. I looked and looked and looked at his face, and his hands with the tiny pink-shell nails, and his feet, so small and perfect, to try to print it all on my mind and keep the picture safe until I saw him again. I breathed in the sweet smell of his head and stroked his velvety cheek. I felt his forehead for fever, but it was cool and whatever the rash had been, it had disappeared.

"I'm your mam," I whispered in his ear. "And I love you. Remember that, remember me, and I'll see you again as soon as I can."

CHAPTER 11

Nine weeks after Teddy was born, I was back in my corsets, and what passed for normal life at Winterton Hall had resumed for me. But I was, at least on the outside, a different person. I asked to join Lady Storton's daily meetings with the housekeeper, Mrs. Oakervee, even getting myself a notebook and writing down the answers to Lady Storton's questions. Where had the Cheddar Lord Storton liked so much come from? When would the estate's venison be at its best? All pointless, when Mrs. Oakervee knew it all and Lady Storton didn't need to, but my mother-in-law nodded her approval at my efforts to learn about what she called "the running of the house." I volunteered to lead the ladies making bunting for the village fair, and at the cottage hospital, instead of trailing behind Lady Storton as she briefly bestowed her presence at each bedside, I offered to visit the elderly ladies while she was in the mens' ward.

On the way back to Winterton in the Rolls that day, she said, "You won't mind me saying, my dear, that I had concerns about you settling into your role here. But you seem to be fitting in at last, and I want you to know I appreciate your hard work."

Hard work?

She wouldn't know hard work if it waved a banner in her face. None of them would. If she thought chatting to grateful old women was any kind of work at all, I'd have liked to see her do a day in the mill.

"Thank you," I said. "I've felt more settled since Teddy was born."

She gave a thin smile. "I was rather hoping that nickname wouldn't stick."

Well, hard luck. They'd christened him without me knowing—Edward, after Lord Storton. Claiming him for themselves. But he was mine too, and I would never, ever call him that. I didn't say so though, did I? I just smiled, like the meek little mouse I'd had to become.

Seven weeks, three days, and four hours. That's how long they kept me away from my son, in the end. When they finally let me see him, he was a different child. Not just bigger, but more solid, like he'd grown into his skin. His face had filled out with chubby little cheeks, and his eyes were focused. I was still confined to my room then, and as Nanny handed him to me, he kept his eyes on her. I whispered hello but when he looked up at my face, he squirmed and whimpered.

He didn't know me.

I didn't cry. I smiled brightly and said perhaps I was holding him the wrong way, could Nanny show me? She stayed in the room the whole time—she'd obviously been told to—and I made pleasant conversation about how he was doing. When she said it was time to take him back to the nursery, I forced down the impulse to cling to him and, still smiling, I offered him up, then sank back on the pillows as though I was glad of the rest. When she was gone, I sobbed for an hour straight.

I was patient though—well, what choice did I have? Each

day, I accepted my time with him, like a good girl, and I talked to him soft and quiet, like I remembered my mother talking to me when I was little. I told him about his other family, his grandfather the cotton king, and his grandmother, who he'd never see but who would have loved him so much. I told him about my childhood and about Haywards. Talking and talking, so even though he couldn't possibly understand what I said, he'd remember the sound of my voice, and know I was his mam. And the first day he settled into my arms, the way he did the day he was born, was the happiest day I'd had for a long time.

When, eventually, I was allowed downstairs again, life went back to the same rigid routines, and for twenty-three and a half hours a day, you'd never have known there was a baby in the house. The only change—apart from my meek and mild act— was that before tea, Nanny brought Teddy downstairs for twenty minutes. I thought I was still on trial, that they were testing me out, so I waited a while before I brought the subject up with Lady Storton, when we were on the way back from the cottage hospital.

"I was thinking, I might take Teddy out in the perambulator in the evening, just round the walled garden. It must be good for him to get fresh air."

"I suppose just this once," she said. "It looks like being a mild evening."

"I didn't mean just this evening. I meant every evening."

She couldn't have looked more surprised if I'd said I wanted to walk barefoot through the village with Teddy in a wheelbarrow. "But you see him just before tea."

"Not for long. I'd like to start spending more time with him."

"Why?"

"Because I'm his mam." I quickly smiled to soften the sharpness of my tone. "You must've spent time with Frederick when he was little, surely?"

"Of course I did. I saw him every afternoon, just as you see Edward. The rest of the time he spent with his excellent nanny, as Edward does."

The penny dropped then. This wasn't just because of all the nonsense about me being mad. This was how it was planned to be anyway. This was how it worked with families like theirs. Because now I thought about it, Lissy didn't spend any time with her boys either, did she?

Very carefully, very calmly, I said, "I know Nanny's capable and experienced, but I didn't realize you meant for her to take care of Teddy all day long. I'd prefer to look after him myself."

"Don't be ridiculous. You're not a washerwoman, Elinor. You are the future Lady Storton. I thought you were coming to understand the duties of your role, but if you see this as a way of avoiding them—"

"That's not it! I just want to be a mother to my son. Why is that so peculiar?"

"You're sounding a little hysterical—"

I took a deep breath to calm my voice. "I'm not, honestly. I'm not. I just didn't expect to have so little time with him, that's all."

"Well, you're still learning how things are done. My dear, you must realize, Edward is the future of this estate. He needs to learn our values, our way of life, and you can't teach him any of that, can you?"

She smiled. "And can you imagine how the poor child would end up talking if he spent all his time with you?"

When we got back to Winterton, I went up to my room and shut the door. I pressed a pillow to my face, and I screamed into it, for quite a long time. Then I sat at my dressing table and looked at myself in the mirror. The face that looked back at me still looked like the cotton king's daughter, but I'd let them change me, hadn't I? Those weeks away from Teddy had frightened me so badly that I'd let them turn me into the compliant wife they wanted, who had nothing better to occupy her mind and her time than choosing the color of the bunting for the hospital bazaar. And now, if I was to have any chance of spending more time with my son, I was going to have to change the one thing I'd sworn I never would. Because Kitty had been right all along, hadn't she?

You can't win this, Elinor.

There was no sense in putting it off. They'd won. So that evening, at dinner, I said to Lady Storton, "I think I'd like to take elocution lessons."

CHAPTER 12

It's such a strange thing, changing the way you speak. The elocution teacher Lady Storton found for me was a flamboyant Londoner, who claimed he'd taught numerous actresses "to throw off ugly accents and become queens of the stage." He knew his stuff, and I was, if not a willing learner, a motivated one. I hated myself for giving in, but I made myself think of Teddy, of being able to spend time with him, the way my mother did with me. Within two months, I could say "baaaath" and "tittle tattle" as though I was born to it. You wouldn't know I'd ever set foot in a cotton mill.

But it's horrible, knowing every time you open your mouth, your voice says you're ashamed of where you came from. Ashamed of the mother and father who brought you up. I wasn't ashamed of them, and I never would be. I'd still thrown away a part of them though, and I hated myself for it. And on top of that, it's exhausting, always taking a fraction of a second to make sure you say the proper words, in the proper way. It's like acting a part, except that Mr. Fletcher's anecdotes made acting sound like fun, and this wasn't fun at all.

When I heard myself making small talk with the bazaar committee, I'd remember the girl who used to go to the mills with her father, checking the accounts for him, helping him choose the season's colors and prints, talking over all the big decisions he had to make. She seemed, now, like someone I used to know but hadn't seen for a long time.

What had Lady Storton said, on my wedding day?

She's only nineteen, easy to mold.

Turned out she was right.

And the worst of it? Changing the one thing about me that I was desperate to cling on to made no difference at all: Lady Storton was still insistent that Teddy was only brought downstairs for twenty minutes each afternoon.

"Nanny has the training, and the experience, to bring Edward up to the life he'll lead when he's older. You don't, and as his mother, I would hope you'd want what's best for him."

I didn't argue; I was too afraid she might decide to allow me even less time with him. All I could do was use the time I did have to make sure he knew he had a mam who loved him. So I held him in my arms and talked to him—if Lady Storton was there, I told him what I'd been doing that day, but if she wasn't, I talked to him about his other family. As he got bigger, I played with him, pat-a-cake and peek-a-boo, or sang nursery rhymes to him, and he'd gaze at me and give a gummy smile that made my heart flip over.

I had no idea how quickly a baby grows and changes, and I only saw those changes in flashes here and there. One day, when he was about seven months old, he reached out to pull at my earring, the first time I'd seen him focus on something and try to grab it. But when I mentioned it to Miss Cairns, she said, "He does that quite a bit now, madam. Nearly upturned a beaker of milk the other day."

I didn't hear his first word; she did. And the first wobbly steps I saw him take weren't his first; they'd already happened in the nursery. He was a year old then, and I worked out, that day, that I'd only spent around a hundred hours with him since he was born. Just over four days, if you added it up. But still I didn't complain. I lived for that twenty minutes, and I wasn't going to give them any reason to take it away from me.

Sometimes when Nanny came to take him back to the nursery he'd cling to me and cry, and letting him go was like a physical pain. One afternoon when he had the beginnings of a cold, he sobbed when Nanny tried to take him, so I suggested I carry him up and settle him. Lady Storton rolled her eyes, took him from me and handed him to Nanny, like a parcel.

After they'd gone, she said, "You're beginning to mollycoddle him, Elinor, and it won't do. I wonder if it might be best if Nanny didn't bring him downstairs when he's out of sorts."

"I don't mollycoddle him," I said quickly. "I just thought it might help Nanny."

"We can't have him turning into a mother's boy. He won't thank you for that when he goes away to school."

As politely as I could manage, I said, "I don't think me settling him in his cot now will make him a mother's boy when he's thirteen."

"Seven, you mean."

"Frederick said he went to Eton at thirteen."

"Yes, of course, but he went to prep school before that, in Dorset."

"A boarding school?"

"Of course. He'd hardly go back and forth every day, would he?"

It was ridiculous. Who in their right mind sent a child of seven to live with strangers? It was a long time ahead, but I'd learned my lesson from the situation with Nanny: if I didn't challenge this, it would just happen, and I'd be powerless to protect him.

I caught Frederick after breakfast the next morning.

"Can I talk to you about Teddy? About school?"

He smiled. "I know our son is destined to be a genius, but isn't it a little early?"

"That's exactly it. Your mother thinks Teddy should go to boarding school at seven, like you did. But that's so young. Wasn't it awful, being sent away when you were so little?"

He shrugged. "I don't really remember."

"You don't remember leaving your family and being sent to live with strangers?"

"All right, yes—I suppose it was a shock. But that's rather the point, with school. It toughens you up."

"At seven? I was still playing with teddy bears then."

He laughed. "I'll let you into a secret—so was I. Well, a toy rabbit. I'd had him since I was a baby. Nanny kept trying to take him away, but I couldn't get to sleep without him. So I smuggled him into my trunk. One of the older boys spotted him, and they set light to poor Rabbit and threw him down the lavatory. I got a bit upset, and they all called me Crybaby Coombes for weeks."

His voice caught, and for a second I glimpsed a frightened little boy. But he covered it with a laugh. "Luckily Forbes Minor wet himself after a nightmare and took the attention off me."

"That's terrible. Didn't your parents know it would be like that?"

"Odd if they didn't—Father and Grandfather went there too. But look, you've got the wrong idea about it. It's a good school. It taught me to be self-reliant and keep a stiff upper lip, nothing wrong with that."

"But seven is so young. Teddy should be here with us, not crying himself to sleep with strangers."

"Don't be silly, no one cries after the first couple of weeks. Besides, it'd be a lot worse if he just landed at Eton when he was thirteen. If you're going to get on there, you've got to have a bit of backbone."

"Don't I get any say in this?"

"There's nothing to have a say about. Coombes boys go to Crown Hill and then Eton. It's the family tradition." He put a hand on my arm. "You're still a little emotional, I think, since Edward's birth, but honestly, there's no need to worry yourself. He'll get the education he needs, and who knows, perhaps in time we'll have a little girl too. Then you can keep her at home and make a pet of her."

No one tells you, when you're young and dreaming of love, what marriage means for a woman. You're encouraged to long for it, and to fear, above all else, being left on the shelf—look at poor Charlotte in *Pride and Prejudice*, who decided marrying the awful Mr. Collins was better than being a spinster. Perhaps some girls learn the truth from watching their own mothers, but you see, I never did. My mother and father agreed on most things, and even after she died, when he discussed business decisions with me he'd still say, "I wonder what your mam would think." I'd never had cause to wonder who'd make the final decision if they disagreed on something important, and it certainly never occurred to me that the law would have anything to say on the matter. So there was a shock in store for me when the family's lawyer, Mr. Conway, came to take instructions about updating Frederick's will.

Lord and Lady Storton were in London that day, but he stayed to luncheon with Frederick, Kitty, and me. The conversation was very dull, Mr. Conway droning on about his legal cases, so I wasn't paying much attention. Nodding and smiling without listening comes easily after months of being frightened to say the wrong thing and knowing no one wants your opinion anyway.

But as dessert was served, he said, "I always say, we can't prevent the worst happening, but sensible planning can mitigate the consequences. It's a pity not everyone thinks to safeguard their child's future with the arrangements we put in place today."

That last bit caught my attention.

"What arrangements?"

Mr. Conway turned to me with an indulgent smile. "Guardianship arrangements, Mrs. Coombes. For Edward, and any subsequent children. A very sensible precaution."

"A precaution against what?"

He looked at Frederick as if asking permission to answer, but Frederick spoke first.

"It's just appointing Father and Mother as Teddy's guardians, in the event of my death."

Mr. Conway chimed in: "Lord and Lady Storton would carry out your husband's wishes regarding Teddy's upbringing and education."

"But what about my wishes?"

Mr. Conway gave an oily smile. "We are only talking theoretically—"

"And in this theoretical situation, I'm still alive, I think?"

"My dear lady, I very much hope you'll be alive for many years to come!"

He laughed as if he'd made a very funny joke, then went on: "It's quite straightforward. A father has, of course, the legal authority to decide all matters concerning his children. If the said father should die while the child or children are minors, that authority is bestowed on the guardians, and they carry out his wishes until the child comes of age."

Kitty laughed. "So you're of no importance, Elinor. Like me."

I looked at Frederick. "Shouldn't I be Teddy's guardian, then?"

"Mr. Conway's advice was that it was more straightforward to nominate Mother and Father."

"Why?"

Mr. Conway said, "It's the way it's usually done. You can rest easy that your husband has made the most suitable decision."

Kitty rolled her eyes. "It's obvious. It's in case you remarry after Frederick dies and want to take the son and heir off somewhere."

"It's a formality, that's all," snapped Frederick. "And this conversation is quite unnecessary because I have no intention of dying before Edward grows up. So can we please talk about something else?"

You could say it made no difference. When I said the words and Frederick said the words at the altar that day, I'd tied my own hands. But I couldn't get that document out of my head. I didn't think for a second that Frederick would die while Teddy was a child and set the arrangements into action, but the casual way they'd brushed me out of the picture made me feel enraged and at the same time frightened. I could scream from the rooftop that I was Teddy's mother and it wouldn't make any difference. I had less say in my life than any of the servants did, because they could at least decide to leave.

Sometimes, I'd lie awake at night and dream up daft plans to escape: running away and becoming a governess, like Jane Eyre, or disappearing off to some remote village and pretending to be a widow, like Helen in *The Tenant of Wildfell Hall*. But they'd find us, wouldn't they?

Edward is the future of this estate, and this family.

They might be quite happy to see me disappear, but they'd scour the earth to find him. It was all just fantasy, anyway. I couldn't go anywhere, and whether I liked it or not, Teddy was going to be handed from Nanny to prep school to Eton, being molded into the future Earl of Storton. To grow up like his father, to marry someone he didn't love, all because they were obsessed with—how had Kitty put it?—"Keeping things the same. Keeping what we've got. Passing it all down to the next man in line, so it stays in the family."

CHAPTER 13

I used to think, back when I was the girl who helped my father choose his managers, that I was a good judge of character. But it turned out Frederick wasn't the only person I'd misjudged. Took me a long time to find that out though, and another wedding.

After Kitty and Mr. Bannerman got on so well at the house party, we'd all expected a proposal, but things went very quiet, and Lissy heard he was paying court to the daughter of a marquess, somewhere in Somerset. But that must have gone nowhere, because then he wrote to Lord Storton, saying he was passing through and wondered if he might call in. He ended up staying three days, during which time Kitty flirted herself silly, and the upshot was that he proposed and she said yes.

Teddy was still too little to be a page, but as Lissy hoped, Kitty wanted her twins, Henry and William, so they all arrived the night before, and we were seven for dinner. After two rounds of a cocktail called a Scorpion's Sting, that Lissy had heard was all the rage in London, everyone was in a good mood. At dinner I was seated beside George, who usually had very little to say for himself, but even he was quite chatty, recounting a long anecdote about an eccentric aunt of his. I laughed out of politeness, and perhaps he realized it was only that.

He nodded at Frederick, across the table talking to Lissy. "I can't tell a story as well as old Freddie. He knows how to make people laugh."

I felt sorry for him then, so I said, "Well, you made me laugh."

"Good, I'm glad."

Just then Lord Storton tinkled his spoon on his glass and proposed a toast to Kitty. When we set our glasses down again, George's hand rested lightly on my leg, under the table. I twitched away, but he slid his hand up my thigh, stroking my garter through the silk of my skirts. After that time he'd touched my bottom, nothing like it had ever happened again, and I'd told myself it was an accident. But this certainly wasn't.

"Don't," I said, turning so no one else could see my face. "Stop it."

He stroked a slow circle, then turned and called over to Lord Storton: "Excellent beef, this. Is it from the estate?"

I looked down at my plate, praying my blush—as much from anger as embarrassment—would subside before anyone noticed. What if Lissy saw? How awful for her to know her husband was that sort. Or worse, imagine if she believed I'd encouraged him?

After dinner, when Lissy put on the gramophone, I said I was going to bed. She pouted.

"Don't be a party pooper."

George was standing by the fireplace, and he'd obviously had a good bit more to drink after we left the men to their cigars; his words were slurred.

"Leave Elinor be. She knows you'll dance with Freddie and palm her off with my big feet. No wonder she wants to escape."

"There," said Lissy, "you've hurt George's feelings. You must stay, or he'll drown his sorrows in this delicious brandy and be hungover for the wedding."

She stretched out her hand to Frederick. "Elinor has to make it up to George, so you get me."

I tried to hold myself away from George, but he pulled me close and whispered in my ear, "Relax. We deserve some fun, you and I."

When the song came to an end, I forced a smile and wished everyone good night. Kitty said she'd turn in too, and we walked out together.

"Are you all right?" she said. "You seem a bit upset."

I was hardly going to confide in her, was I?

"I'm fine," I said. "Just tired."

The soft knock on my door that woke me was a surprise; Frederick never came to my room when there were guests in the house. I sat up, irritated, but when the door opened, it wasn't Frederick who slipped in, wearing his nightshirt. It was George.

"Sorry to keep you waiting, that damn husband of yours wouldn't go to bed."

"Get out or I'll scream."

"That's not very friendly."

"Get out!"

To my astonishment, he completely ignored me. Strolled over and sat on the bed, then reached out to wind a lock of my hair round his finger. "About time we got to know each other better, you and I. Like I said, we deserve some fun."

Before I could even answer, he was on me, kissing my neck, pawing at my breasts, his breath rank with cigars and stale wine.

I pushed him off and slid out of bed on the other side, so it

was between us. My heart was pounding; I just couldn't believe this was happening.

"Get out. If you go now, I won't tell Frederick or Lissy."

He laughed. "They're hardly in a position to judge."

He looked at me for a moment, then shook his head. "Don't
tell me you didn't know? Oh come on, Elinor! You've seen
what they're like together. She can hardly keep her hands off
him."

So strange, that moment. His words made no sense, and
then they did.

Don't ask me who, because I won't tell you.

I could almost feel cogs grinding in my brain as it all slid
into place. How could I have been such a fool when it was all
there right in front of me? It wasn't that I hadn't noticed how
she laid her hand on his arm when they were talking, or rested
her head on his shoulder for a second when they were dancing,
but it was Lissy—she was affectionate with everyone. And she
was my friend.

"They're together right now," said George. "So why
shouldn't we enjoy ourselves too?"

Of course they were. It wasn't having guests in the house
that kept him from my room; it was her.

He walked round the bed toward me. "Come on, it'll be
good, I promise. Old Freddie's not the best at everything, you
know."

I backed away but lost my footing and fell back onto the
bed. As he leaned forward, fury—at him, at them, at the whole
thing—flashed through me. I pulled back my knee and drove
my foot into his groin. He yelped and tumbled back, grabbing
at the bedside table. The carafe of water spun through the air
and smashed on the mahogany floor.

"Bloody hell," he said as he got to his feet, clutching his
groin with one hand. "There was no need for that."

"Don't come near me again!"

"Shush, I won't. Look, I'm sorry. I've had far too much to drink, and I thought you were keen. You said I made you laugh!"

"How did you know? About them?"

"Oh, she told me. Two days before our wedding. Said she thought I should know she was in love with him and she didn't think she could ever give him up. Very honest woman, my wife."

"But you still married her?"

"I was hardly going to call it off and tell the world my beautiful, charming fiancée was at it like a rabbit with another man, was I? What a bloody fool I'd have looked. She promised she'd keep out of his bed till we had an heir and a spare, as they say, and I thought he'd lose interest, find someone else's wife to play with. But things generally go the way Lissy wants them to—it happened quickly, and we even got the spare at the same time. So they took up where they left off."

He ran a hand through his hair. "I'm sorry, again. It really would be best to keep this between ourselves. You do see that?"

"Just get out."

As he stepped outside, I heard him say, "Oh shit."

I went cold all over. Someone had heard. I'd done nothing wrong, but who'd believe me?

The voice outside was Kitty's.

"If I were you," she said crisply, "I'd scurry back to your own room. Before I wake the whole household."

She came in, her hair in rags for her wedding-day curls.

"Kitty, it's not how it looks—"

"I know that." Her eyes took in the glass and water all over the floor. "I saw him pawing at you earlier, but I didn't think he'd dare try anything more. I couldn't sleep, so I went downstairs for a bit, and I heard a crash. Are you all right? He didn't—"

I shook my head. "I kicked him. You know, there."

"Good for you. It's just a shame that's all the punishment he'll get."

"You're not going to tell everyone?"

"Don't be idiotic, what good would that do? It'd all be brushed under the carpet, and the only difference would be, you'd be in disgrace here. People always think it's the woman's fault. I'm sure even naïve little you must realize that."

"Well, you know what, Kitty? I'm even more stupid and naïve than you think. He said Frederick and Lissy were together. In bed."

She didn't look the slightest bit surprised.

"You *knew*?"

"I suspected," she said. "He's been smitten with her for as long as I can remember. And if you're going to ask why I didn't tell you, think who you'd have believed the worst of—the crabby sister-in-law who resents your very existence, or sunny-faced Lissy whom everyone loves, and who did such a good impersonation of being your friend?"

She sighed. "Will you tell him you know? Because you should realize, it probably won't make any difference. They'll carry on anyway."

"So you think I shouldn't?"

"If I were you, I'd keep it up your sleeve. I know my brother; he's not a total shit. So wait till you want something from him, then face him with it. He'll feel guilty, and you might as well get some use out of the situation."

CHAPTER 14

Kitty was right. Nothing to be gained by telling Frederick, or Lissy. It was humiliating enough that it was going on behind my back—how much worse if, knowing I knew, they carried on anyway? So I kept quiet.

At first it was hard not to say to her, "Stop pretending you're my friend." Or to him, "Stop pretending you made the noble sacrifice for your family. You didn't make any sacrifice at all; you got my money and kept her love." But I satisfied myself instead with finding ways to gouge little holes in their smug bubble of happiness. The next time Lissy called for dancing, I took Frederick's hand before she could palm me off with George.

After a couple of dances, she said, "George, that's the third time you've stepped on my toes! You take him, Elinor. He doesn't dance so badly with you."

I gave a merry little laugh and said, "No, thank you, I don't want my toes trodden on either."

She looked as though she hadn't understood, standing

there with her hand out to Frederick. But I just smiled, and she had to retreat back to George, saying, "My feet will be black and blue tomorrow, you wait and see."

Sometimes I let them have one dance before I said, "I'm claiming my husband back now, Lissy." Sometimes two. Never more. One evening she said, with a silvery laugh, that it wasn't fair of me to "hog" Frederick.

I gazed up at him, all adoring, and said, "Perhaps he's hogging me."

Of course he wasn't. But he couldn't say so, could he? There was a nasty little twist of pleasure in knowing he must be longing to touch her too, and I'd made him pretend to be happy dancing with me.

Those little victories, and the time I could snatch with Teddy, got me through the days, but I was sad to my bones that this was all the life I'd ever have. Living in this cold house with this cold family, seeing my son being brought up the same cold way they were, and now on top of all that, having to watch my husband and his mistress make a fool of me.

I was sadder about her than I was about him. I'd known long ago that he didn't love me, but I really did think she was my friend. But that was just convenient for both of them, wasn't it? They'd cooked it up between them, I suppose. It stopped me seeing what was in front of my eyes, and on top of that, I'd been fool enough to think she was trying to help me with her advice, but she was just making life easier for him. If I was lonely before I met Lissy, it was nothing to how lonely I was now.

So when a letter arrived from my father and tickets for the maiden voyage of the *Titanic* fluttered out onto my bed, I'll admit, I cried. I hadn't thought about the trip for a long time, but the slips of paper with White Star Line at the top brought back that day, when I tore out the article about the ship, and spotted the announcement of our engagement.

Until then I hadn't spilled a single tear over Frederick and Lissy. I'd worked hard at being angry instead. But I couldn't help it then. What a fool I'd been, right from the start. Thinking he'd put the announcement in the paper so quickly because he couldn't wait to tell the world he loved me, when he was just reeling me in, in case I saw the light and backed out. He needn't have worried: I was too naïve, too gullible, and too stupidly romantic to see anything at all. He was right; I'd read too many novels, and Jane Austen and Charlotte Brontë and all the rest of them had sold me a lie.

From the pile of books on the bedside table, I picked up the top one: *Pride and Prejudice.* A bundle of lies. Mr. Darcy was just like Frederick, with his great estate and his illustrious lineage. Probably had his own Lissy. I hurled the book across the room and it hit the door with a satisfying thud. As for *Jane Eyre*—we didn't hear the mad wife's story, did we? Perhaps she was driven mad by her husband being in love with someone else and only wanting her for her money and bringing her to live in a horrible cold house where she didn't fit in and never would. That one hit the wall. *North and South* followed, *Far from the Madding Crowd, Great Expectations*—all ridiculous. What were they thinking of, peddling lies like that? Making people—no, not people, girls and women—think love always found a way and a wedding day was a happy ending.

I didn't stop until *Middlemarch*, which is a big book, narrowly missed the dressing table mirror. I sat on the bed and looked at the books lying around the room. The tears had stopped, and I was strangely calm. I unfolded my father's letter.

> *My dear Ellie*
>
> *Here you are—tickets for an adventure! Imagine young Teddy seeing the other side of the world when he's barely more than a baby.*
>
> *The clerk at the shipping office said first-class passen-*

gers take their maids and valets. I shan't bother, but I bought five tickets for you, and the servants here are very envious of Rose's luck, I can tell you.

I am so looking forward to spending time with Teddy on the ship and getting to know Frederick a bit better too. And of course, seeing you, my daughter, who I miss so much.

Your loving father
Robert Hayward

I picked up one of the tickets and read the words on the front.

WHITE STAR LINE
First Class Passenger Ticket
per Steamship Titanic
Sailing from 10/4 1912

The return tickets were dated 20 April. I'd read the voyage took six days, so we must have four in New York, and six back again. Sixteen days away from Winterton Hall. And my father—thank goodness—had obviously not even thought of us taking Nanny. I'd have Teddy entirely to myself for all that time. I'd see my father again, and he'd meet his grandson at last. I'd been too afraid to suggest taking Teddy to Clereston in the terrible early months when I was trying to show I wasn't mad, and then later on, every time I asked, the Rolls was needed for something else, and of course it always would be— they didn't really want me in Teddy's life, and they certainly didn't want my father in it. So when I wrote to him, I made excuses: the journey was very long; Teddy didn't travel well in the motor car; I was so busy with Lady Storton's charitable endeavors. But these sixteen days would finally be a chance for them to get to know each other.

Had it been down to me, I'd have rather my father hadn't bought a ticket for Frederick, but of course he'd no idea how things were between us. And anyway, it tickled me to think how it would annoy Lissy for Frederick to be out of her clutches for a few weeks. Perhaps I'd get her to come shopping with me when I bought clothes for the trip, just to rub it in. I wiped my eyes and swore those would be the last tears I'd cry over either of them.

Next morning I caught Frederick alone in the morning room. I put the tickets beside his plate and sat down.

"What's this?"

"A present from my father. You must remember me telling you he'd offered to take us on the *Titanic*'s maiden voyage? He's bought tickets for us and Teddy, as well as himself, and for Rose and Terence to look after us."

He looked up, frowning. "Five first class tickets? Must have cost a fortune."

"Probably, yes. It's not any old ship, after all."

He flicked the tickets with his finger. "I'd rather he gave us the money, to put toward the roof repairs. Perhaps we could ask him to do that instead. I'm sure he could get a refund on the tickets."

So casual, as though he was saying no thank you to an extra helping of beef. A jolt of panic ran through me. I'd been so excited about getting away from Winterton that it hadn't occurred to me he might not want to go.

"I think it sounds marvelous," I said. "And you did once, too."

"But you must see, it's quite ridiculous of your father to be flashing money around like some kind of English Rockefeller when we have responsibilities here."

The contempt in his voice! My retort came out before I had time to think about it.

"He earns his money, and he's entitled to do what he likes with it. He's already given you more than you deserve, in the marriage settlement that you got under false pretenses. And if you think I'm going to ask him for more, you can think again."

It pleased me, how shocked he looked. Wasn't expecting that, was he? He thought we'd put all that behind us, now that we were "rubbing along together." Well, the time had come for him to find out we weren't. And to see if Kitty was right, that he could at least be made to feel guilty about Lissy.

I know my brother; he's not a total shit. So wait till you want something from him, then face him with it.

I was shaking inside, but I forced myself to speak calmly.

"I know about you and Lissy. You humiliated me, encouraging me to be friends with her when, all the time, you were leaping into her bed. And you told me that people like us didn't marry for love, and I was silly and naïve to expect love, when all the time, you had it, both of you. Well, if I can put up with all that, you can put up with a leaking roof. And with lowering yourself to spend time with my father. So we won't be throwing his generous gift back in his face."

A flush colored his cheeks. He picked up the tickets, fanned them and, without looking at me, said, "Well, we can't take Edward. There's no ticket for Nanny, and I'm certainly not paying for one."

Not a word about him and Lissy. No attempt at denial, no apology. Nothing. The silver coffee pot was right by my elbow and I could happily have tipped the contents over his head, but instead I screwed my napkin into a ball and stood up to leave.

"We're going on that ship," I said. "And Teddy is coming with us. When your mother objects, you'll tell her that. It's the least you can do."

CHAPTER 15

Lady Storton did object to us taking Teddy, of course, but Frederick told her, quite brusquely, that it was only just over a fortnight and I'd have Rose to help me. Her face was a picture.

He and I were back to barely speaking to each other, but the night before we were due to set off, I asked him if I could have a word about the voyage.

"I don't want my father to know how things are between us. He has no idea how badly everything turned out, and it would break his heart to know I haven't been happy."

He sighed. "Elinor, I wish you'd—"

I put up a hand to stop him. Nothing he could say was worth hearing.

"I'm asking you to pretend, that's all, for sixteen days. Can you do that?"

"If I can ask something of you in return."

"What?"

He ran a hand through his hair. "Don't tell Lissy that you know . . . about us. I don't want her embarrassed, and for things to become awkward."

I had to laugh at that. "I think they're already quite awkward, don't you?"

"She helped you when you were lonely."

"Yes, because it made life easier for you! That's all our so-called friendship was ever about."

"That's not true. She's genuinely fond of you."

That word again.

"I doubt that. But all right, there'll be no confrontation, as long as you play your part on this trip. Are we agreed?"

He nodded and walked away.

We traveled down to Southampton in the Rolls, driven by Wilson, with Rose and Terence, Frederick's valet, following behind in the smaller car. The whole way, Frederick sat silent, staring out of the window. Face like a wet Wednesday.

As we reached the harbor, there it was: the *Titanic*, towering over the dockside. So big that from inside the motorcar I couldn't even see the top of it; I had to duck my head and peer up through the window to see its full height, and four huge funnels standing proud against the overcast sky. The biggest ship ever built, the newspapers kept saying, and the most luxurious. I was looking forward to seeing the swimming bath I'd read about, the French restaurant, and the promenade deck where you could stroll right around the ship, but not nearly as much as I was looking forward to seeing my father again. He'd traveled down from Lancashire by train, so we'd agreed to meet on board. I smiled to myself; he'd probably be running a keen eye over the bed linen by now, pricing the fabrics to the yard.

The dockside was teeming with people, and Wilson had to edge the car through the crowd. Teddy stood on my lap, his little feet in their shiny new shoes digging into my thighs as he gazed wide-eyed at all the people. To my surprise, there were twice as many men as women, and most of them looked far from wealthy. It hadn't occurred to me people would be travel-ing on such a luxurious ship for anything other than pleasure, like us, but judging by the tearful farewells taking place on all sides, far more of the passengers were sailing to a new life in America. Right beside the car, a couple was saying goodbye to two lads in well-worn suits, each clutching a bulging sack. The man shook their hands, and the woman hugged them both, then gave each of them a soft little slap on the cheek and wagged her finger at them.

"Work hard, don't get yourselves into trouble, and be sure to write every month," she said. "Now, off you go, we can't be standing round here all day."

When they walked away, she burst into tears. The man gently patted her back as she sobbed.

"It's for the best, love. A new chance for the boys, you know that."

As the car nudged its way forward, I caught her answer. "But we'll never see them again, will we?"

I'd already had nightmares about saying goodbye to Teddy when they sent him away to school, so how must it feel to know you were saying goodbye to your sons forever? I hugged him close but he squirmed, pushing me away to carry on watching all the hustle and bustle. I couldn't help a dart of sad-ness: he was changing from a baby to a little boy, and I'd seen so little of the baby time. I nuzzled his head, trying to push those melancholy thoughts away; this trip was my chance to make up for it all, at least for a little while.

"This is quite ludicrous," said Frederick. "It's complete chaos. Surely they could have got these people aboard before the first-class passengers arrived."

These people. You'd have thought he was talking about a dif-ferent species. I didn't bother to reply.

"Look, Teddy," I said. "Look at the big ship. That's the *Ti-tanic* and we're going to sail across the sea on it."

"Big ship!" he said, in his half-baby, half-boy babble. "Going cross de sea!"

The Rolls pulled up close to a gangplank where a sailor was yelling, "First-class passengers this way! First class only!" Teddy chose that moment to kick off his shoe, and I had to scrabble on the floor for it. Frederick rolled his eyes and muttered, "This is what we have a nanny for," then stepped out of the car. By the time I'd got the shoe back on, everyone else was out on the quayside. Terence was helping Wilson unload our baggage, but Rose was just standing there, her face a picture of misery. I knew Terence was among those who'd been snooty to her at Winterton; had he upset her during the journey?

"What's the matter, Rose?"

She turned to me, her eyes wide, and said, "I can't do it. I can't go on that ship."

"Don't be silly, of course you can."

"It's too big; it can't be right for a ship to be that big. It can't be safe."

I sighed inwardly. Rose all over, my own personal Cassandra.

"Rose, it's the safest ship there's ever been. It said so in the newspapers."

She shook her head. "I didn't want to say, madam, but I've had dreams about it. Bad dreams."

Frederick gave a snort of laughter, and his valet echoed it in a smirk. I ignored them both.

"This is nonsense," I said. "Now come on, we'll get aboard and get settled, and you'll be fine."

Her lip trembled, and she shook her head.

"Please, Rose," I said. "I need you to help me with Teddy."

"I can't do it. I'd rather resign my position than step on that ship."

"You can't mean that."

"I do."

Frederick, of course, was enjoying the whole thing.

"Well," he said, "that rather puts the kibosh on the trip, doesn't it? We can't drag her onto the ship, and you can't travel without a maid *and* without a nanny."

"I'm sure I can manage—"

"I doubt that. But even if you could, what would people think? No, we'll have to cancel. It might not be too late to get a refund on the tickets."

My sixteen days were slipping through my fingers, and I couldn't bear it.

"I'm going," I said. "You can do what you like, but I'm going."

"Don't be ridiculous." He turned to his valet. "Find the shipping office, ask what we have to do about canceling the tickets, and how we get a message to Mr. Hayward on board."

Teddy was wriggling, wanting to be put down. Nervous about him getting lost in the crowd, I held on to him. He started whining, and I tried to distract him but the whine was threatening to turn into wails.

"You see?" said Frederick. "Coming without Nanny was ridiculous enough, I should never have agreed—"

"Excuse me, madam?"

We both turned to see a young woman, about my age, plainly but neatly dressed and carrying a battered suitcase.

"I couldn't help overhearing," she said in a Manchester accent as broad as mine used to be. "I've experience as a ladies' maid, and I'm good with children too; I had five younger brothers. I'm sailing on the ship anyway and I could do with earning some extra for when I get there. So if you'd take me on—just temporarily—I could help you out."

"I don't think so," said Frederick, at the same time as Rose said, "What a nerve!"

The young woman ignored them both and said to me, "I

know you don't know me from Adam but I have a good reference."

She scrabbled in her bag and handed me a letter. It was
from a Mrs. Fieldwood, at a smart address in London, and it
confirmed that she—Molly Mortimer was her name—had
been employed there as a ladies' maid, was honest and reliable
and recommended for further employment.

"Why did you leave this post?" I asked.

"I've family in New York. They've done well for themselves
over there, and they invited me to join them."

As I passed the letter to Frederick, she said, "I was paid
twenty-four shillings a week at Mrs. Fieldwood's. I'd be happy
to accept the same from you for the length of the voyage."

"The cheek of it!" said Rose. "Madam, surely you won't—"

"I think this solves our problem," I said.

Frederick looked up from scanning the letter, his face a picture of irritation, but before he could reply, I said, "You owe me
this."

He looked at me for a long moment, then said, "All right.
You win."

CHAPTER 16

My father had booked us a suite, and as we were shown in by a steward, even Frederick had the grace to look impressed. We had two large bedrooms with bathrooms, a sitting room and separate servants' quarters. The walls were panelled with pale blue silk brocade, the dark blue and gold carpet was soft and thick, and the furniture, all elaborately carved in gleaming dark wood, made some of Winterton's heirlooms look quite shabby.

"It's beautiful," I said. "I never imagined it would be like this."

"Wait till you see the rest," came my father's voice, and there he was in the doorway, smiling fit to burst. A little less hair, a rounder stomach, but then it had been over two years. Did I look different too? I sounded it, obviously. But though his face told me he'd noticed, he didn't comment; he just kissed me on the cheek and said, "I've missed you, Ellie." He smiled at Frederick. "Hope you've been looking after our lass."

"Good to see you again, Mr. Hayward."

They shook hands, Frederick's smile so easy you'd almost

have thought it was sincere. Teddy stared up at my father curiously.

"And this must be my grandson." My father crouched down to him. "What a big boy you are! Are you excited to sail across the ocean, lad?"

Teddy hid behind my skirts, his little hand holding fast to mine.

Frederick frowned. "Edward, say hello to your grandfather."

"It's all right, he doesn't know me yet. But we'll get to know each other better on this adventure, won't we?" He swept a hand round at the cabin. "Pretty special, eh? I won't deny, when I saw the price of the tickets, my eyes boggled, but you don't get luxury like this for the price of the Thelwell Ferry."

Frederick's smile got very thin at that.

The steward gave a polite cough. "May I ask if you've sailed on a liner before, madam and sirs?"

"We haven't," said Frederick.

"Well, people usually like to be up on deck as we set sail," said the steward. "The band'll be playing, and everyone down on the quay will be waving us off. I can show you the way if you like—she's so big, this one, I've got lost myself a couple of times."

Leaving Molly and Terence to unpack the baggage, we followed the steward up to the deck. I balanced Teddy on my hip, holding him tight as he waved at the crowds of people on the quayside—such a long way down now, it made me feel dizzy. I told my father what had happened with Rose, and how Molly had overheard our conversation and offered to step in.

"That was lucky. Silly of Rose though, to miss a chance like this. She'll regret it when she reads all about it in the papers."

Our cars were nowhere to be seen now. They must all have gone straight back to Winterton. Rose was very upset when we left them, and I'd promised to write straight away to Lady

Storton and ask that she didn't lose her position. She was my only link to home and the nearest I had to a friend now, and she knew how much I'd been longing for this trip. She wouldn't have let me down unless she was genuinely terrified, however silly that fear might be. I'd have to pray that Lady Storton wouldn't want the bother of sacking her and finding a new ladies' maid for me.

At twelve o'clock exactly, a whistle shrilled, so loud that Teddy shrieked and put his hands over his ears. My father copied him, wide eyes and all, which made Teddy giggle. Was there a likeness there, in the way they laughed? I hoped so. I'd never seen anything of myself in Teddy; he had the Coombes features and coloring, just like his father and grandfather, and all the ancestors that stared down from the walls of Winterton Hall. But seeing them together, there definitely was something of my father in his smile. That would annoy Frederick. Not that he could have noticed; he was staring moodily over the crowds, more like a man on his way to the gallows than someone heading for New York on the world's biggest ship. What had he said, the night we met, when I'd told him we planned to travel on the *Titanic*'s maiden voyage?

How marvelous. I'd love an adventure like that!

Perhaps it was true, back then. Who knew? I'd given up trying to work out when and where he'd lied to me. I wasn't even sure he knew himself.

As the band struck up "Land of Hope and Glory," and the gangways were pulled away, I gave myself a little shake. Frederick could be as miserable as he liked; I wasn't going to let him spoil this trip for me. For sixteen whole days, I wouldn't have to breathe Winterton's frosty air. My father's voice broke into my thoughts.

"Look at them!" He pointed down to the dock, where four men in overalls were running toward the ship, crew kitbags over their shoulders. "Come on, lads," he yelled. "You'll miss it!"

The men made it to the last gangway but the officer guarding it refused to let them board, and after much arguing and gesticulating, they stepped back, defeated, as the gangway was pulled away.

"They'll kick themselves for having that last pint," said my father. "Imagine missing this trip."

The crowds down on the quayside cheered as we edged away from the dock, Teddy watching fascinated as tugboats guided the huge ship out, looking like children's toys beside it. As we turned toward open water, the funnels belching smoke and the ship speeding up, we passed two more liners moored together. My father was just saying that the *Titanic* made even them look small, when there was a series of almighty cracks, like guns going off. Ropes tying up one of ships whipped up in the air and snapped back onto the quay, scattering the crowd down there. The outer ship had come loose from its moorings and it was drifting toward us, slowly at first but very quickly speeding up.

"Good God," said Frederick, steering me away from the rail. "It's going to hit us! Get back!"

The liner was heading straight for the side of the *Titanic*. Clinging tight to Teddy, I pressed myself against the outside of the saloon. There was chaos down on the other ship's deck, crew running around and red and white flags being raised and lowered, bells ringing and orders being shouted through a megaphone. In the water the little tugs tried to pull the ship back, but it kept coming, as though the *Titanic* was sucking it through the water. A few people had moved back, anxiously, like us, but mostly the passengers continued to hang over the rail, watching the scene as if it had been put on for their entertainment.

I tensed myself for the impact, but suddenly the *Titanic* stopped moving and the other ship slid past. There was a cheer from the passengers around us, and excited conversations broke out, everyone speculating about what had caused the problem.

"Well," said my father, "that was a bit more excitement than we wanted, but all's well that ends well."

"Looked dangerously chaotic to me," said Frederick. "How on earth could they let that happen?"

"This ship's built to stand up to worse than a little nudge like that," said my father. "Would've been a good test for it, in a way, but anyway, no harm done and we're on our way."

I hated to think what Rose would have made of it, and a guilty little part of me was glad she wasn't here. I was going to have enough trouble keeping the peace between my father and Frederick without having to calm her fears too. In the moment, it had been frightening, seeing the liner swing closer and closer, but it probably looked more dangerous than it was.

Even so, a couple walked by and the man said, "That's a bad omen if I ever saw one. If you ask me, it's a good thing we're getting off in Cherbourg."

My father shook his head when they'd passed. "Never heard anything so daft! Still, all the more champagne and fillet steak for us."

By the time we got back to the suite after watching all the fuss, Molly had the trunks unpacked and our clothes put away. She held out her hands to take Teddy.

"Is he hungry? Would you like me to give him something to eat and then put him down for a nap?"

The question threw me off for a second; nobody ever asked me anything like that.

"Yes, please."

I hesitated a moment . . . no, I would say it. Frederick was out of earshot in his own stateroom; he needn't even know.

"But once Teddy's had a nap, could you bring his crib in here?"

If I'd said that at Winterton, they'd have called the doctor again, but Molly didn't turn a hair.

"Of course, madam. It'll be nice for him to be near his mama, being as he's in a place he's not used to. Come on then, Teddy, we'll get you something to eat, and then you can have a little sleep."

Teddy was usually shy with strangers, but he went to her quite happily, and she took him off to her cabin. I wasn't a great believer in miracles, not by then, but surely Molly happening to stand beside us on the quayside when she did was one. I'd come so close to losing this precious time, and she'd saved me. Me and Teddy.

If I'm honest, when she made her offer, I think I'd have bitten her hand off even without the reference, but so far, she was living up to her own recommendation and her former mistress's. For a few minutes, I indulged myself in a little daydream: Nanny Cairns had run off with the coalman, or died—I honestly didn't care which—but Molly came back with us and replaced her, and everything was different. Silly nonsense of course, they'd never allow it, but at that moment, I let myself think that anything was possible. We were sailing to New York, on the world's biggest ship. If that could happen, perhaps anything could.

CHAPTER 17

My father was keen to explore the ship, and though Frederick plainly had no wish to be in his company, nor mine, manners won out; he could hardly slink off alone when my father had paid for the tickets. We started at the heart of the first-class quarters, where a grand wooden staircase descended seven levels from the Boat Deck, and a huge glass dome above flooded it with light. Up and down it we went, peeking into the dining saloon, where there must have been over a hundred tables set with snow-white cloths and crystal glasses; a beautiful white-paneled reading room; and a vast lounge with carved wooden paneling, huge mirrors, plush green velvet armchairs, and a gigantic electric chandelier hanging from the ceiling. It was magnificent, and everywhere you looked, people were open-mouthed at it all. Hard to believe that all this luxury and comfort was afloat on the ocean—you could barely notice the ship moving. I'd wondered if I might feel seasick, but it was so smooth we might have been sailing on a millpond.

"Look," said my father, pointing to a sign on the wall.

"There really is a swimming bath! Do you remember, how we couldn't believe it when we read that? Let's go and see."

It was in a lovely light room, with portholes to one side and changing cubicles to the other. It was about thirty feet long, and filled with clear blue water that was rippling with the motion of the ship—almost the only sign that we were moving at all. A notice on the wall said it cost twenty five cents to use the pool, rental of a costume included, and gave the separate times for men and women.

"Well, I'll be blowed," said my father. "Imagine, swimming *on* the sea, but not *in* the sea. That's worth a thousand pounds of anyone's money."

Pure disgust flashed across Frederick's face. He muttered something I didn't hear, turned away and said, "Shall we take a stroll around the deck?"

My father didn't seem to have noticed anything amiss, thank goodness. We walked the length of the deck and then stood for a while at the back of the ship, watching England disappear.

I'd heard someone say the Chief Purser decided who sat where in the dining saloon, and as we went in for luncheon, I was hoping we'd be put on one of the big tables that filled the middle of the room. Partly because I was on edge about my father noticing how frosty the atmosphere was between Frederick and me, but also because I really wanted to meet some Americans—they looked such a lot of fun. But we were shown to a smaller table for three, toward the edge of the room. I couldn't help looking over at the bigger one beside us where a group of eight, two older couples and two about our age, were having a high old time, raising coupes of pale gold champagne to a toast of "Going home!" and then "Going home *on the Titanic!*"

My father smiled at them, but Frederick rolled his eyes. "Noisy lot, the Americans. Not our sort of people at all. Thank goodness we got a table to ourselves."

"Thank you for bringing us," I said to my father.

"Yes," said Frederick. "Absolutely marvelous, thank you."

If you didn't know him, you'd have thought he meant it, and my father couldn't tell.

"It's a pleasure," he replied. "I've missed Elinor a lot, and I hope you and me will have a chance to get to know each other a bit better on this trip."

Ignoring the last part, Frederick answered smoothly, "Elinor's been kept very busy learning to run Winterton Hall, when the time comes."

"Of course," said my father. "She's got a good brain, and a good head for business. I bet she's given you a few new ideas about that estate of yours, hasn't she?"

Oh heck, I didn't want Frederick getting on his high horse about Winterton not being a business, not with my father. I jumped in quickly.

"It's more the house I'm learning about. You know, dealing with the servants, and entertaining guests, that kind of thing. Frederick and Lord Storton run the estate."

"Entertain a lot, do you?" said my father.

I could have bitten my tongue off. I hadn't told him, in my letters, about the house parties. I didn't want him to be hurt that he was never invited.

"It's expected, in our position," said Frederick. "Not always much fun, but one has to do it."

That was a lie; Frederick had quite a lot of fun at those house parties, with his mistress. But at least it spared my father's feelings and gave me a chance to move the conversation on.

"I wonder how many passengers there are in all," I said. "There must have been hundreds on the quayside."

"Less than they expected," said my father. "I was talking to a steward when I came aboard. He said the ship can take two and half thousand, but only just over half that booked. People are superstitious about maiden voyages, apparently. Completely daft, but that's people for you."

"That's still a lot," I said. "Where are they all?"

"Second and third class have their own quarters," said Frederick. "It'd hardly be worth buying a first-class ticket if they mixed everyone together."

"Twice as many down there in third class as up here," said my father. "Over seven hundred, the steward said."

I'd seen the captain strolling the deck as we came in to luncheon, smiling and glad-handing the first-class passengers; he hadn't looked at all like a man who had that many people to worry about, but then I supposed he was used to it.

Frederick said, "That girl, the maid, did rather well for herself, then. Paid for a third-class ticket, travels in first—I really can't see why we're paying her a wage as well."

A frown flickered across my father's face. He opened his mouth to speak, but luckily at that point our desserts arrived, cherry soufflés with a velvety chocolate sauce, and by the time the waiters had ceremoniously made a hole in the soufflés and poured the sauce with a flourish, the moment had passed. After that, the conversation flowed smoothly and for once I was grateful for the ability Frederick and all his circle had, of making pleasant conversation without saying much. We talked about what New York might be like, and what we should do there. I'd read about buildings called skyscrapers, more than forty floors high, an enormous park with a zoo—Teddy would love that—and a huge statue that you could climb up inside and then come out at its head. It sounded like a different world, and I was excited about seeing it all.

"They've department stores that make Kendal's and Lewis's look like village shops," said my father. "I thought you and me might have a nosey round and see what's selling, if Frederick can spare you for a morning." He turned to Frederick. "Ellie always had a good eye for the next big thing. I miss her advice, to be honest."

I had to turn away then, unexpected tears pricking my eyes. It had been so long since I'd been properly useful, and it meant a lot to hear him say that. I made a promise to myself that when we were in New York, I'd find him the next big thing, something he could be the first to sell in England.

For all the marvels of the ship, what I'd longed for was time with Teddy, so I was pleased when my father said he needed to write a letter to go with the mail when we docked at Queenstown in Ireland next morning. When he'd gone, Frederick mumbled something about having a cigar in the smoke room. I didn't bother to answer. He didn't want to be with me, and that was fine—I didn't want to be with him either. I knew perfectly well why he'd been so silent and sullen in the car that morning. The previous afternoon, I'd heard him ask the butler to get Bellingham Hall on the telephone, so I stood upstairs in the gallery and eavesdropped. His hearty "Good afternoon, George" didn't fool me; he was talking to her. And by the sound of it, she wasn't very happy with him. Twice he said, "Of course I'm not," and then there was a long pause when she must have been speaking, and he said, "Well, I can't do that, obviously," and it went quiet. I peeked over the banister; he was striding away. She must have hung up. So quite likely he had a letter to write too, his last chance to send his love before we sailed across the Atlantic.

For a moment I toyed with the idea of writing to her myself, telling her that we were having a lovely time together. I could still see her tight little smile when I'd lied about how pleased Frederick was when the tickets arrived. He'd have told her otherwise, but I liked to think she couldn't be certain which of us was lying.

No, I wouldn't bother. I wasn't going to waste a moment of the trip on her, or him. I was going to enjoy this time with my son and my father and store up some memories that I could bring out to comfort myself when it was all over and I had to go back. As Frederick walked away, I poked my tongue out at his retreating back, then went downstairs to fetch Teddy.

CHAPTER 18

As I came down in the lift to our corridor—a lift on a ship, it was so peculiar!—Molly was just coming out of our suite, holding Teddy by the hand. His little face lit up; he called out "Mama!" and my heart flipped over.

"I was going to take him up on deck, madam," said Molly. "He's got ants in his pants now that he's had a nap."

I hadn't heard that phrase in a long time. My mother used to say it about my father, when he had a new idea for the business. It was like hearing her voice when Molly said it, and I couldn't stop myself asking.

"You're from Manchester, Molly, aren't you?"

"Yes, madam."

"I thought so. That's where we're from—my family, I mean. My parents both grew up in Ancoats."

Her glance at my French silk dress and the pearls at my throat told me she didn't know what to make of that, so I put her out of her misery.

"Have you heard of Robert Hayward?"

"The cotton king? Of course I have."

"I'm his daughter. He's traveling with us."

Her mouth dropped open. "Well, I never!" she said, and then, embarrassed, "Sorry, milady. It's just you don't . . ."

"Don't sound like a girl from Ancoats?" I said. "No, well, I've rather had the corners rubbed off since I married."

And with every single "Rain in Spain" and "Look at the books on the hook," another little bit of myself scrubbed out.

"But by 'eck," I said, slipping back into my old accent and hamming it up a bit, "I've got Manchester running through me like a stick of Blackpool rock."

It came out as easily as breathing. She laughed, and I did too, and then there was an awkward silence. One didn't laugh with the servants, she knew that as well as I did, and she wasn't to know that I hadn't laughed with anyone for so long—not honestly, anyway—that I'd almost forgotten how it felt.

"Well," she said, "should I take Teddy up on deck, then, for a walk?"

"I'd like to take him," I said, and even then, I couldn't keep the hesitation out of my voice—so used to always being told I couldn't or shouldn't.

She must have thought it strange, but she just said, "Of course, madam."

As she turned to go, on impulse I said, "Why don't you come with us?"

There was a quite a crowd up on the deck, and excitement in the air: people were smiling, and little groups, all beautifully dressed, stood around chatting and laughing. They were American, mostly: so fascinating to hear snatches of conversation in their unfamiliar accents.

As we passed one group, Teddy holding my hand and Molly's, a very pretty woman in a cherry red coat and a lovely hat trimmed with feathers was saying, "Of course I'm excited! It's something special, this ship, and we're the first ones on it.

There'll be photographers when we reach New York, you wait and see."

"And you'll be sure to get in the pictures," the man beside her said.

She laughed. "Of course. A girl has to be seen if she wants to stay ahead."

She sounded so bold and confident, but then they all did, these people who reached up and scraped the sky.

Molly was staring at her, and when we'd passed them, she said in a loud whisper, "Did you see who that was, madam? Dorothy Gibson!"

"The actress?"

"Yes! I'd know her anywhere," she said. "She was in *Miss Masquerader*. I saw it at the Gaiety."

"The Gaiety on Peter Street? The theatre?"

"It's a picture house now. *Miss Masquerader* was the first one they showed."

"I used to go to there with my mam," I said.

I hadn't said that word in a long time, but there's something about hearing the accent you grew up with that makes you feel comfortable with a person. Perhaps that's why I said such a daft thing next.

"Funny to think we might have known each other in Manchester, if things had been different."

She smiled. "I think things would've had to be *very* different for us to have known each other then, madam. I doubt I'd have bumped into you at the tripe stall in Church Street market."

Lady Storton would have been apoplectic at a servant speaking to her like that, but I couldn't help laughing.

"No, it's true, I didn't spend a great deal of time there. And I don't think I've ever eaten tripe."

"Well, you've missed nowt in that."

"Do you know what I do miss, though? Rag pudding. We had it every Wednesday at home."

It was my father's favorite: minced meat, onions, and gravy, in thick suet pastry, cooked in a muslin cloth.

"Our cook was under strict instructions to follow the recipe my mother used when they were first married," I said. "The first time we had it after she died, it made us both cry."

I hadn't thought of that evening for years, the pair of us weeping into our dinners because she'd never be there on a Wednesday night again. I hadn't thought of rag pudding for a long time either, but now I could almost taste it.

"Aye," said Molly, "grub can be like that, can't it? Pease pudding's what makes me think of my mam. She taught me to make it, before she passed, but I could never get it to taste the same."

"When did your mother die?"

"Six years ago, when I was fifteen."

"The same as mine," I said. "It's a hard age for a girl to lose her mother. And you had—what was it, five little brothers as well?"

"That's right. The youngest was only a babby, so I had to bring them up, really."

Just at that moment Teddy, who'd toddled on ahead, took a tumble and fell headlong on the deck. He lifted his head and opened his mouth to cry out, but quick as a flash, Molly ran and lifted him to his feet, gave him a big smile and said, "Don't cry, Teddy, you're all right! Didn't hurt, did it?"

She made a shooing motion and he set off again, none the worse.

"Does that always work?" I said.

"Only if you nip in quick before they start. I learned it with my second brother—he had summat wrong with his ankles, poor Bob, he was forever falling over."

"Who's looking after your brothers now?"

"They've a stepmother—my father married again."

"Was that strange for you? I can't imagine how I'd feel if my father got a new wife."

"I didn't like it much, to be honest. We didn't get on, her and me, and that caused a falling-out between me and my father. That's why I took myself off to London and got the position with Mrs. Fieldwood."

"What do they think about you going to live in America?"

She shrugged. "They don't know. I'd no reason to tell them—it's five years ago I left. I wrote with my address, but my father didn't write back, and I've not heard from them since. Don't suppose the youngest even remembers me."

"That's very sad."

"It is, but there's nowt I can do about it. And if I'd stayed at home, I don't suppose I'd be sailing to a new life in America now. So perhaps they did me a favor."

Dinner that evening was delicious—cream of barley soup, asparagus vinaigrette, salmon mousseline, filet mignon that cut like butter—and it tasted all the better for not being eaten with thirteen generations of ancestors glowering down at me.

"You'll never guess who I got talking to in the library this afternoon," said my father. "Only the man who designed the ship! Nice fellow, worked his way up from being an apprentice. He told me he goes on the maiden voyage of every ship, just to see if anything needs improving. Likes to oversee every detail."

"Like you," I said, smiling.

"Never hurts to keep a close eye. It's the same with the estate, Frederick, I should think?"

"Absolutely," replied Frederick. "We have a manager, of course, but Lord Storton and I are on top of the big decisions."

I had to hide a laugh at that: if they were on top of anything, I was Cleopatra. My father's eyes would have popped clean out of his head if he'd seen the ropey set of accounts I'd once spotted on Lord Storton's desk in the library.

"Very interesting to hear how it all came together," my father went on. "No expense spared, he said—they've used the best of everything. The only thing the shipping line quibbled about was the number of lifeboats. He wanted more, but they said they'd ruin the view from the decks."

"There are enough, though?" I said.

"Oh aye, more than they're required to have, there's no worry there. And he told me all about the construction, how exactly they've made it so safe."

As I've mentioned before, on the subject of machinery and suchlike my father would give you the ins and outs of a pig's backside, and it sounded like the chap he'd met was the same. My father had the whole story to tell us—something about watertight compartments that they could close off at the flick of a switch, so even a hole in the side wouldn't sink the ship. Frederick nodded here and there, but he wasn't really listening, and to be fair, nor was I. I was just enjoying eating the wonderful food, eavesdropping on the conversations of the Americans around us, and knowing this was only the first day of a whole sixteen of them.

When the coffee and brandies arrived, Frederick stood up and, with a ridiculously exaggerated yawn, said, "The early start is catching up with me. You'll excuse me if I go to bed?"

When he was gone, my father took a sip of his brandy, leaned back in his chair and said, "It's good to see you, Ellie. And Teddy—he's a fine lad."

"I'm sorry you haven't seen more of him up till now," I said. "It's just . . ."

"Difficult? I'm not daft, lass. Doesn't take a genius to work out that Frederick and his family don't think me suitable company for the future Lord Storton. But I'd like to know that you don't think the same, that it hasn't been your choice to keep Teddy from me."

"Of course it hasn't!"

How awful that he'd realized what they thought of him, though I should have known; he was cleverer than any of them.

No point in denying it, but I didn't want that conversation to go any further. Because even though I had no choice about it, it felt disloyal, letting myself be absorbed into Frederick's family when they thought so little of mine. I remembered my father's face, down there in the suite that morning, when he heard me talking like they did. Like I was ashamed of where I came from. I wished I could say, I had to do this, in the end, and tell him why, but I still couldn't bear for him to know they looked down on me as much as they did him.

So I said, "I think Teddy's got a look of you about him, don't you?"

"Perhaps, yes. I wish your mam could have known him. She'd have been so proud of you."

"He knows all about her though, and about you. I've been telling him since he was a little baby. All about Clereston, and the mills as well."

"I hope he'll come and see them for himself, one day."

So did I, but if Frederick had anything to do with it, Teddy'd be more likely to fly to the moon. I changed the subject.

"Have you decided on the management committee yet?"

After my father took the decision not to leave the company to me in his will and instead to put it in trust for all the workers, he'd been enjoying playing all his managers off against one another with the carrot of a seat on the committee. He happily launched into an explanation of the final list and why he'd picked them, and if he noticed I'd not answered his remark about Teddy visiting the mills, he didn't say so.

We sat on for about another hour, chatting and listening to a band playing jazz, and then went back to our rooms. Teddy was sound asleep in a crib by my bed, and after Molly had helped me into my nightgown and brushed out my hair, I lay down to sleep in the same room as my son for the first time. As I fell asleep listening to his breathing, my last thought was that I could happily stay on this ship forever.

CHAPTER 19

I woke early next morning to the sound of Teddy chatting happily to himself in his crib, and honestly, it was one of the best moments of my life. His little face lit up in a smile as I reached in and picked him up, then took him back to bed with me. We spent a happy twenty minutes or so looking at one of his picture books, and it was only when he said he was hungry that I realized I had no knowledge at all of his routine. Rose had been given a list of instructions by Nanny, and my plan was that, once we were on board, she'd pass them on to me so I could look after Teddy myself. But now, here I was, with my own son, and I didn't know what he had for breakfast—I'd never even seen him eat. And though I was aware that Nanny had trained him to use the pot before he was six months old, I had no idea of his toilet requirements now either. So there was nothing for it but to ring for Molly.

"I'm sorry, madam," she said as she hurried in, looking a little pale. "I didn't want to disturb you if you were still asleep. I can take him now though."

"No, it's fine, I want to spend time with him—I don't get

much chance at home." I laughed to cover my embarrassment. "I don't even know what he likes for breakfast."

"Well, my brothers were all very fond of bread in milk at that age. Shall I ask the steward to bring that, and we'll see?"

By the look on his face, Teddy had never seen bread in milk, but under Molly's guidance, I sprinkled brown sugar on top, blew on a spoonful to cool it, and when I spooned it into his mouth, his face creased into a smile. It took half an hour to get the small bowlful into him—he was keen to feed himself but not very accomplished, and on top of that a slow and contemplative chewer—and I loved every second of it. I loved washing his face and hands afterward too, and tickling him as I got him dressed in a little sailor suit. And while I can't truthfully say I loved getting my new satin slippers covered with urine (he was less expert at using the toilet than Molly predicted), his giggle at the shock on my face was so infectious I found myself laughing too.

I was so caught up with him that I didn't notice Molly wasn't just pale, she was what my mam used to call "green about the gills." Just as I'd got Teddy dressed, she put her hand to her mouth, muttered "Oh no," and rushed into the bathroom. Not seasickness, surely? You could still hardly feel the ship moving. Had she eaten something that disagreed with her? But she'd said the food in the servants' dining room was very good, and surely no one got food poisoning on a ship like this? I could only imagine what Lady Storton would have made of a servant being sick in her bathroom; she'd had a face like she'd sucked a sour plum when I'd once had to rush out of the morning room when I was expecting Teddy. And with that thought, the penny dropped.

When Molly came out I saw what I hadn't noticed before; a tell-tale thickening of the waist on her otherwise delicate frame, and buttons that had obviously been moved to accommodate it.

"I'm so sorry, madam," she said. "It's the movement of the ship, I think."

"It isn't that, is it? I'd rather you told me the truth, Molly. Are you expecting a baby?"

"Yes," she said flatly.

"Is that the real reason you left your position?"

She nodded. "The mistress said she was sorry to see me go, but . . ."

She didn't need to finish the sentence. No respectable household would keep a servant on in that situation. Frederick would be livid if he found out.

"But honestly, apart from the sickness—which passes quickly, I'm fine by mid-morning—I'm perfectly able to work."

I couldn't let her go; I needed her help. But besides that, I liked her already—and she was in enough of a predicament without me sitting in judgment.

"I think we can keep this to ourselves—just stay out of my husband's way," I said. "Now, I'd better get dressed for breakfast."

I was only just ready when Frederick knocked on the door. I didn't want him to know I had Teddy's crib in with me, so I slipped out and closed the door behind me. We met my father at the table and the conversation over breakfast was quite cordial, though when Frederick said he thought he'd go for a swim, I prayed my father wouldn't suggest joining him. He didn't, and after collecting Teddy and dropping off my letter to Lady Storton about Rose at the purser's office, the three of us went up on deck.

The sea was calm and the weather mild. More passengers had come on board at Cherbourg the evening before, and now we stood at the rail as the ship sailed toward Queenstown in Ireland, the last stop before we crossed the Atlantic. Obviously too big for the harbor, the *Titanic* anchored outside it and two small boats brought out about a dozen new passengers, then took away sacks of mail. Was there a letter in there for Lissy? Probably, but I couldn't even bring myself to care now. About half a dozen passengers left too; how could they bear it, to watch this beautiful ship sail away to New York without them?

The whistle blew and the ship began to move again.

"Next stop, New York!" said my father.

How strange to think that for the next five days, we'd be out on the ocean, miles from any land. What would happen if, say, someone was taken ill when we were so far from help? I shook off the silly thought: there must be a doctor on board. They had everything else, after all.

As the ship sailed serenely along the coast of Ireland, the motion still barely noticeable, we took a stroll, the three of us, Teddy holding my hand and looking curiously all around him. It made my heart happy to see how people smiled at him as we passed. Still a little shy at first, he clung to me, but whenever my father spoke, he seemed fascinated, and after a little while, he reached up and took his hand, to my father's obvious delight. Was it because my father sounded like I used to, back when he was a baby? Perhaps that was also why he'd taken so easily to Molly—after all, I'd done the same.

Near the front of the ship, a little crowd had gathered; someone said they'd seen porpoises. My father picked Teddy up so he could see, and just then Frederick appeared, his hair slicked back after his swim.

"There you are!" He smiled, and ruffled Teddy's hair. "Look at this little sailor, in his uniform."

His words might have been pleasant, but his face said he wasn't happy to see Teddy in my father's arms, so I said quickly, "He likes walking round the deck, looking at all the people. Shall we take a turn around together, before luncheon?"

"Good idea," said Frederick, and then, as my father set Teddy down, "Will you hold Papa's hand, Edward? We don't want you getting lost."

He held out his hand, but Teddy reached up for my father's hand instead.

I said quickly, "Hold Papa's hand now, there's a good boy. Let's show him all the things we've seen this morning."

He took Frederick's hand then, and I avoided my father's curious glance.

We stopped to watch three portly American men playing a game of shuffleboard, using long sticks to scoot a flat black disc across a court painted on the deck. Teddy was fascinated, clapping his hands every time the disc skated across the court, and one of the men held out his stick.

"Want to have a go, little fella?"

The stick was taller than he was, but I helped him hold it and he whacked the disc surprisingly hard, scoring an eight. The three men cheered.

"Got yourself a champion there," said one. "You oughta teach him to shoot pool next."

Teddy wasn't keen to relinquish the stick, but he was distracted when my father crouched down beside him and talked to him about how the game was played. Teddy hung on to his every word, gazing up at him. It warmed my heart to see it, but at the same time, it made me sad to think they'd both been deprived of this up till now, and they would be again, as soon as we went home. It wasn't right: Teddy was a part of our family too, he had Hayward blood in his veins, and for all they knew, he might grow up better suited to running cotton mills than the Storton estate. But he was never going to get the chance to find out, was he? Frederick's frown, watching them together, said it all. There was only ever going to be one grandfather allowed in Teddy's life.

* * *

All day, my thoughts kept straying to Molly's revelation that morning. It worried me, her going off to a different country, in her predicament. That evening, when she was doing my hair before dinner, I asked her if she'd thought about going home to her family, when she found out she was expecting.

"Not for a minute. They didn't want me before, so they certainly won't now, and I wasn't going to beg for their charity. My mam was always talking about her cousin in New York, how well she'd done for herself over there. Mam wanted to go with her when she left England, but my father wouldn't take the chance. So I thought, I'll do what she wasn't able to. I wrote to Ruth, and she said to come."

"So you've somewhere to stay when you get there?"

"Oh aye, it's all arranged. They've only a small place, but there's room and they can arrange work for me."

"And they don't mind about . . ."

She bit her lip. "They don't know. I thought if I told them they might say no. Because they don't know me yet; I'm just a name on a letter. But once I'm there, on their doorstep, they're not going to throw me and the baby out, are they?"

"Goodness. It seems . . . well, a bit of a risk."

"I know . . ." She lifted her chin and said, "But sometimes you have to take a risk, if you want to get on in life. That's why I went to London, when I could've just got a job in—pardon me for saying this—in a cotton mill. And all right, it didn't go the way I'd planned, but I'm blowed if I'm going to give up and go home with my tail between my legs. I've got even more reason to make something of myself now—I want to give my baby a good life. And America's the place to do it."

She pinned back a wayward curl at my temple, then teased out the front a little until it was flatteringly full around my face. She was a lot better with hair than Rose.

"Will you wear the diamond earrings, tonight, madam? Or the emerald drops?"

"The diamonds, thank you. It sounds exciting, all your plans. Is she nice, your mother's cousin?"

"I've never met her. I wasn't born when she went to America. But Mam used to read us her letters. She found herself a husband, not long after she got there, and they live in an apartment—that's what they call it in New York, when you've got lodgings in a building with other people—with his mother and their children, a boy and a girl."

"Is he American, the husband?"

"No, he's from Sweden. She says there are people from all over, where they live—Italians, Germans, Irish, Jews from Poland and Lithuania—but everyone gets along, even though they're all living cheek by jowl. The mother-in-law sounds a bit of a baggage, mind you—Ruth says she likes to rule the roost."

Well, I knew what that was like, and I felt sorry for Ruth.

"Won't you be homesick, so far away?"

"I've nothing to be homesick for, have I? My family you know about, and the father of my child turned out to have a wife and three daughters living happily in Deptford."

"I'm sorry. Were you very fond of him?"

"I thought the sun shone out of his eyes. And he told me the sun shone out of mine. More fool me to fall for a line like that."

I'd fallen for a lot less.

Her eyes met mine in the mirror. "My mam used to say, everything happens for a reason, and now, I'm getting the chance to turn something bad into something good. Perhaps it sounds silly to you, madam, but that's the way I look at it."

She looked so determined. In that moment I went from feeling afraid for her to being envious of her courage. She'd done the same with us back on the quayside in Southampton, hadn't she? Seen an opportunity and reached out for it. A bit like my father did, all those years ago with the shop. And yet here was I, the cotton king's daughter, not reaching out for anything at all, just accepting that my life was decided by other people. And Teddy's life, too.

"It doesn't sound silly," I said. "It sounds brave, and I wish you luck with it all."

CHAPTER 20

Much as I loved the ship and the adventure of sailing to New York, I'd have happily done the trip in a fishing boat, just for the time I was able to spend with Teddy. Even when he woke up grumpy on the second morning and whined his way through his bowl of bread and milk, then squirmed and yelled when I dressed him, I treasured those ordinary little snatches of his life that were usually kept from me. At Winterton, I only ever saw him fed and dressed and presentable, and now I could hold him in my arms and comfort him without worrying that Lady Storton would decide I was mollycoddling him.

I tried, really hard, not to think about the trip ending. I'd looked forward to these sixteen days for so long, and I wanted to keep them whole and perfect, and not let reality creep in. But the more time I spent with Teddy, the more I got to know my own son and he got to know me, the more the shadow of going back crept over me.

On the third night, I sat by his cot, just watching him sleep. The sea air made me drowsy, but I tried to keep my eyes open and capture every precious minute. Every so often, his mouth twitched into a little smile and I hoped he was having happy dreams. It was unbearable to think that when we returned to Winterton, he'd be taken away from me again. How on earth, after this, was I going to hand him back to Nanny after twenty minutes? I worried, too, that I'd made things worse for him, getting him used to being with me, when he'd have to go back to the nursery when we got home. Had I been selfish to bring him at all? Perhaps I'd at least have given him some happy memories from these sixteen days. But they wouldn't be enough to protect him when he was sent away to school, to be "toughened up."

I kept thinking of Molly, and how brave she was, taking such a risk for her child's sake. I hoped she was right, that her relatives would take her in anyway, but even if they didn't, I had the feeling that Molly would pick herself up and find another solution. She didn't seem to let anything stand in her way.

We'd chatted, that evening as she did my hair for dinner, about Manchester, the places we both knew. I might have seen them from the backseat of a chauffeured motorcar, and Molly from the tram, but we had a lot of memories in common. And when we took up the conversation again later, as she brushed out my hair for bed and hung up my evening clothes, she got to talking about her family: her mother who was rarely well, her father who sounded like an out-and-out bully and was none too fond of work, the five little brothers who were always getting into scrapes. She didn't say so, but it was plain she'd been holding the household together from a very young age. And then her father had thrown it all back in her face, bringing in a stepmother who made it plain Molly was no longer needed, and not welcome either.

"Sorry, madam," she'd said as she buttoned up my nightgown. "I'm talking your ear off, aren't I?"

"Not at all." I handed her my rings to put away, slathered

my hands with cream of lavender and slipped on my sleeping gloves. "I'm just sorry you had such a difficult time of it at home."

"Leaving my brothers was the worst of it," she said. "The little ones all confused, and the oldest, Sam, biting his lip so he wouldn't cry."

"You haven't heard from them since?"

She shook her head. "I thought a clean break was better for them. My father's wife, she'll care for the boys—I wouldn't have left them if I wasn't sure of that—but she wanted them to think of her as their mam, and Sam would've struggled to do that with me still in the picture. The youngest ones probably don't even remember me now, and that's for the best."

She looked down at her stomach. "If this one's a boy, I'm going to call him Sam. And maybe one day I'll tell him about his uncles in Manchester."

"But you don't think you'll ever come back?"

"And have my child grow up poor, like me?" She shook her head. "Ruth's children go to a good school, completely free, and she says that in America, if you get yourself an education, you can do anything. That's what I want for him. Or her."

Before she went back to her own cabin, I asked her if, when she was settled, she'd write and tell me. I wanted to know there was a happy ending to Molly's story.

CHAPTER 21

We settled into a pleasant morning routine, my father and I taking a stroll around the deck with Teddy while Frederick had a swim, and by the fourth morning, Teddy had completely taken to his grandfather. He held his hand as we walked, chatting happily away, and my father, even when he couldn't make out Teddy's babble, conversed back for all the world as though they were the same age.

We walked to the back of the ship and stood at the rail, watching long frills of white foam stream out as the ship carved its way through the ocean.

"I think we've picked up speed," said my father. "Perhaps it's true, they're trying to beat the *Olympic*'s time."

We'd read in *The Times* that the *Titanic* might try to get to New York faster than a sister ship from the same line had on its maiden voyage.

"I hope not," I said. "I love being on here. I wish it would go slower."

He laughed. "Well, there's still the return journey to look forward to."

I didn't answer. The thought of that return journey was like a big dark cloud hanging over me. Life at Winterton Hall was going to be more miserable than ever, now I'd tasted something else.

Even on the *Titanic*, with all its pleasures, my father didn't break the habit of being early to bed and early to rise. As part of our agreement not to let him see the coldness between us, each evening Frederick and I sat on in the saloon for ten minutes or so after he said goodnight, just for the look of the thing. Then, when I could be sure my father was safely tucked up, I'd leave Frederick to it and go back to my stateroom.

On the fifth night, after my father left, Frederick mentioned that he'd seen me and Teddy in the gymnasium that afternoon, as he walked past on his way to have a cigar in the smoke room. It'd got quite chilly after luncheon, and I'd spotted that children were allowed in there between one and three. He'd had a good time on the electric horse, me holding him steady while it lurched backward and forward and he giggled fit to burst, his little face beaming.

"He looked like he was enjoying himself on that horse contraption," said Frederick. "We'll have to see about a pony for him soon."

"Perhaps I should learn to ride too," I said. "Then we could all go out together."

I'd no intention of going anywhere near a horse, but a few weeks before, I'd happened to walk past Frederick as he came in from his afternoon ride, and smelled roses in full bloom. No wonder he went out so often. And now there it was, a satisfying glimpse of panic in his eyes at the thought of losing the chance to snatch a little secret time with Lissy.

"I don't think it would be something you'd enjoy," he said.

"Probably not as much as you, no. But, then, you've had such a lot of practice."

He didn't rise to that, just picked up his whisky glass, swirled it around and took a gulp. We sat in silence for a few moments, him looking out of a window, me watching the band without really seeing them. He put down his glass.

"I thought we were paying that girl to look after Edward? She wasn't with you this afternoon."

"We're paying her to be my maid. I'm looking after Teddy. He's sleeping in my cabin, and I get him up in the morning and put him to bed at night. Molly only sits with him for his afternoon nap and when we're at luncheon and dinner."

"I see."

His face gave nothing away. I regretted, now, irritating him with the comment about riding. It meant this really wasn't the best time to say what was on my mind, but since it had come up, perhaps I should? No sense in leaving it till the last day—this way he'd have time, after I'd planted the idea, to see that it could work.

"Look, I was thinking, when we go back, what if we don't have a nanny, but just two nursery maids? Then I could look after Teddy, mostly, but there'd be someone to take care of him when I was busy. I'd still have time for my duties at Winterton, so your mother couldn't complain about that."

"You know she wouldn't like the idea, regardless of that."

"Because she thinks I'd mollycoddle him. Well, my parents didn't mollycoddle me. They wanted me to be happy and loved, that's all, and that's what I want for Teddy. I know it's not how your family usually does things, but it's how I was brought up, and he's my son too. And I like looking after him."

"You seem to have managed very well."

I could hardly believe my ears.

"So you'll back me up? I'm sure if you said—"

"But what comes next?"

"What do you mean?"

"Even if I thought this was a good idea, which I don't necessarily, it wouldn't be enough, would it? The next thing would be that you don't want him to go away to prep school."

"I already don't want him to go away to prep school."

"Exactly. But he has to."

"Why does he have to?"

"Because it's what people do. It's what everyone does. If we didn't send him away to school, people would think there was something wrong with him."

"We could send him to the village school."

He ran a hand through his hair and sighed. "Come on, Elinor, now you're being ridiculous. Edward is the future Lord Storton. He can't go to school with the baker's son and the butcher's son and, for all I know, the local poacher's son."

"What I think is ridiculous—and cruel—is sending a child of seven away from home. You told me yourself how miserable you were when you went."

He waved a hand. "I was upset for a few days, that's all. It did me no harm."

"It didn't sound like that to me."

"Well, on that we'll have to agree to disagree."

It was the same tone his mother used, the one that meant: "The subject is closed." Once again, the reality crashed over me like cold water: this was just an interlude, and when it was over, I was going back to all that.

"You've seen how happy Teddy is; you've seen how much happier I am, but none of that matters to you, does it? Everything's got to stay the same, whatever the cost."

I realized I'd raised my voice when a couple of women at the next table turned to look, but I was beyond caring.

Frederick glanced round. "Keep your voice down, people are staring," he muttered.

"Why do you care? They're not our sort of people, you said."

Now people were definitely listening. Heads turned our way and the conversations at the nearest two tables fizzled out.

"Elinor! What on earth has got into you?"

"You! You, and your family, and your house, and your . . . your stupid, stupid traditions." I slammed down my glass and stood up. "I need some fresh air."

CHAPTER 22

When I stepped out onto the promenade deck, a wave of cold hit me. The temperature dropped every evening, but it hadn't been more than chilly before; now it was bitter. I turned to go back in—my evening dress had bare shoulders, and I hadn't thought to grab my angora stole—but there was Frederick, coming up the stairs, two at a time.

"Well, that was a fine display! You've got half the room gossiping about us now."

"Like I said, what do you care? You look down on the people in there, just like you look down on my father. And, let's be honest, on me."

"Don't be ridiculous; you're my wife. Of course I don't look down on you."

He reached out to take my hand, but I jerked it away.

"Why do you have to be like this?" he said. "I know you struggled at first, but I thought we were rubbing along together quite well now."

"Oh, *you* are. You got a wife with bags of money, and a mistress whose bed you can jump into any time you like. So, yes, I'd say you're rubbing along rather well. But I'm not."

"So this is all about Lissy?"

"It isn't. It's about Teddy. But since we're on the subject, did you really think I'd never find out? Or didn't you care?"

"Elinor—"

"Do you know how humiliating it was, to know the pair of you were laughing at me?"

"We weren't laughing at you! I promise we weren't! You were lonely; I thought it would be good for you to have a friend."

It was ridiculous. But he really meant it; it was there in his eyes.

"I was lonely because you wanted my money and not me."

I was shivering now, and infuriatingly it made my voice tremble. I wanted to sound angry, not upset.

"I was trying to help," he said. "I didn't want you to be unhappy."

"But how could you think tea and shopping trips with your mistress would fix that?"

"Stop calling her that."

"It's what she is, Frederick. And that was your choice. She told me there was someone she loved but couldn't marry, because she wasn't rich enough. It was you, wasn't it?"

He sighed. "Yes."

"You loved her too. You still do."

"Look, do we have to do this? It's cold, let's go inside."

"I've got a right to know. Do you love her?"

"All right!" He threw out his hands. "Yes. I do. I have for as long as I can remember, and I always will."

"You should have been brave enough to marry her then! All three of us would be happier if you had."

"It wouldn't have been brave; it would have been selfish. Do you *still* not see? There was more at stake than what I wanted or what she wanted. She understood that."

"And you were happy to see her marry someone else?"

"Of course I wasn't happy! I hated seeing her marry that idiot, and I hate seeing her with him now. But that's not the point!" He ran his fingers through his hair. "How can I make you understand? Look—let's say you were a boy, and you inherited your father's company, the company he'd worked hard all his life to build up. The decisions you made then, they wouldn't just be about what you wanted, would they? You'd have the weight of his expectations on your shoulders, and on top of that, you'd have all the workers to think about—you'd be responsible for their livelihoods. That's the position I'm in. I can't just do what I want to, I can't just think about what I want. I don't have choices. I've got the weight of thirteen generations on me, and I can't let them down."

He sounded so sad. Did I feel sorry for him, at that moment? No, I can't honestly say that. But I did realize I wasn't the only one who was unhappy.

"Suppose . . ." he went on. "Suppose your father's business was in trouble, and he wanted you to marry someone who could invest and save it. Wouldn't you have done it?"

"My father wouldn't ever have wanted me to marry someone I couldn't love."

"I didn't marry someone I couldn't love. I liked you, and I knew I could come to love you as my wife and the mother of my son."

"But you were never going to love me the way you love Lissy."

"What do you want me to say, Elinor? I love her, I've said so. And I won't give her up, if that's what you're going to ask."

It came to me then, what to do.

"I'm not going to ask for that," I said. "I'll put up with you being with her, whenever you like, and I won't complain, and I'll even act as though she and I are still friends, if that's what you want. But in return, I want you to back me up about Teddy. Let me be a proper mother to him now, like I said in there, and don't send him away to school when he's still so little."

He sighed. "This is ridiculous. Anyone would think we were talking about sending Teddy down a mine! He'll go to Eton, just as I did and my father and grandfather did, and he'll go to prep school before that, because that is the best way to prepare him for the life he is going to have. As for what you will and won't put up with, I'm afraid we are where we are, and putting up with it is what you're going to have to do."

I took a deep breath. "No, it's not. Because if you don't do what I'm asking, I'll tell everyone we know just what you two have been up to, and what kind of a woman Lissy Harcourt is."

We stared at each other for what seemed like a long time, and then he just laughed.

"And have your father read all about it in the gossip columns? I don't think so, Elinor. You know perfectly well that it would be as painful and humiliating for you as it would be for us, and he'd be devastated. And you might well take pleasure in causing Lissy and me unhappiness, but you would never do that to him. Now, let's get inside—it's freezing out here."

CHAPTER 23

We parted company at the grand staircase. Frederick went to the lounge; I trudged back to our suite. He was right, of course. I would never have gone through with the threat. It had just come to me in the heat of the moment, and I'd done what my father would never have done, named my price without thinking it through. Frederick was right: it would break my father's heart, and even if I could bear that, it still wouldn't have got me what I wanted, would it? It would have made everything worse.

Nothing was going to change now. Eleven more days and then back to Winterton, back to seeing Teddy once a day, until he was sent away to school to prepare him for the life that had made Frederick so miserable, weighed down by generations of tradition and trapped by duty. As for my own life, when Teddy went to school there'd be nothing good in it at all. If we had another son, I'd have to lose him to boarding school at seven too, and if we had a daughter, I might have her for longer, but what kind of future was there for her? My money was propping up the estate, and the way things were going, there wouldn't be much left for a marriage settlement. She'd be married off to the first man who'd have her, like Kitty.

We were trapped, all of us. Me, Frederick, Teddy, and even the children we didn't have yet were trapped. Lissy too, come to that. And there was no way out.

When Molly had hung my clothes up and left, I sat by Teddy's cot, watching him sleep. I must have drifted off in the chair, but I woke at the sound of Frederick coming back to his cabin. I got into bed then, but I couldn't sleep. I was wondering if I could ring for some warm milk when there was a juddering noise— not very loud, but peculiar, like an enormous piece of calico being ripped. I sat up to listen, but the noise didn't happen again. I glanced into Teddy's cot, but it hadn't woken him, so I lay back down and nestled into the cozy bed, hoping to sleep.

Something was different, though. What was it? I sat up again. Yes: the hum of the ship's engines, usually just audible in the quiet of the night, had stopped. Why would that happen in the middle of the night?

Hearing movement in Frederick's room and the main door of the suite opening, I pulled on my wrapper and joined him at the door.

"Did you hear something?" he asked, but before I could answer, one of the stewards came along the corridor.

"Has something happened?" asked Frederick. "We heard a noise."

"Nothing to worry about, sir," said the steward. "Little problem with the engine, I believe—soon be sorted out. I'd get back to bed if I were you."

Other doors opened along the corridor and heads poked out. The steward cheerfully reassured them all as he passed by. My father's door remained closed; he wasn't a light sleeper, and I guessed the noise hadn't woken him.

We went back inside, awkward with each other after ending the evening on such bad terms, and I think we were both relieved to see Molly and Terence had woken too and were emerging from their respective quarters.

"What's happened?" asked Molly.

"There's a problem with the engines," I said. "That's why they've stopped."

Just at that moment, Teddy called out for me. He'd slept through all the other nights, but the noise of conversation must have woken him. I retreated into my cabin and Molly followed, leaving Frederick and Terence to go back to their beds.

I picked Teddy up from his cot and held him close. He was warm from sleep and his head smelled sweetly frowsty.

"I can settle him, madam, if you'd like to go back to sleep," said Molly.

"No, there's no need. I'm wide awake now. You go back to bed."

"If you're sure?"

"I'm sure."

I sat on the bed with Teddy on my lap and gently rubbed his back. He curled his little arm round my neck and rested his cheek against my shoulder. His breathing slowed, and mine slowed to match it.

When I was sure he'd drifted back to sleep, I got up to put him back in his cot, but just then there was a knock on the door, and Frederick said, "Can I come in?"

He smelled of cold fresh air. He'd put on trousers and a sweater over his pajamas—the stripy legs were just peeking out at the hem—and his cheeks were red.

"I saw your light still on," he said stiffly. "I've been up on deck with Terence. It seems we've struck an iceberg. Nothing to worry about, I just thought you'd want to know. There's great chunks of ice up on the deck, and the most fearful noise—they're letting out steam from the boilers, apparently."

"How can that be nothing to worry about?"

"I heard a crewman explaining—it's made a bit of a gash, but the ship'll be fine for the rest of the voyage; they'll patch her up in New York. All part of the design, he said."

Hadn't my father heard about that from the ship's architect? Something about watertight compartments down below that could fill up with water and still the ship wouldn't sink. I hadn't given it much thought at the time, but it was a comfort to remember it right then. Not that I thought we were in danger, but I kept remembering how I'd stood on deck that morning, seen nothing but ocean in every direction, and realized just how far away we were from land.

Frederick looked at Teddy, curled against me with his arms round my neck.

"I wish you'd try to understand," he said. "I love him too, you know. But I've lived the life he'll have to live, and you haven't."

"What if he doesn't want that life?"

"We can't always have what we want. We have to do what's expected of us. We have to accept our responsibilities."

"And that's what marrying me was. Accepting your responsibilities."

He sighed. "Elinor—"

"But it wasn't, was it? You talk as though you made a great sacrifice, but what did you actually give up? You've still got Lissy, and she's still got you."

As he opened his mouth to reply, there was a sharp rap on the door, and a voice called out, "Everybody up on deck! Lifejackets on!"

Frederick strode to the door and called out to the steward, who was knocking on all the other doors and repeating his message.

"Thought you said there was nothing wrong?"

"Just a precaution, sir. But I must insist you come, and quickly please—captain's orders."

Frederick came back in, and a second or so later, my father appeared in the doorway in his dressing gown and night shirt.

"What's going on?"

Frederick told him what he'd discovered.

"Well, it's ridiculous," said my father. "There's no danger. Why the heck are they getting us all out of bed for nothing? But I suppose we'll have to go up."

"I'll tell Terence and Molly," said Frederick. "And I'd advise you both to put on something warm. It's freezing up there."

Expecting to stroll the streets of New York in spring weather, I'd only brought a light coat, and even my warmest day dress was only fine wool. It had tiny buttons up the back and my fingers fumbled with them; it was the first time I'd ever dressed myself, and I was only halfway there when Molly appeared, in just a coat thrown over her nightdress. She dressed Teddy while I stripped a blanket from his cot to wrap him in and then we put on our lifejackets—bulky things in white canvas with big square pockets filled with blocks of something light but stiff. As Molly was tying the strings at the side of mine, I suddenly remembered Rose and her bad dreams.

It's too big, it can't be right for a ship to be that big. It can't be safe.

So silly. There couldn't possibly be any real danger. The ship was as steady as a rock under my feet, and my stateroom, with its solid dark wood furniture, thick carpets, and electric light, looked so much like a bedroom on land that the idea of any harm coming to us seemed ridiculous. As the door closed behind us, I fully expected to be back in my bed before long.

CHAPTER 24

Up on deck, people were already milling around. A few had had the foresight to dress warmly: there were women in furs, and some of the men looked as though they were setting out for a walk in the country. But most were either still in evening dress or had just thrown coats on over their nightwear. The sea looked reassuringly calm and still, but it was bitingly cold and the noise from the escaping steam was deafening, so the people standing around in little groups were having to shout to each other to be heard. Quite a few were complaining about being ordered out of their cabins onto the cold deck, but other than that no one seemed concerned. We were near the middle of the ship, by the lounge, and from inside it came music—the band playing a quickstep, just as though it was a normal evening.

As more and more people came up the stairs, the middle of the deck got crowded—not least because everyone was either wearing or carrying a bulky lifejacket. Frederick pointed toward the front of the ship.

"Let's get out of this crowd, there might be more room down there."

As we got near the front, the crew were swinging out the lifeboats that hung from metal frames around the edge of the deck. A chill ran down my back. Why would they do that if there was no danger?

Suddenly there was a hiss from the very front of the ship. A flash like a firework went up, up, up, and then exploded in a shower of stars. Frederick and my father looked at each other.

"Distress rocket?" said my father.

Frederick frowned. "I don't like the look of this."

He walked across to one of the crewmen and had a brief conversation, then turned back to us, his face serious.

"He said the ship's badly holed, and taking on water. There's no danger, they're radioing for another ship to pick us all up, but getting everyone into the lifeboats will take a while, so they're going to start as soon as they've lowered them down to the deck below. It's easier to get on there, apparently, so I suggest we go down now. It'll be women and children first, so you three will have to go and we'll follow later."

"I've left my savings in the wardrobe," said Molly. "I need to fetch them."

"Well, you'd better go now," snapped Frederick, "and be quick back."

On the deck below, we stood, silent, as the lifeboats were lowered to come alongside the rail. It was like a bad dream, impossible to take in. Just that morning, we'd been crossing the ocean in the sunshine, watching people play quoits, thinking about what might be on the menu for dinner, and now we were about to get into lifeboats and be lowered down to the icy sea. The lifeboats, which we'd barely taken notice of before, just looked like big wooden rowing boats. How could we possibly be safe on the huge ocean in one of those? How long would we be out there, in the cold and dark? And come to that, how were we going to get into them? There was a big gap between the rail and the boats and I kept thinking how far down it looked when we'd stood at the rail and watched the waves below. I was shaking by then, whether with fear or the cold, I didn't know.

"It will be all right," said Frederick. "That crewman said other ships will be on their way already."

"He's right," said my father. "We'll be picked up, and we'll have an exciting tale to tell when we get home."

Molly still hadn't come back. I looked over at the stairs, hoping to see her coming up, but there was no sign of her. Where on earth had she got to?

Just then a crewman stepped forward, his hands cupped around his mouth, and shouted, "Women and children, come forward! Women and children only!"

A couple of women walked over, but most people carried on standing and chatting, some with drinks in their hands, waving their cigarette holders around as though it was a cocktail party. The two sailors beside the boat kept calling for women and children to come forward, but no one was really taking any notice.

One woman, still in a silver satin evening dress with a white fur stole, laughed and said, "If you think I'm getting in that thing, you can think again." Hugging her stole around her, she turned to another woman, "Let's go into the lounge and have a whisky, while they sort this nonsense out."

"Right," said Frederick. "Let's get you and Teddy into that boat."

"No, I'll wait for Molly—there's no rush, no one's moving."

"I think you should get in now."

"What about Molly?"

"She can go in another boat."

"No, I'll run down and get her. God knows why she's taking so long."

He caught my arm. "No, you will not. Get in the lifeboat."

"Don't talk to me like that! There's plenty of time, and I'm not just leaving Molly."

"We'll go and find her once you and Teddy are in that boat." He turned to my father. "Won't we, Mr. Hayward?"

"Of course," said my father. "Go on, Ellie, I think you should do as Frederick says."

"No, I want to know she's safe. She's . . . well, she's expecting a baby."

Frederick rolled his eyes. "For God's sake!"

I ignored him and passed Teddy into my father's arms. "Take him for a minute. I'll just run to the top of the stairs and see if I can see her."

I hurried off toward the stairs, but the deck was so crowded it was hard to weave my way through the people. Before I even got near the staircase, Frederick caught me up.

He grabbed my arm and said in my ear, "Elinor, listen to me. Right now, people are not panicking. But when they let the second- and third-class passengers up, and the deck gets crowded, they may well be. I want to see you and Teddy safely away before that happens."

"But they said there was no danger."

"And I'm sure they're right. But all the same, better go now than once everyone's jostling and pushing. That'll be frightening for Teddy."

"You promise, you absolutely *promise* you'll find Molly?"

"I promise. Now hurry up."

Just as we got back to where my father was standing with Teddy, one of the crewmen shouted, "Let's get this one away then."

"What?" said Frederick. "It's half empty!"

He marched over and said something to the crewman, gesturing back toward me. They seemed to be arguing for a minute or so, and then Frederick strode back, beckoning me.

"He'll take you. But be quick."

* * *

My legs were shaking as the crewman, balanced with one foot in the boat and one on the rail, helped me over it. Frederick held Teddy until I'd sat down on one of the benches that went widthways across the boat, and my heart was in my mouth as he was handed down to me. I wrapped the blanket tight around him, so only his face was out in the cold, and held him close to try to keep him warm and lull him back to sleep.

There were about twenty-five women in the boat, with room for thirty or forty more, but the sailor who'd been calling people forward said, "Right, *now* let's get this one away."

Three crewmen got into the boat with us. They weren't in uniform like the ones on deck—judging from their white jackets, I thought they must be cooks. In a funny way that made me feel safer; if we were going to be in the lifeboats for long, they'd surely have given us proper sailors. The boat began to be lowered, foot by foot, in frighteningly rough jerks.

Frederick, my father, and Terence stood watching, and just as we were about to disappear out of their sight below the rail, my father cupped his hands to his mouth and shouted, "Don't worry, we'll see you soon."

CHAPTER 25

The lifeboat smacked down hard and water splashed over the side, dousing all our feet. It was so cold, I caught my breath.

"Oh really!" said an elderly American woman sitting in front of me. "Now we'll have wet feet until we get back on the ship."

"For goodness' sake, Mother—we won't be going back on the ship," said a younger woman sitting beside her. She had to yell to make herself heard over the noise from the funnels. "I told you what I heard—the damage is bad. It's going to sink."

"Don't be ridiculous," said another woman—American as well, but the accent was harder, more clipped; she sounded a bit like Lady Harcourt, Lissy's mother-in-law. "Of course it won't sink. It's the finest ship in the world."

"Then why do you think they're getting everybody off?" said the younger woman. "For a pleasure cruise?"

Two of the crewmen sat in the middle of the boat and began rowing us away. The third fixed an oil lamp to a hook at the front, then picked his way across to the tiller.

"Is this true?" the woman with the clipped accent asked as

he passed. "Because I was given to understand this was merely
a precaution."

"It's to keep everyone safe," he said.

"Until we go back on the ship?"

"I'm afraid not, madam. But there's no need to worry; another ship is on its way. Shouldn't be out here too long."

"But I've left two thousand dollars' worth of jewelry in the
safe. This is dreadful! Why weren't we told? I shall complain—"

Others joined in:

"Outrageous! Hundreds of pounds for a ticket and we're
treated like cattle!"

"There'll be a stiff letter from my husband, I can tell you."

"If this is what the White Star Line considers acceptable—"

The crewman on the tiller said, "Ladies, please, calm down.
We're doing our best and—"

Another woman, behind me, cut in then, panic in her voice.
"What about the men? If it's really sinking, what about the
men?"

Before the crewman could answer, the younger woman
who'd spoken earlier gasped. "Oh my God, look!"

We'd all been facing ahead, but as every head turned, we
saw what wasn't visible when we were on the ship. The long
horizontal rows of cabin lights blazing out into the night were
higher at the back than the front. A lot higher. The great ship
was tipping downward and even as we watched, the front end
of the lowest row of lights dipped under the water. The *Titanic*
really was sinking.

I hadn't really believed it myself until that moment. Even
as I'd heard what the crewman told Frederick and seen the
sense in getting into a lifeboat before the panic started, even as
I'd clambered over the rail and sat down, the reality of what
was happening was too difficult to contemplate. Like when you
look up at the moon and know, as a fact, that it's big like the
earth, but in your heart of hearts, you can't really imagine that

it is. Every one of those lights disappearing into the sea was a cabin, where someone had slept at night and woken up each morning. Now those cabins must be completely flooded. I was frantically trying to work out where our stateroom was in those rows of lights, but I couldn't tell.

Frederick will have found Molly. He promised.

There was a second's silence before a clamor of questions started.

"What's going to happen now?"

"When will the men be taken off?"

"How long are we going to be out here?"

The crewmen stopped rowing, and one stood up. "Ladies, there is no need to panic."

He pointed at the ship, where lifeboats were being lowered from both ends now. 'As you can see, all the lifeboats are being launched. Men will be allowed on as soon as all the women and children have been accommodated. Now, our job is to keep you safe until a rescue boat comes, and you can help us do that by staying calm."

There was some muttering from the woman who'd left her jewelry behind, but once she'd shut up, the boat fell silent. The crewmen resumed rowing, but they were the only ones looking forward. The rest of us couldn't take our eyes off the ship. More lifeboats were lowered, faster now, in sharp, long jerks. The passengers were just silhouettes against the still-blazing lights, but it was obvious that, like our boat, none of the lifeboats being launched were full. There were still a lot of people visible on deck. Hadn't they realized by now that they needed to get off the ship? And if the boats were being sent off half empty, how could the crew be sure there'd be room for everyone in the end?

Molly would have got off by now though. Frederick would have found her and got her into a lifeboat, like he promised. And as soon as they were allowed, he and my father and Terence would get in a boat too. Frederick had spotted the danger while everyone else was still milling about like they were at a cocktail party. He'd got me and Teddy off safely, and he'd get the four of them away too.

As soon as each lifeboat hit the water, they moved off, fanning out in all directions. In the dark, the lights from the ship were dazzling, and once a lifeboat got more than a few yards away, it disappeared, but for the oil lamp at the front of it, seemingly floating through the dark. I peered through the blackness, desperate to find Frederick, my father, Molly, and Terence in one of them, but it was impossible to see.

The front of the ship was still slipping into the sea, as though a giant thumb was pushing it downward. It was listing to one side now too. And even though it was happening right in front of me, I was still struggling to believe my eyes. Nobody spoke, but behind me, a woman began sobbing, and then another, and another.

When we were a good distance from the ship, our crewmen stopped rowing and turned to see. They looked at each other, and one shook his head. That was when I understood. Lifeboats were still being launched; one smacked down in the water just at that moment. But there wasn't going to be time. There couldn't be. I didn't know what 1,300 passengers looked like—once we were on board we'd never clapped eyes on the second- and third-class ticket-holders—but it had all happened so quickly, they couldn't have got anything like that many people in the boats.

I prayed then. I wasn't a particularly religious person, but I prayed and prayed and prayed. *Let them be on a lifeboat, God, and I won't complain again. I'll go back to Winterton, and I'll be the way they want me to be.* They had to be on a boat. They had to be.

I couldn't take my eyes off the ship; no one could. It was so huge—even from a distance it towered above us—and yet it was being upended like a child's toy. Gasps and a whispered "Oh sweet Jesus" came from behind me as the front of the ship dipped under the water. We'd stood there, just that morning. The horizontal rows of lights were still shining out into the night, and as the front of the ship slid downward, they were meeting their reflections in the water, like a huge arrow pointing nowhere. More lifeboats were lowered and rowed away, but there were still so many people on the deck.

A woman sitting in front of me said, "How will they ever get it back up again?"

You might think that was a stupid question—certainly the crewmen didn't bother to answer it—but you see, even as we watched, it was impossible to believe that the *Titanic* would sink completely. It was so big, and so solid, and we'd walked on it and slept on it and eaten dinner on it. How could it just disappear into the ocean? And yet it was doing exactly that, right in front of our eyes.

Minutes later, the whole front of the ship slipped under the water. The back tipped up as though it weighed nothing at all, revealing the propellors, and then the front funnel broke away, crashing into the sea in a shower of sparks.

"That's it," said one of the crewmen. "She'll go fast now."

There was an almighty noise of crashing and clattering and roaring, as though every single thing in the ship was coming loose from its moorings and being hurled downward, and under that awful noise there were screams. The lights flickered, then went out. The ship seemed to break in two, and for a moment the back half settled back, as though it might continue to float, quite contentedly. Then it tilted up, pointing diagonally into the sky, and just slid down into the water and disappeared. In front of us stretched nothing but ink black sea. The *Titanic* was gone.

CHAPTER 26

From out of the dark came screams and cries, and under them a terrible, pitiful groan, like a wounded animal. Hundreds of voices together. Hundreds of people out there in the icy sea, calling for help.

"We have to go back," said the younger American woman. "There are people in the water!"

Other voices joined in the clamor, and I did too. But one of the crewman held up a hand for silence.

Looking round at all of us, he said, "If we go back, we'll be swamped, and we'll sink."

"But the boat's only half full," I said. "We could take forty more people, easily."

"And do you think the forty after that will just step aside?" he said. "You can hear how many there are in the water. It's our lives or theirs."

The woman who'd complained about losing her jewelry piped up then. "He's right. We can't take the risk."

From the back another woman called out, "We have to listen to the crew; they know what to do."

For a few minutes, there was a cacophony of voices—me, the younger American woman, and a few others, perhaps three or four, saying we couldn't just leave the men drowning in the water, we had to at least fill the boat, but the rest arguing that it was too dangerous to go back.

The crewman at the tiller stood up, making the boat rock. The movement shocked us into silence.

"Shut up!" he said. "All of you, shut up! We are not going back. Those people in the water, it's too late for them. It's too cold. You, by the grace of God, are still alive, and the captain gave us the duty of keeping you that way. So will you please be quiet and let us do it."

In that moment, I wished I was a man, so I could have grabbed the oars and made them turn round. But perhaps even a man couldn't have done it, not when most of the people in the boat were in agreement with them.

A woman sitting near the front cried out, "Did none of you leave your husbands on that boat? Because I did! Please, please, we have to go back."

"Calm yourself," someone answered. "The first-class passengers were brought off first; your husband is safe."

It shocked me, that, and it disgusted me. But, to my shame, it comforted me too. And I don't think I was the only one; after that, there were no more calls to turn back. The crewmen rowed on, and we sat in silence, listening to the awful cries, knowing all those people floating in the ice-cold water could see the lights on the lifeboats. They were begging us to rescue them, and they must be gradually realizing there was no hope. No one was coming. It was at least an hour before, gradually, the voices died away.

It got colder and colder. I didn't know you could be that cold and still be alive. My hands burned and I couldn't feel my feet at all. I was terrified that the freezing air might get into Teddy's little lungs and stop him breathing. I'd wrapped the blanket around him so that only his nose and mouth were out, and I cuddled him close in to me, curving my body around him as best I could with the stiff panels of my lifejacket between us. Thank goodness we'd tired him out with running around on deck that afternoon; he'd been dozy when we took him from his crib, and once we got into the boat he slept again. Every few minutes, I put my hand in front of his mouth to make sure he was still breathing.

The sky was completely clear and speckled with stars, but there was no moon, so it was pitch dark. The one lamp at the front of our boat cast a small circle of yellow light ahead of us, and here and there the lights of other lifeboats glowed weakly through the blackness, but that was all. Our crewmen's white jackets showed up in the darkness, but it was impossible to make out the faces of any of the passengers. I only knew there were twenty-five or so of us, all women, and there'd been no other English voices, only Americans.

Not long after the ship went down, the younger American woman had asked the crewmen whether they knew where the nearest other ship was.

"Distress signals were sent," said one of them. "Someone will have picked them up, don't worry."

"But how far away is the nearest ship? How long will it take to get here?"

"We don't know, is the honest answer, madam. But they'll come. There'll be dozens of ships here before long, don't worry."

For the first, I suppose, couple of hours, the two crewmen rowed, but in the darkness, there was no way of knowing where to head and eventually they stopped. Without the creak of the oars, it was silent out there in the middle of the ocean. There was no breeze and the sea was so still there wasn't even the slap of it against the side of the boat. Every now and then, someone would spot a light and say "Look!" or "There!" only for it to be a star, or the lantern of another lifeboat.

I kept remembering how we'd stood by the rail that morning and seen nothing but ocean in all directions. No land, of course, but no other ships either. How long could we last, in that cold? What if the nearest ship was just too far away? How could we even be sure the distress signals had reached any ship at all?

It seemed as though dawn would never come, but at last, the sky began to lighten. As it did, there they were: mountains of ice floating in the sea, dozens and dozens of them, their jagged crags catching the morning sun and turning gold and pink. Most of them rose fifty or sixty feet out of the water, but some were much, much bigger. If we'd wondered how the ship could have been damaged so badly, so quickly, the answer was right in front of our eyes. And yet we'd plowed on through them at what now seemed a terrible speed.

We could see other lifeboats now too: one, perhaps three hundred yards away, looked full, and there were men in it as well as women and children. But others were like ours, half empty. One only had around a dozen people in it and, straining my eyes in every direction, I couldn't make out more than eight boats in all. I told myself the ones launched from the other side of the ship would have rowed away in the opposite direction from us, that they were out there but we just couldn't see them. But those dreadful cries were still in my ears. How many people hadn't been saved? And though I hated myself for it, I kept reminding myself of what the woman had said last night. The first-class passengers were brought off first. Frederick and my father and Molly and Terence must be safe. They were in a lifeboat, and they were safe.

As the sun rose higher, dazzlingly bright, a stiff wind came with it, and the sea that had been so calm all night was ruffled with choppy little waves that rocked the boat. The wind cut into my face and my eyes streamed; my lips were already so chapped that it hurt to move them. My arms were stiff with the effort of holding Teddy close to me, and I wondered if I'd ever be able to feel my feet again.

A movement near the boat, and a color—emerald green—caught my eye. The remains of one of the plush velvet seats from the first-class lounge floated by us, its filling spilling out behind like a wake. Less than twelve hours ago, someone had sat there, sipping a cocktail, perhaps laughing and joking. How could that be possible?

Hopelessness washed over me. No one was coming to rescue us. It couldn't have been true that there were ships nearby; if there were, they'd have arrived by now. We couldn't last much longer in that cold, and the sea was getting rougher, nudging the boat up and down, splashing against the sides. The crewmen had had to start rowing again to avoid the icebergs, but they were tired and struggling to steer between them. One of those icebergs had ripped a hole in the *Titanic*. Ripped clean through steel that must have been inches thick. Our little boat was only made of wood; what chance would we stand if it was dashed against one of these jagged mountains of ice?

Well, we knew the answer to that, didn't we? No chance at all.

Those people in the water, it's too late for them. It's too cold.

I had to make a plan. If the worst happened, I couldn't let Teddy suffer like that. He wouldn't last long, being so little, but the thought of him slowly dying in that ice-cold water was unbearable. I looked down at his face. If it came to it, could I bring myself to suffocate him? I could do it with the blanket; at least it would be quick and he wouldn't suffer. And then I'd take off my lifejacket, and hold him close, so that when they found us we'd be together.

Please let us survive, I begged God silently. *It's not fair, he's only little; he hasn't had a life.* I thought of the day he was born, so tiny and helpless. It was my job to keep him safe, and here, now, I couldn't.

I jumped when one of the women at the front of the boat said, "What's that?" She pointed off to the left. "There, look!"

On the far horizon there was a dark smudge.

"Please God," someone behind me whispered. "Please God, let it be a ship."

The crewmen stopped rowing, and everyone was still as the scribble of black slowly got bigger.

"Lights!" said someone. "I can see lights!"

I stared into the distance, squinting my eyes, trying to see what was really there.

Not more false hope. Please let this be real.

Were they lights? Yes! Tiny pinpoints, but they were lights. And they were coming toward us. I think every single person in the boat was holding their breath, and then there it was, the unmistakable shape of a ship's hull, the black smoke coming from a red funnel. At that distance it looked like a toy boat, but sooner than we could possibly have hoped, it was looming up toward us. The women in the lifeboat broke out into tearful cheers, and the noise woke Teddy. He squirmed and cried, but I held him tight.

"It's all right," I said. "We're going to be all right."

CHAPTER 27

The ship was called the *Carpathia*. By the time it was close enough to see the name painted on the side, the mood in the boat had turned from hopeless exhaustion to tearful relief. We were saved. One of the women began to say the Lord's Prayer, and everyone joined in.

We were the fourth lifeboat to come alongside. It had taken a long time to unload the first three, and we'd watched as their passengers, stiff with cold and exhaustion like us, climbed, agonizingly slowly, up the rope ladder hanging from the deck. Our boat was close enough for me to see that none of them were my father and Frederick, nor Molly or Terence, but still I told myself, they were on another lifeboat. They'd got on one launching from the other side of the ship, probably; if those lifeboats had rowed off in the opposite direction, they might not even have sighted the *Carpathia* yet.

The ship was very much smaller than the *Titanic*, but the deck was still high above us, and our little lifeboat was dancing and jerking on the waves. Anxious faces looked down over the rail, but no familiar ones. They must be the ship's own passengers and crew.

A sailor called down from the deck, "We'll bring the child up first. I'll send down the sling."

As a canvas sling was lowered down, panic rose through me. It looked so flimsy, and Teddy was wriggling and crying now.

"I can't put him in there!"

The second crewman, the one who hadn't said much before, stepped across to me.

"I know it looks frightening," he said gently. "But I promise you it's safe. I'll strap him in tight, and he'll be up there and safe in no time."

I didn't have any choice; I couldn't carry him up the rope ladder.

I'd held him so tight for so long that my arms had cramped around him. Thinking I was just refusing to let him go, the other crewman snapped, "Come on now, madam, we need to get everyone off."

"Let her alone," said his colleague. "Here, let me help you."

He lifted Teddy from my arms and held him tight against his chest as he turned and reached for the sling. He tested the straps three times before shouting up, "All right. Slowly now."

I held my breath as the sling was pulled up, Teddy's little legs dangling. But within just a few moments, he was safely on board the ship. I followed, my legs trembling, and found him in the arms of a kindly-looking woman.

"Here's Mama," she said. "Now, let's get some warm milk for you, young man, and soup for your mother. There's nothing to worry about now, you're safe."

Part of me wanted to stay there and wait, but the deck was already crowded with crew and the *Carpathia*'s own passengers, and I needed to get Teddy into the warm. So I followed the woman into the ship's lounge, where I was given a mug of hot soup and a blanket, and the woman gave Teddy some warm milk. I was so exhausted, I couldn't even drink the soup. I put it down for a moment and closed my eyes.

I don't know how long I slept, but when I woke up, the lounge was full of passengers from the *Titanic*, those wearing evening dress or nightwear now wrapped in blankets. Almost all of them women, some silently weeping, others just staring, blank-eyed, into space. The kind woman had Teddy on her knee; she was telling him a story, and he looked none the worse for the terrible night we'd had. She looked over as I stretched my stiff arms above my head.

"You needed that sleep. Now, if you can take this little lad from me, I'm going to see about finding you some dry shoes. What size are you?"

She stood, and it was only because she reached for the table to steady herself that I realized.

"The ship's moving."

"Yes, we got underway about twenty minutes ago. Full steam ahead to New York now."

"Everyone from the lifeboats is on board?"

"Yes."

"Could you look after my son for a little bit longer? I need to find my family."

I still believed they'd be there. Even after hearing all those voices calling for help. Even after seeing so few lifeboats, and most of them half-loaded, I was sure they'd been saved. I checked the saloon, the library, even the barber's shop, and when they weren't in any of those places, I ran around like a mad thing, asking people if they'd seen them, getting only a shake of the head and a "Sorry, no" in reply. Finally, I went up on deck. There were fewer people up there now, and most, from their clothes, were passengers of the *Carpathia*. I stood there, staring round. They had to be there; there was nowhere else.

A young crewman looked at me, concerned. "Are you all right, madam?"

"I'm looking for my father and my husband, and my maid and his valet," I said. "I've searched everywhere. And someone said everyone from the lifeboats is on board, but they can't be. Is that where we're going now, are we going to look for the rest?"

He looked down at his feet. "We're heading for New York, madam. We picked up everyone from the lifeboats."

"But they're not here. My husband promised he'd make sure they all got into a boat. They must have got off the ship, so where are they?"

"I can't say, madam."

An older crewman spoke up then. "There's no sense hiding it, Joe. People have got to know sometime."

He came over and said, "It looks like only about a third of the passengers got off. Mostly women and children. We found every lifeboat, and the captain went back to look for survivors in the water. If your people aren't on board, I'm afraid they didn't make it."

I don't know how other people heard the news, but it soon spread. Everywhere you looked, there were women weeping, some quietly, others with great racking sobs. I searched again; it was better than standing still and taking the news in. In the smoking room there was a young woman saying, "My son, where's my son?" over and over again. Had people lost children too? If there hadn't even been time to get all the women and children off, what chance had the men had?

That's when I finally let hope go. I went back to the lounge and took Teddy from the woman I'd left him with. I don't think

I even said thank you; I just picked him up and walked out, holding him tight to me. There was a corridor outside, and I walked up and down it, up and down, I don't know how many times. I didn't cry. I was too numb, too bewildered. I just kept thinking, how could it have happened? How could so many people be lost?

I kept remembering my father waving from the deck, and shouting, "We'll see you soon." How was it possible that he was dead? Or Frederick, and Terence? Or Molly—oh God, poor Molly, looking forward to her new life, so brave and so full of hope and excitement. How could she be dead? It hit me then that her baby hadn't even had the chance to live. That's when I cried. My tears frightened Teddy, and he started crying too. I stopped pacing and tried to comfort him, but it was no good. Soon he was bawling, his face red and tears coursing down his cheeks.

"Can we help?" said a voice behind me, and I turned to see two elderly ladies. The one who'd spoken had a foreign accent, perhaps German.

"Would you like to have somewhere quiet to rest?" she said. "You can gladly take our cabin. Come, it is just here."

I followed them to the end of the corridor, where the other lady unlocked a door and gestured for me to go in.

"It's for you now. Stay here; we will sleep in the lounge." She reached out and stroked a tear from Teddy's cheek. "We are all so sorry for this."

The cabin was small and simply furnished, with two narrow bunks, one above the other, a tall cupboard, and a washstand. I thought of my room on the *Titanic*, all the silk and mahogany and gilt, the heavy wooden bed, and the cot beside it. The place where I'd woken to Teddy gurgling happily beside me for the first time, and where I'd laid him down to sleep, and watched him dream. All of it gone, tumbling down to the bottom of the sea. I still couldn't believe it. I couldn't believe any of it. That my father, my fearless, clever, force of nature father was dead? That my husband was dead, and my son was fatherless? That at the age of twenty-one, I was a widow? None of it was possible and yet it was true.

Teddy had stopped crying, his attention caught by the ladder up to the top bunk. I unhooked it for him and laid it flat on the floor, and he was soon amusing himself, stepping in and out of the rungs. I sat on the bottom bunk, watching him. Thank goodness he was so little still, oblivious to everything that had happened, and too young to understand that his father was gone.

In that moment it hit me, what Frederick's death meant for us. The future that was all mapped out had just been swept away. Frederick would never be Lord Storton. Teddy was the heir now, to the title and the estate. It was the most peculiar feeling, realizing that: like going to sleep in one place and waking up in another. And then, like a punch in the stomach, I realized something else. The legal document that I'd dismissed as annoying but irrelevant, because Frederick wasn't about to die, had just taken effect. Lord and Lady Storton were Teddy's guardians. I'd never had much say in his life before, but now the law itself said I was no one to him.

Even before, I'd dreaded going back to Winterton. The few short days I'd had away from it had only made me see more clearly how unhappy I was there. How lonely, too, without even Lissy as a friend. Now it would be so much worse, not just for me, but for Teddy too—I was certain of that.

And when we went back, what would I be? Even when things were at their lowest ebb with Frederick, after I learned about him and Lissy, there was at least a certain protection in being his wife. There was a place for me. What was my place now? Not Frederick's wife, not the future Lady Storton, and not even really Teddy's mother. And yet I was still trapped there, for years to come. What had Kitty said, about the guardianship arrangements?

It's in case you remarry and want to take Teddy off somewhere.

Remarrying was the last thing on my mind, but the same would apply if I wanted to leave Winterton for any other reason, wouldn't it? So even though I'd inherit Clereston, I couldn't go there. They might be happy to be rid of me, but they'd never let me take Teddy away from Winterton, and if I did go, they'd be able to cut me out of his life, the way they'd done with my father. And if I stayed, in five years' time, they'd send him off to school, and I would have to live there, unwanted, seeing him only in the holidays, until he was old enough to make his own decisions. And who could say what kind of boy they'd have made him into by then?

I looked at him, playing on the floor.

You are all I have now.

My mother was gone; my father was gone. Frederick had never loved me as I'd hoped he would, but he'd cared for me a little and now he was gone too. There was no one in England who'd be praying I was alive. As far as Lord and Lady Storton were concerned, it would probably have been more convenient if I'd died too, as long as they got Teddy back.

And then Teddy, poor Teddy, growing up to live like Frederick had, a slave to the title and the estate and the generations of ancestors who stared out from the portraits on the wall. What I saw now, after that last argument on the ship, was that he'd been miserable too.

I've got the weight of thirteen generations on me, and I can't let them down.

I sat there, looking at the future that stretched ahead of me and Teddy, and I kept thinking of all those people begging for help in the darkness after the ship sank. The cries and the screams were still in my head. So many voices at first, but then the horror of that awful sound fading away as, one by one, people died of the cold, or slipped underwater and drowned. And now, when that sound haunted me, it was with the terrible knowledge that my father and Frederick and Molly and Terence must have been among them. I don't know if anyone could live through something like that and not go a little bit mad, and perhaps I did, because in that moment, the most ridiculous thought came to me.

We'd been given the chance to go on with our lives, when so many others had lost theirs. What if I decided not to waste that chance on a life that would make us both miserable? What if we didn't go back?

CHAPTER 28

For a few minutes, I indulged myself in a daydream where we stayed in America, made a new life for ourselves there, and never went back to Winterton at all. But it was just that—a daydream. Because I couldn't keep Teddy with me, could I? The guardianship papers that stopped me taking him if I re-married would apply just the same way. He wasn't mine to take; he was theirs now, and I had to be where he was. So there wasn't going to be a new life, just the old one—but worse.

At around lunchtime, there was a knock on the door. The kind German ladies had brought us sandwiches, with coffee for me and a cup of milk for Teddy. They said the captain had asked that all *Titanic* passengers come to the lounge by seven that evening and give their names, so they could compile an official list of the missing. Then all the usual arrival formalities would be suspended when we docked, in order to get everyone off quickly.

"And this," one of the ladies said, handing me a pen and a piece of paper. It was the form for a marconigram. "They will send it for you. To tell your family you are safe."

When they left, assuring me again that we could stay in the cabin for the night, I pulled one of the sandwiches into pieces for Teddy. He ate happily, his little face cheerful and contented. I sipped the coffee, strong and bitter, and looked at the marconigram form. How do you write the words that will break someone's heart? In their own strange, cold way, Lord and Lady Storton must have loved Frederick, and the sorrow and shock of losing him this way was unimaginable. The news of the sinking would have reached England by now; they'd be mad with worry. They had to know, and they'd need to tell Terence's family as well, but how was I going to find the words?

Then there was Molly's family. Who'd tell them? All I knew was her surname, and that she was originally from Manchester. I'd no idea where her father and stepmother lived. But, then, I realized, they wouldn't even have known she was on the *Titanic.*

I left, went to London and got myself the position with Mrs. Fieldwood, and I haven't seen or heard from my family since.

They wouldn't be waiting anxiously for news, like so many other families. It seemed so unfair, that. People who'd loved and cared for their daughters and sons, sisters and brothers were about to be dealt a blow that surely no one could ever really get over, and yet Molly's father and stepmother, who'd let her go without a thought, would go on with their lives, not even knowing that she was dead, let alone the awful circumstances.

I picked up the pen, then put it down again. Because suddenly I saw that there might be a way. It was . . . well, it was completely crazy. I couldn't quite believe I was even considering it, and yet once it was in my head, I couldn't ignore it.

With Frederick taking against the American passengers, we'd barely spoken to anyone on the ship, and certainly not introduced ourselves to anyone. In the lifeboat, people hadn't really seen each other's faces, much less exchanged names, and the two German ladies had no idea who I was. So until I sent the marconigram, no one knew whether Teddy and I had survived or not. No one knew yet that Molly had died, either. And the list they were taking this evening would be the only record of who'd made it onto the *Carpathia*. If I left Teddy here in the cabin, went to the lounge and gave Molly's name instead of mine, he and I would be listed as missing and no one would ever know we'd survived. I could take him and escape. We wouldn't ever have to go back.

But we'd have to disappear, utterly and completely. Because those guardianship papers meant that if I didn't take Teddy back to Winterton, I'd be kidnapping my own child. If Lord and Lady Storton ever discovered we were still alive, they'd look for us, and if they found us, the law would let them take Teddy from me.

It was ridiculous and impossible. We'd have nowhere to live and nothing to live on. I'd brought quite a lot of money with me, hoping to go shopping in New York, but that was at the bottom of the sea now, along with all my jewelry. Even my engagement and wedding rings—I'd taken them off to put on my sleeping gloves before bed, and now they were lost with all the rest. I couldn't claim my inheritance either. We'd be penniless. So how could I hope to disappear even on my own, let alone with a two-year-old? But even as I was telling myself how impossible it was, I was working out how to do it.

Molly had relatives who were expecting her, but they'd never met her, had they? We were about the same age, we'd come from the same place, and I could slip back into my old accent as easily as blinking. They weren't expecting her to turn up with a child, but they weren't expecting her to turn up pregnant either, and Molly hadn't let that stop her.

They don't know me yet; I'm just a name on a letter. But once I'm

*there, on their doorstep, they're not going to throw me and the baby
out, are they?*

I'd have to think of some sort of story, but that wasn't impossible. I could base it on Molly's own tale of woe—just a
little further along the line. It would be somewhere to go, just
till we got on our feet. I could work, just as Molly would have
done, and as soon as I'd earned enough, we'd move on.

I knew it was wrong. Wrong to steal another woman's life,
wrong to deceive her family. Most of all, wrong to inflict such
terrible pain on Lord and Lady Storton, to make them believe
they'd lost their grandson as well as their son. A little voice in
my head kept saying they'd only care because Teddy was the
heir to the title and the estate, but I knew in my heart that
wasn't fair. They weren't monsters; they loved Teddy in their
own way. All the same, it was because he was the heir that any
of this was even in my head. If he'd been a girl, they wouldn't
have bothered to put guardianship arrangements in place, and
we could both have gone to live happily at Clereston.

All afternoon, I thought about it, went backward and forward. Told myself over and over that it was impossible, and
crazy, and wrong. And then I would think about going back to
Winterton, and what that would mean for both of us, and it
seemed impossible and crazy and wrong to do that too. Molly
had tried to turn a bad choice into something good, to make a
new life for herself and her child. She couldn't have that life
now. But if I could, if we could, shouldn't we seize that chance?

When the German ladies brought us dinner, I asked them if
they'd sit with Teddy for a few minutes, and they happily
agreed. I walked slowly to the lounge. Was I seriously going to
do this? Tell this terrible lie, fake my own death and Teddy's,
and then step off the ship into a life I knew next to nothing
about? It was completely mad. And yet I kept walking.

In the lounge, a row of three tables had been set up, each with a crew member sitting behind them. People were filing past, giving their names. I joined the little queue, my heart pounding and my legs shaking. The closer I got to the front, the more terrifying and ridiculous and impossible it seemed. But I kept thinking about Molly. She'd had none of the advantages in life that I'd been blessed with, but she was so much braver than me. She'd been fooled by a man, just as I had, but she'd picked herself up and found an opportunity to start afresh, on the other side of the ocean.

I didn't want to be Elinor Coombes anymore, living a life where other people made all the decisions. I wanted to be Molly—brave, bold Molly who decided for herself where she wanted to live and how. Who hadn't been given the chance to go on with her life, but who certainly wouldn't have wasted it if she had.

My turn came. The crewman looked up, pen poised.

"May I take your name, miss?"

I swallowed, took a deep breath.

"Molly Mortimer," I said.

CHAPTER 29

Four days after the *Titanic* sank, we reached New York late in the evening, in the middle of a horrendous rainstorm. The sky was charcoal gray, and the rain was teeming down in sheets. Perhaps it was better that way: a sunny day would have been a horrible reminder of the happy arrival we'd all expected, the end of a glamorous voyage on the greatest ship in the world. All the same, it was a grim experience. I'd left Teddy sound asleep in the cabin, and gone up on deck, where most of the passengers from the *Titanic* had gathered. By then, despite the rain, I think we were all just desperate to see land.

The downpour was so heavy that the buildings looming up ahead were just vague shapes, but as we approached the harbor, there was a volley of flashes. A flotilla of tugboats was speeding toward us, cameras pointing up at the deck.

"Damn journalists," said someone behind me. "Parasites, the lot of them."

I stepped back quickly, into the shadows. How had it not occurred to me that we'd be news? Of course we were: over a thousand people had died, on a ship that was supposed to be unsinkable, and we were the ones left to tell the story. And if one of those journalists got a picture of me or Teddy, and printed it in a paper, the whole thing would unravel. Lord and Lady Storton would know we were alive, and they'd find us, and take Teddy away from me.

When, at last, we walked down the gangplank, dressed in the muddle of clothes the *Carpathia* passengers had donated, Teddy was swathed in a blanket I'd taken from one of the bunks, and I'd fashioned a headscarf from a section of silk ripped from my petticoat. It covered my hair completely, and with Teddy held high in my arms, facing me, I could conceal my face as well. Even if someone took a photo of us, we wouldn't be recognizable.

I stepped onto the dock on shaking legs. There must have been hundreds of people waiting there, but the crowd was completely quiet, and in the distance bells were tolling. Making my way through, holding Teddy tight, I saw only a few tearful reunions. Mostly people were just standing there in the pouring rain, looking anxiously toward the gangplank.

We'd been told that if we were expecting to be met, there would be partitions to head for, with the initials of our surnames. It was hard to see through the crowds, but eventually I spotted the partition for M. And there they stood. An elderly woman and a couple in their forties, the man holding a sign saying "Molly Mortimer." Molly's mother's cousin, Ruth, her husband Per, and his mother, Anna. Their eyes searched the crowd, skimming over us because of course they were looking for a young woman on her own.

Before I could let myself think, I stepped forward. Slipping back into the voice that used to be mine, the words I'd prepared tumbled out, breathless and garbled.

"I'm Molly, and this is my son, Teddy. I know you were

expecting me to be on my own, and I'm sorry I didn't tell you, but I thought you might not let us come if you knew."

There was a moment when they all looked confused, and then Ruth threw her arms around us.

"Thank God," she said. "We've been so worried! We saw your name on the list but then people were saying the list wasn't right, so we didn't know for sure."

She stepped back, looked at me full in the face. Her hand flew to her mouth. She knew immediately I was lying, of course she did. I opened my mouth to say I'd made a mistake, got the wrong people, but she spoke first.

"Oh my Lord. You look so much like your mother."

Per offered to carry Teddy, saying it was a long walk to their apartment, but I made an excuse. Clinging on to him was the only thing that seemed real. It was like being in the most peculiar dream, hardly able to believe what I was doing, and at the same time trying to keep my thoughts straight so I could answer Ruth and Per's questions about the sinking without slipping up.

It was such a relief when the older woman, Anna, who'd barely spoken till then, said firmly, "I think Molly has answered enough questions."

Per sounded like the Americans on the ship, but Anna's singsong Swedish accent was strong. Had Molly said how long she'd been in America? I couldn't remember, and that added to my panic. What else was there going to be that I didn't know?

I jumped when she put her hand on my arm, but she just said, "There is no need to talk of this more, if you don't wish to."

I didn't wish to, and I couldn't afford to. If I was going to go through with this I had to concentrate, and that meant blocking out everything else that had happened in the past few days. Thank goodness, Per followed his mother's lead and changed the subject, but I couldn't tell you what he talked about. I was looking around me at dirty cobbled streets, strewn with stinking rubbish, and rows and rows of tall, narrow, red-brick buildings with iron fire escapes zigzagging all the way up to the roof, like the ones on my father's mills. But these couldn't be mills—there were curtains at the windows and plants on some of the windowsills.

This can't be right.

Where were the skyscrapers, the department stores, the big park I'd read about?

Eventually Ruth stopped outside one of the red-brick buildings.

"Here we are."

As we stepped inside the front door, my heart plummeted into my shoes. The stairway was lit by one dim light and the steps snaked up into darkness. From inside a door to the left came the voices of a man and a woman shouting at each other in a language I didn't understand, and there was a revolting smell of cabbage that got stronger as we walked up the stairs. On the third floor, Per stopped at one of the four doors that led off the stairway. But the stairs continued on up: there must be at least four, perhaps five floors. And if they all had four apartments to a floor, that was twenty families. How was that even possible?

The door opened straight into a very small room with a cast-iron stove, a little table with benches on either side of it, and a large wooden chest. Curtains in red checked cotton hung at the single window, and the benches had seat cushions in the same fabric. The table was covered with a white cloth embroidered in red, and a simple painting of a lake ringed by birch trees hung on the wall. In one corner stood two sewing machines with foot treadles. Two strange internal windows, with curtains, each revealed a bedroom, both furnished with just a bed and a chest. The place was cheerful and looked spotlessly clean, but how on earth did five people live here, let alone seven? Where were we going to sleep? And where was the bathroom? After the long walk from the dock, I was already in need of the lavatory, and then Teddy started jiggling around in a way that I'd learned, over the past few days, meant he was in the same need as I was, and probably more urgently.

"Um . . . where's the lavatory?" I asked.

Three faces looked at me blankly. Lady Storton's strictures on the words we did and didn't use had sunk in so deeply I'd completely forgotten normal people didn't call it that. But Ruth spotted Teddy's wriggling.

"Oh! Downstairs and round the back," she said. "Use the one on the right—I gave it a good scrub this morning so I hope that filthy man from the second floor hasn't been in there since."

The outhouse was a wooden shack with five doors, and I smelled it before I saw it. Following Ruth's instructions, I gingerly opened the door on the right, to see a toilet that was nothing more than a wooden box with a hole cut into the lid, and squares of newspaper hanging on a hook beside it. The smell of strong disinfectant didn't hide the underlying stench, sharp and pungent. Holding my breath, I helped Teddy and was just pulling up his trousers when to my horror I heard footsteps and one of the other doors opening and closing. A man's voice began to sing in a foreign language, and then the song was accompanied by the most horrendous noises and smells. Teddy giggled. I shushed him and relieved myself as quickly as I could, unsure whether I was most embarrassed about hearing the man or him hearing me. How could people live like this?

I'd realized, of course I had, that Molly's family wouldn't be wealthy, but I hadn't expected this. The cottages on the Winterton estate had outside toilets, but they weren't down three dark flights of stairs, and they certainly weren't shared with twenty other families. And five people in three rooms! Even the little houses my father's mill workers lived in weren't as crowded as that. I didn't want to think about how washing themselves was managed, either. The only tap I'd seen was out in the hallway, dripping into a rusty iron sink.

At the bottom of the stairs, Teddy hung back, dragging on my hand.

"No, Mama," he said. "Dark."

There was a tearful wobble in his voice and I was close to crying myself. What had I brought us into? Before the wedding, I'd been nervous about going to Winterton and having to live with strangers, and I'd turned out to be right about that. Yet here I was, about to be crammed into a tiny space with five people I didn't know, and sharing toilets with who knew how many others I'd never even clapped eyes on. We had nothing but the clothes we stood up in, no possessions, no money, and no idea how I could support us. And on top of that, the idea that I could keep up the pretense of being Molly looked more and more ridiculous. The family hadn't questioned it so far because they'd no reason to. They were expecting Molly; they'd never seen her, and I was roughly the right age and spoke with a Manchester accent. Ruth had even imagined a resemblance to Molly's mother, because she'd seen what she expected to see. But I'd never so much as made my own bed or peeled a potato. How was I going to make them believe I'd grown up poor and worked in service?

Why had I been so foolish? It was a crazy idea, born in a moment when I wasn't entirely in my right mind. We couldn't stay here. We had to get back to the port, tell someone there'd been a mistake, have a marconigram sent. No one at Winterton need ever know I'd tried to run away—things had been chaotic at the docks, and hadn't Ruth said, no one was sure if the lists were right? As long as I was quick, I could make it all right.

I almost did it. But then I thought again of the piece of paper that I'd paid so little attention to at the time, the one that made Lord and Lady Storton Teddy's guardians. If I went back, that piece of paper would rule our lives. They'd have control over Teddy, and that meant they had control over me, too. Yet another situation that had been decided over my head.

I remembered all the cries in the dark, all the people who'd lost the chance of any life at all, and how I'd told myself, back there on the *Carpathia*, that I wouldn't waste the chance I'd been given. For once, I'd made my own choice and taken responsibility for what happened to me. Either I stuck by it, or I'd have to go back to having other people choose my life for me.

You're Molly now, and Molly made her own decisions.

"Come on," I said to Teddy. "I'll carry you up."

CHAPTER 30

When we reached the top of the stairs, Ruth was at the door of the apartment.

"All right, love? I was just about to come and find you. It's easy to mistake your floor in the dark."

She put her arm around my shoulder. No one had done that since my mother died.

"You poor thing, you must be tired out. Come and have some soup, then we'll get you both to bed."

I sat at the table next to Per and Anna, Teddy beside me, his face turned shyly into my shoulder. Ruth put a bowl of soup down in front of me, golden yellow, thick and hearty, with chunks of ham floating in it, and a smaller one for Teddy. I managed to get him to turn round and eat, but I was so nervous, I wasn't sure I could swallow even a mouthful. But when I tried, I realized I was ravenous. I'd been so anxious about this whole idea of pretending to be Molly that I'd barely eaten on the *Carpathia*.

I wanted to get the story I'd concocted about Teddy out of the way, so I told it as soon as I could, saying that I'd lost my previous position when I fell pregnant, but my employer had felt sorry for me and given me enough money to tide me over till he was born.

"She gave me a reference too, so when I'd found a woman to look after Teddy, I was able to get another position. But I wanted a better chance in life for him, and I remembered what you said in your letters, about children here getting a good education so they can make something of themselves."

The words I'd rehearsed slipped out so easily, I was shocked at myself. I hadn't ever been in the habit of telling lies, even as a child. Was it because I'd become so used to being someone I wasn't at Winterton? That was one kind of lying, and perhaps this was just another.

Ruth patted my shoulder and said, "You did right. Over here, if you get yourself an education, you can do anything. Micke wants to be an engineer, to build bridges and roads, and if he works hard at school, he'll be able to. It's not like at home, where they keep you in your place." She nodded at Teddy, dozing off on my knee. "Micke and Lena will be excited about getting a cousin. Or nearly a cousin."

"Where are they?" I asked.

"Staying with a neighbor downstairs. They've been looking forward to meeting you, but we thought you should have some peace and quiet tonight."

There was a knock at the door, and Ruth opened it to two women, one about her age, with dark hair and eyes, the other older and almost the first one's opposite, pale and freckled with red hair. She was carrying a small wooden crate.

"We saw you come in," she said in an Irish accent. "The lists were right, then, thank God."

"Molly, these are our neighbors," said Ruth. "Eileen lives downstairs and Giovanna is across the hall."

"We won't disturb you, just wanted to say welcome, and bring this," said the Irish woman, handing the box to Ruth. "A few things you might need, clothes and so on. Everything's clean. But I see there's two of you, we didn't know . . ."

"This is Teddy," said Ruth. "Molly's son."

There was an expectant pause, but when Ruth offered no explanation, Eileen said, "Well, I'll sort out a few of Liam's old things for the little fella."

"Thank you," I said. "That's kind of you."

"We're sorry for this terrible thing that happened," said the dark-haired woman, who I thought must be Italian. "Everyone want to help."

When the two of them had gone, Anna said, "So nosey, that Irish woman! You saw she wanted to ask, where's the husband?"

"She is nosey, but her heart's in the right place," said Ruth. "I'll tell her the story tomorrow, and as long as she's first with the news, she'll be satisfied." She turned to me. "I won't say there won't be gossip, but people here mostly take you as they find you. There's plenty who've come to America to escape worse than you have."

As she spoke, she was unpacking the crate, taking out an assortment of clothes and underclothes, a bar of soap, and a small pot of face cream.

"That'll be from the Colemans, downstairs," said Ruth. "He works at Bigelow's Pharmacy. And these . . ." She took out half a dozen oranges and a dish with a cloth over it, lifting the cloth to reveal little pastries that smelled of honey. "Fruit from Eileen—her Patrick's in the trade, and the pastries will be from Eleni next door."

She took out the last item in the box, a little tin, and opened it. To my horror, it was full of coins. These people who lived twenty families to a building and probably earned less in a week than I used to spend on a pair of shoes had scraped together a collection for me.

"I can't take their money," I said.

Even as the words came out of my mouth, I realized how ridiculous they sounded coming from someone who was penniless.

"Sorry," I said quickly. "I just meant . . . it's so kind of them."

"Like Giovanna said, they want to help. She's been lighting a candle at the church for you every day too, till we knew for sure you were safe."

"Superstitious nonsense," said Anna.

"Mama!" said Per.

"Well, it is," said Anna, and then, grudgingly, "but she means well. They all do."

That first night, Anna insisted that Teddy and I had the bed she usually shared with the two children, in the smaller of the two bedrooms. The mystery of where we'd be sleeping otherwise was solved when she took out a featherbed, pillows, and blankets from the chest under the window and spread them on the kitchen floor. I protested, but she held up a hand and said sternly, "No need for this English politeness. We Swedes say what we mean, and I have said you are welcome to take the bed, just for tonight. You and the boy need to sleep well after this terrible time you've had. So good night."

Sleep well? Even exhausted as I was, there wasn't much chance of that. Lying there in the dark, curled around Teddy like a mother cat with her kitten, all the horror of that night out on the ocean came back again, and with it, the worst imaginings. When had my father and Frederick and Terence realized there was no seat in a lifeboat for them? I kept seeing the moment just before the ship disappeared, the silhouettes of people jumping from the decks into the icy water. Were they with them? Were their voices among all those crying out for help, and realizing no one was going to come? And then Molly, poor Molly. Why hadn't she come back up on deck? Why had I let her go back to the cabin in the first place? I could have replaced her savings without a thought, and then she'd be safe now, and her baby would have had a chance to live.

I still couldn't believe what I'd done, either. Declared us dead. Taken another woman's name. And what now? These kind people had believed me, because they had no reason not to. But if I couldn't keep up the pretense, we were lost—if they threw us out, there'd be no choice but to go back. And if Lord and Lady Storton could decide I was mad for wanting to see my baby in the hours after he was born, they'd have no trouble proving it after this.

CHAPTER 31

When I woke the next morning, a loud, rattling whirr was coming from the front room. I couldn't think what it was but clearly the rest of the household was up and about. In a panic, I dressed quickly from the pile I'd been given, picking a plain white blouse and brown wool skirt that seemed the best fit, and trying not to think about the fact that I was putting on someone else's undergarments and woollen stockings that, though perfectly clean, still sagged with the shape of the previous owner's knees. But when I tried to dress Teddy, he pulled and picked at the flannel trousers Eileen had brought up the night before.

"Itchy, Mama, don't like it!"

"Don't be silly now, leave them on. You'll get used to them."

As I struggled to get him into a worn cotton shirt, he squirmed and wriggled, holding himself rigid. I did my best to be gentle, but in the end I had to force his arms into the sleeves, and by the time I'd got it buttoned up, I was hot and flustered and he was red-faced and crying, the noise only covered by the rattle from the parlor.

"Teddy, please, be quiet now."

I took him in my arms to comfort him, but he pushed me away, his little arms stiff, and cried harder. I'd only ever seen him a little bit grouchy, and I had no idea how to calm him down and stop him crying. Molly had taken care of five brothers; if Ruth and Anna saw us like this, they'd know straight away that I wasn't used to looking after even one child. How on earth was I going to keep up the pretense of being her, when it was falling apart before we'd even shown our faces?

I promised him breakfast; I told him he was naughty, but nothing worked. How on earth had Nanny dealt with this? Or did he never act like it with her? Suddenly I couldn't hold back my own tears of fear and frustration. His eyes widened, and the crying suddenly stopped. He let me hug him then, and after a few minutes, I wiped his tears and mine, and we went out to face the day.

When we emerged, Teddy holding tight to my hand, the front parlor was wreathed with steam. A big pot of water was heating on the stove, and Ruth, red-faced with tendrils of hair crinkling round her brow, was scrubbing clothes in a zinc tub, with another big pile of laundry on the floor beside her. The strange rattling noise came from one of the sewing machines; Anna sat at it, feet flashing backward and forward, operating the treadle that made the needles stab in and out of the fabric at a frightening speed. There was no sign of Per or the children, and I guessed he must already have gone to work and them to school.

"I'm sorry," I said, "I didn't realize it was late, and Teddy's been a bit upset by everything."

"It's as I said," said Anna, without looking up from the machine. "You needed to sleep."

"Poor little lad probably doesn't know where he is," said

Ruth. She smiled at Teddy. "A big boy's breakfast for you, like Micke has, how about that?"

She poured me coffee from a red enamel pot, then dished out two bowls of thick porridge from a pan on the stove. Teddy tucked into his breakfast, his tears apparently forgotten, thank goodness, but I struggled to swallow mine, my throat tight with fear that at any moment I was going to give myself away. I had to concentrate even to remember to speak with my old accent—how was I going to manage everything else? Remembering what Molly had told me about herself and her family, doing the things she'd know how to do?

Ruth plucked a shirt from the murky-looking water and rubbed it ferociously against a ribbed board. Molly would know how to do that, but I'd never given a thought to how my clothes were washed: they were just taken away by Rose and then reappeared, freshly laundered, in my wardrobe. My mother cooked and cleaned in the early days of her marriage, and I suppose she must have done laundry too, but by the time I came along, they had servants to do everything, so there'd been no need for her to pass any of that on to me. It looked like hard work; Ruth's hands were rough and red.

Anna came to the end of a seam and looked up. "Have you used a sewing machine before?"

"No," I said, wondering why she was asking. "If the mistress's gowns needed repairing, I sewed them by hand."

Despite—or perhaps because of—my nerves, the lie came easily. I might not have been a ladies' maid but at least I'd seen that from the other side.

"I hadn't either," said Ruth, "but with a bit of practice you'll soon pick it up."

What was she talking about? But as she continued, the penny dropped. I'd completely misunderstood how they earned their living. When Molly said her relatives were in the clothing trade, I'd imagined a little dress shop, but that wasn't it at all. They worked, Ruth explained, right there in their own front room. So that was why they had two sewing machines. It had seemed odd, with so little space in the apartment, but it hadn't occurred to me that the tiny room became a little factory during the day.

"We make shirtwaists—blouses, really, but that's what they call them here." Ruth pointed at the one I was wearing. "That's a shirtwaist. They're cut like a man's shirt, so apart from the sleeves, it's mostly straight seams."

Anna came to the end of a hem, bit off the cotton and held up a blouse in blue lawn, sprigged with daisies.

"See," she said. "Very easy."

"You've made one already this morning?"

Ruth laughed and pointed at a pile on the floor. "We've made all those this morning. It's piecework—we're only paid for as many as we make, so you have to be fast."

"Got to keep up with the girls in his factory as well," said Anna. "Not many contractors using home workers these days; they'd rather have you under their eye all day. If we're not quick, he could get to thinking it's not worth his while."

"We usually make ten a day," said Ruth. "Mr. Klein sends the pieces every evening; we make them up, and his foreman collects them when he brings the next lot."

I looked down at my bowl of porridge to hide my shock. The clothes I used to wear took weeks to make, trims sewn on by hand, hems taken up with stitches so tiny you could barely see them. I'd no idea what a shirtwaist might cost to buy here, but how could they be paid so little to make them that they had to do that many in a day? And how on earth was I going to be able to do that? I'd done a little hand sewing, but I'd never so much as touched a sewing machine.

Deep breath. It can't be that hard. You understand fabrics, that'll help. You'll pick it up in a week or two.

Ruth said, "You've no need to start today, not after what you've been through. Tomorrow will be fine. Mr. Klein will want you to make one as a test, but if we send that with tomorrow's work, he'll bring your machine the next day. It's always busy this time of year, so he'll be glad of another machinist."

I wasn't going to get weeks to practice; I was going to get, at best, a day. And if I couldn't do it, what then? I'd only been able to carry out this mad plan at all because Molly had somewhere to live, and the promise of work to earn a living from. This household obviously couldn't carry two extra people, and we had nowhere else to go but back to Winterton.

No.

Whatever it took, we weren't going back. I forced down the last spoonful of porridge and pushed the bowl aside.

"I can get started today," I said.

Ruth frowned. "Are you sure you feel up to it?"

"Work is the best medicine," said Anna. "No point in wallowing, much better to occupy your mind."

"Thank you, Dr. Svensson," said Ruth tartly. "But Molly's had a bad time—"

"Anna's right," I said. "I'd rather get started."

"Well," said Ruth, "if you're sure, it would be easier today. You can practice on my machine, while I get this washing done."

As I stood up and made to leave the table, I noticed Anna looking at me curiously. What had I done? I glanced down.

Idiot! The cup and the dishes.

The night before, Ruth had taken my soup bowl and everyone's coffee cups out to the sink in the hall, so, doing my best to make it look as though I'd always intended to, I did the same, wincing at the ice-cold water as I rinsed them. I had the feeling Anna's shrewd blue eyes didn't miss a lot; if I was going to stop them seeing me for the imposter I was and throwing us out before I had a chance to earn some money, I'd have to be much more careful. Think on my feet, and watch and learn, without anyone realizing I didn't already know all the things a girl like Molly would know.

After fetching some toys of her son's for Teddy to play with and finding a worn old pillowcase for me to practice on, Ruth showed me how to work the sewing machine's treadle with my feet, while holding the fabric taut with my fingers and passing it under a little metal plate, then lifting up the needle to change direction. I felt sick: it was even more difficult than it looked.

"You'll soon get it," she said. "Practice what I've shown you, and when I've got this lot done and hung out, we'll try a shirtwaist."

Nothing for it but to put my head down and get on with it. So, while Anna clattered away on the machine beside me, stopping now and then to press a seam with an iron heated on the stove, and Ruth scrubbed the laundry against a board, I sewed up and down, up and down, painfully slowly. Terrified of getting my fingers caught under the needle and struggling to keep the needle moving smoothly and the stitching straight.

After about twenty minutes, Anna sighed and got up from her machine. "Stop," she said. "You have long legs, like me. Try like this." She bent down and repositioned my feet on the treadle, my left foot at the top, my right at the bottom. "Now, you must get the rhythm, backward, forward, backward, forward . . . When it's smooth, you can get faster."

After a couple of minutes, I saw what she meant; your hands and feet had to work together. Soon I could keep the stitching straight, row after row, and I made myself go a bit faster each time. I was concentrating so hard, jaw clenched and shoulders stiff, that when Ruth spoke, it made me jump.

"That's it, you're getting it now." She pointed at the zinc tub, full of water and laundry. "Help me take this lot out to the sink, will you?"

We each took a handle of the tub and lifted. It was so heavy! We lugged it to the sink in the hallway and tipped out the water, Ruth holding the clothes back with her hand.

"I hate Mondays," she said, running cold water over the clothes in the tub. "All this work, and then it just starts getting dirty again tomorrow."

Stirring the clothes around in the water, she said, "It'll be a big help having you here though. Anna insists she's fit as a flea, but her knee gives her trouble so I don't like her doing too much lifting and carrying. Right, let's get this lot hung up."

We hefted the tub up, and for a horrible moment I thought we were going to have to carry it down the stairs, but Ruth led the way out onto the fire escape. There, strung between their building and the next, from top to bottom, were dozens of washing lines, with shirts, petticoats, socks, and even drawers flapping in the breeze, and between every other pair of buildings, the same. I opened my mouth to ask if everyone in New York did their washing on a Monday, but then thought better of it. Perhaps everyone in the world did their washing on a Monday, and everyone who did washing knew that.

Ruth picked a shirt from the tub and twisted it hard between her hands, making the water drip out, so I did the same, copying what she did as best I could and trying to look as though I'd done it many times before. I must have done all right; when we were down to just a few items, she left them to me, and reached out to reel in the washing line, which was on a sort of pulley system. So I was feeling quite pleased with myself until I realized I was holding a pair of Per's drawers and, in a sudden flush of embarrassment, dropped them. They slipped through the struts of the fire escape and floated down to the ground, landing on the dirty cobbles.

Ruth laughed at my stricken face. "Run down and fetch them, and we'll just rinse them under the tap. I won't tell if you don't."

* * *

Back inside the apartment, once another batch of laundry was soaking in the tub, I showed Ruth the stitching I'd done.

"See, I told you you'd get it," she said. "We'll try you on a shirtwaist then—but take it slowly. The ones we've got this week aren't too tricky, no lace or ruffles, but the fabric's very fine. If you go wrong, it's a devil to unpick."

"And if you ruin a piece," said Anna, "the cost is taken from our pay."

That stopped me short. My father routinely deducted pay if work wasn't up to scratch, and at the time I'd considered that perfectly reasonable. I hadn't ever thought about what it would be like on the other end of it, much less expected to be there myself. This wasn't like sewing bunting for the village fete; it was what Ruth and Anna did to put food on the table, and I had to do it well enough for someone to pay for it. I'd been all buoyed up and confident, but as I started to sew the first two pieces together, my hands were trembling.

The fabric was much more delicate than the pillowcase had been. It'd show the slightest flaw. Fearful of making a mistake, even on the straight pieces I went so slowly I'd have been quicker to sew them by hand. And the sleeves! Horrible curved seams that you had to ease the fabric into, and even with Ruth's gentle advice to take my time, it brought me out in a sweat. But, eventually, there in my hands was a complete shirtwaist, that a couple of hours before had been just pieces of fabric.

Ruth took it from me, still inside out, and held it up. She turned to Anna. "It's good," she said. "I think it's good enough to show him, do you?"

Anna peered at the stitching. Frowning, she pulled at a side seam, then stretched the hem out straight between her fingers. I held my breath.

"It's good enough," she said.

I smiled, very pleased with myself.

"But you will have to get much quicker. Let's see how many more you can make today."

Teddy, thank goodness, behaved himself all day, playing quietly with some wooden bricks Ruth gave him, and settling down easily for a nap in the afternoon, just as he had on the ship.

"He's very good at amusing himself, isn't he?" said Ruth. "Micke was into everything at that age. He'd never play quietly like that."

Had he learned that in the nursery with Nanny? I'd no idea; I'd never even seen him playing with toys before.

Late in the afternoon, Ruth's children bounced in from school: eight-year-old Lena, slight and blonde, like a little fairy, and ten-year-old Micke, blond too and tall for his age, with spectacles and a serious look in his blue eyes. They chorused hello, and then Lena took something from her school bag and came over to me at the sewing machine.

"This is for you," she said, holding out a handkerchief embroidered round the edges in red, like the tablecloth, but not as neatly. She nodded at her grandmother.

"Farmor helped me with it."

She'd made it for Molly. And now here I was, accepting it under false pretenses.

"Thank you," I said, feeling sick with shame. "It's lovely."

She looked at Teddy, who'd come and half-hid behind me.

"We don't have anything for you, because we didn't know you were coming. But you can share Micke's toys."

By the look on Micke's face, he hadn't been consulted about that idea. But he looked at the pile of wooden bricks Teddy had been playing with, three or four stacked precariously on top of each other, and said, "Shall I show you how to build a tower that doesn't fall down?"

Teddy continued to cling to my legs, but as Micke quietly started building, he watched intently.

"Want to help me?" said Micke.

Teddy looked up at me.

"Go on," I said.

He toddled over and squatted down, listening intently as Micke explained—in quite a lot of detail—how to stack the bricks to give the tower a solid foundation.

"I think," said Ruth, "those two are going to be friends."

By the end of the day, I'd made another shirtwaist and started a third, gone out to the fire escape with Ruth to hang up two more batches of washing and bring in the dry garments, and then, once I'd watched carefully how she did it, I offered to do the last batch myself. Ruth gratefully accepted, then sat straight down at her machine. By the time I'd scrubbed the washing clean—even harder work than it looked, and despite the last batch all being dark colors, I was sweating when it was done— she'd added to the pile of completed shirtwaists. I helped her carry them all downstairs to be collected, and bring the next day's work back up, and by then Anna was starting to cook dinner.

I was so tired it was an effort to walk up the stairs, and I could happily have fallen into bed right then. But I'd got through it. I'd done the work; I hadn't slipped up, and in con- centrating so hard, I'd driven thoughts of the *Titanic* out of my head. They'd be lying in wait for me as soon as I closed my eyes, but perhaps the tiredness would rescue me this time. The whole thing still seemed like a very peculiar dream, but if I'd got through one day, couldn't I get through another, and an- other, until we got on our feet and we could leave?

When Per came home he was holding a newspaper. He put it down on the table and there, smiling up from the front page, was a photograph of me.

CHAPTER 32

Tragic victims of the *Titanic* the headline said. Beneath it were two rows of photographs, and right in the middle of the bottom row, Frederick and me on our wedding day. Smiling straight at the camera. My blood turned to ice. I glanced round at Teddy, playing on the floor. Could I grab him and run? No. It was already too late. They wouldn't keep this quiet—why would they help me when I'd lied about Molly? And after I'd taken their charity when, back in England, I was rich beyond their dreams? Once the news got out that I wasn't a tragic victim at all, I was alive, there'd be nowhere for us to hide. I put my head in my hands and waited for the world to collapse.

"Per!" snapped Ruth. "Molly doesn't want to see that!"

She snatched the paper up and shoved it in a drawer of the dresser.

"Sorry," he said, hanging his coat on the hook behind the door. "I didn't think. It's going to be hard to avoid though, I'm afraid—the whole city's talking about the *Titanic*." He went over to Anna, who was stirring a pan on the stove. "What's for dinner, Mama?"

My heart was pounding so hard I was sure they could hear it.

"Stop that!" said Anna, smacking Per's hand as he dipped a spoon into the stew. "Sit down and wait till it's ready."

"Lena, can you set the table please?" said Ruth.

The little girl started packing away her homework, and as she did I remembered where Ruth had taken the soup spoons from the evening before.

"I'll do it," I said, jumping up. But Ruth shook her head.

"No, you sit down. The children both have jobs to do. Lena just forgets once she's got her head full of sums."

I froze as Lena went to the dresser. Would she see the photograph? Would her sharp young eyes notice it was me?

But she just pushed the paper aside and took out the cutlery. When she closed the drawer a corner of the newspaper was poking out. I couldn't take my eyes off it.

Anna served up meatballs in a thick brown stew, and it was probably delicious because everyone tucked in, even Teddy once I'd cut it all up for him. But it could equally well have been roast pheasant or the meanest gruel for all I tasted of it. From my seat, against the wall, that little triangle of paper was shouting at me. I was frantically trying to think what I could say when they saw my picture. Could I beg them to keep my secret, explain to them why I'd done what I did?

Don't be ridiculous!

The story of the poor little rich girl who wasn't happy with her life in the great house wasn't going to mean much to people who shared a toilet with twenty other families, was it? And it wasn't going to mean much when they found out poor Molly was dead and I'd taken advantage of that to escape my fancy life.

They'd be furious, they'd have every right to be. And once they knew we were running from a family with power and money, who could blame them for seeing the prospect of a reward for turning us in? All I could think of to do was make sure they didn't look at that newspaper tonight, and once everyone had gone to bed, find a way to get rid of it.

So as soon as the children went to bed and a very sleepy Teddy was settled in a nest of blankets, I plied them with questions about life in New York. They told me how strange they'd all found it at first, but how they soon got used to it, and I would too.

"We came from a very small village in Sweden where everyone knew everyone," said Anna in her singsong accent. "But here, there were so many strangers. I thought my head would burst with all the noise, and the streets and the buildings scared me—no forest, no meadows, only bricks and iron."

She glanced at the painting on the wall, of the calm blue lake surrounded by trees.

"It was hard, the first few years, for a widow on her own with a child. Per was only a little older than your boy, and we had to live with another family to afford the rent. They were Swedes, at least, so we could feel at home there, but outside, there were so many languages in my ears, and I didn't understand any of them. But then Per learned English at school, and I learned from him, and it was better. Most of the Swedes we knew only stayed a while and then went to the countryside, to Minnesota, to farm. But I thought, did we travel halfway across the world just to have the life we had at home? So we stayed here."

"And now look at you," said Per. "Grandmother to two proper little Americans, who say hot dog instead of varmkorv."

Anna scowled. "Stupid word."

"It was easier for me in that way," said Ruth. "At least I didn't have to learn a new language. But it's still strange and frightening, coming to a new country, especially on your own. I didn't really feel at home here till I met"—she jerked her head at Per—"this one."

She reached over and patted my hand. "But you've got us; you've got family already. I was made up when you wrote and said you wanted to come. We were like sisters, you know, your mam and me. I begged and begged her to come with me, and I know she wanted to, but your father wouldn't take the chance. But you coming is the next best thing."

I didn't answer. I couldn't. All that time on the *Carpathia*, trying to figure out if my ridiculous plan could work, I'd barely given a thought to this family, had I? I'd assumed they were just giving a relative a helping hand, till she found her feet and moved on. So if I did the same, got some money together then left as soon as I could, there'd be no real harm done. But Molly was someone special to them. They'd have been worried to death when the news of the sinking came, and now they thought she was alive. I hadn't thought it was possible to feel more guilty than I already did, but hearing them talk about her, I felt sick with it.

"I know we're cramped here," Ruth went on, "but we won't always be. We won't send the children out to work, like a lot of people do. We want them to get their education. The rent's low here because the landlord's dodging the sanitation rules, so we put up with it for now, and put a little aside each week till we can move somewhere nicer. Brooklyn, maybe—the Goldbergs from downstairs went there last year, brand-new building with toilets on every landing, and running water."

"And one day, we'll get a little house of our own," said Per. "It's a long time away, but if we work hard, we can do it."

Ruth gave a wry smile, and stood up. "But in the meantime, it's the long walk downstairs."

Before I realized what she was doing, she strode over to the dresser, took out the newspaper and said to Per, "You finished with this? We've nearly run out in the outhouse."

My heart hammered as she sat back at the table, unfolded

the newspaper and began methodically tearing pages off it, stacking them on top of each other.

"Let me help—"

"No need, it'll only take a minute."

She'd turned the paper over, I suppose still thinking I wouldn't want to see the stories about the *Titanic*. So the front page with my photograph on it must be at the bottom, face down; they wouldn't see it. All the same, I could hardly breathe as she tore the pages off one by one, and I had to stop myself letting out a sigh of relief when she placed the last page on the top of the pile. Then she folded the pile in half and there was our wedding picture, facing up.

She glanced down, then looked closer. I had to stop her and I could only think of one way.

I clapped my hand to my mouth and said, "Oh heck, that's Mr. and Mrs. Coombes. Can I—"

I held out my hand for the page.

"You know those people?" asked Per.

"Only from the ship. Of course, I haven't said, have I? I ended up traveling as Mrs. Coombes's maid, went in first class with them."

I told them the story, the way I thought Molly would have told it. How I'd seen a chance to make a bit of extra money, and it'd turned out Mrs. Coombes was from Manchester too, originally, though she'd married into a titled family. And then, with the feeling that I was stepping out onto a tightrope, I said, "She was the same age as me as well. She kept saying we looked alike."

Ruth peered at the photograph. I kept my hand over the text below it. They might swallow this, but if they read that Mrs. Coombes had a son the same age as Teddy, I'd be in trouble.

"You do have a look of her. Poor woman, so young!"

"Why couldn't she get into a lifeboat?" asked Per. "Said in the newspaper that first-class women and children got away first."

"I keep asking myself that," I said. "But we got separated in all the chaos, so I don't know."

"All that money, and it couldn't save them," said Anna.

"Saved more of the rich ones than the poor though," said Per. "They're saying most of the dead were down in steerage, women and children as well."

Ruth shook her head sadly. "It doesn't bear thinking about. If you hadn't been traveling in first class with them . . ."

"Enough of these morbid thoughts," said Anna. "She was saved and we thank God for that. And for the fact that we're all here in America and we'll never have to travel across the ocean again."

When everyone was in bed, and I'd laid out the featherbed and blankets on the kitchen floor, I took out the newspaper page—no one seemed to have noticed that I'd kept hold of it, or perhaps they didn't like to say. Our picture was one of a dozen, the rest mostly rich and famous Americans. I recognized some of them, though at the time I'd had no idea who they were: the man I'd seen talking to the actress Dorothy Gibson was a millionaire businessman called John Jacob Astor, and an elderly couple who'd been at the table beside us in the dining saloon turned out to be the founders of a department store. Under our photograph, it said:

Mr. Frederick Coombes was the son of Lord Storton, an English aristocrat. He was traveling with his wife, Elinor, and their infant son, Edward, who also perished.

The words seemed to dance in front of my eyes. My own death, written down in black and white, for anyone to see. I'd got away with it tonight: there's nothing like fear to sharpen your thinking. Because I'd pointed out the resemblance before any of the family noticed it, they'd readily accepted that the woman in the ridiculously expensive wedding dress, with the veil held on by diamond pins, just looked a bit like the one sitting there at the table with them, in her borrowed clothes with a shiny face and frizzy hair from the washing-day steam. But they wouldn't be the only people who'd have seen that picture and read those words.

The whole city's talking about the Titanic.

CHAPTER 33

I disposed of the page in the morning, in the outhouse. But now the thought of stepping outside, where anyone might recognize me, was terrifying; I kept picturing accusing faces and pointing fingers. So when Ruth asked me if I wanted to come with her when she went out for provisions, I made an excuse, saying I wanted to keep practicing my sewing. As she'd predicted, my shirtwaist had passed muster with their employer, Mr. Klein, and a machine had arrived for me that morning. I'd disappeared into the bedroom when two lads delivered it, afraid of seeing recognition in their faces.

I was nervous about trying to sew faster, but I told myself that I hadn't thought I could make a shirtwaist at all and then I had. So I could do it again, and in less time. By the end of the morning, I'd done two, and only had to unpick one seam. We ate a very quick meal—bread and cheese and strong coffee—and then went back to the machines.

"This is the busiest time of the year," Ruth explained. "He'll take as many as we can make, so we work all hours now, to ease us through when there's less work available."

Teddy played happily with Micke's toy cars for most of the morning, submitting to a nap in the children's room in the afternoon, and Lena and Micke entertained him when they came home from school. I made five shirtwaists that day, and when I submitted them for Anna's inspection, she raised an eyebrow and said, "This is good work. Well done."

Ruth laughed. "Have you had sugar in your coffee today, Mama? It's not like you to be so complimentary."

"I say as I find," snapped Anna. And then, to me, "It was a good day's work. And you'll sleep better for it tonight."

About that, she was both right and wrong. I was so bone-tired at the end of that day that I fell asleep as soon as I lay down, beside a sleeping Teddy, on our featherbed on the kitchen floor. But in the early hours, I woke quite suddenly, as if from a noise. I don't know if I'd been dreaming about the *Titanic* or not, but memories of that last night came flooding into my mind, and I couldn't stop them. The sound of the ship hitting the iceberg. The confusion up on deck. Molly disappearing. Frederick arguing with the crewman to make sure we got away safely. My last sight of my father, cupping his hands round his mouth to shout to me as the lifeboat was lowered.

Don't worry, we'll see you soon.

A sob rose in my throat as I remembered the conversation we'd had on the ship, about the committee he'd appointed to run the company after him. "I've picked young'uns," he said, "because I've no plans to fall off the perch for a while yet."

How could he be dead? It wasn't possible, and yet it was true.

And Molly—how could Molly be dead? She was a survivor; she'd grabbed life by the scruff of the neck and shaken it, and she was going to make such a good life for her baby. I kept seeing that line of cabin lights dipping down into the sea. The decks below must have been flooded by then. Had she got lost on her way back up and been trapped by the water? Had she known, before any of us up on deck, that the ship must be sinking and she couldn't escape?

Under and over all those thoughts, the cries of the people in the water echoed round in my head. Screaming, calling for help that was never going to come. I knew the sound was only in my mind but it was so clear, and the cries so distinct, that I might have been sitting in that lifeboat again. I don't know how long those sounds kept me awake, but when I heard Per tiptoe past on his way out to work in the morning, I felt as though I'd hardly slept at all.

All that first week, I didn't dare step outside the apartment block. Because there were people who knew we weren't dead, weren't there? People on deck, who'd seen us get away in the first lifeboat. People who'd been in the lifeboat with us—we'd barely seen each other's faces in the dark, but I was the only Englishwoman, as far as I knew, and certainly the only one with a child. And if any of them saw that photo in the newspaper, saw me and Teddy listed as among the dead and knew it couldn't be true, surely they'd tell someone? There might already be people out there looking for us.

Even going down to the outhouse, panic darted through me if a neighbor came out of their apartment or passed me on the stairs. Any of them could have seen the newspaper, and they all knew I'd been on the *Titanic*. It would only take one of them to comment on the likeness for Ruth, Per, or Anna to look closer and see what they hadn't seen before—and I couldn't prevent anyone else from reading that Elinor Coombes had an infant son.

So when, on the Friday evening, there was a rap on the door, I froze. They'd found me. Someone had seen that picture and known it wasn't right, and now Lord and Lady Storton knew we weren't dead, and they'd got someone to track us down. I wasn't going to be able to talk my way out of this. I glanced at the fire escape. Could we run? But before I had a chance to move, Anna had opened the door.

In walked an elderly man carrying a bundle of shirtwaist pieces.

"Mr. Klein, this is Molly," said Ruth.

The man they worked for. My legs went weak with the relief of it. I remembered now, hearing Anna say something about him coming on Fridays with their wages.

"The new recruit," he said. "Welcome to New York."

My heart was still jittering as he checked through each of our bundles of work, and at first I didn't take in his words to me.

"Your work is very neat. Were you in the garment trade back in England?"

"No, I was a ladies' maid."

"Living in the big house, huh?"

"Quite a big one, yes."

"I guess the Lower East Side is a bit of a change, then. You like it here?"

"Yes, I do."

"Good. Right . . ."

He took out a little leather pouch and counted out my pay. Ruth had explained that in the first week, he'd deduct some money for supplying the machine, but as he put the coins into my hand, he said gruffly, "No charge for the machine, in view of what's happened to you."

He handed Anna and Ruth each their money too, tipped his hat to us and said, "There we are, ladies. Don't spend it all on diamonds and pearls."

I was still so panicked from that rap on the door that it took me a couple of attempts to count my wages; for the first time in my life I couldn't think clearly enough to get numbers to make sense. When I'd finally calmed down and got to grips with the unfamiliar coins, my first thought was that they wouldn't have bought me a petticoat in my old life. But my second was that I couldn't have been prouder of myself if it had been a thousand pounds. With all the fear and the nightmares and the strain of pretending to be Molly, I had earned a wage. It wasn't a lot, but if I saved the bit left after I'd given Ruth some for our keep, I could work toward being able to look after myself and Teddy, and get away from this kind family who made me feel sick with guilt every time I opened my mouth and lied to them. Even get away from New York, eventually, to somewhere no one would even know we'd arrived on the *Titanic*. As long as I could keep our secret till then.

Stretching her arms above her head, Ruth said, "What a week! You've worked hard. We all have. One more day, though, and then on Sunday we'll get out and have some fresh air."

CHAPTER 34

Each morning, we'd all washed hurriedly in water heated on the stove, but on Sundays, Ruth explained, they went to a public bathhouse, a few streets away.

"You can have a nice hot soak there, all free." She rubbed her shoulder. "Reckon we need it after six days bent over those machines. And then after, we usually take the children to the park."

All day Saturday, I worried about what to do. Could I pretend to be ill? But if I did, Ruth might offer to take Teddy, and I was terrified to let him out of my sight. I couldn't think of any way to refuse to go without looking suspicious, and the last thing I needed was to give Ruth and the rest of the family any cause to start wondering about me.

So when Sunday came, I dressed in the dowdiest garments I could find from the pile I'd been given. None of them were exactly glamorous anyway, but I looked least like myself in a sack-like black skirt that was worn to fraying at the hem, and a faded blue ticking shirtwaist. My hair, without a maid's attentions, was flat and dull anyway, and I scraped it back, winding the telltale curls into a tight bun that made me look like a cantankerous schoolteacher. I looked a sight, but at least I didn't look like Elinor Coombes on her wedding day. And in his patched trousers and flannel shirt, Teddy certainly didn't look like the heir to an English estate. At the last moment, I got the idea to ask Per to carry him, saying he wasn't used to walking near busy roads. If anyone was looking for us, they'd be searching for a woman with a child, not a family of seven in three generations.

All the same, my legs were shaking as we went down the front steps to the street. I kept my head down and my eyes fixed on the ground, terrified that if I looked up, I might see a "Wanted" poster on a lamp post, or a policeman running to arrest me. Was it screaming out of me that I shouldn't be there? Because it does, doesn't it, when you're somewhere you don't belong? It made me think of Lady Burnham's ball, where my dress and my jewels were as expensive as anyone else's, but I'd have bet that every single person there could see I wasn't one of them. And here, walking down the dirty cobbled street, I might be dressed much like Ruth, and that woman across the road, and that one there, coming toward us, but surely they could see I was an imposter, who'd done an awful thing and deserved to be found out?

A couple of elderly women in long black clothes passed us, carrying a heavy shopping basket between them and chattering in a language I didn't recognize. A family strolled along on the other side of the road, the father and two boys in skull caps like the one my father's Jewish tailor wore, and a young woman in a smart green coat and high heels clicked past us, waving to a man who stood waiting at the corner. None of them so much as glanced at me, but it made no difference; my shoulders were up around my ears with tension. Ruth was talking all the way, but my ears were so pricked for the sound of someone shouting my name that I didn't take in a word.

"Here we are," she said as we approached a huge white stone building with carvings of dolphins over two arched entrances, one for men and one for women. It can't have been more than a ten-minute walk, but I was so relieved at the thought of getting inside that it was all I could do not to run up the steps. We collected towels and then, at last, a fierce-looking woman showed us each to our cubicles, and barked, "Twenty minutes only, and no adding hot water."

I almost shoved Teddy in, locked the door behind us, and leaned against it, taking deep breaths to try to calm myself down. We'd got here. For a little while, at least, no one could see us; no one could find us. The cubicle was plain and sparse with white tiles on the wall and well-worn green ones on the floor, and the bathtub, filled with about six inches of water, was less than welcoming, but it all looked clean. I'd tried very hard all week to ignore the grubby feeling of putting on the same clothes every day, after just a quick wash at the sink, but now I let myself think about it, I was itchy all over.

I tested the lock—twice—then hurriedly undressed us both and got into the tub with Teddy. He sat at one end, splashing happily, just as he'd done when I bathed him on the ship. Such a short time ago, but it felt as though I'd climbed a mountain on my knees since then. My muscles ached from the hard work that I wasn't used to, my back was stiff from sleeping on the floor, but worse than either was the fear and tension that whirled through my mind every moment of the day, so that by the time I lay down to sleep, my head was banging and jangling, and I could barely think straight.

Every conversation I had with Ruth was a potential trap. Molly had told me quite a bit about her life and her family in the four days on the ship—she was chatty for a servant. I'd liked it at the time, and now I thanked my lucky stars for it. But still there were big gaps—how could there not be when we'd known each other so briefly? I was constantly having to word my answers carefully, so as not to show I didn't know the names of all Molly's brothers, or what she'd been good at in school, and at the same time, making myself memorize any details Ruth let slip so I could fill in some of the missing parts.

On top of that, all the time I was watching Anna and Ruth, so I could see how to do the things that any ordinary woman would know: peel a potato, sweep a floor, make a bed. Anna always made the dinner—"She doesn't like my cooking," Ruth told me, "so I let her get on with it"—but one day that first week, a problem with her sewing machine made her late to start the meal.

"Here, Molly," she said, passing me a dish of potatoes she'd just peeled. "Slice them thin."

I'd never cut up a vegetable in my life. Suddenly I had hams for hands: the potatoes kept slipping under the knife, and the slices came out ragged and uneven. When I glanced up, Anna was watching me.

I took a steadying breath to keep the panic from my voice and said breezily, "I think I've forgotten how to cook. I was in service such a long time, and a ladies' maid never sets foot in the kitchen—the cook wouldn't allow it."

"A strange job," said Anna. "They must be lazy, these women who need someone else to brush their hair and run their bath."

"Lucky, more like," said Ruth as she tied a bundle of shirt-waists with string, ready to be collected. "I wouldn't mind someone waiting on me hand and foot."

What would they think if they knew I'd had just that, all my life?

That I was getting away with the pretense so far must be down to all the practice I'd had at Winterton: speaking in a voice that wasn't mine, acting the compliant little wife, pretending I'd become what they wanted me to be. But if that was hard—and it was—it was a picnic on a summer's day compared to pretending to be Molly. And I was going to have to keep that pretense up for a long time yet. After giving Ruth a share of my wages for our keep, there was very little left. As I stashed the coins away in the tin that contained the collection from the neighbors, I told myself I was one week closer to being able to move away. But it was going to take a lot longer than I'd hoped.

The hard, green soap we'd been given smelled of disinfectant, but I washed myself and Teddy and then lay back in the water, what there was of it. I was so tired. Every night that week I'd woken from dreams of the *Titanic*, and as I surfaced from sleep, those awful cries for help filled my head again. One night, I thought I heard my father's voice among them, and when I woke the next morning, my pillow was wet with tears.

The partitions separating the cubicles only went part of the way to the ceiling, and people were chatting freely over them, some in English, though the accents were Irish and American, others in languages I didn't understand. All these people, coming from all over the world to build a better future for themselves and their children, working all hours to scratch a living in tiny apartments, and I'd left behind a life they couldn't even dream of. Even in the hardest moments of the past week, I didn't for a moment wish I could go back there. But had I done the right thing by Teddy? Depriving him of his inheritance, and the position in life that he'd been born to?

A rap on the cubicle door broke into my thoughts.

"Time's up, out you come!"

The park that Ruth had mentioned turned out to be a big square a few streets away, with swings, seesaws, a slide, and a kind of permanent maypole with long metal arms instead of ribbons. It was swarming with children, some of them very scruffy, but all of them having a high old time, squealing and yelping as they played, or ran around chasing each other. Parents and a few grandparents stood around the edge of the square, chatting and watching the children play. Panic rose in me again, and I kept my head down.

Micke and Lena dragged Per and Anna off to push them on the swings, and Ruth said, "There are some box swings over there in the corner, for the smaller ones—d'you want to give Teddy a go?"

He was nervous at first, his face pinched as I put him into the seat, then pushed the swing gently. Then a skinny little girl, perhaps about three, came over with her mother and clambered onto the swing beside him.

"Push me high!" she said, and Teddy watched as she swung past, faster and higher.

"Push Teddy high!" he said.

"Hold on tight, then."

I pushed harder and within minutes he was giggling, joy all over his face, and copying the girl, pumping his chubby little legs to try to propel the swing himself.

Ruth laughed. "Your mam was like that, when we were kids. Always a bit timid at first, but once she got going, she'd want to do better than everyone else. She could have done so well for herself, if she'd come here."

She turned to me. "You were shocked, I think, when you got here and saw how we live."

My insides turned to water. How did she know? Why hadn't she said before?

"I—"

"It's fine," she said. "I know it's not what you've been used to, lately. And even back in Manchester, we didn't share an outhouse with all the neighbors, did we?"

Breathe. She's talking to Molly.

"But the difference is, at home they keep you in your place. Here, you can make something of yourself. So if you're worried about him, don't be. You've done right by him, bringing him here."

I hoped she was right.

CHAPTER 35

The *Titanic* was in the news for weeks and weeks. A fund was set up to build a memorial, millionaires writing checks, schoolchildren sending in nickels and dimes. An inquiry began, to find out why so many lives were lost; only 705 people had survived, the papers said. I knew, of course, that one more had been carried off the *Carpathia* in my arms. The hearings picked over who did what and when, how many lifeboats there were, why we weren't rescued sooner. All questions that churned through my mind too, when I lay awake at night, the cries of the dying always in my ears.

The weather in New York turned mild, and when the window was open during the day, the shouts of the newsboys calling out the headlines as they patrolled up and down the street drifted up to the apartment. It made me even more terrified to go out, and apart from the unavoidable Sunday visit to the bathhouse and the park, I didn't step outside the building for weeks, using the piles of shirtwaist pieces that arrived, bigger each day, as an excuse not to leave my machine, and thanking my lucky stars I'd arrived in the busy season.

After that first evening, Per always put his newspaper straight into the pile they kept for wrapping rubbish and lighting the stove, but I'd dig it out when everyone was in bed. I didn't want to see it, any of it, but I couldn't afford not to look. I didn't dare believe I'd got away with it, that no one had remembered seeing me get into a lifeboat, and then seen me named as one of the dead. Every time I pulled a paper from the pile, I expected to see my face again, but this time with the question: *Where is she?*

The inquiry reported, telling me things I already knew—that there were too few lifeboats, and most of them were sent off half-empty—and some that I didn't. I felt sick to my stomach when I read that there'd been another ship close enough to see the *Titanic*'s distress rockets. The evidence its captain gave was full of excuses—they didn't think there was a ship that close, they'd tried to send a message but got no response, even—and I wanted to scream when I read this—that he'd thought the flare was a shooting star! And the upshot of it all was, they'd done nothing. They'd been close enough to save people, and they'd done nothing.

Gradually, though, the *Titanic* slipped from the front pages, and then was shoved aside completely by a horrible axe murder that had the newsboys yelling gruesome details for days on end. As the weeks went on, I began to tell myself that if anyone had recognized me and let loose a search, I'd know by now. It had been chaos on deck, that night; I didn't remember who I'd seen and when, did I? Surely others would be the same. In the lifeboat, it was dark, we'd barely seen each other's faces, and on the *Carpathia* I'd spent most of the time in the German ladies' cabin. They were the only two people who'd seen me properly, and they didn't know my name. As long as they hadn't seen the paper on the day my photograph was printed, they'd be none the wiser, and there was every chance that they hadn't.

I was still careful when we went to the bathhouse and the park, always dressing as dowdily as possible and scraping back my hair, but even from that short walk, I was coming to realize that I couldn't have found a better place to disappear into than the Lower East Side of New York. You'd hear six different languages just walking to the corner, and who was going to care much about where you'd come from, or ask for your story, when everyone had pretty much the same one? They'd come to make a better life than they'd had at home, and they were too busy doing it, working from early in the morning in factories and shops or, like Per, on construction sites, to take any notice of yet another arrival from somewhere else.

One Friday, after Mr. Klein had delivered our wages, Ruth pointed to the sensible lace-up ankle boots I'd been given on the *Carpathia* and said, "The hot weather'll be here soon, you should get yourself some shoes. I'll take you down to Grand Street on Sunday."

Grand Street was where she went to buy provisions each day, but I'd never seen it. Up till then, I'd never seen anything but the first night's walk from the port, and to and from the bathhouse and the park. But now it was clear we were going to have to stay for a good while, I'd have to get over my nervousness at going out. I was still anxious about letting Teddy out of my sight, but he'd be less conspicuous with the rest of the family than with me, so I left him at the park with Anna, Per, and the children. A few streets from it, we turned a corner and Ruth said, "Here we are. Best place to shop on the whole Lower East Side."

The street was lined with little shops, each with a striped canopy and their merchandise spilling out onto the street: here a rack of cheap-looking men's shirts; there a pile of blankets; across from them a row of plucked chickens, hung up by their feet and looking none too fresh. In front of all the shops, on each side of the road, was a line of carts, wooden trays about eight feet long by four feet wide with handles on each side, set on tall metal wheels, and piled high with everything from potatoes to prayerbooks. Crowds of shoppers picked over the goods on the carts, and it was noisy: an organ grinder tootled out a tune, and as we passed, the vendors yelled out their wares in a cacophony of different accents.

"Peaches from sunny California!"

"Pots and pans, good pots and pans!"

"Getcha herrings, getcha herrings!"

I'd never seen anything like it, and Ruth smiled at my astonishment. "Makes Church Street market look quiet, doesn't it?"

I'd never seen Church Street market, but I nodded and then followed as Ruth jostled our way through the crowd. At first, I kept my eyes to the ground, but when I'd glanced up a couple of times, I realized: no one was taking the slightest notice of me. Everyone was too busy going about their own business, whether it was buying or selling, and not one person was giving me a first glance, let alone a second one.

"Is it always this busy?" I asked Ruth.

"This is nothing. You should see it on a Friday, when all the Jews do their shopping. Now listen, you'll get the best bargains from the pushcarts, but you've got to haggle. Only greenhorns fresh off the boat pay the price they ask. The shoe man is usually here on Sundays . . . yes, there he is."

We walked over to a cart stacked with rows of women's shoes: along the top, sensible-looking flat lace-up Oxfords, all in brown; in the middle, Mary Janes with straps across and a little heel; and on the bottom row, high-heeled court shoes, fashionable and in the prettiest colors, dark plum, jade green, and midnight blue.

The seller, a short man with bushy eyebrows and a very shiny bald head, smiled. "What can I help you with, ladies?"

Taking my cue from Ruth's shoes, I pointed at a pair from the top row.

"Can I try those?"

Ruth shook her head. "You don't want a frumpy pair like mine. You're young! Try these."

She took down a pair of Mary Janes, still brown, but they were nicer than the Oxfords, with a neat almond toe. I sat on the little stool by the cart and tried them. The leather was stiff after the butter-soft kid I was used to, but they fitted.

"Perfect fit," said the seller. "Sixty-five cents to you."

You've got to haggle—only greenhorns fresh off the boat pay the price they ask.

Well, that was something I did know how to do. I gave him my best smile.

"I think you've made a mistake. Did you mean to say twenty?"

His eyebrows shot up. "Twenty cents? Young lady, you're mocking me, surely?"

"I'm not. Twenty cents is a good price."

"For leather of this quality?" He shook his head sorrowfully. "They're good shoes, they'll last you."

He looked at me expectantly, and I looked back at him, smiling.

For a long moment, neither of us spoke, and then he said, "All right, I can give you them for fifty."

Very slowly, I took the shoes off, put my boots back on, stood, and handed the shoes back. Then I turned to Ruth. "Didn't you say you saw some like this elsewhere?"

Before she could answer, the seller threw up his hands. "You young women, you drive a hard bargain. Forty cents."

I sighed. "Well, I don't really want to look somewhere else. I'll give you thirty."

* * *

As we walked away, me in the shoes I'd just bought for thirty cents, Ruth chuckled. "That was good bargaining! I've never got more than a third off."

"Beginner's luck," I said.

I couldn't tell her, could I, that I'd learned from a master? When you'd seen my father bargaining for consignments of cloth worth hundreds of pounds, knocking a few cents off the price of a pair of shoes was easy. I'd instinctively followed his rules: look them in the eye and smile when you name your price; hold your nerve once the bargaining starts; don't miss the moment when you've got them where you want them.

"Well," said Ruth, "we need potatoes, a cabbage, and a piece of pork for dinner. Let's see if your beginner's luck holds."

Of course it did: a cabbage seller was no match for the cotton king's daughter. I got the vegetables at half the starting price, and when I'd haggled the butcher's price down as far as I could, I persuaded him to throw in bones for soup for nothing. My father would have been proud of me, and for the first time since the sinking, I thought of him with a smile. I really hoped he was looking down and chuckling.

When we got back to the apartment block, young Lena was on the front steps of the building, talking to a very pretty older girl, perhaps eighteen or nineteen, dressed in a plum-colored coat, cut elegantly slim, with a matching hat, and high-heeled court shoes like the ones on the cart.

"That's Erin from downstairs," said Ruth. "Eileen's daughter. Lena thinks she's the bee's knees."

As Erin handed Lena a magazine, a couple of girls the same age, similarly smartly dressed and heeled, were strolling up, arm in arm, on the other side of the road. Erin waved to them and skipped down the steps just as we got there. Closer to, the fabric of her outfit was poor quality, but the style was as fashionable as anything I'd have worn in my old life.

"Hello, Mrs. Svensson," she said. "And you must be Molly, hello. Sorry, can't stop, we're off to the movies."

She ran across the road to her friends, high heels wobbling on the cobbles, as Lena clutched her magazine and gazed adoringly after them.

"I'm going to have clothes like that when I'm a secretary in a bank," she said. "And I'll look different every single day, like Erin does."

"Well, that's very easy to do when you've nothing to think about but clothes," snapped Ruth. "Let's see what Erin looks like when she's got a husband and children to look after."

That evening was, I think, the first time Ruth and I sat up together after everyone else had gone to bed. We were drinking coffee at the little table, and flicking through the magazine Erin had given Lena, full of sketches of fashionable clothes. Looking at them made the ones I was wearing feel even uglier, and I thought longingly of being able to put on fresh, clean, pretty clothes that hadn't been on anyone else's body but mine.

Though the prices in the magazine weren't in the cents, like my pushcart shoes, even the cost of the dearest summer dress wouldn't have paid for a sleeve of the last one I bought, handmade in fine lawn and trimmed with Calais lace. But Ruth sighed as she turned the pages.

"Imagine not having to haggle." She pointed at one of the pictures. "Imagine just strolling into Lord and Taylor and paying that much for a dress, without a quibble."

"How does Erin afford to?"

She laughed. "Erin doesn't shop at Lord and Taylor! She gets her clothes from the carts, all the girls do."

She explained that factories like Mr. Klein's made clothes

for the shops uptown, but other factories copied them in cheaper fabrics.

"A shirtwaist'll be poplin instead of lawn, and maybe the sleeves won't be as full, but as long as they're the latest style, the girls don't care. It's like a fashion parade when they all go off to work in the mornings, even though most of them are only going to the factories to sit at a sewing machine all day."

She sounded wistful as she went on. "I was like that myself once. I worked in a dress shop uptown, and the owner liked us girls to wear the clothes, to show them off. Make them want what we've got to sell, he used to say. I wore a different outfit every day, and people would come in for something else, and then they'd see a blouse or a skirt on me and buy one. But that was a long time ago."

She drank the last of her coffee, closed the magazine, and stood up. "Anyway, I don't think I'll ever need to haggle again—next time I'll get you to do it for me."

CHAPTER 36

After that, it became my job to go out for the provisions each day. It was Ruth's idea—"You haggle for the bargains, lass, and I'll stay here and get an extra shirtwaist made"—but now that I felt less frightened outside, I was thankful for the chance to get out of the cramped apartment for a little while. I'd wondered, that first day, how five people could live together in such a small space, let alone seven of us, and it was proving every bit as difficult as I'd imagined. Bad enough during the day, with just us three women and Teddy; when all the sewing machines were going, there was no room to move, and the rattle and whirr bounced off the walls. But once Per and the children came home and Anna started to make dinner, it got hot and airless, and someone was always in someone else's way. By that time of day, everyone was tired too. Ruth would snap at Per to hang his coat up and not throw it over a chair, Anna mithered the children to be quiet. When the squabbling got too much, Per would pick up his newspaper and stomp out onto the fire escape—"To get some peace from all this!"

Worst of all was washing day, when there was constantly a pot boiling on the stove, steaming up the place and fogging the one window at the front, so you couldn't see out. Anna couldn't abide drafts, however mild the weather, so she didn't like the window open, but Ruth hated the room being full of steam. So they bickered all day long. My back ached even more than usual from helping Ruth carry the washing out, and if it rained and we couldn't hang it from the fire escape, the apartment would be festooned with damp garments that took two days to dry and made the place smell like a wet dog.

Even at night, it was impossible to forget that there were seven of us in that tiny space. Anna's thundering snores rang out from the bedroom she shared with the children, and when she made brown bean stew for dinner, the effects on everyone's digestion were nearly as loud. And then, on a Saturday night not long after I arrived, just as I was dropping off to sleep on my featherbed on the floor, there came a rhythmic creaking from Per and Ruth's room, and my face grew hot as I realized what they must be doing, and that, surely, they must know I could hear.

I never expected to be grateful for the practice Winterton had given me at hiding my feelings, but it was a godsend now, to be adept at biting back a snappy remark and concealing the times when I was tired and irritable myself. And no longer just because I was afraid of them asking us to leave, but also because I felt so guilty. It was clear now that it would be months and months, perhaps even more than a year, before we could think of finding a place of our own. But even though the two of us, and the extra sewing machine, were making the place more cramped, they never once made me feel we were unwelcome.

The worst of it was that the longer we stayed, the more lies I had to tell, and now I wasn't telling them to strangers, but to three people I'd come to know. Gentle, quiet Per, who brought home scraps of wood from the construction site to make toys for Teddy, and took a bowl of cold water into their bedroom each night, so he could wash and shave there in the morning and not wake me earlier than he had to. Crotchety old Anna, who was never slow to complain if you took too long at the sink in the morning or made her coffee too weak, but when she was in a good mood, made us cry with laughter at her mishaps and misunderstandings when she arrived in New York, a shy young widow with a child. But most of all, Ruth. It was hardest of all to lie to her, because Molly was her link to someone she'd loved, and because despite the difference in our ages— she was only a few years younger than my mam would have been—I was coming to think of her as a friend. She and I would often stay at the table chatting after Per and Anna went to bed.

"I've been outnumbered by Swedes here for years," she said once. "It's nice to have someone I can have a good gab about England with."

At first, when she reminisced about life back home, I was terrified I'd slip up. But as there'd been no contact since Molly's mother died, there was plenty that Ruth didn't know anyway. And by listening carefully, I kept picking up more about Molly's background.

She told me all about her early days in America too. How she'd been lonely at first, until she met Per when she caught the wrong streetcar, and he walked twenty minutes out of his way to make sure she got on the right one.

"I liked the look of him straight away, but he was so shy, he hardly said a word all the way there. But I thought, I'm not letting this one slip through my fingers. So when we got to the stop, I made out I'd twisted my ankle . . ." She looked up, batting her eyelashes at an imaginary Per. *"Oh heck, I can't walk on it—would you come with me, so I can lean on you?"* She laughed. "But then we got to my stop, and he still hadn't asked me out, so I said it had got a lot more painful and could he carry me? By the time we got to my boardinghouse, you could say the ice had been broken."

We laughed a lot, but she told me sad things too, about the three babies they'd lost before Micke was born, two girls and a boy, all born too early.

"And you've seen what a baggage Anna can be, but she was so kind to me each time it happened. Per didn't want to talk about it, you know how men are, but she held my hand and just let me cry until I'd cried enough."

I made a daft sort of bargain with myself that I'd try my best not to tell a straight-out lie unless I had to. So I didn't repeat the stories Molly told me as if they'd happened to me; I just nodded along when Ruth talked about home, and the things Molly's mother had written about in her letters, and only answered a question with a lie if there was no way not to. But there was no difference really, was there? Because that was what Frederick had done too. He'd taken care never to say he loved me; he just helped me think it, but it was still a lie.

Talking to Ruth about Molly's mother was the worst, because I knew how much they'd meant to each other.

"You remind me so much of her, you know," she said one evening. "She had a bit of grit about her, like you've got. Mind you, she needed it with your father. I never thought they were suited, but your mother wouldn't listen. She was besotted with him. It broke my heart when she used to write and tell me how unhappy she was. It can't have been easy for you children, either."

There was a question in her voice, and I looked down at the table, fiddling about with a pencil Micke had left there, so I didn't have to meet her eyes as I said, "No, it was difficult for all of us."

There was a moment's silence, and I was about to change the subject when she said, "She'd be chuffed that you're part of our family now."

The words were like chalk in my mouth.

"Yes," I said. "She would."

And yet, for all the difficulties and the guilt, a couple of months after we arrived, I lay back in the bathhouse's six inches of water, thought over the week just gone and realized I was proud of myself. What would the old me, who'd never even run her own bath, think if you'd told her she'd be setting two great pans to boil on the stove every morning, so six of us could take our turn to wash at the sink? Let alone groping her way down the dark staircase to the outhouse, carrying the stinking pail we tipped our nighttime chamberpots into.

Hard to believe I'd worried that I'd never master sewing a shirtwaist—now I could do ten a day. It was hard work, though, bent over the machine for hours, and tedious. Every couple of weeks, the pattern and the fabric would change a little—a ruffle here, or a lace trim there—which relieved the monotony for the first few, but that aside, I was almost cross-eyed with the boredom of it. So the challenge of haggling down at Grand Street became the high spot of the day. I'd never had to count the cost of anything before, but making the household's money go a little further by getting a cent or two off a quart of potatoes or a bit of bacon made me feel useful again. And every time I got a good price, I felt close to my father. Sometimes, as I walked home from Grand Street, I talked to him in my head, telling him all about the clothes I saw the young girls wearing, how fashionable they were but how cheap the fabrics, and how the factories brazenly copied all the new styles. What did he think of it, I'd ask—was it clever business, or did he disapprove of copying someone else's work? I'd play out the argument we might have about it, and for those few minutes a day, I could pretend he was still alive.

I can't say I was happy, not when I still woke in the darkness, hearing and seeing that night again, thinking about my father, Frederick, and Terence, up there on the deck watching lifeboats leave and realizing there'd be no place in one for them. And Molly—I could hardly bear to think of what happened to her, when she realized she was trapped. I wondered, sometimes, if any of us who lived through that night would ever really feel happy again. But despite that, despite being bone-tired at the end of every day, despite still having to watch every word that came out of my mouth, even despite the horrors of the outhouse, I didn't regret what I'd done. It struck me once, as I listened to Micke telling Teddy about how he was going to be an engineer when he grew up, why they were so different from Frederick's family. Everyone at Winterton was obsessed with the past, with their history. Desperate to keep things the same, at any cost. But Ruth, Per, and Anna and even the children were looking forward, building the future they wanted for themselves. Just like I'd seen my mother and father do. Perhaps that was why, even after such a short time, I felt more as though I belonged in that crowded apartment than I ever had in Winterton's huge, cold rooms.

And thank goodness, Teddy was thriving too. I'd felt so guilty when we arrived and I saw how the family lived. He was destined to have servants and silver candlesticks, and I'd brought him to a place where we didn't even get hot water. Yet in the warmth of that tiny apartment, he flourished, hero-worshipping Micke, happily holding Per's hand when we walked to the bathhouse and then going into the men and boys' section with them, and even being the only one allowed to "help" when Anna rolled meatballs. Sometimes, in the early weeks, he'd said "Papa" or "Nanny," but his speech was still babyish enough then that no one noticed. And now he showed no sign of remembering Winterton at all.

When we first arrived, he'd fall asleep on my lap after dinner and then sleep beside me on the floor, his little arms clasped round my neck. But one evening, he and Micke had been playing with their cars on the floor, and when Micke and Lena's bedtime came, he got up and followed them into the bedroom.

"You want to sleep with us?" said Micke, laughing. "Like a big boy?"

"Yes," said Teddy, quite decisively.

When Anna went to bed later, she beckoned to me. "Look at this."

Teddy was snuggled up against Micke, the older boy's arm thrown protectively around him. All three children were fast asleep, and though I slept that night in fits and starts, worried he'd wake up and not know where he was, the night passed peacefully.

As he found his feet, though, away from Nanny's beady gaze, Teddy was less and less content to play quietly on the floor with a pile of bricks. Feeling safer now, I took him with me when I went to Grand Street, and by the middle of the morning, he'd be asking, over and over again, when we were going out, and I gave in earlier and earlier, worried he'd drive Anna and Ruth mad with his whining. The noise and the sights and smells of the shops and carts entertained him while we were there, but as soon as I'd bought what we needed and turned for home, he'd drag his feet and pull on my hand, grizzling and grouching all the way, and being so annoying that I'll admit, now and then I shocked myself by thinking that I'd really quite like to have Nanny to hand him over to.

One particularly bad morning, as we reached the steps to the front door, he let go of my hand, stamped his foot and shrieked. "No! Not going in."

"Don't be silly," I said. "We have to go in; Mama has to work."

He shook his head and took a step back from me.

"Teddy, come on."

I held out my hand but he turned and ran. He was fast, and I had to put down the shopping basket before I could run after him. Even as I shouted at him, he kept going, his little legs like pistons. By the time I caught him up, I was cross and grabbed at his hand, almost falling over as I reached down. He yelled "No!" and held his hands behind his back. I had to pick him up, tuck him under my arm and lug him up the front steps—he was getting heavy to carry by then—but when I put him down to pick up the basket, he went to run away again, and I only just managed to grab his hand.

Red with temper, he squirmed, and as he twisted, he kicked me in the shin, hard. The pain was such a shock that I almost let him get away again, but I managed to keep hold and dragged him, shrieking and crying, up the three flights of stairs to the apartment. When we got there, me sweating and panting, my leg throbbing, and him bawling, I couldn't help it, I shouted at him, "You are a bad, horrible boy! Now shut up!"

Red-faced, he opened his mouth, but nothing came out. He went silent, his mouth a perfect O. He wasn't breathing! What had I done? I snatched him up and bashed on our door. Ruth opened it.

"He's dying!" I said. "He can't breathe!"

His eyes stared up at me, terrified, and then, to my horror, his lips turned blue.

Ruth leaned over and gently blew on his face. He gasped, and a second later, he gave a breath, and then tears filled his eyes and he clung to me, sobbing.

"Always worked with Micke," she said. "He'll be fine now."

My legs suddenly felt weak, and I sat down heavily by my sewing machine, Teddy on my lap, his arms round my neck.

"I thought he was going to die."

"They just get themselves into a state and then forget to breathe. Lena was worse; she used to pass out completely."

She looked at me curiously. "Didn't any of your little brothers do it? I thought all children did."

I scrabbled for something to say but I was still so shocked

that I couldn't think how to reply without giving myself away. Was this a normal thing, then? Something the real Molly would know all about? There was a horrible pause before, to my relief, Anna chimed in: "Per never did that."

Ruth laughed. "Because he was a good little Swedish boy?"

"No, because all children are different. That's why it gave Molly a shock."

Ruth shrugged and turned back to her machine. "Well, you'll know what to do now. They grow out of it in a couple of years."

That afternoon, as I sewed, I kept glancing at Teddy as he sat looking at a picture book that used to be Lena's, chatting happily away to himself about the cat in the story. Partly reassuring myself that he was all right, but also thinking, how can that be the same child I dragged screaming up the stairs? I didn't recognize myself in the woman who'd shouted at him to shut up either. I loved him more than anything, and as I looked at him now, the thought of anything upsetting or hurting him was unbearable. But for those few moments, he'd felt like my enemy. And then to go, in a moment, from that to being so desperately frightened that I'd lost him . . . It made me feel ill to remember it, even though I knew now that he hadn't been in danger. I'd longed to be Teddy's mother, properly, but I'd had no idea how hard it was going to be.

No idea, either, how hard it would be to pretend that I was used to taking care of him. It must have looked so odd to Ruth when I panicked, but thank goodness for Anna. Even if it was true that Per had never held his breath like that, it was obviously something very common, and she must have seen Lena and Micke do it. But she could never resist an opportunity to be contrary with Ruth, and this time it had saved me. We'd survived, him and me, once again.

CHAPTER 37

I missed Teddy's warm little body beside me now that he was sleeping with Micke and Lena, but the mild weather meant that if I woke in the night, I could go out and sit on the fire escape for a while, instead of lying there, seeing and hearing the sinking all over again. The cries from the people in the water still haunted me, and I couldn't stop them coming, but out there it was easier to distract myself. I could watch the stars, or look over at the windows opposite, and think about the people who might live there, where they came from and why. Sometimes it worked, and I got drowsy and went back to sleep; sometimes it didn't. Sometimes I couldn't block those sounds out at all, and on one of those nights I was sitting out there, tears rolling down my face as I imagined my poor father's terror in his last moments, when Anna came outside.

"You can't sleep again," she said.

"Have I woken you before? I'm sorry—"

"I'm old, I'm often awake in the night these days. But it's not the same as this. It's not the same as when memories won't go away. Will it help to tell me what's the worst of it?"

I hadn't ever talked to anyone about the *Titanic;* the family had been kind enough not to ask, and I'd no wish to relive it all in the daytime as well as at night. But there was something so touching about the way that Anna—normally so gruff and get-on-with-it—asked.

I took a deep breath, and said, "The worst was the sounds, after the ship went down. People screamed and they cried and they called out for help, and it went on and on. And no help came, and they must have realized no help was going to come, they were just going to be left to die. And then . . ." I swallowed back a sob at the thought. "And then gradually, the screams and the cries stopped. Dead, all of them. I was relieved when it stopped, because I couldn't bear to hear it anymore."

I hadn't admitted that to myself before, but it was true, and it was a relief to say it. "And now I hear it almost every night."

She sat beside me, wincing as her bad knee creaked.

"It's a terrible thing you've lived through," she said. "And you won't forget it easily. Perhaps you won't forget it ever. But we have a saying in Swedish: you cannot prevent the birds of sadness from flying over your head, but you can stop them from nesting in your hair."

In spite of my tears, I couldn't help laughing at the picture her words painted, and she laughed too.

"Yes, it sounds comical in English. The Swedish language is much better for melancholy. But it's true."

She looked out over the silent street, but her eyes were far away, as though she was seeing somewhere else.

"My husband, Per's father, was in an accident, felling trees in the forest. They brought him home to me, his poor body all broken. He lived for six days, crying out in pain until at last God showed mercy and took him. For a long time, I couldn't close my eyes without seeing and hearing it all again. I wanted to die myself, and it was only for Per that I chose to live, to come here and make a fresh start. I thought I could leave the memories behind, but they followed me here."

"Do they never go away?"

"I won't tell you a comforting lie. They never leave you— even now, sometimes I wake and see it all again. But they get weaker, in time. I think you are a strong woman, and you made a good start, here, applying yourself to work—when your mind is occupied, bad memories will fade. So I have found, anyway."

Down on the street, two cats were squaring up for a fight. We watched them, circling each other, yowling and growling, until one eventually lunged and the other took to its heels and ran off down the road.

"Ha, coward!" said Anna. And then, "Do you like to read?"

I wasn't expecting that question, and it gave me a jolt. Of course I loved to read, but she wasn't asking me, was she? In my surprise at Anna confiding her own troubles, I'd almost forgotten she was talking to Molly and not me. I had no idea whether Molly liked to read. But Anna didn't know either, or she wouldn't have asked.

"Yes. I used to read a lot, when I was younger. But I got out of the habit."

For a moment I saw my copy of *Middlemarch* flying across the bedroom at Winterton, almost hitting the mirror on my dressing table. I hadn't opened a book since that day.

"It saved me," said Anna, "when the nights were very bad. I kept a book, and a candle, by my bed, and if I woke in the night, as soon as I opened my eyes, I lit the candle and I—oh, what do you call it, when you go from one world into another one?"

I knew exactly what she meant; hadn't I done it since I was a little girl?

"Escape."

"Yes, that's it. I escaped, from the sights and sounds I

couldn't bear, and went somewhere else, until my eyes began to close again." She waved a hand at the view in front of us. "It's what you hope to do, coming out here, I think. But a book is better. The ones I have are in Swedish and no use to you, but you could go to the public library, perhaps."

"There's a library here?"

"A big one, yes."

She stood up.

"What I told you," she said, "was only for your ears. Per believes that his father died instantly with no pain, and there is no need for him to know otherwise. But I think you are some-one who can keep a secret."

"Thank you for telling me," I said. "And for the advice, about reading. I think it'll help."

"Good. Now don't stay out here too long, or you'll get cold."

The public library was only a few minutes' walk from the apartment, by the park where the children played. How had I not even known it was there? But, then, I'd never used one before; in my old life, I could buy all the books I wanted. It was a big, solid-looking building in red brick and stone, and as I walked up the steps, clutching Teddy's hand, I'd no idea what to expect. I followed the signs to the circulating library and as we walked in, my heart thumped at the sight: hundreds and hundreds and hundreds of books. I walked around, and there they were, on the shelves: *Pride and Prejudice*, *Middlemarch*, *Jane Eyre*, *The Return of the Native*. Even *Lady Susan*! It was like meeting old friends again. Old friends that I'd fallen out with, but now the disagreement seemed so far in the past, and so much had happened since, that it didn't matter anymore.

I filled in the form to get a borrower's ticket, and chose four books: *Pride and Prejudice* and *Jane Eyre*, and then two by au-thors I didn't know.

As the librarian stamped them, she smiled down at Teddy and said, "You know we have a children's room downstairs? You can borrow for him too."

I won't say that the books chased the terrible memories away, and Anna hadn't promised that they would. But they helped. I spent a few cents on a little lamp, and before I went to sleep, I'd read a bit from one of my old favorites—it was like a comforting cup of hot milk to send me to sleep. And when I woke in the night and knew what was coming, I opened whichever of the new ones I was reading, and escaped into it. It didn't always work, but if I was quick and the book was good, I could keep the sounds and the sights at bay long enough for my eyes to feel heavy again.

Each time we went to the library Teddy chose a picture book, and I chose one that my mam used to read to me, and read it to him for a little while before he went to bed. We read *Alice in Wonderland*, *The Jungle Book*, and Hans Christian Andersen's stories, and I did the voices, the way my mam used to. And it was funny: all the way across the ocean, in a place she'd never seen, I felt closer to her than I had for a long time. When my father said, on the ship, that she'd be proud of me, I knew she wouldn't—not then, when I'd let my son be brought up by someone who was paid to do it. But perhaps now, she would.

CHAPTER 38

The sights and sounds of Grand Street were never the same two days running. Some of the pushcart sellers kept to the same place every day, but you could take a cart anywhere in the city, stopping wherever a spot looked promising, so others came and went, and there were always new faces. Most of the vendors were men, but not all of them—I'd bought shoes for Teddy from a Greek woman, and I always got the pickled herrings that Anna loved from a German lady with long blond plaits, who reminded me of a doll I once had. And most days there was a cheese cart belonging to a woman from Leeds— one of the few English people, apart from Ruth, that I'd met in New York. She'd noticed my accent the first time I bought from her and thrown in a bit extra "for a fellow Englishwoman, even if you are from the wrong side of the Pennines." Her name, she told me, was Della, and after that, if she wasn't too busy and I wasn't in too much of a hurry, we'd have a few minutes' gab.

One day, when she'd watched, smiling, as I haggled down the price of a pair of trousers for Teddy from the pushcart opposite, she said, "You should get into this lark, duck. Buying your goods at the right price is half the battle, and you'd be good at it."

I laughed when she said it but, walking home, I started to wonder. As I got quicker at making shirtwaists, I'd got my wage from Mr. Klein up to eight dollars a week, like Ruth and Anna, and it still gave me a sense of pride when he counted it into my hand on a Friday. But it wasn't going to go far toward buying us a better life. By the time I'd put my share into the household pot, there still wasn't much left, and no matter how hard I worked, it wasn't possible to earn more, because I could only make so many shirtwaists a day without the quality dropping. Unless I grew another pair of hands or there were suddenly more hours in the day, I was stuck, and if I wanted to work toward an apartment of our own, I needed to make more money. Could a pushcart be the way? My father used to say the same as Della had: you get your profit when you sell, but you make it when you buy. I'd have to find something I could buy cheaply, and sell at a decent profit, but that couldn't be impossible, surely?

That evening, as Anna fried onions and Ruth and I packed up the day's work, I mentioned the idea.

Ruth frowned. "A pushcart? Why would you want to do that?"

I didn't want to say how boring I found the sewing, not when they'd been kind enough to get me the work.

"I think I might be good at it. If I can get a low price for what I buy, and a decent price when I sell, there's profit to be made."

"Well, you say that, but those pushcart people don't go home to Fifth Avenue mansions at the end of the day, do they?"

"No, but some do pretty well from it. That man who sells herrings, on the corner, Della says he's built up to three more pushcarts in different places, and his sons work them for him. And you know that shoe shop on Hester Street? They started out with a pushcart. If I work hard, perhaps I can make more money than I do now and save a bit more for our future."

Ruth tied a knot in the string around the shirtwaists, and without looking at me, said, "I didn't realize you thought making shirtwaists wasn't good enough for you."

"I don't think that at all. I'm grateful to you for getting me the work, you know I am."

"Doesn't sound like it, if you think you can do better being a peddler on the street."

"I just thought it might be something I could do well, that's all. I'd like to try it and see. Della says you can get away without having a license for a couple of weeks, so if it didn't work out, I'd stop."

She looked at me. "And you think Mr. Klein will just take you back? Maybe it's different for ladies' maids in England, Molly, but here, good employers are hard to come by. Very few of them are as fair as Mr. Klein, and most of them don't want home workers anymore. But if you don't mind sweating in one of those factories all day, with a supervisor watching you every second and docking your pay on the slightest excuse, you just go ahead."

With that, she picked up the bundle of shirtwaists and slammed out.

Anna stirred the onions for a few minutes, then said, "You touched a sore spot there, I think."

"What do you mean?"

"Perhaps my daughter-in-law also thinks sewing shirtwaists is beneath her. This is the way with modern women. When I first came here, we had to do whatever work we could find, and we were grateful to earn a crust."

She stopped as the door opened and Ruth came back in, followed by Per. As he hung up his coat, they were talking about something on the front page of his newspaper, and she didn't look at me. Obviously our conversation was over, but the set of her chin and the way she thumped down the dinner plates told me she was still annoyed.

Apart from the occasional irritation over something daft like who'd used more of the morning hot water, it was the first time we'd ever fallen out, and I hated to think that I'd annoyed her, or made her think I considered myself too good for the work she'd found for me. But I didn't! They were saving for a better life, so why shouldn't I? They'd three wages to put aside money from; I couldn't hope to save much unless I could find a way to earn more. The children were playing out in the street, and when I went down to call them in, it was me who gave the door a bit of a slam.

We ate dinner all together as usual, both of us joining in with the conversation, but not once speaking to each other directly. It was stuffed cabbage, and as soon as we started eating, Anna began a familiar tirade about how American cabbages weren't as tasty as Swedish ones. We'd heard the same about beans, about pork and even milk, and usually Ruth and I shared a smothered smile, but that day we didn't even look at each other. So I wasn't surprised when, after we'd had coffee, Ruth said a rather stiff good night and went to bed at the same time as Anna and Per, instead of staying up for a chat. Well, that was up to her. I hadn't done anything wrong, and she could just stew in her own juice until she realized that.

CHAPTER 39

The coldness between us continued the next day. We didn't speak at breakfast, and though there was rarely much chatter as we sewed anyway, even the way Ruth asked me to pass her the scissors had an edge to it, or so it sounded to me. When we stopped to drink a cup of coffee, late in the morning, Anna was talking about a rumor she'd heard that the Greek family across the way were moving to Brooklyn.

When Ruth said nothing and I only managed an "Are they?" before we sipped our coffee in frosty silence, Anna said, "And I hear that the O'Reillys downstairs are buying a big house on Madison Avenue, twenty bedrooms and a stable for their horses."

She raised an eyebrow at our puzzled faces. "So you can still hear, even if you can't speak? *Herregud*, what is wrong with you two? Like children, sulking and giving each other cold eyes."

She stood and reached for the shopping basket. "Today, I will go and buy the provisions. You two can stay here and talk to each other. When I come back, I want to find two grown women and not two silly little girls who fight over a doll."

As the door closed, Ruth said, in Anna's singsong accent, "Swedish women would never fight over a doll."

We looked at each other warily for a second, then both of us burst out laughing, and the ice was gone.

"I'm sorry," said Ruth. "I shouldn't have got annoyed with you. I was jealous."

"Jealous? What do you mean?"

She sighed. "You remember me telling you I used to work in a dress shop? Well, I loved it there. I loved wearing the clothes, meeting the customers, and I got a thrill from seeing money that was in the till because of me. I felt like I was in a movie, sometimes. And then I married Per, and straight away . . ." She scooped the air in front of her, mimicking pregnancy. "I couldn't wear the clothes anymore, so I was no use. Anna was already working for Mr. Klein, and he took me on as well. Then when the baby died, and the next one and the next one, I was glad I didn't have to go uptown every day and be bright and cheery for the customers. And by the time the children did come along, I was stuck. We needed a steady income, and I couldn't risk giving it up for a job that might not work out, or that I'd lose if I was expecting again."

She picked up a reel of thread, twirling it in her hands. "That's why I got annoyed. Because when I came here, I was like you. I took risks. I crossed the ocean to find a new life; I found a place to live. When I saw that dress shop, I thought it would be fun to work there, so I just walked in and asked for a job, and I got it. When you talked about getting a pushcart, you were so excited, you reminded me of how I used to be. I was jealous of that, and I'm sorry I took it out on you."

Before I could reply, the door opened and Anna walked in, brandishing a little parcel of waxed paper.

"I bought you apple cake from the bakery, but you don't get it unless you're friends again."

Ruth looked at me.

"We're friends again," I said.

"Good. What was your silly argument about, anyway?" Ruth shook her head at me, just slightly.

"Nothing," I said. "Just a misunderstanding."

"About a doll," said Ruth.

That evening, as we sat at the table after the others had gone to bed, she asked, "So are you going to do it? Get a pushcart?"

"I don't know. Like you said, it's a risk, giving up the sewing work."

"It was a risk coming here, but it's worked out, hasn't it? For both of us. And I think you're right, you'd be good at it. Lord knows where you got it from, because no one else in our family ever had a head for money."

If only you knew.

"What would I sell, though? I don't know anything about food, and I wouldn't know where to start with pots and pans or anything like that."

"It's obvious, surely? You should sell clothes."

"There are quite a few carts selling clothes already, though. It'll be harder to get a good price if there's a lot of competition."

"Yes, but who's got those carts? They're all men. You're young and pretty, Molly. The girls who like their fashion will want to buy from you. That's why the shops uptown get the girls to wear the clothes. You'll make them want what you've got to sell."

She got up and fetched a magazine that Erin had given Lena that morning. "Whatever's in here, the factories on Seventh Avenue will be making cheap copies of."

We looked through and made a list of garments that we

thought might not cost too much to buy from the factories: a shirtwaist with a ruffle round the neck, a plain skirt dressed up with braid around the bottom, a simple dress with a lace collar and cuffs.

"Now you just need to do what you're good at," said Ruth. "Go there and get a good price."

The first factory was in a loft, three floors up. As I climbed the metal stairs, the familiar whirring of sewing machines got louder and louder, and at the top, I saw why. There must have been a hundred women in there, seated on either side of three long tables, all heads down, treadling away. Just inside the door was an office, where a man I took to be the owner was sitting at a desk.

He glanced up and said, "No vacancies for machinists at the moment. Try Gold's, down the street."

"I'm not looking for a job. I'm looking to buy from you, for my cart."

He peered at me over his spectacles. "Buy what?"

I smiled. "What's your best price for a dozen shirtwaists?" I pointed to a rack of waists like the one we'd seen in the magazine. "Like that, with the ruffle round the neck."

"For a dozen? Thirty cents a piece."

"How about seven?"

He laughed. I'd gone in too low. Much too low.

"I can't even make them for that price."

"Well, then, could you do a dozen for a dollar fifty?"

He laughed. "Not even close."

"But surely—"

My father used to say that if you got off on the wrong foot in a negotiation, you'd mostly likely lost the deal, and he was right.

Before I'd even finished the sentence, the man leaned across the table, and said, "Young lady, you're new to this, aren't you?

And maybe you think you can drive a hard bargain because you have a pretty face. Well, your pretty face won't pay this lot's wages. Now, get outta here, and stop wasting my time."

My legs were trembling as I walked down the stairs. I hadn't expected that at all. Not just that I'd messed the negotiation up so badly, but that the prices obviously weren't as low as I'd thought they'd be. Of course, if I hadn't annoyed him by going in so low, I might have got him down a bit, but thirty cents was nowhere near what I thought I'd be paying; there'd be barely any profit in it.

I spent all day trying factory after factory. There were so many, surely I could find a deal at one of them. But although I didn't make such an idiot of myself again, I couldn't get the price below twenty cents, and the response when I tried told me the best haggler in the world wouldn't have had any more luck. The peddlers who sold clothes might be making a living from it, but it couldn't be much of one. Any fool could get a cart and sell something from it, but unless you got the margins right, it'd only ever be hand to mouth. No point giving up steady work for that.

"You were right," I told Ruth later. "It's not going to work. It's not worth taking the risk of throwing in the work for Mr. Klein unless I can be sure of earning quite a bit more with a cart."

"I still think you could do it."

I shook my head. "It's only worth doing if I can find something to buy much more cheaply than I'd sell it for. And I can't."

She put her head on one side and looked at me. "When you came here, you couldn't use a sewing machine. Don't think I didn't see how terrified you were when you saw how many shirtwaists we had to make in a day. But you got your head down and learned how to do it. So don't tell me you're just going to give up on this. We're not busy this week. Anna and me can cover all the shirtwaists Mr. Klein sent round for tomorrow. Take one more day, and if it doesn't work, at least you'll know you gave it a good go."

Buoyed up by her enthusiasm, I set out early the next morning. If there was a factory where I could get a good deal, I was going to find it. I climbed the stairs to the first with a spring in my step, and gave him my best smile when I named my price. He laughed in my face.

The second and third weren't much better, and when I wearily climbed the stairs to a fourth factory, it was only to find they weren't even making cheap copies to sell on Grand Street. There was a rack of shirtwaists right by the door, but the fabrics were good quality and the trims more detailed, needing longer to do. Completely hopeless to ask there, then.

I turned to go, and as I did, an elderly man in a well-cut coat was coming up the stairs. They were narrow, so I waited for him to reach the top, and as he got there, he said, "That's a very sad face. What's the matter, dolly?"

"Nothing you can help with but thank you for asking."

He smiled. "You're English! I've got cousins over there, place called Bethnal Green?"

He seemed to think I'd know it, but I'd never heard the name. For politeness's sake, I said, "That's nice, do they like it there?"

"Well, it never stops raining, apparently, but apart from that, they do, yes. So, what brought you to New York?"

"The same as everyone else. I wanted a better life."

"And have you found one?"

"I have, thank you."

"Then why the sad face?"

"I had an idea for making it better still, a business idea, but now I don't think it's going to work."

"A business idea, eh? What was that, then?"

He smiled indulgently. Well, since he'd asked, he could hear it. He knew the trade, maybe he'd have some advice for me. And what did I have to lose? So I told him my plan, and explained what I'd learned from going round the factories, that it just didn't look like it was going to be possible to buy clothing cheaply enough to sell at a good profit. He looked quite surprised when I finished.

"Well, at least you've worked out the problem. Most people come here fresh off the boat, get a pushcart and think they can sell any old thing and make a fortune, but it sounds like you might have a business head on your shoulders."

He pointed at the rack of shirtwaists just inside the door. "Come here, look at these."

He pulled one out to show me. I felt the fabric; it was good quality cotton. Probably from Sea Island fibers. The sort of thing that my father's mills made, and it gave me a sudden pang of sadness to think of them still churning out cotton over there, but without him.

"They're lovely," I said, hoping he didn't hear the catch in my voice.

"There's thirty factories along this street making cheap copies, but there's only three of us doing this sort of quality, and that means we can get a good price from the stores. That's the reason I got out of the cheap shirtwaist trade and went upmarket—when you're selling what everyone else is selling, the profits just ain't there. It's a different kettle of fish with a pushcart, I know, but the principle's the same."

I thanked him for his advice; at least he hadn't been rude like the other three, even if the advice itself was pointless and the delivery patronizing. I already knew you couldn't make a good profit when there was too much competition, but he wasn't to know I'd been hearing that kind of thing since I was knee high to a grasshopper.

Dejected, I turned to leave. As I did, a door to the side opened and a young lad came through it with a huge box that he couldn't see over. Before I could stand aside, he bumped into me, and the box tipped forward, spilling out bits of fabric, lace, and trim. Cursing, he kneeled to pick them up, and I stooped down to help. There on the floor was a strip of lace that looked like the kind we'd seen on the collar and cuffs of a dress in Lena's magazine—I remembered it because I'd especially liked the color of the dress. I picked the scrap up and had a closer look. It was the exact same stuff. There was more of it, too, as well as pieces of fabric, the same lovely quality as the shirtwaists on the rack.

I looked up at the factory owner.

"How much for these?" I asked. "The boxful?"

He looked at me as if I was mad. "They're just cutters' scraps, dolly."

"Will you sell them to me?"

"They're no use to us, just a fire hazard," he said. "If you can carry them, you can have them."

By the time I'd lugged that box down the stairs, onto the streetcar, and then up to the apartment, I was drenched in sweat, my lungs were bursting, and my arms were like cotton wool. And all the way, I was thinking, is this what I think it is? Or have I just hauled a box of rubbish across the city?

Ruth's eyes lit up as I came through the door with the box and dumped it on the table. "See, I told you you could bargain them down! How much did you get them for?"

I was still getting my breath back as she opened the box and peered inside.

"Oh no! Molly, he's cheated you. Look, it's just bits and pieces!"

"No, he hasn't," I said, rummaging in the box for the scrap of lace I'd seen. "Look at this."

The magazine was on the table. I found the picture of the
dress with the lace collar and cuffs, then wrapped the lace
round my neck, tucking it into the neckline of my shirtwaist.

"Ten cents, say, and there's a new dress from an old one."

"You mean we'd make them, the collars and cuffs? But how
would we get time? We're working all hours as it is."

"No, we don't make them. We take that . . ." I pointed at the
magazine. "And we have it on the cart to show them what they
can do with ten cents' worth of lace. It's what you did when
you worked at the shop, wearing the clothes—making them
want what we've got to sell. And we'll be selling something no
one else has got."

She frowned for a moment, but then said, "You know what,
that could work. What else is in the box?"

"There's more of that lace, for a start. But I didn't have a
chance to look at the rest."

We each pulled out a bundle of scraps and sorted them out
on the table. By the time the box was empty and we'd weeded
out all the small pieces of fabric that were just left after cutting
out armholes and necklines, we had twenty offcuts of the
snow-white lace we'd seen in the magazine, about the same of
some very pretty ivory lace, a pile of remnants of cotton lawn,
plain and sprigged, and lots of lengths of satin ribbon, in eau
de Nil, lavender, and rose pink.

"That's forty lace collars, for a start," I said. "And I didn't
pay a cent for any of it."

"The ribbons'll trim a hat, easily. And we can think of something to do with these." She picked up one of the remnants.
"They must be the ends of rolls, but there's still a decent
amount of fabric."

"Thirty cents' worth, do you think?"

"For anyone handy with a needle and thread, that's a bargain."

"Della said a cart costs ten cents a day. But after that, whatever I make would be profit."

"But can you be certain of getting more of this to sell?"

"I'm sure I can. He was glad to be rid of it."

"Well," said Ruth. "You'd better see about hiring a push-cart, then."

CHAPTER 40

A week later, at six in the morning, I joined the pushcart vendors on Grand Street for the first time, and it felt like my wedding day all over again. As I pushed the heavy cart past the pickles man levering open his barrels, the meat seller hanging up bright red salamis, and the Jewish grandmother on the corner uncovering her stacks of dark rye bread, all their eyes followed me. I wasn't the only woman there, but I was the youngest by a couple of decades, and their faces were curious. It was a relief to see Della waving.

"Molly, over here!"

She maneuvered her cart to make room for mine between hers and the one next to it, where a grumpy-looking man was stacking up pots and pans.

"Shift over a bit, Ivan love," she said. "Molly's new at this, and she's no competition to you."

The man moved his cart so I could get mine in, and then stood with his hands on his hips, watching as I set out my goods. The evening before, Ruth and I had practiced it on the table, working out exactly how to display everything so it would entice passersby. Right in the middle, the picture of the lace collar from Lord and Taylor. I'd stuck it onto card with flour and water paste, and Per had made a little wooden block that it slotted into so it would stand up. To either side of it, stacks of the white lace and the ivory, and then the remnants of lawn, neatly folded, and coils of ribbon.

We'd been so excited when it was all set out beautifully, but now, under Ivan's baleful stare, I felt daft. Peering at my cart, he scratched his thick gray beard.

"Rags, is it? You'll want some junk as well; you'll never make money with just rags."

"It's not rags," I said with as much dignity as I could muster. "It's remnants and trims. For making collars and things."

He shrugged and went back to his pans, and I finished setting everything out.

"That looks nice," said Della. "And I wouldn't worry if you don't make much at first. Sometimes it's trial and error before you work out what people will buy."

So she thought it was a daft idea too. And she wasn't the only one. As the first shoppers appeared, crowding round the other carts, the air began to fill with the sounds of customers and vendors haggling, but all I got were curious glances as they passed by. No one stopped to look. It had sounded so clever, when the factory owner talked about selling something different from everyone else, but what if no one wanted it?

I stood by my cart, with what I hoped was a welcoming smile pinned on my face, trying not to think about how many shirtwaists I could have made in the time I'd been there. Mr. Klein had been surprised and none too pleased when I told him I wouldn't be able to sew for him anymore.

"You're getting a pushcart?" he said. "Out in all weathers, making a pittance? What do you want to do that for?"

"I'm not planning to make a pittance," I said. "I'm planning to do well enough to have a shop one day."

He laughed. "That's not a plan; it's a dream. Same dream they've all got, but you won't see many of them come true. Anyway, I'll get the machine collected tomorrow—we need another one in the factory, so don't come running to me asking for it back."

What was I going to do if no one bought anything? All very well getting my stock for free, but if it didn't sell, we couldn't eat lace or pay the rent with ribbons.

You are your father's daughter. Make them want to buy what you're selling.

My cheeks flaming, I held up one of the pieces of white lace, took a deep breath and yelled out, "Straight from the fashion magazines! Exactly the same as at Lord and Taylor!"

I wasn't very loud—it seemed so rude—and people continued walking by. But then a couple of women about Ruth's age glanced over.

"Come and have a look, ladies!" I called.

They looked at each other, one shrugged, and they walked across. I picked up a length of the lace and pointed to the picture.

"This is the exact same lace," I said. "You could go all the way uptown to Lord and Taylor . . ."

They both laughed; all three of us knew they were never going to shop at Lord and Taylor.

". . . or you could make your own—very easy, takes five minutes, and then you can put this over any plain shirtwaist, or a dress, and you've got a new one for, what shall we say? Ten cents?"

As their eyes lit up I realized; in my excitement at the possibility of making a sale, I'd said the price I wanted to get, and not the price I expected them to knock me down from, and now I was stuck with that as my opening bid.

"Four cents," said one of the women.

I pretended shock.

"For this?" I pointed to the text under the picture. "See what it says here? A fine lace collar updates an old favorite dress or waist and makes it as good as new. That's worth six cents, surely?"

"Five," she said.

"You drive a hard bargain," I said. "But I can do two at five cents each, how about that?"

They looked at each other and nodded. I had my first sale, and if it was the subject of a beginner's mistake, well, I wouldn't be making that one again. It spurred me on and as the street got busier with shoppers, I found my courage and raised my voice like the rest of the vendors. It was hard work—by ten my feet were killing me, and my throat was hoarse from shouting. But I'd sold three more pieces of lace and a remnant of cotton lawn and bargained a decent price on all of it.

When Ruth came along just after midday, holding Teddy by the hand, I was haggling with the Italian fruit seller's wife, who'd brought him his lunch and spotted my cart as she passed by. She'd picked through the remnants of fabric and found a piece of pale blue lawn just big enough to make a shirtwaist for her daughter, and she was determined to get it for ten cents. I was equally determined not to let her have it for less than fifteen—it was a whole shirtwaist's worth!—and we were at a stalemate when Ruth chimed in.

"Your daughter will look beautiful in that color, Mrs. Petrassi." She turned to me. "Sophia's such a pretty girl. When people see her in that, they'll all be wanting the same."

It took a moment and a subtle wink from Ruth for me to get the message.

"All right, Mrs. Petrassi," I said. "Ten cents, and you tell Sophia to make sure she tells everyone where you bought the fabric."

As Mrs. Petrassi went off happy with her bargain, Ruth said, "That girl looks like a movie star; she'll bring you some customers for certain."

"Maybe you should be standing here," I said. "I wouldn't have thought of that."

"We're a good team." She looked over the stock left on the cart. "Looks like it's going well. You've sold a fair bit. Meanwhile . . ." She pulled a face. "We've had a morning of Anna's rheumatism playing up. She's been quite grumpy, hasn't she, Teddy?"

Teddy nodded.

"Very grumpy," he said solemnly. "Teddy makes too much noise."

"He was only playing with his car; I don't know how she could even hear him over the machines, but you know how she gets when she's in pain."

"Leave him here with me, then—give Anna a bit of peace."

Not surprisingly, Grand Street was a lot more entertaining to a small boy than playing by himself in the apartment, and Teddy happily sat perched on the side of the cart, swinging his legs and watching the comings and goings. He greeted anyone who came to look at the cart with a cheery hello and echoed my "Thank you" as I handed over their goods. When an organ grinder came along, I got him down, and he ran over to listen to the music, but when he came back he still had the coin I'd given him clutched tightly in his hand.

"You were supposed to give that to the man. For the music."

He looked at the coin in surprise, then shrugged.

"Teddy's money now," he said, and tucked it into his pocket.

Beside us, Della laughed. "Smart boy. He'll make you rich one day."

* * *

Ruth sent Lena to fetch Teddy at about five, but the Grand Street pushcarts plied their wares well into the evening, catching people who worked uptown on their way home. By then all the carts were lit with lamps—Della had warned me to bring one—and the street was strewn with the rubbish of the day, but shoppers still kept coming. And whereas the daytime customers were older people and mothers, now came girls on their way home from the garment factories, and from shops and offices uptown, dressed in Grand Street's cheap copies of Fifth Avenue fashions. My shouts of "Straight from the fashion magazines!" caught their attention straight away, and I sold five of the lace strips, two fabric remnants, and most of the ribbons in the space of half an hour.

By the time I'd wheeled the cart back to its shed and set off home with the remainder of my goods, I was worn out, but smiling all over my face. Had it really been me, standing there, yelling out my wares, and then bargaining hard for every cent? It was hard work, but I'd done a good job. With that first day alone, I'd already covered the cost of renting the cart, and made a little more money than I would have done stitching shirtwaists. As I walked up the steps to our building, I wished my father could see me.

Sitting at the table with Ruth that evening, I was buoyed up by how well the day had gone, and she was almost as excited as I was.

"I'm so proud of you," she said. "When I walked down Grand Street at lunchtime, I could hear you hollering 'Straight from the fashion magazines' and honestly, you looked like you'd been doing this for years. It's a proper talent you've got, and I'm made up that you've found a way to use it."

"I can learn a thing or two from you, though. I saw Mrs.

Petrassi with her daughter a bit later on, and you're right—the other girls will want anything she's got."

"It's just what we did when I worked in the shop. Put clothes on someone who looks glamorous in them, and the glamour rubs off on the clothes and makes people want them."

"I might think about a special price for Mrs. Petrassi every week. And there's Erin as well; she always looks stylish—I'll ask her to spread the word around her friends and the girls she works with."

Ruth traced a circle on the table with her finger, then looked up at me. "Were you serious, when you told Mr. Klein you wanted to have a shop one day?"

"I was, yes. I know Mr. Klein says it's just a dream, but other people have done it, so why shouldn't I? I want a good life for Teddy, and I'm willing to work hard for it. I want him to grow up and think I made the right choice, coming here."

She couldn't know, of course, what I really meant by that. She thought I was talking about something completely different.

"Was there ever any prospect of marrying his father?"

Sticking close to the story Molly had told me, I said, "No. I thought we were walking out together, but it turned out he had a wife and three children. I was just a dalliance."

But then she asked if I was in love with him, and I didn't want to lie to her about something as important as that. I couldn't tell her the true story, but I could be truthful about my feelings for the man who was really Teddy's father.

"I thought I was in love, but then I found out I didn't really know him at all. And I don't believe you can love someone if they're not who you thought they were. So I don't think I was in love, really. I think I was just naïve and stupid."

I looked down at my hands, remembering Frederick on that last night, saying he loved Lissy and he always would.

"We were never like you and Per," I said. "He looks at you,

sometimes, like you're the best thing he's ever seen. Teddy's father never looked at me like that."

She laughed. "He only looks at me like that when he's feeling frisky! That's men for you."

I wasn't sure if I should ask what I wanted to ask then, but I was really curious about it. Most Saturday nights, I heard the tell-tale rhythmic creaking from Ruth and Per's bedroom, but where I'd always been mortified to face Frederick on the mornings after he visited my bedroom, Ruth never seemed embarrassed at all. In fact, they were especially affectionate with each other on those mornings. Per might pat Ruth's bottom as he squeezed past her, or she'd smile across the table at him when she thought no one else was looking. It was so puzzling—surely she couldn't like the thing men needed to do? So when she said that about men feeling frisky, I screwed up my courage and ignored the embarrassment warming my face.

"Ruth, can I ask you something about . . . men's needs?"

"Of course you can. What is it?"

"Well, do you like it? Because I didn't."

"There's plenty of women who would agree with you there—you should hear Eileen downstairs on the subject. But I can only speak for myself, and what I think is, it makes a difference if you love the man and he loves you, and he's kind and gentle."

She reached across the table and took my hand. "You trusted someone who didn't deserve it, that's all. It'll be different with someone you love."

"You didn't mind me asking?"

"Of course not. You didn't have a mother to ask these questions of, did you? That was what upset me most, you know, when Mary died. The thought of you being without her, just when a girl really needs her mother. So if I can step in now, I'm proud to."

She wagged a finger at me. "And I'll tell you what she'd tell you—get a wedding ring on your finger before you let them have their way next time. A decent man will wait."

I shook my head. "I'm not looking for another . . . man."

I almost said husband, but stopped myself just in time.

"I can see why you say that, after what happened. But life can be hard for a woman on her own. You'll always have us, of course you will, but I'd love to see you with a good man who cares for you." She gave a wry smile. "Ideally one who doesn't come with a mother attached."

"You love Anna really."

"I'd love her more if she lived somewhere else. But yes, I do. And anyway, Per wouldn't be Per if he didn't want to take care of his mama."

She poured out the last of the coffee for both of us, took a sip, and said, "There are plenty of good men, you know. And you're not that girl who was so naïve anymore, are you? You'll be wiser next time and pick a good one. So don't close your heart to it."

"I don't know. Perhaps you should choose for me. Perhaps your judgment is better than mine."

Her eyes twinkled. "Are you setting me a challenge? Shall I find you a husband?"

"No! Honestly, right now I don't want one. If I change my mind, I'll let you know."

That night, lying on my featherbed, I thought of my mam, of all the times she and I could have sat and talked, like I'd done with Ruth, if she hadn't been taken from me too soon. About all the things a girl should be able to ask her mother, all the things a mother needs to tell her daughter. I told myself perhaps it wasn't so wrong, letting Ruth think she was being a mother figure for Molly, when she wanted to do that, and I needed it. But a little voice in my head said, *Tell her the truth, then*, and I knew I was fooling myself. Her kindness to me was based on a lie; the truth would make it disappear, and that was no less than I deserved.

But I was glad of her advice; it was a relief to think that if I ever did marry again, it wouldn't have to be the same sort of ordeal. And after that, seeing Ruth and Per together, sometimes I'd wonder what it would be like to have what they had. But right then, and for the foreseeable future, I didn't want another husband. Sometimes I thought back to the girl I used to be, reading novels and imagining the happy ending that my own wedding day would bring. How could I have been so daft? All the heroines I admired could have ended up just like I had, couldn't they? Jane and Elizabeth Bennet, for example—all very well going off to live at Netherfield and Pemberley, but if Mr. Bingley and Mr. Darcy decided they were only going to see their children for twenty minutes a day, there wouldn't be a thing they could do about it. And maybe they wouldn't mind, like Lissy didn't, but that wasn't the point. The point was, it wouldn't make any difference whether they minded or not. They'd been bought and sold, like I had—like a roll of cotton, and with about as much say in what happened to it.

I didn't blame the books anymore. It wasn't their fault I'd been too naïve to think beyond the last page, and it certainly wasn't their fault that Frederick and his family had got the benefit of that. It wasn't anyone's fault, really. I believed Frederick when he said he'd never meant to make me unhappy. He'd deceived me into thinking he loved me so my father didn't hold them over a barrel on the settlement, but he honestly thought— the whole family thought—that I was lucky to be "marrying up," and that life as the next Lady Storton had plenty to recommend it. And my father had thought that too. None of us realized we were reading two different stories.

So I wasn't going to fall for another happily-ever-after promise from a man. What I wanted now was to make my own living, to be able to look after Teddy and to look forward, like Ruth and Per did, to making a better life for us.

CHAPTER 41

By the end of my first week with the cart, I felt as though I'd been run over by a streetcar, but I'd sold almost everything. On the Friday morning, Ruth looked after the cart for a couple of hours so I could go back to the factory where I'd got the scraps and give the owner there my proposal.

"You want to what?" he said.

"Pay you for your cutters' scraps."

"Like I said before, dolly, you can have them. They're no use to me."

"I'd rather make a deal. I need to know you'll keep them for me each week, and not throw them away. How does fifty cents a box sound?"

He laughed. "I may not be John D. Rockefeller, but fifty cents ain't much of a persuasion to me."

"But you're a good businessman, and when a good businessman makes a deal, he sticks to it."

He shook his head. "You're a funny one, but all right, you're on. Saves my lads getting rid of it all, anyway."

* * *

I did another deal too, this time with Erin downstairs: her pick of the cart each week, in exchange for her magazines when she'd finished with them. Nothing in the box this time was an exact match for anything in the latest issue of *Ladies Home Journal*, but Ruth wasn't daunted.

"Here we are!"

She read from the magazine, putting on a voice that, if she'd only known it, was comically like my mother-in-law's: "Of course, you are going to have a bordered frock this summer. Every shop on the Avenue is showing the most charming styles, and you can have the border wide or narrow, simple or elaborate, just as your fancy dictates."

The drawings were of plain cotton dresses, with borders of print fabric at the hem and on the sleeves. Ruth picked up a remnant of sprigged cotton and held it round her arm.

"This would work—strips of a different fabric sewn on at the hem and the sleeve, and there's a new dress. We cut the remnants into strips and sell them like that, so it's obvious."

"I think I should be giving you a cut of the profits," I said.

"Buy me a diamond necklace when you make your first million."

At the end of each week, I gave Ruth our keep like before—she wouldn't take more, even though I offered it—and squirreled away the rest in the tin. If the cart continued to go well, we'd be able to get our own apartment sooner than I thought, so I was strict about not buying anything unless we really needed it. I did make one exception though. Since the night we'd talked on the fire escape, Anna had never mentioned our conversation again. She was back to being her usual gruff and grumpy self, but I couldn't forget her kindness in sharing a secret with me that must have been painful to remember, even so many years later. So when her birthday approached, I wanted to do something special for her.

She often talked about the spiced biscuits—pepparkakor—that her mother baked when she was a girl in Sweden, and which she couldn't make because the apartment had no oven. So I decided to try to find some.

One afternoon, I left Grand Street early, and walked and walked, asking people if they knew of a Swedish bakery. I had to go all the way to Fifty-first Street, but I found one, just round the corner from the cathedral, and proudly carried home a box of pepparkakor, tied with a blue and yellow ribbon.

"Oh, you'll be the favorite now," said Ruth when I showed her the box. "And we'll get a lecture on how no one makes biscuits like the Swedes do."

It was worth the long walk to see Anna's face when I presented the box to her, after dinner on her birthday.

"Jaha, pepparkakor! I haven't tasted these in years."

She took a bite. "Not as good as my mama's. But very good all the same. Where did you get them?"

"They're from a proper Swedish bakery, up on Fifty-first Street."

"Well, of course—only a Swede could make pepparkakor properly, because . . ."

Sure enough, we got the lecture Ruth had predicted. I couldn't look at her, and she had to turn to the window to hide her laughter. Inevitably, it led on to Anna reminiscing about Sweden, and the three children sat wide-eyed as she told a long (and, I'm fairly sure, much embroidered) story about seeing a bear in the forest. As she came to the end, Teddy said, "Farmor, did the bear bite you?"

He'd never called her that before, and Lena, who liked to be precise about things, said, quite kindly, "She's not your farmor, Teddy. You have a different farmor."

He looked around, puzzled. "Where?"

Anna glanced at me and then said to Teddy, "You know, on her birthday, a farmor can choose an extra child to be farmor to, forever. And I choose you."

Teddy threw Lena a look that said, "So there," and then, as if the previous matter was resolved to his satisfaction and he was now going to get to the root of this one, leaned forward, raised a questioning finger and said, "Did the bear bite you, Farmor?"

Anna lingered a little after Ruth and Per went to bed that night, and as I spread my featherbed on the floor, she said, "That was a long way to go, to find the pepparkakor. And a kind thought. Thank you."

"Thank you for what you said to Teddy. About being his farmor."

She shrugged. "I left behind my family, but I have learned that family can be anywhere you find it. I think perhaps you are learning the same."

The trouble was, she was right. When I made my crazy decision on the *Carpathia*, this was—almost literally—a port in a storm. That Molly had a place to go was what made the whole plan possible, but I'd never intended to stay for long, and certainly never to get to know them all or come to think of them as family. And yet, sitting crammed round the table that evening, laughing with Ruth, watching Teddy's face as he listened to the story of the bear, that was exactly how it felt. And not just for me but for him, too. As much as I wanted our own apartment, I couldn't imagine not being part of this family anymore—but I had to keep reminding myself, I wasn't. I was lying to them all, and I didn't deserve to stay.

The strips of dress fabric did so well on the cart that we kept them going for a couple of weeks, and I got a little dart of satisfaction seeing the office girls in dresses they'd remodeled with them. On Fridays, when the girls got paid, I usually stayed on Grand Street a little later, yelling out my wares for all I was worth, while they had money in their pockets. On one of those evenings, a man, about my age, in workman's overalls, stopped to look at the cart. I was talking to a couple of girls who couldn't choose between a set of strips in polka dot poplin or a pretty daisy print, but when they eventually decided— with a little help from the cotton king's daughter—to take both, he was still there. I didn't get a lot of male customers, but when they did come, after presents for a wife or sweetheart, they were an easy sell, because they didn't have a clue what they were looking at.

"Looking for something for your wife?" I said, picking up some broad satin ribbon I'd got in that week's box of scraps. "This would be pretty on a hat, or if she's handy with a needle, these strips of lace for a collar and cuffs are very popular."

"You're English," he said. "I thought so."

So was he. That took me by surprise; among all the accents you heard on Grand Street, English wasn't common. A Southerner though, by the sound of it.

"Not that many of us around here," I said. "Have you been in New York long?"

"A while now, yes." He gestured around at the bustle of Grand Street, still crowded even as the evening drew in. "Takes a bit of getting used to, doesn't it?" He nodded at the cart. "Still, you do a good trade, by the look of it. Land of opportunity, they say, don't they? Haven't found mine yet but I keep looking."

He gestured at the ribbon I was holding.

"I don't have a wife," he said, "so I'm afraid I'm not much of a customer. Just wanted to say hello to a fellow traveler from England."

He held out his hand. "Tommy. Tommy Jenkins."

"Molly Mortimer."

"Pleased to meet you, Molly." He tapped his hat. "Perhaps I'll see you again sometime."

He strolled away, whistling, just as Ruth came up.

"Who was that?" she said.

I shrugged. "He's English, just came up to say hello."

"Well, from the smile on his face, he was very pleased to have said it. Perhaps you've got an admirer."

"I've told you, I'm not looking for a man."

She grinned. "We'll see."

CHAPTER 42

The early summer weather in New York had been very similar to England's, and despite Ruth's warnings, I was completely unprepared for the heat that suddenly descended on the city. Within a day or two it went from pleasantly sunny and mild to oppressively hot and sticky. Pushing the cart to Grand Street was like walking through a thick, damp blanket, and I was dripping with sweat before I'd gone two blocks. But it was worse at the end of the day, when the tiny apartment was suffocating. The front parlor window was the only opening to the street, and even with it wide open, the air was so still and humid that it was like sleeping in an oven. So, along with everyone else in our building and all the others along the street, we took to spending the night outside.

Some people took their bedding and pillows out onto the fire escapes, but we dragged ours up to the roof, where you could sometimes catch just the breath of a breeze. Each family would claim their regular spot—ours was in the corner at the front—and by about ten o'clock, the roof was full of little encampments. Children drifted off to sleep while the adults, all in their nightclothes, sat and talked until the sky grew dark, the stars came out and gradually the conversations died away and snores and snuffles took their place.

It was quite bizarre at first, looking around and seeing all the neighbors in their nightclothes, but it was such a relief to get out of the stifling apartment that, once we all lay down to sleep, it was never long before my eyes closed. I slept better out there than I ever did on my featherbed on the kitchen floor, rarely waking before the sun came up. One night, though, I did wake in the early hours. I'd stopped keeping a book beside me then, I was sleeping so well, so to distract myself from the memories that still threatened, I got up quietly and stood by the wall that surrounded the roof, looking out over the street below. The fire escapes opposite were dotted with sleeping families, and others had bedded down on the steps up to their front doors. So many people, just in this little block, and so many more in the next and the next, all of us here to start again, to find a new life and a better one. And against all the odds, Teddy and I were doing just that.

Teddy losing his shyness meant he was also less easy to amuse quietly while Ruth and Anna sewed, so by then, I usually took him with me to Grand Street. All the regular vendors knew him: the fruit seller would slip him an apple or a tangerine, and the pickle man let him stand on tiptoe and stir the barrels. He'd listen to the organ grinder or wander over to look at the hustlers with their dice games, but most of all, he liked to stand and watch grumpy Ivan, whose cart of pots and pans was usually beside mine. Ivan didn't hold with enticing customers: he sat, hunched over a stool beside his cart, until someone came up, and then he'd stand up wearily and say, "Don't offer me less than ten cents, lady, these are good pans," or "Let me warn you, if you want five cent rubbish, you've come to the wrong place."

I hadn't realized quite how intently Teddy had been studying him until one day I was haggling over the price of a remnant of candy-striped cotton and Teddy, perched on the cart, leaned in and said, with Ivan's New York accent, "Don't offer me less than ten cents, lady."

Della and the customer laughed, both at him and my open-mouthed surprise, and even Ivan joined in, shaking his head and saying, "You're learning well, little man."

Of course then Teddy repeated the line all afternoon, sounding more like Ivan each time and grinning when people laughed at him.

"He'll turn into a little American, like my boys did," Della said. "To hear them now, you'd never know their mam and dad came from Yorkshire."

I thought about that as I stood there on the roof, looking out over the streets, as our neighbors snored all around me. Della was right, of course. Now that the evenings were light, all the children from the building played together outside, and though most of their parents revealed their homelands as soon as they opened their mouths, the shouts and shrieks that carried up to our open window had nothing of Naples or Kerry or Småland in them. America was the only home they knew, and it would be the same for Teddy. As far as I could tell, he had no memory of Winterton Hall, and I was certain he wouldn't miss it if he had. He didn't need servants and silver candlesticks; he could learn to make his own way in life, just like my father and mother did, and I was doing now.

This place, that had once seemed so strange and intimidating, had become our home. And even though this life was so different from the one I'd been brought up to, I'd come to feel like myself again. When Ruth and I looked through the magazines and found ideas for what to sell on the stall, it was like the days when I argued with my father about colors and prints. And when I struck a good deal with a customer, even though it was only over a matter of cents, I heard the voice of the girl who knew she could run Haywards as well as any man.

I wondered, often, what was happening there now, with my father gone and the management committee he'd picked running things much earlier than any of them had expected. There'd have been a seat on that committee for me, if things had been different, but it shocked me to realize how little I wanted it now. While he was alive, the managers at the mill had to listen to me, but without him, would my voice—a woman's voice—even have been heard? He'd done his best to give me what I wanted, a place in the business, but I'd never have been more than the founder's daughter, tolerated but not listened to. The cart might be small beer compared to Haywards, but it was mine, and I was proud of it and the money it earned me. It gave us a future, and that future was here.

The next morning, as I left the apartment with Teddy, a young lad was loitering outside.

"You Molly Mortimer?" he said.

"Yes, why?"

He thrust an envelope at me. "Fella asked me to give you this."

As I opened it and glimpsed the first words, my stomach turned over.

"Who gave you this?" I said.

"Just a fella."

"What fella? Where?"

He shrugged. "I dunno, he just paid me to give you that."

He walked away, and I opened the letter and read the first words again.

I know you're not who you say you are.

CHAPTER 43

I stuffed the letter into the pocket of my skirt; I couldn't stand and read it there, outside the apartment, when Ruth or Anna might come down to visit the outhouse, and I didn't want to read it in front of Della either. I needed to go somewhere to calm myself down, and think. My heart pounding, I took Teddy's hand and hurried down the steps to the street.

"Where we going?" said Teddy, when we didn't turn down toward Grand Street.

"To the park," I said.

"Hooray!" he cheered.

I'd only ever seen Seward Park on a Sunday, the square thronged with children, but today it was quiet, just a couple of old Greek ladies in their long black dresses chatting on one of the benches, and an elderly man walking a little dog whose legs looked as stiff as his own.

Teddy ran up to the slide, always his favorite, and I sat down on a bench where I could watch him. My hands shook as I unfolded the letter. No address and no greeting at the top. Just three sentences.

I know you're not who you say you are. Your name is Eli-
nor Coombes, and your son is Edward Coombes.
If you want to keep your secret, meet me tomorrow at
seven, by the fountain in Madison Square Park.

I went hot and then cold. So it had happened. Someone had
seen me, and knew who I was. So often, in those early weeks,
after my photograph was in the newspaper, I'd imagined this
moment, but when the weeks and then the months went by
and it didn't come, I thought I was safe. Thought I was building a future here for me and Teddy, so we could truly leave our
old lives behind. But all the time, I was fooling myself.

I read the words again, my heart hammering. No casual
stranger would have known my face from a picture after all
this time, much less recalled our names. The person who wrote
this letter had seen me before, and knew we'd got off the *Ti-*
tanic alive. Then they'd spotted me here in New York. Madison
Square was a good long walk away, but it was in the direction
of the Swedish bakery where I'd bought Anna's biscuits. Whoever it was had probably seen me when I went there. So much
for a good deed being its own reward.

I'd become so used to being able to blend into the background here on the Lower East Side, I'd got out of the habit of
being scared, of always checking to see no one was following
me, or giving me more than a casual glance. Why hadn't I been
more careful? But with the area being unfamiliar, I'd been concentrating on street names so I could find my way back, not on
the people I passed as I walked. And then a thought sent a chill
down my back. Whoever this was, they'd not just seen me.
They'd followed me home. In my panic, it hadn't struck me
before, but they must have done. They knew where I lived.
And—oh God, this was worse—they'd found out what name
I was using.

Now I was really scared. How had they found out that I was

calling myself Molly Mortimer? Had they been asking around, about an Englishwoman who'd been on the *Titanic*? But apart from Ruth's immediate neighbors, no one here knew that about me. I looked around, suddenly afraid whoever it was might be here, watching us. But there was no one but the two old ladies and the man with his dog.

I don't know, now, how I got through that day. I worked the cart, as usual, but I was so distracted that I'm sure I all but gave things away. It was a Friday, so Grand Street was busy, and I nervously scanned the crowds, even though I'd no idea who I was looking for. Poor Teddy got the rough edge of my tongue when he wandered over to the herring man, and I suddenly turned round and couldn't see him.

"He's over there," said Della, seeing my panic.

When I'd fetched him back, scolding him all the way, she said, "Are you all right, Molly? You seem a bit on edge today."

"I'm fine," I snapped, and then, "Sorry, just a bit distracted, that's all. I've got a few things on my mind."

"Anything I can help with?"

It was tempting to ask if anyone had been asking around about me, but I'd never told Della or any of the other cart vendors that I came on the *Titanic*, and it certainly didn't make sense to tell anyone now.

"No, but thanks all the same."

She shrugged. "You've only to say if there is. Us English should help each other out, like the others do."

She turned to attend to a customer, but I must have stood there staring. Because that's when the penny dropped. There was someone who'd found out the name I was using, only, what, about a week ago? Someone I didn't know, who I'd never seen around here.

Just wanted to say hello to a fellow traveler from England.

* * *

I knew I wouldn't sleep that night. Up on the roof, once the conversations had all faded away and everyone was settling down to sleep, my mind was a whirl of questions. It was the man who'd come up to me on Grand Street, it had to be. What was his name? Tommy something . . . Jennings, Jenkinson. No—Jenkins. Tommy Jenkins. It meant nothing to me, but, then, why would it?

He must have seen me somewhere when I went to the Swedish bakery, recognized me and followed me home. He'd even followed me from there to Grand Street. Which meant he was certain he knew me. But how? I kept trying to picture him: about my age, fairish hair, brown eyes . . . or perhaps blue? Not distinctive enough for me to remember them, anyway. I was sure I'd never seen him before. And what was puzzling me was his clothes—his general appearance, really. Workman's overalls, a scruffy cap. He needed a haircut, and hadn't I seen scuffed old boots as he walked away? If he was on the *Titanic*, he must have been in third class, surely? And the few men I'd seen on the *Carpathia* were first-class passengers. So how had he ever seen me?

When I was certain the family were all asleep, I got up and stood by the wall, looking over the rooftops. He was out there somewhere, this man who knew who I was. Probably sleeping quite peacefully, while I stood here sick with fear, knowing he had our fate in his hands. If he chose to, he could take away this life I'd built in a moment: a call to the White Star Line would do it, or a tip-off to a newspaper. And as soon as it was out, as soon as it was known that we were still alive, they'd come looking for us and take Teddy back.

I couldn't let that happen. But I had no idea how I was going to stop it.

CHAPTER 44

This time, I saw him before he saw me. Standing by the fountain, looking toward the Flatiron building, because he was expecting me to come from the direction of Broadway. But I'd taken a roundabout route instead, so I was walking toward him from the other side of the park. It had come to me, as I stood there on the roof the night before, that I should get a good look at him first, see if he looked nervous or confident, try to work out what I was dealing with.

He did look nervous, hands knotted in front of him, shifting his weight from foot to foot, craning his neck to see if he could spot me. Good. And if he thought he was about to see a frightened little woman, he had another think coming. I *was* frightened—I was terrified—but if it killed me, I wasn't going to let him see that. You should never go into a negotiation looking vulnerable, and I kept telling myself that was what this was. He had the power to wreck everything for me, but I must have something to bargain with, or he'd have done it already and we wouldn't be here.

He jumped as I walked up and said, "Mr. Jenkins. I believe we have some business to discuss."

I'd thought long and hard about who to be in this conversation. He plainly knew I wasn't Molly Mortimer, so there was no point pretending. And if I was going to be Elinor Coombes, I'd nothing to lose by employing the accent she'd worked so hard to acquire. I'd seen how effective cutglass vowels and crisp consonants were at intimidating anyone who didn't have them.

He turned. "You worked it out, then. And don't you sound different when you're not hawking from a pushcart?"

Doing my best to emulate Lady Storton's manner, I stood up tall and said, "I'm well aware that that's not a surprise to you. So let's not waste time. Why am I here?"

He shook his head. "You people never change, do you? Well, you know what? You don't get to speak to me like that. We're not on the ship now, and you're not in the first-class saloon, snapping your fingers to order a cocktail."

I think my mouth must have fallen open, and when I found my voice again it didn't sound at all like Lady Storton.

"You were part of the crew? On the *Titanic*?"

What was a sailor doing here, dressed like a workman?

"Well, I wasn't a first-class passenger, was I?"

"I don't remember seeing you."

The words just came out, and as soon as they did, his face said they were the wrong ones.

"Of course you don't. We were invisible to the likes of you."

My heart sank. I couldn't have made a bigger mistake, trying to carry off Lady Storton's haughty manner. He scowled.

"You didn't see me when you walked past me the other week either. Just a navvy having a beer after digging the road all day, nothing to you. But I've got a good memory for faces, and I remembered yours. Couldn't place it at first, but it kept nagging at me." He looked me up and down. "And then half an hour later, there you were again, strolling back the other way, swinging a box tied with ribbon and looking pleased with yourself, and it came to me. You were with the toff who threatened to have me sacked if you and the kid weren't on the next lifeboat."

Now I remembered. Frederick had argued with a crewman who was going to send the first lifeboat off half empty. I'd only seen the argument from a distance, and the crewman's back was to me, though I admit, I don't suppose I'd have remembered him even if it wasn't.

"You got into a lifeboat," he said. "I saw you, you and your boy. And then I see you walking around here in New York, but you're not Lady Muck anymore, and I get to wondering, what's going on here?"

"So you followed me home."

He shrugged. "I don't have much to do, of an evening, and I couldn't run to another beer."

"How did you find out my real name?"

"I've still got the newspaper with the lists of who was missing and who survived. A lot of my shipmates—my mates— were on the wrong list, and I kept it, because from time to time I've had to remind myself I was on the right one. I was *lucky*."

He said the word as though he was anything but.

"Wasn't hard to work out who you were—no other woman the right age in first class, with a child. So I thought, this is interesting—she's taken the kid, and she's got herself listed as missing, what's that about?" He shrugged. "Can't blame a bloke for being curious, when he's got nothing to occupy his mind but digging holes and wondering if he'll be able to pay his rent this week."

"I don't understand. Why aren't you still working on the ships?"

"Can't face it, can I? Can't even go home on one, let alone work on them again."

He gestured off to his left, in the vague direction of the East River. "Thought it would pass, eventually, but I still can't even go near the water. Can't look at it, can't bear the smell of it. Can you?"

I shook my head. I hadn't been near the river since the day I stepped off the *Carpathia*. I was always aware of it, out there on the edge of the Lower East Side, and I avoided anywhere that might give me even a glimpse of it.

"So you've had to stay here and find work?" I said.

"White Star Line cut us off without a penny—we only got paid up until the day the *Titanic* sank. I got myself a job in a restaurant at first—they were happy to have me, White Star still has a reputation for service. But word got round to the customers and every day, there were questions. Did I see the iceberg? How big was it? Is it true the band played on till the last? What song did they play? Can you imagine, asking someone who was there that night, what song the bloody band played? I couldn't take it; my nerves got bad."

He thrust out his hands; they were trembling. "You try doing Silver Service in this state."

"I'm sorry. I thought the White Star Line would have looked after you all."

"Looked after us? Don't make me laugh. You read what the inquiry said, I suppose? Crew didn't carry out their duties. Well, that's an easy accusation to make, when most of them are dead and can't speak up for themselves. We did our best for the passengers that night, every one of us. But no one stuck up for us. No one even thanked us."

I hadn't expected this, and I didn't know what to do. I'd come here, steeling myself to get the upper hand, frightened of what this man could do to us, and I was still frightened of that.

What I hadn't expected was to feel sorry for him. My father hadn't ever taught me how to negotiate with someone when you pity them.

He looked down at his hands. "They call us the lucky ones, but sometimes I wish I'd just died with my mates. I've got no life here, and no future. When I followed you, I was just curious, looking for a distraction, and that's the truth. But then I saw you, with your boy, and that nice family you live with, making a living from your little cart. You looked happy and I hated you for it. And then I thought, there'll be people back in England who'd pay good money to know where she is, and the kid. What's to stop me getting the news back to them?"

I took a deep breath. This was the bit that mattered.

"Do you still hate me?"

He shrugged, and didn't answer. Well, that was a start.

"If I'm happy here," I said carefully, "it's because I was miserable before. I was rich—you know that. And you think that means I had a good life. Well, I didn't. I'm not going to tell you my story, because it's none of your business, but if I'd rather be here, working all hours, sharing a tiny apartment with five people and a stinking outhouse with twenty families, than living that life, do you think it can possibly be as wonderful as you imagine? When the *Titanic* went down, I saw a chance to escape, and I took it."

"Good for you. But you still came down here and spoke to me all hoity-toity, didn't you? Not above playing the toff when it suits."

"I was frightened. You said I was to meet you here if I wanted to keep my secret. I thought it would be easier to persuade you not to expose us if I sounded . . . like I used to."

"Well, you got that wrong."

"Yes, I did. And I'm sorry."

"Well, since we're down to brass tacks, here's the situation. I can't go home, and I can't stay in this hellhole of a city, or I'll lose my marbles completely. I want to start again somewhere else. Somewhere where there's trees and fields and not too many people, and no one will know I was ever on the sodding *Titanic*. And I need money to do it. You can help me with that little problem, or I can get it another way."

"You can't think I'm still rich—look at me! I left the ship with the clothes I stood up in, that's all."

"You've earned money since. And I'm not asking for a fortune—just enough to get me a train ticket and a few weeks' rent. I can take it from there."

"I don't even have that much!"

"Then get it. Borrow it, steal it, I don't care. Look, I didn't have to give you this chance. I could have just spilled the beans and asked for a nice reward, couldn't I? But I'm not a bad lot. I wouldn't be doing this at all if I didn't have to. So, here's the deal. You bring me that money here, a week from Friday, and I'll disappear. If you don't, your vanishing act will be over."

CHAPTER 45

I knew to a cent how much was in my tin, and it wasn't even close to the amount Tommy Jenkins wanted. I believed him when he said he wasn't a bad lot—if he'd gone straight to the White Star Line, I'm sure he could have got a lot more money as a reward from Lord and Lady Storton than he'd asked for from me. But that was what was frightening: I could almost smell his desperation. I could see it, in the shaking of his hands. He didn't want to expose me, but if he had to, if it was him or me, he would. So somehow I had to find that money, and get him on his way before he thought better of the deal.

Borrow it, steal it, I don't care.

On the top shelf of the dresser, there was another tin, a little bigger than mine. It was white, and painted with blue and yellow flowers. Anna had brought it with her from Sweden, and every week, she and Ruth and Per put the little they could spare from their wages into it. I'd no idea how much was in there; they dipped into it for things like clothes or shoes and the children's birthday presents, and I'd heard Ruth say that it helped tide them over when the slack season for the garment trade came, but it was also where the money for moving to a bigger, better apartment would eventually come from. Would there be enough in there to make up the shortfall?

I couldn't ask to borrow the extra I needed without a good reason, and there wasn't one I could offer. But it would be so easy to take it, when everyone was asleep.

No.

What was I thinking of? How could I even contemplate stealing from the people who'd been so kind to me? Who had so little themselves, but willingly shared it with us? It was unthinkable. I had to get that money, but I'd have to find a way to borrow it, fair and square, from somewhere else.

There was only one person I could think of to ask. Hadn't Della said that we English should help each other out? But I wasn't surprised when, after I'd asked her, quietly, she shook her head.

"I've no savings to speak of, duck. What I make here pays the rent and feeds us but that's about it. What do you need that sort of money for?"

"I'd rather not say. And I trust you not to tell anyone I was asking."

She tapped the side of her nose. "Safe with me." She looked hard at me, and I think she could see the worry in my face. "Do you really need this money?"

"I've got to get it, Della, that's all there is to it."

"If you get it, can you definitely pay it back?"

"Yes. It's just that I need it quickly."

"Well, if you're really desperate, you could try Bill at the tavern on Orchard Street. But be careful."

She agreed to watch the cart for me, and I set off for Orchard Street, feeling a shred of hope for the first time since I'd heard Tommy Jenkins's demands. If I could just borrow the extra money, I could get rid of him. It'd be all my savings gone, I'd be back to square one and with a debt on my shoulders, too, but what choice did I have?

I'd seen the tavern before, a scruffy place that always had five or six rough-looking men hanging about outside. I usually crossed to the other side of the street to avoid their eyes, and I had to steel myself to walk toward the door. A few steps from it, one of them stood in front of me and looked me up and down.

"Can I help you, miss?"

"I'm looking for Bill."

"If your old man's sent you here to beg for more time to pay, you're wasting your time. A deadline's a deadline."

"No, I want to borrow some money."

He looked at the other men and laughed. "Another one's sent his woman because he thinks a pretty face'll get him a better rate. No shame, some of 'em."

"I haven't been sent here by anyone," I said. "I want to borrow money on my own account."

"Oh," he said in a mocking voice. "Well, that makes quite the difference." He opened the door and gestured me inside, shouting to a man sitting in the far corner, "Customer for you, Bill."

As the door closed behind me, I heard him say, "That'll give him a laugh, anyway."

The tavern was gloomy inside, and a smell of stale beer and old sweat hung in the air. My shoes stuck to the grimy floor as I picked my way through the handful of tables, ignoring the heads turning my way. The man sitting at the table in the corner was dark and stocky, and on a chair beside him sat a small black dog, wearing a red bandanna round its neck. In front of both of them, on the table, was a book, open and laid out like an accounts ledger, and a knife. The man stared as I walked across, no expression in his eyes at all.

"Are you Bill?" I said, trying not to look at the knife.

"That's my name," he said. "Don't wear it out."

"I was told you lend money."

He turned to the dog. "Young lady was told we lend money, Snapper," he said. And then to me: "What if I do?"

"I'd like to borrow some."

"I see. What are we talking about? A thousand dollars? A million?"

He laughed. "I'm joking with you. How much do you want?"

I told him and he looked at the dog again. "What do you reckon, Snapper?" He paused, for all the world as though he was listening to the dog's answer, then said, "Two hundred percent interest if you keep up the payments—"

"What? That means I'd be paying you back three times what I borrowed."

"Whaddaya know?" he said to the dog. "This one can add up." And then to me, "And it goes up ten percent every time you miss a payment."

"If you cut the interest by half, you'll get your money back quicker—I could pay you back in six months."

He looked at me, his eyebrows raised, looked at the dog, then back at me. "Are you trying to make a deal with me?" He threw back his head and laughed, then leaned forward. "Just for that, the interest'll be two hundred and fifty."

He picked up the knife and ran it under his thumbnail, then inspected the line of grime it had scraped out and wiped it on the table. My mind was racing. It was such a lot of money. I'd be paying the debt off for months and months, with nothing left to save. But it was better than stealing from Ruth and her family.

"I'll take it."

He pulled the ledger toward him. "What's your address?"

"Why do you need that?"

He looked at the dog and shook his head. "Why, she asks.

Why do you think? So I can make sure I'm going to get my investment back, one way or the other. You need this money fast, right?"

"By the end of the week."

"Well, I can send one of the lads round tomorrow morning, to see what you've got, and if there's enough there to make it worth my while, we're in business. You can collect the money tomorrow afternoon."

"I don't understand . . . What do you mean, to see what I've got?"

He sighed. "You walk in here, trying to make a deal, then suddenly you're the Virgin Mary, all wide-eyed and innocent." Very slowly, emphasizing each word, he said, "I need to know what you've got, in case you can't pay."

"But I can pay. I won't even miss a payment."

"Lady, if I had a dollar for every time I've heard that, I'd be dining out with Rockefeller. If you can pay, that's fine and dandy. And if not, I take what I can sell and get the money back that way. Furniture, pots and pans, whatever—as long as my lad tells me you've got enough stuff to cover it, we're good. So—" He picked up a pencil. "What's the address?"

"I need to think about it. I'm not sure if I want to do this after all."

He shrugged. "Think away. But don't keep me waiting, or I might have to put that interest rate up."

I couldn't go straight back to Grand Street. I walked and walked, trying to think what to do. I couldn't take the loan, that was obvious. Apart from my clothes and Teddy's, I didn't own anything. And part of me was relieved. I might be certain I could make the payments, but if anything went wrong, I didn't want to think of Bill's "lads" going anywhere near the apartment. They didn't need to be that big and burly just for the purposes of shifting furniture, and that knife had been there on the table as a message, hadn't it?

But where was I going to get the money now? At one point, I remember, I laughed as I walked along. It was so ridiculous! I was the daughter of a millionaire, and here I was with the life I'd built hanging in the balance, for want of less than the cost of a good silk petticoat. I was the cotton king's daughter, brought up learning how to bargain, but I had nothing to bargain with. And I was desperate enough that if I could've taken the loan, I would have, even though it was skinning me alive.

I only stopped walking when a dank smell in the air told me I was getting close to the river. I turned back then, and hurried to Grand Street. Thanked Della for looking after the cart, and spent the rest of the day yelling "Straight from the fashion magazines" and "New styles this week" at the top of my voice, for all the world as though it was going to help.

Up on the roof that night, I tossed and turned, unable to sleep. How the heck was I going to find the money to get rid of Tommy Jenkins? I kept picturing the flower-patterned tin on the top shelf of the dresser, and my thoughts whirled round and round in a sickening circle.

Should I just look and see how much is in there? If there's not enough, I can rule it out completely.

You've already ruled it out completely. You're not touching that tin.

But if there's no other way . . .

In the end I couldn't stand it any longer. I sat up and looked around. They were all asleep. I got up and crept down the fire escape, and into the apartment. I had to stand on tiptoe, but I could just about reach the tin. Slowly, slowly, watching the door all the time, I lifted it down, holding it with both hands so as not to make the coins rattle.

It was heavy. I opened the lid. Half full. No need to take the risk of counting the coins; it was plain to see there was enough there to add to my savings and pay off Tommy Jenkins. But not enough that it wouldn't be obvious at a glance that it was missing.

My hands trembling, I put the tin back on the top shelf, crept back up to the roof and lay down. The money was there. I half wished it wasn't, that the decision was out of my hands. But it was. I kept imagining Ruth's bewildered face when she opened the tin at the end of the week and saw there was money missing. I'd be the obvious culprit, wouldn't I? They'd hardly steal from each other. She'd know, they'd all know, that I'd stolen from them, and I wouldn't even be able to tell them why. Even now, even before it had happened, the thought of it made me hot with shame.

Even if I could push my conscience aside, what then? They'd throw us out, of course they would. And with no savings of my own left, where were we going to go? I lay there looking up at the stars, trying to think of another way. But apart from praying for a miracle, there wasn't one, and while I was willing to try that, I didn't hold out much hope.

CHAPTER 46

I took the money on Thursday night, when it became obvious that praying for a miracle, unsurprisingly, hadn't worked. Waited until I was sure everyone was asleep, crept down the fire escape and helped myself. All the time thinking about the hours Anna and Ruth had spent hunched over their machines, and the aches and pains Per suffered from long days on the construction site. And hearing Ruth's voice, saying how glad she was that I was part of their family now, and how proud my mother would be of me. It didn't help one bit to tell myself she was speaking to Molly, and talking about Molly's mother, because what would my own mother think if she could see me now?

I couldn't think of an excuse to give Ruth for why I'd be going out that Friday evening, so I put the cart away early and took Teddy with me. He was excited to go somewhere we hadn't been before, and trotted happily along, holding my hand and singing to himself. When we were nearly there, we walked past a little playground, and he stopped and pointed.

"Look, Mama, swings!"

He went to run in, but I held onto his hand.

"Not now, Teddy, we're in a hurry."

Tommy Jenkins was waiting by the fountain. If anything he looked more nervous than last time, wringing his hands as he shifted from foot to foot.

As we walked up, he said, "You came, then."

"You didn't give me much choice."

Teddy looked up at him curiously and in the same cheery voice he used to greet customers on the stall, said, "Hello, mister."

"Er, hello, lad." His eyes flicked quickly away from Teddy and back to me. "You've got the money?"

I handed over the bag of coins. He opened it and looked inside.

"Count it if you want to," I said. "But it's all there, what you asked for."

He looked at me—shamefaced but, at the same time, righteous, like he'd done something bad but he could justify it to himself. "Can't have been that hard to get it, then."

I didn't want to antagonize him, but I couldn't just take that.

"It's all my savings," I said, as calmly as I could manage. "Every penny. And on top of that, I had to steal from the people who took us in. I've no idea what's going to happen to us when they find out. So it wasn't easy to get, and if you were thinking you might come back for more one day—"

"I wasn't. I won't." He held up his hands. "Look, I told you, I wouldn't be doing this if I didn't have to. I've got to get away from here. My nerves are getting worse."

"Where will you go?"

I didn't care, as long as he went and never came back, but I wanted to be sure he had a definite plan in mind.

"Nebraska. Farming country. They're desperate for workers there. And it's a long way from the sea."

"When?"

"Tomorrow. The trains run every day, I checked, and the rent on my room's due on Saturday, so that's another reason not to stick around."

"Right, well, I—"

Just at that moment, a piercing wail came from the direction of the playground. For a second, Tommy froze, then he dropped to a crouch, his hands over his eyes, his whole body shaking pitifully as he turned his head from side to side.

Before I could think what to do, Teddy put a hand on Tommy's shoulder and said, "Don't cry, mister. You're all right; it didn't hurt."

It was what I always said to him if he fell over, to stop any tears before they started; I'd learned it from Molly on the ship. Tommy didn't take his hands from his face. Teddy looked up at me, his face concerned.

I crouched down and said, "Tommy, what's wrong?"

He shook his head, his hands still over his eyes. And then I realized.

"There's a playground back there," I said. "It was just a kid, screaming. They'll be playing a game, that's all." I put out my hand and covered his. "It's all right; it's just children."

He sighed and stood halfway up, his hands on his knees, head down and facing the ground, as if he was trying not to be sick.

"You hear them too, don't you?" I said. "The people in the water."

He looked up. "Do you?"

"At first, it was every night. It's less often now, but they're still there."

"Do you think they'll ever go away?"

He sounded like a little boy, and I was tempted to comfort him with a fib, like a mother would. But he'd know as well as I did that it wasn't true.

"I don't think we'll ever forget that sound," I said. "Any of us who were there."

"But I can't live like this. I get no peace from it. It's all in my head, what happened that night, and it's bursting to get out, but I can't speak about it because I can't have people knowing I was there."

"Will it help to talk to me?"

He looked down at his feet. "I'm a man. I shouldn't be like this."

"You're a man who lived through something terrible. Do you think there's anyone who survived the *Titanic* who wasn't changed by it?"

A smartly dressed couple walking by glanced curiously at us.

"Look," I said, "there's a bench over there. Come and sit down."

We sat on the bench, in a shady corner out of the way, and I pulled Teddy onto my knee. Tommy looked off into the distance for a moment, and then he said, so quietly I had to lean in to hear, "I should have gone down with the ship. We knew, those of us left, that we had no chance. But right at the end, right before she sank, we were trying to launch the last of the collapsibles—the deck was awash, water coming in all over the place—and I don't know what went wrong but it flipped over and landed upside down. Then everything tilted. I couldn't see or hear and the next thing I know, I'm in the water."

My stomach turned over. "I thought you'd been assigned to a lifeboat. I thought that was how you survived."

He shook his head. "I managed to swim to the collapsible, a few of us did. We couldn't turn it over, so we just clambered up onto it. And then more came, and more, we stood up to make room, until there were about thirty of us, balancing on it. First Officer Lightoller was there, and he got us sorted into two rows, on either side, so we could keep it steady. Then we looked up and . . . well, you know."

Neither of us spoke for a few moments. I was seeing that great ship slip under the waves, and I knew he was too.

"We balanced on that upturned boat all night. Wet through, stiff with the cold, and terrified we might pass out and fall into the water. Or worse, upset the boat and tip the others in. It was so cold, I thought my blood must be freezing in my veins, but I kept saying to myself, *You've got to live, Tom, you've got to live.* Because I could hear all the ones who weren't going to live. I could hear them crying out for their mothers, and calling for help that was never going to come. But sometimes now I wish I'd died with them."

"Listen to me," I said. "You survived. And so did I. And we've got to keep going, because of the ones who didn't get a chance to. We'll never forget what we saw and heard that night, but a very wise friend of mine, who has reason to know, told me that even the worst memories get easier to live with, in time. She's someone who doesn't sweeten the truth, so I believe her. And you're doing the right thing, getting away from here. I think it'll help."

He put his head in his hands. Teddy looked up at me and said anxiously, "He's crying again."

Tommy looked up, wiped his eyes with the heels of his hands and smiled at Teddy. "I'm not, mate, look, I'm all right. Just being a bit silly, that's all."

He twisted the bag of money closed and handed it to me. "I can't take this. I should never have threatened you. You've got your reasons for wanting to disappear, and as you said, they're none of my business. I won't say we should stick together, us survivors, because I daresay you want to see the back of me and I can't blame you. But we're members of the same club, me and you, and I can't take your money."

I didn't know what to say. It was a relief, but at the same time, I needed Tommy Jenkins to be far away, starting a new life and forgetting all about me.

"What will you do, then?"

"I'll stay here, navvying, till I've made enough money to go."

"If you don't go mad first." I opened the bag. "Could you get there on a bit less money? Go part of the way, perhaps, get some work and then move on?"

"I don't want any of it—"

"I don't care. Look, I'll be straight with you. I do want to see the back of you. It would be a great relief to me to know you were miles away in Nebraska, starting a new life, so I don't have to worry about seeing you coming round the corner one day. Because I don't want to be reminded of the *Titanic* either. So let me give you the part of this money that's mine. You can get away then, and I can give back what I stole."

He thought for a minute. Looked at Teddy, looked back at me. "I'll pay you back. Every penny. As soon as I get settled."

"I won't say that wouldn't be welcome. I worked hard for that money."

"I'll work hard to get it back to you, I swear."

When we parted, I wished him luck, and I meant it. If I'd thought sitting in that lifeboat all night was an ordeal—and it was—what he'd been through was unimaginable. No wonder he was in such a state. I hoped Anna's advice was true for him too, but it was plain that it would be a long time before those memories faded, if they ever did.

I was back at square one with my own savings, nothing left at all, but at least I could put back the money I'd taken from Ruth's tin. I'd do it that night, creep down the fire escape when they were all asleep. I could already feel the relief of it.

As we passed the playground, Teddy tugged on my hand.

"Go on the swings, Mama?"

"All right, just a short go, then we have to get home. Anna will have dinner ready, and you know she gets cross if we're late."

We were longer than I planned at the swings. Teddy was having such a good time, laughing and yelling at me to push him higher, and I smiled from pure relief.

We're going to be all right.

I've lost my money, but I've still got everything that's important.

I've started over once before, and I can do it again.

We strolled back together, hand in hand, Teddy chattering all the way. It was a long walk for his little legs, so when we arrived home, I carried him up the stairs. The smell of Anna's meatball stew wafted out of the apartment as we reached the third floor.

"Your favorite," I said. "Hope they haven't eaten it all."

I pushed open the door, Teddy still in my arms. Anna was stirring a pan on the stove. Per and the children were sitting at the table. And Ruth was standing on tiptoe, reaching up and putting the tin back on the top shelf of the dresser.

CHAPTER 47

They'd been talking when I came in, but the conversation stopped abruptly. My heart jumped but Ruth shoved the tin back on the shelf and said brightly, "You're late home. Busy down there today?"

Why didn't she say the money was missing? Before I could answer, Teddy piped up: "Teddy went on the swings. Not our swings, different swings. And we saw Mama's friend. Tommy."

Teddy's speech was still babyish at times, but he had to choose that moment to be as clear as a bell. Ruth raised an eyebrow at me, and Anna stopped stirring the pot, her ears all but waggling. I brazened it out as best I could.

"Tommy Jenkins," I said. "The Englishman who was at Grand Street the other day."

"I remember," said Ruth.

"Turns out he was on the *Titanic* too, had quite a bad time of it. He just wanted to talk it over with someone else who was there."

"He was crying," said Teddy. "And Mama said—"

"Teddy, be quiet," I snapped, and then said to the others, "Sorry, it was just a bit upsetting, raking it all up again."

"Well, we have no need to speak of it," said Anna. "Sit down, dinner is ready."

I sat there, rigid with fear, as they all chattered on as though everything was quite normal. About Lena getting a star for her homework, Per's irritation with a new worker on the site who didn't pull his weight, a story in the paper about a gangster getting killed. Micke pinched one of Lena's meatballs when she wasn't looking, just for a joke, and was told off by Per; Ruth asked Anna if she'd left something out of the meatball gravy because it tasted different, and got the sharp retort that there must be something wrong with her tongue. And all I could think was, *They all know. Why aren't they saying?* They'd been talking when we walked in, and they'd all stopped, and there was something so odd in Ruth's tone when she spoke to me.

It was only when Micke was in the middle of a long explanation about how the Brooklyn Bridge was built, that he'd got from a school book, that it suddenly hit me. Had they called the police? Had they realized, straight away, that it must be me who'd taken the money and now they were just waiting for the police to come? In all my worry about being found out, that prospect hadn't occurred to me, because no one ever called the police for anything there. I'd heard Per say they were all in the pockets of the neighborhood gangs, and if you were an honest person, it was better to have nothing to do with them.

Surely they wouldn't do that, without even accusing me? I looked around the table. No. It couldn't be that. They couldn't pretend like this, and they'd hardly want the police turning up and scaring the children. If the police would even come, anyway.

Calm down. Think. What are you going to say?

But there was nothing I could say, was there? I couldn't tell them the truth, and there was no lie that could possibly save us. The best I could hope for was to beg them not to throw us out there and then.

We got through dinner and still nothing was said. Everything was completely as normal until, as darkness fell, Per and the children started gathering up the bedding to go up on the roof. I went to get mine, but Ruth caught my arm and gestured to the table.

"I want to talk to you."

It was almost a relief, after the tension of the evening. I sat down, and she sat opposite.

Once the others had gone, she said, "I heard something today that's got me worried."

Heard something?

"Eileen downstairs says she saw you coming out of the White Horse. I said it couldn't be, but she was certain. Was it you?"

I couldn't think quickly enough to stop my face from telling the truth and she saw it.

"Have you borrowed money from that Bill?"

"No."

"You swear?"

"I haven't. I swear."

"Thank goodness for that at least! But were you trying to?"

Why lie more than I had to?

"Yes, I was. But he turned me down."

"I knew it!" She hit her hand on the table and I jumped. "This is about us moving, isn't it? I said to Per and Anna earlier, Molly thinks they're in the way here, that's what it is. You think you need to get a place of your own when we go."

Was that what they were talking about when I came in?

"You daft thing," she said, giving me a gentle smack on the arm. "You and Teddy will come with us. If you've saved enough for your own place by then, all well and good, but if not, we'll work something out until you do."

It was all I could do to stay upright in my seat and not collapse in a heap of relief. She couldn't have looked in the tin. She didn't know the money was missing.

I couldn't trust myself to speak, and when I didn't answer, she said, "That's if you want to?"

"Yes! Of course I do, I just didn't want to be under your feet forever. You've done so much for us already."

"Well, you're family, aren't you? Anyway, I don't suppose it'll be for ages yet." She looked up at the tin. "I haven't done a count-up for a while. I meant to have a look this evening. But what with the kids growing like beanpoles lately, we're still going to be a good way off."

She looked at me curiously. "Unless, of course, you've got plans with a certain Mr. Jenkins. You kept that little rendezvous secret."

"It wasn't a rendezvous."

She raised an eyebrow. "You sure?"

"Completely sure. He's moving away from New York, and he just wanted someone to talk to about what happened. Before he went, and put it all behind him."

Poor Tommy. I didn't think he ever would.

Ruth put her hand on mine.

"I've never asked you about it, because I didn't think you wanted to be reminded. But you know you can always talk to me, if you want to."

"Thanks, Ruth. But I don't, honestly. I want to put it behind me too."

"Well, you know where I am if you change your mind. Now, let's get up on that roof, it's sweltering in here."

* * *

After I'd put the money back, sometime in the small hours of
the night, I sat out on the fire escape by myself for a while. I
didn't try to distract myself with a book; I let the cries of the
people in the water come and made myself bear it. It was daft,
really, but I wanted Tommy not to be alone with them, that
night.

CHAPTER 48

Right up until the day I said goodbye to Tommy Jenkins, I'd thought of our life in the apartment as a temporary one. Even once I realized we'd need to stay longer than the few weeks I'd originally imagined it would take to get on our feet, I always had in my mind that we'd have to move on. And in the beginning, I wanted to. It was hard, always having to be on my guard about what Molly would or wouldn't have known, what she'd be able to do that I couldn't, and though I intended to keep her name, there'd be so much less pretending needed once I moved away from them and we lived on our own, with neighbors who'd only know what I chose to tell them. As the months went by though, and I got to know our adopted family so well, I wished we didn't have to go—but I still thought we would.

But that evening, when Ruth told me off for thinking that I needed to leave, and said that I could go with them when they moved, I could see she meant it. I was so relieved, in that moment, that she hadn't found the money missing, I'd said yes without thinking about it. But afterward, I went over and over it in my mind, and I couldn't see a reason not to. I hadn't given myself away in all this time, had I? I'd learned to do everything Molly would know how to do—including looking after Teddy—and all those late-night conversations with Ruth meant there couldn't be anything important about Molly's background left to catch me out.

I kept remembering what Anna said, that family can be anywhere you find it. I had found it, for me and for Teddy, and I didn't want to lose it. And they didn't want to lose us either. I'd done wrong, lying to them, but mightn't my lie, in the long run, have hurt them less than knowing the truth, that Molly had died a terrible death? And so I made up my mind: we'd have a new and better life, Teddy and me, one day, but when we did, it would be as part of the family we'd both come to love.

By the time I'd had the cart for a couple of months, I'd learned what kind of things sold best, and how to sell them. I was buying three or four boxes of scraps a week from Mr. Walden, the factory owner, and after plucking up my courage to go and see the owner of the hat factory downstairs from his, I paid twenty cents for a box of damaged trimmings from him every week too. A lot of it was rubbish, but there were always bits and pieces that, with Ruth's help, I could salvage and make sellable. She had such a good eye—Lissy used to say that about me, but it's one thing knowing about good quality fabrics and completely another to look at bits and pieces that could easily have been thrown away, and see a way to make something pretty from them.

Each week, we'd comb through the magazines Erin from downstairs gave us, cutting out pictures to have on the stall as inspiration. I watched the girls tripping off to work each morning to see what they were wearing and, on Saturdays when Grand Street was quieter because it was the Jewish Sabbath, I'd sometimes take the El train uptown and look in the windows of the department stores to see if there was anything we could copy. We changed the selection every Friday, so there was always something new to see when the office girls and the shopgirls came home with their wages, and on Erin's advice, I'd got a little mirror on a stand for the cart, so I could show how a new collar could lift someone's plain dress, or a bunch of paper flowers, the torn bits turned to the inside, would freshen up an old hat. And then one day Ruth came up to the cart, smiling all over her face, with the top half of a shop window mannequin in her arms.

"Look! That dress shop on Orchard Street was closing down; they're moving to Jersey. I got this for fifty cents. We can put a shirtwaist on it, and use it to show the trims."

It worked perfectly. Anna ran up a plain white shirtwaist for me, and each week, we'd trim it with whatever looked good from the boxes—a frill of lace round the neck, a ribbon pinned round the yoke, a row of braid tacked round the sleeve. No one else had anything like it, and in the sea of carts, it caught the eye. We named it Dolly, and the office girls would come along saying, "What's Dolly got on this week?"

Teddy, for some reason, found Dolly fascinating, and kept asking it questions.

"How old are you, Dolly?"

"Where d'you sleep, Dolly?"

"D'you like cats, Dolly?"

One quiet afternoon, grumpy Ivan on the pots and pans cart answered him in a squeaky voice.

"I haaaate cats. I like lions," and then gave a great roar.

Teddy almost jumped out of his skin, then burst into giggles, and after that it became their game, when the street was a little quieter in the middle of the afternoon, for Teddy to question Dolly and Ivan to give silly answers. Sometimes, as I watched him creased up with laughter at Ivan's daft voices, or at home, playing with Micke and Lena, I thought about what his life would be like now, if we'd gone back to Winterton Hall.

Shut up in the nursery all day with Nanny Cairns, who, for all her qualifications and her duchesses, had never shown an ounce of affection for him. Brought downstairs at four o'clock like a parcel, then taken back again, even if he cried and clung to me. Then, in a few years' time, bundled off to school to learn to be as unhappy as his father was. He might not have servants and silver spoons here, but he was a happy little boy, surrounded by people who loved him.

Besides, we were already on our way to a better life here in New York. I did a steady trade through the week, and then on Friday evenings, girls clustered round the cart and it would be almost picked clean by the time they'd finished. I was earning seven or eight times more than I did working for Mr. Klein, so the new pile of coins in my little tin was growing fast. And I kept thinking about something my father used to say, about how he built Haywards up from that one drapers' shop. In business, he'd say, you can't stand around feeling pleased with yourself—you've got to be looking for the next thing. And I had an idea what the next thing should be.

One night, as we sat sorting through a new box of scraps, I said to Ruth, "What do you think about getting another cart? To take to Fifth Avenue, and catch the office girls up there?"

She frowned. "How could you do that? You can't be in two places at once."

"You could be in one of them."

She pulled a face. "Don't be daft. You're the one who's got the gift for bargaining."

"I could teach you that. Easily. Ruth, none of this would have happened without you. It's you who has all the ideas, and we're a good team, you said that yourself, right at the start."

"But I'd have to give up working for Mr. Klein. That's a big risk."

"Do you remember what you said to me when I first had the

idea to get the cart? You said, when you came here, you were like me. You took risks. You told me how you crossed the ocean to find a new life; you found a place to live, and you walked into that dress shop and asked for a job. And all of it worked out, didn't it?"

"I know, but that was a long time ago."

"You're still the same person. Honestly, Ruth, I think we could make a success of this. If we could earn double what I'm taking now, we could think about getting a little shop in a few years' time."

"From factory scraps?"

"It doesn't have to be factory scraps forever. This is just our start, and it's a good one."

She was tempted, I could see it.

"I've got a deal for you," I said.

She laughed. "Oh no, I'm not haggling with you."

"No, listen. I'd get the second cart, and pay for the license. And whatever we make, we just split between us. Mine's bringing in enough to cover what Mr. Klein paid you, so even if it takes a while to get the second one going, you won't lose out."

"I'd have to see what Per thinks."

"But if he agrees, you'll do it?"

She thought for a moment, looking out of the window, and I don't know for sure, but I think she was remembering that girl who walked into a dress shop and asked for a job.

"Yes," she said. "I'll do it."

CHAPTER 49

That summer was a long one, still very warm right through October. It was Micke's birthday at the end of the month, and for weeks before, he'd been badgering Ruth and Per for a day trip to the seaside at Coney Island. A classmate, Buddy, had been there, and Micke was desperate to see the amusement parks he'd talked about, where you could ride a camel, see a miniature city complete with real live little people, and even take a trip to the moon. When he came home grinning from ear to ear after getting top marks in a test, it was agreed that we'd go on the following Sunday.

I was nervous, I'll admit, about seeing the sea again. Since the night we arrived at Pier 54, all those months ago, I'd still never gone anywhere near the river. I couldn't imagine looking at the cold, dark water, and not being transported back to that lifeboat, watching the ship sink and hearing those awful screams. But when we got off the train at Coney Island, nothing could have been less of a reminder of that awful night. The sun was shining, and the place was a giant carnival, with sideshows and beer stands and barkers yelling about the wonders in the parks. A trio of black men in striped shirts and straw boaters was playing jazz by the side of the street, and the smells of cotton candy and toffee and fried onions hung in the air.

We followed the crowds to Luna Park, which Buddy had assured Micke was the best, and as we walked through the gate, all of us looked around in astonished wonder at a fairy-land of minarets and onion domes, castellated towers and col-onnades covered in cascades of flowers. Everywhere you looked there was something comical or strange or both: a man and woman on stilts, striding through the crowds hand in hand; a troupe of clowns with enormous shoes, pretending to trip each other up; a swarthy-looking man swirling flaming torches and then, right in front of our eyes, opening his mouth wide and swallowing the fire. A young lad led a camel past us, a couple perched up on its back, swaying precariously, and I couldn't believe my eyes when that was followed by an ele-phant, its mournful eyes surveying the crowd as it picked its way through, led by a pretty young girl in a sequined dress.

"See?" said Micke, his blue eyes shining. "It's just like Buddy said: everything in the world is here."

Ruth had promised that he could choose what we did first, and his answer was instant: "Go to the moon!"

Inside a big white building, we took our seats in a "space-craft" with enormous red canvas wings. The children whooped as the wings began to flap. The lights went out, and suddenly we seemed to be rising up into the night sky, surrounded by stars, a wind whipping our hair, and looking down on the city. That part was very cleverly done: even though I knew per-fectly well there was a roof on the building and we were still underneath it, it really did feel as though we were flying. Our landing on the moon was less convincing, since it was plainly made of papier mâché that had seen better days, and the green-faced moon-dwellers who sang us a song of welcome couldn't have looked more weary of the task if they'd tried. But the children loved it, clutching their gifts of green cheese as we climbed back down to earth on a rope ladder.

After we'd visited the North Pole, met mermaids, and raced on mechanical horses, we stopped at a shack to eat baked clams, butter dripping down our chins, and drink cold German beer straight from the bottle. The children had root beer—none of them had tasted it before, and Teddy giggled as the bubbles went up his nose. Over the past few months, he'd lost his chubby cheeks and shot up a couple of inches. He was a little boy now, not the baby I'd carried off the ship all those months ago.

Per's voice broke into my thoughts. "Right, who's ready for the beach?"

The three children cheered, and as Per handed back the beer bottles and collected the deposit, they ran on ahead, Lena dancing with excitement, Teddy trying to keep up with Micke's longer legs. And then there it was in front of us: the sea. Glittering in the sunshine, full of laughing people splashing in the frothy waves. It looked so harmless, so different from the ink-black water that night. But it was still the sea. I lifted my eyes to the horizon. Somewhere out there, that enormous, beautiful ship lay under the waves, and with it so many people. It was as hard to believe now as it had been when I watched it sink right in front of me.

Teddy turned and waved at me. "Mama, look! The ocean!"

He didn't remember anything of that night, and I was glad of that. But all the same, the thought of him—of either of us—going near the water that had claimed his father and grandfather was making me feel sick. I hadn't mentioned my fears to anyone, not wanting to spoil the day, but Anna, shrewd as ever, noticed my steps slowing as we walked toward the beach.

She slowed too, so we were a few paces behind Ruth and Per, and then said quietly, "A difficult day for you. But you are a strong young woman; you don't run from things that frighten you."

"I don't want Teddy to see that I'm frightened and be frightened himself."

She pointed to Teddy, already skipping onto the sand with Micke and Lena. "I don't think you need to worry about that."

We rented bathing costumes at a booth with a sign declaring "All suits sterilized."

"How do you think they do that?" I asked as we struggled into the itchy wool dresses and voluminous drawers in a tiny cabin, Ruth and I and Lena together. Anna had already said cold water was for cod, not human beings, and she wouldn't be going anywhere near it.

"That's what I was wondering," said Ruth, pulling at the drawers. "You couldn't boil this stuff; it would shrink." She shrugged. "Well, they'll get a good rinse in the sea, anyway."

I bit my lip. If just looking at the sea made me want to turn and run, how on earth was I going to get up the courage to go into the water?

From outside came an impatient little voice.

"Mama! Come out, we're waiting!"

I pasted on my best Molly Mortimer smile, the one I used when a customer was haggling hard, and stepped outside. There were so many people on the beach, you could barely see the sand, but we managed to find a patch to spread out the plaid blanket we'd brought and sit down. Long red ropes, anchored to vertical poles, stretched from the beach out into the water, where they were attached to a series of floating barrels painted in red and yellow stripes. A sign said, DO NOT BATHE BEYOND THE LIFE LINES, and most people were holding on to the ropes as they stood thigh high in the water, though there were some men splashing about in between the lines, out by the furthest barrels. Children were playing in the shallow waves lapping onto the beach, kicking up spray or scooping up handfuls of water and throwing it around. It was perfectly safe; you could see it was.

Micke, skinny in a baggy wool bathing suit that came to his knees and elbows, was hopping up and down with excitement.

"Can we go in the water now? Can we?"

"Papa will take you," said Ruth. "Stay close to him, and don't splash your sister."

Per reached down and took Teddy's hand. Teddy smiled up at him, then said, "You coming, Mama?"

"In a minute," I said. "You go with Per but stay in the shallow water."

I wanted to grab him and hold him tight, but instead I forced a smile as the four of them threaded their way down to the water's edge.

"That water looks cold," said Anna as the three children squealed at their first steps into the sea.

"It'll be refreshing," said Ruth, leaning back on her elbows and lifting her face to the sun. "I'm going to get properly hot, and then I'll go in."

I watched the three children splash about in the shallows. They'd started a game, badgering Per to pick them up by their hands and sweep them through the waves. When it came to Teddy's turn, he threw back his head and laughed as his legs splashed into the water and up and out again. Per had become like a father to him, and he didn't know any different, but one day he would feel the lack of a father of his own. Perhaps, in time, I should think about marrying again, for his sake, though I still couldn't imagine wanting to for mine.

"Shall we go in, then?" said Ruth, sitting up.

"I don't know . . . It does look cold."

It was ridiculous, to be afraid of walking into the sea where so many people were frolicking quite happily. But I *was* afraid. It was like walking into the arms of an enemy.

Ruth stood, hands on hips, and looked down on me. "Come on, just a quick dip. You can't come to Coney Island and not go in the sea."

I stood and brushed the sand from my costume, glanced at Anna. She nodded, just slightly.

You are a strong young woman; you don't run from things that frighten you.

"Right," I said. "Let's go."

Ruth went in front of me, one hand lightly on the rope, squealing and laughing as the waves lapped at her legs. The water was so cold, even on this hot, sunny day. How much colder must it have been that night? All those people, floating in the icy sea, waiting to die. I tried to shut out the thoughts and listen to the sounds around me, the splashing and the laughing and the music drifting down from the street, but the cries in the darkness were there behind it all.

My legs were trembling, but I couldn't turn back and let Teddy see me afraid. Gritting my teeth, with my eyes half closed, I gripped the rope and took tiny steps, half forward, half sideways. When the water reached my knees, I had to stand still for a moment, clenching my toes in the soft sand to keep my balance against the waves rolling in.

Not like that night, when the sea was so calm and still. There hadn't been a breath of wind, just that biting chill in the air. No wonder we thought there was no danger. All those people standing around on deck with their drinks and their cigarettes, like it was a cocktail party, when the ship was already slipping down into the ocean.

Like a film playing in my head, I could see it all again.

The cabin lights at the front meeting their reflections in the water.

The people still up on deck, when it was too late.

That green velvet chair from the first-class lounge drifting in the sea, only hours after someone must have sat in it, sipping champagne.

When had they realized, my father and Frederick and Terence, that there wouldn't be any lifeboats left for the men? Had they stayed on till the last, or jumped? And Molly, trapped in those endless corridors below deck, seeing the water rising, she must have been so frightened . . .

A wave splashed my thighs; I whimpered and opened my eyes just as Ruth turned round, laughing. She saw my face and her smile faded.

"What's the matter?" She clapped a hand to her mouth. "Oh, Molly, I should have thought! Let's get out."

I shook my head. "No, I'm all right." I lifted my eyes and looked ahead. "I'm going to get to the first barrel, so Teddy can see I'm not afraid. Even though I am."

She let go of the rope, came and stood beside me. "Hold my hand, then, and we'll do it together."

I grasped her hand, fixed my eyes on the barrel, and slowly we out into the waves. All the way, Ruth chattered on, just quietly, talking about how she'd always wanted to go to the seaside at home, and then one day they'd gone, but it was freezing cold even though it was July, and wasn't it much nicer when it was properly hot? I listened to her so I wouldn't think about that night, and I looked straight ahead, watching the sunlight dancing on the water like sequins. One foot in front of the other, her supporting me and me supporting her when a wave made us wobble. And then we were there, standing beside the red and yellow barrel, the water edging up to our thighs. I didn't like it, not one bit. But I'd done it.

She squeezed my hand. "Well done. Now let's go and dry off in the sun." She plucked at the skirt of her costume, wrinkling her nose. "Though I reckon these will still be wet next Wednesday."

* * *

We stayed for the fireworks at Luna Park, so it was late by the time we got on the train, and within ten minutes, I was the only one not asleep. Per and Ruth sat opposite me, her head on his shoulder, the children on either side. Teddy had his head in my lap, and Anna was beside us, her chin every now and then dropping to her chest and jerking her half-awake for a second before she settled back in to sleep with a grunt. Hard to believe that when we were on the ship, these people had been nothing more than names to me, and this life as strange a prospect as walking on the moon. As the train rattled back to Manhattan and I began to drift into a doze myself, I thought how lucky we'd been to get our second chance.

That was the last hot Sunday of the year. Autumn descended suddenly and then slid into winter. New York's bitter cold came as a shock, but Anna, who'd grown up with Sweden's snowy winters, taught me how to stay warm—"Tuck every-thing into everything else and leave no gaps"—and lent me a big fur hat she'd brought with her from home. It made me look like I was going out to hunt bears, but it kept me warm, along with the hot chicken soup Della and I took turns to fetch from the Jewish deli on the corner of Grand Street.

We celebrated Christmas the Swedish way. Anna cooked a spiced ham that filled the apartment with the warm smells of cinnamon and cloves, and Per brought home a little tree. On Christmas Eve we danced round it, holding hands, Anna laughing till she cried at my attempts to get my tongue round the traditional Swedish songs.

In the spring, the memorial lighthouse, the one funded by schoolchildren's pocket money and rich people's checks, was dedicated, on the anniversary of the sinking. Ruth asked if I wanted to go to the service, and offered to come with me if I did, but I said no and she didn't question it. That night, I sat out on the fire escape and let myself hear the voices again, so

Tommy wouldn't be alone with them. I hoped he was in Nebraska by then, far from the sea, with people who didn't know he'd ever been anywhere near the *Titanic*.

With each season that passed, my old life slipped further away, and with it, my fear of being discovered. It's a funny thing, pretending to be somebody else; it becomes easier and easier, until one day, you almost forget you're doing it. It wasn't that I'd become Molly Mortimer, exactly—how could I, when I barely knew her? But I wasn't helpless Elinor Coombes who couldn't peel a potato anymore, and I certainly wasn't the meek little wife that Winterton Hall had turned me into. I was what Molly had wanted to be: a New Yorker, earning my own living and working toward a good future for myself and my son. Now, when someone said "Molly," I answered automatically, no longer having to remember that they meant me.

By the time I'd been in New York for two years, I'd long since pushed from my mind the thought of what Ruth, Anna, and Per would think if they found out the truth about me. There was no reason, now, to think they ever would. My old life seemed so far behind me that when I saw Lissy again, it was like seeing a ghost.

CHAPTER 50

It was a bright, sunny spring afternoon, and I'd taken the El train up to Sixth Avenue to have a look at the new stock in Bloomingdales and Macy's. Ruth and I had been doing a good trade in braid trims and we were hoping something similar would be in style for summer. I stopped to look in Macy's windows—lots of bright, fresh colors; they'd catch the eye nicely on the carts—when right behind me, a cab pulled up.

The door opened, and I heard a familiar voice say, "Thank you, driver, this will do nicely."

It couldn't be. And yet I knew it was. The voice was so familiar, light and silvery, as though she was on the point of laughing. I stood there, frozen to the spot. Reflected in the gleaming glass window, Lissy stepped out of the cab, followed by her American mother-in-law. Lady Harcourt had often said, after Lissy and I had been shopping together in London, "One day I'll show you the shops in New York. They knock Harrods and Selfridges into a cocked hat." And now here I was, standing outside Macy's when she was doing exactly that.

I had to get away. I was about to turn and head off in the

opposite direction but as Lady Harcourt paid the cab driver, Lissy strolled over to look at the store window. I honestly thought my heart would stop. She was no more than two feet from me, chic as ever in toffee-colored wool with a matching hat. So close I could smell the perfume she always wore, the scent of roses in full bloom.

Her gaze was fixed on a mannequin in the window wearing a buttercup-yellow spring coat—it would have suited her perfectly, but then, almost everything did—and I was afraid to move in case I attracted her attention. I turned my face away and looked down at the feet of the mannequin in front of me, so she couldn't see my face reflected. Stood completely still, my eyes on the mannequin's shoes. Hardly daring even to breathe, willing Lady Harcourt to finish paying the cab driver so they'd go inside. I knew Lissy—when we went shopping in London, she'd quite often strike up a conversation with a doorman, or a shop assistant, or another customer, just, I think, to see the effect of her charm on them. I could see it—she'd turn, with that wide, open smile, the one I used to trust, and say, "Isn't that a lovely coat?" or, "So much to choose from!" Her big blue eyes would widen, she'd say "Elinor?" and I'd be done for.

We stood there, side by side, for what can only have been a minute or two, but felt like an age. And then, at last, Lady Harcourt said, "Right, shall we see if we can find that new hat for you?"

Lissy turned to answer, and I took my chance and walked away in the opposite direction. The street was busy with shoppers, and I wanted so badly to run, run, run, and get away from that place as fast as I could. But I forced myself to stroll as casually as everyone else, weaving my way through the gaggles of women laden with bags and parcels, and slowing my breathing to calm myself down and stop my heart pounding. It was such a shock, seeing her, that I almost couldn't believe it

had happened. I wouldn't have been at all surprised to find myself waking up from a dream.

I got safely to the corner, a hundred yards away, and then I
did one of the stupidest things I've ever done in my life. I
turned and glanced back. Lissy and Lady Harcourt must have
stood looking at the window a bit longer; they were only just
going into the store. And at that very second, Lissy turned to
her left. At almost any other time, I'm certain, two people
standing a hundred yards apart wouldn't have spotted each
other through the crowd, but nevertheless, our eyes met. I
turned away instantly, ducked into the side street and then ran.
Not caring who stared, not daring to look back, I didn't stop
till I got to the El station and took the stairs two at a time up
to the platform, where a train was just coming in.

Faces turned to stare as I flopped into a seat, my face hot
and my breath ragged. The conductor was just poised to shut
the gate on the train when there was a shout of "Wait!" from
the direction of the stairs. Had she run after me?

Shut the gate. Please, shut the gate.

Usually the conductors were impatient to set off, and I always suspected they enjoyed slamming the gate closed just
when a passenger got to the platform. But this one was in no
rush—he was busy eyeing a pretty blonde sitting at the end of
the carriage. He called out, "Hurry along there, lady!" but he
still didn't close the gate.

In panic I stood, but I couldn't get off without running
straight into her. The carriage was half empty. There was nowhere to hide. If she got on the train now, I was trapped. My
heart was pounding so hard I thought it must be audible, and
by the looks on the faces of the other passengers, I must have
looked like a crazy woman, poised to run, but with nowhere
to go.

The top of a head appeared on the stairs, then a face. I

slumped into a seat, head in my hands. It wasn't her. A plump woman carrying a suitcase struggled over to the train and got on; the conductor gave the blonde a "See how helpful I am?" look, and then at last he shut the gate and we rattled out of the station.

The train picked up speed, and I turned my hot face to the open window, not even caring about the smuts that blew in. It wasn't her. She hadn't chased me. She hadn't recognized me; she couldn't have done. In the cool of the breeze, I could breathe again, and I began to calm down. The shock of seeing her had made me panic, but she could only have caught a split-second glimpse of me. And the woman she saw wasn't Elinor Coombes, in an outfit that cost hundreds of guineas, with her hair done three times a day by a maid. It was Molly Mortimer, in a homemade shirtwaist and her only good skirt, her hair pinned up in two minutes flat and then forgotten about.

A memory of the day I arrived flashed through my mind: Ruth looking at me and seeing a resemblance to Molly's mother that couldn't possibly be there. We see what we expect to see, and there was no way on earth that Lissy was expecting to see me. So it might have struck her for a second that Molly Mortimer looked like Elinor Coombes, but no more than that. If she'd even registered my face at all, she'd have forgotten it already.

The El track threaded through the narrow streets back down to the Lower East Side, passing so close to tenement buildings like ours that you could look right into the windows of the front apartments and get little glimpses of people's lives: a couple arguing, a mother cooking dinner, a man making faces at himself as he shaved in front of a mirror. It always reminded me of a dolls' house I used to have as a girl, but the tiny, exquisitely made furniture in that dolls' house was more expensive than anything in those apartments, or ours. What would Lissy think, if she knew I'd chosen this life over one like hers? She'd never understand why I'd done it, that was for certain. The way of life that I'd hated so much was entirely natural to her, just as it was for Frederick.

I didn't want to think about what she'd have done if she had seen me. There'd be no question in her mind about where Teddy belonged, would there?

Families like ours are the backbone of this country, and we've a responsibility to future generations to keep the line going.

CHAPTER 51

The next day was Sunday, and we went to the bathhouse as usual, but I couldn't enjoy my precious twenty minutes of hot water and privacy. I'd tried hard to push the encounter with Lissy out of my mind, but as I lay there in the tub my thoughts kept straying back to that moment when I turned back and looked into her eyes. Over and over, I told myself she couldn't have known me. It had been so quick. And yet, when I pictured that moment again in my mind, could I be absolutely certain there wasn't a flicker of recognition there?

It was a huge leap for her to suspect the truth, but it wasn't impossible. Lord and Lady Storton wouldn't want me back, after what I'd done, but they'd want Teddy, the heir. And the law was on their side. They'd carry him back to England to bring him up as the next Lord Storton, and I'd never see him again.

How could they find us though? Hundreds of women must walk along Sixth Avenue every day, and they could come from anywhere in the city. Or even outside it: there were trains into Grand Central from all over the place. They wouldn't know where to start looking. But even as I told myself that, a chill ran down my spine. They didn't need to know where to start, did they? They wouldn't be doing the searching; their money would.

They wouldn't go to the police—the whole thing would end up in the papers then, and there'd be a scandal. But you could get private investigators to find people, I'd read about one in the newspaper just the other day. A private investigator would know the city, and it wouldn't take them long to work out that the Lower East Side might be where I'd gone. It was where everyone went who came to New York with no money and needed a job and a place to live. And even if it was teeming with people, as an Englishwoman I stood out more than most; how often had customers buying from the cart commented on my accent? And oh God, what had I been thinking of, bringing Teddy out with me so often? All they had to do was go to Grand Street and ask after an Englishwoman with a young son, and someone would know exactly who they meant.

I jumped at the rap on the door.

"Time's up," yelled the attendant. "Out you come."

As I rubbed myself dry with the bathhouse's rough towel, I couldn't stop wondering what Lissy was doing now. And wondering how long it would take, if a person wanted to send a telegram from America to England.

That night, for the first time in ages, I dreamed about the *Titanic*, but this time, the crew were telling people to get in the lifeboats, and I couldn't find Teddy. Someone had taken him, and I didn't know who. I woke up sweating, and even though I managed to get back to sleep, in the morning the dream came back to me, and I couldn't shake off a feeling of dread.

I took the cart out as usual, but I didn't take Teddy. I bribed him with the promise of doughnuts later and told Anna he seemed to be coming down with a cold and would be better staying at home. She didn't question it, and he was happily playing with his cars when I left.

* * *

The customers on Grand Street were always a mixture. Some you saw most days, others only occasionally, and because every ship brought new people, there were always unfamiliar faces too. I could spot a greenhorn by then: if they didn't give themselves away with their homespun, un-American clothes, their wide-eyed astonishment at the sights and sounds of Grand Street did it for them. But as that morning wore on, I found myself searching the crowds for a different sort of unfamiliar face, one who did know their way around, one who looked as though they were searching for someone. I kept telling myself it was ridiculous, that no one was coming after me, but I couldn't get that moment when my eyes met Lissy's out of my head.

Hearing Della yell out her wares to passing customers, it struck me just how much her English accent stood out among all the others that made up the hubbub of the street. Mine must too: I couldn't bring myself to shout out like I usually did, and I had to bite my lip to stop myself asking her not to.

The afternoon turned sunny, bringing out a crowd, and making it harder to spot a face that didn't belong. I got more and more tense and anxious, and by about five, I had such a raging headache that I packed up early to go home. I dropped off the cart at the shed, and then even though there was no sign of anyone suspicious, I walked ten blocks out of my way. With every step, I told myself I was being daft, but I still looked over my shoulder every few minutes until I was absolutely certain there was no one following me home.

By the time I reached our building, I was exhausted. As I plodded up the stairs, all I wanted was to get inside, shut the door behind me, and then pick Teddy up and hold him tight. But when I opened the door, the apartment was empty. Teddy's bricks lay on the floor, as though he'd been torn away in the middle of playing with them. Where was he? I threw open both bedroom doors: empty.

Had they come? Had they taken him? For a second I couldn't breathe, and then I ran across the hall and bashed on Giovanna's door. She opened it, her eyes startled.

"Molly! What's the matter?"

"Did anyone come here today? Did you see anyone go to our apartment?"

"No, why—"

"Teddy's gone. He's not there." Panic made my voice shrill. She touched my arm. "Isn't he with Ruth?"

"I don't know, she's not there either! None of them are!"

She looked at me as though I was completely mad. "Well, then, that's where he must be. With them, surely?"

I must have stared at her blankly for a moment, and then just as I took her words in, footsteps came bounding up the stairs.

"Mama, we had ice cream!"

I turned and there he was, his little face smeared with the pink of his favorite flavor, strawberry. There they all were, Ruth, Micke, and Lena, Anna half a dozen steps behind, grimacing as she bent her bad knee.

I wanted so badly to pick him up and feel that he was really there, he was really safe, but I couldn't let them know how scared I'd been. I forced a laugh and said, "There you are! I thought you'd all gone back to Coney Island and flown to the moon."

I was hoping Ruth hadn't heard my panicked conversation with Giovanna, but her puzzled face told me she had.

"Are you all right?" she said. "You sounded worried."

"No, I just came home early because I had a headache, and then I wondered where you all were, that's all."

"Bunch of new office girls started across the way this week, and they bought practically everything I had on the cart today," she said. "So I thought I'd finish early and take the children out for a treat. Teddy seemed fine. I don't think he has a cold after all, so . . ."

I faked a smile. "Nothing ice cream wouldn't fix, anyway." I held out my hand to him. "Come on, let's get in and wipe your mucky face."

That evening, I saw Lissy again. Not in the flesh, thank goodness, but in the pages of the newspaper Per brought home. I was flicking through it while Anna was cooking dinner and Ruth was telling us about Eileen downstairs having problems with her husband, when I turned a page and there she was, smiling out from a photograph.

"What's the matter?" asked Ruth, and it was only then that I realized I'd gasped.

She leaned over and looked at the page. "Who's that?"

I said the first thing that came into my head.

"Just someone Mrs. Fieldwood used to know—you know, the lady I worked for in London. I was surprised to see her, that's all."

"Nice hat. Anyway, I said to Eileen . . ."

As soon as everyone was in bed, I opened the paper again. The photo of Lissy was with a story about a new hotel, the Biltmore, which had just opened up. Hers was one of half a dozen photos of some of its first guests. The caption underneath said that Lady Rosemary Harcourt was in town from England with her daughter-in-law, and would attend a ball at the British Embassy on Tuesday, before returning home on the *Mauretania*.

Lissy was smiling into the camera, as beautiful as ever. She looked happy, carefree even. No one would ever have guessed the man she'd loved all her life had been dead only a little under two years. But then that was Lissy, wasn't it? You never could trust what you saw in that face.

* * *

I'd have liked to hide indoors until the *Mauretania* took Lissy back across the ocean, but if anyone was looking for me, I needed to know. All the same, I asked Anna if Teddy could stay at home with her for a week or so, making an excuse about him having a cough. She didn't mind; they were so fond of each other, those two, and he was always well behaved with his adopted grandmother.

Grand Street was even busier the next day, and the warm weather brought me plenty of business: everyone likes to refresh their wardrobe a little when spring comes. There was a craze just then for hats with big feathery plumes, and I'd got hold of some feathers in lovely pastel colors. They were a bit battered because the box had been dropped, so the stores wouldn't take them, but perfectly fine if you bunched a few together—and at five cents to make a hat look brand new, they were so popular, Ruth had joked that we should tip the factory's delivery boy a nickel to drop another couple of boxes. I had remnants of a pretty sprigged cotton too, and some new lace, perfect for collars and cuffs, which always did well. So there was a steady stream of customers, and they all went away with bargains because all I could concentrate on was looking through the crowds for a stranger's face.

I was just packing up, relieved to be going home, when Della called across, "Molly, your surname's Morton, isn't it?"

"No, Mortimer."

Why was she asking that?

"That's it, knew it began with an M."

She came over, a little parcel of cheese in her hand. "Here, take this home for Teddy. I've only a scrap left and it's his favorite. No, I was just asking because there was a man in the chicken store by the El station, asking if anyone knew an English woman with a little boy. But he said her name was Coombes."

CHAPTER 52

It was all I could do not to abandon the cart and run home, but if I'd done that, it'd have been the talk of Orchard Street, and that man, when he came, as he surely would, would discover instantly that he'd found who he was looking for. So I finished packing up as quickly as I could, took the cart to the shed, and then hurried home. And all the way, I was thinking, *This can't be happening. But it is.*

Lissy had recognized me; she must have done. Perhaps sailing across the ocean meant I was on her mind, so when she saw me, there wasn't such a great leap to make. Perhaps I just didn't look as different as I imagined. Whatever the reason, it had happened. She must have sent a telegram to Winterton Hall, and the fears I'd told myself were ridiculous had come true. There was a private investigator looking for me, and he wasn't far away.

Why had I convinced myself she couldn't have recognized me? If I'd been more cautious, I'd have given myself time to think, but now there wasn't any time at all. It was only luck that their detective hadn't started his search on Grand Street, but sooner or later, he'd go there. Perhaps even as soon as to-morrow.

By the time I got home, I was in a complete panic, my head spinning. As I got to the third floor, Anna's sewing machine was rattling away. I needed to think clearly, to decide what to do, so I carried on up the stairs and went out onto the roof. I stood by the low wall that surrounded it, taking deep breaths to try to calm myself down. The private investigator had obviously figured out quite quickly that a woman with no money, wanting to disappear, might end up here on the Lower East Side, where it was easy to find work and accommodation. They couldn't know the name I was using—in the lists of the dead and the survivors, Molly would still have been down as a third-class passenger, so no one could possibly know we were even acquainted, much less suspect I'd taken her name. And no one in New York would know me as Elinor Coombes. But if the detective asked on Grand Street about an Englishwoman with a little boy, he'd soon know that the person Lissy had seen was me, and I wasn't far away.

There was only one thing I could do. I had to take Teddy and run. Disappear to some other corner of America, where they'd have no reason to suspect we might be. America was a big place; they couldn't search all of it, could they? I'd put by some savings since paying off Tommy Jenkins, enough to get us a place to stay while I looked for some way to support us. Work in a shop perhaps, or a factory. I wasn't Elinor Coombes with no skills anymore; I could talk my way into something, if I had to.

But the thought of starting all over again, and this time knowing no one, was terrifying. From up there on the roof, I could see the places that had been our life, these past two years. The corner of Grand Street, and the deli where Della and I got the chicken soup that kept us warm through the winter days. The bathhouse where we went on Sundays, and the gap between buildings that was Seward Park, where the children played. The roof of the library, where I'd found my old friends again in the pages of its books. This place that I'd found so strange at first was my home now, and I didn't want to leave it, or the life we'd built here. But most of all, I didn't want to leave the people I thought of as our family.

It was only then that it dawned on me. I wasn't just going to have to leave them, I was going to have to tell them I'd been lying to them all along. We couldn't just disappear—how could I do that to them, leave them wondering where we were and why we'd gone?

No, if we were going to go, I'd have to tell them why. And there was no explanation I could give other than the truth, that I wasn't who they thought I was. I'd let them take us in when we had nothing, let them share what little they had, and now I'd have to tell them what we could have gone home to. I was going to have to tell them that I'd lied and lied to them, and that poor Molly was dead and I'd stolen her life.

CHAPTER 53

Per was just hanging up his coat as I walked in; he must have arrived home just before I came down from the roof. Ruth and Lena were looking through the latest magazine Erin had brought up, and Teddy and Micke were building yet another complicated-looking bridge in the bedroom. Anna had just started the dinner: minced pork and onions were sizzling in the pan, and she was peeling the leaves off a crinkly green cabbage. I'd seen her cook stuffed cabbage so many times, and now this would be the last.

I stood in the doorway for a moment, and looked at the apartment, remembering what I'd seen that very first time. How tiny it was, and how it couldn't be possible for five people to share it, let alone seven. I didn't know then that the picture on the wall, with the calm blue lake, was of the place where Anna was born, or that the embroidered tablecloth was her wedding gift to Ruth and Per. I didn't know that Per had made the wooden trunk himself when they knew Molly was coming, or that they'd used money they'd saved to buy the featherbed inside it, that I'd eventually get used to sinking into gladly after a day's work. I didn't know I would come to love this place and the people in it.

I didn't want to tell my sorry story in front of the children; I'd wait until they'd gone to bed. Have one last dinner round that little wooden table as Molly, so I could remember it when we were far away, and on our own. Then I'd tell them, and we'd go tomorrow, take whatever train would get us farthest away from New York without too much of a toll on my savings. If they didn't throw us out now, tonight.

I looked round the table, trying to print it all on my mind: Micke teasing Teddy that he'd never be able to eat all his cabbage, Lena telling us she'd seen Erin going off to a dance, and describing her outfit in minute detail, Per praising the dinner—stuffed cabbage was his favorite—and Anna saying, "Well, I do my best, but they don't know how to rear pigs in America. In Sweden the pork was always tastier."

Ruth threw me her here-we-go-again look, and it hit me like a kick in the stomach that it was the last time she'd do that. By the end of this evening, our friendship would be over, and I could hardly bear to imagine what she'd think of me. I'd lied to all of them, but my lies to her were the worst of all. With the others, yes, I'd said I was Molly, and when necessary I'd told lies to explain why I couldn't slice a potato and I'd never used a sewing machine. But I'd sat at this table with Ruth, and I'd talked about Molly's mother, who she'd loved, as though I knew her. I'd told her an entire story about who Teddy's father was, and if what I'd said about my feelings for him was actually true of his real father, well, I didn't think she'd see it that way. And I couldn't blame her. I knew what it was like to be deceived by a friend.

I looked across at Teddy. Micke had buttered a piece of bread for him, and he smiled as he took a big bite. Lady Storton would say that was eating like a starving urchin, wouldn't she? Well, she wasn't going to get the chance to. I wasn't going to let them find him, and if that meant I had to leave all this, then I'd do it, even though I wished with all my heart we could stay.

All too soon, dinner was over. The children went off to bed, Ruth took the dishes and pots out to the sink in the hallway, and I followed with the pan of water that had been simmering on the stove. She washed and I dried, as always, and as she handed me the last of the pots, she sighed and said, "Won't it be nice when we get a place with running water? We won't know ourselves."

When I didn't answer—I couldn't—she looked up from the sink.

"You're very quiet this evening. Are you all right?"

At that moment, I'd have given a lifetime without running water to say, "Yes, I'm fine." But the time for lying was over.

"Not really," I said. "Let's go back in. There's something I need to tell you."

Anna was just putting the coffee pot on the stove as we came back into the apartment.

"Shall we play Kille?" she said. "Per, get the cards."

"Not now, Mama," said Ruth. "Molly has something she wants to tell us."

"This sounds very serious," said Per.

"It is," I said.

Ruth sat down beside Per; Anna and I opposite them.

Ruth reached over and touched my arm. "Molly, what's the matter? You look like someone's died."

I hadn't known how to start the story, but there it was.

"Well, someone has," I said. "Molly died."

CHAPTER 54

They looked at me, puzzled, and there was nothing to do but say it.

"I'm not Molly Mortimer. My name is Elinor Coombes."

Ruth and Per exchanged puzzled glances.

"What?" she said. "What do you mean, you're not Molly?"

"I'm sorry," I said. "Molly . . . she didn't survive."

"What are you talking about? Of course you survived, you're here."

"I'm here, but I'm not Molly. I took her name, so I could get off the ship without anyone knowing I was alive."

She looked at me as though I was mad. "This is ridiculous. What's got into you? Are you ill?"

"I think," I said, "I should start at the beginning."

If I hadn't been so worried that they'd hate me, their faces as I told my story would have been comical. There was disbelief in their eyes when I said how rich my father was, and when I said Frederick's father was the Earl of Storton, Ruth shook her head.

"I'm sorry, this is just crazy, it's—"

Anna stopped her with a raised finger. "Let her tell her story."

I told them, as briefly as I could, the story of my marriage: how unhappy I was at Winterton Hall, how I hated the life they insisted on for Teddy. Every so often, Per would shake his head, and in Ruth's eyes there was just shock and bewilderment, but they all believed me now, I could see it. But how ungrateful I must sound, talking about a life wealthier than they could even dream of. The millionaire's daughter who didn't get the happy ending she'd read about in books.

I was telling them about meeting Molly on the dock, when Anna got up and went to the stove. I stopped talking, but she waved a hand.

"Go on with your story. We don't need to add burnt coffee to the drama."

As I told them about Molly being pregnant, and how hopeful she was about a new life for her and her baby, tears prickled my eyes. I didn't want them to think I expected sympathy, so I fixed my eyes on Anna as she poured the coffee and blinked to keep the tears back.

Per said to Ruth, "Did you know she was expecting a baby?"

"No, she never said."

I told them why, that Molly hadn't been sure they'd want her to come if they knew.

"Of course we would!" said Ruth. "I wish she'd known that."

She traced a circle on the table with her finger, then looked at me, cold-eyed. "So how did it happen that she didn't survive?"

I told them then about that last night on the *Titanic*, and Molly going back to the cabin to get her savings.

"I know this is hard to believe but, at that time, nobody thought we were in danger. And my husband promised he'd see she got into a lifeboat. If I'd thought there was any chance of her not getting off the ship, I'd never have let her go back."

"What do you think happened to her?" asked Per.

So many times, in the quiet of the night, I'd wondered that.

"I can only think she must have got lost trying to get to the cabin or trying to get back up to the deck. The ship was so big, it was easy to lose your way at the best of times. And it sank so quickly . . ."

I stopped, seeing it again in my mind, unsure whether to share that horrible picture. Ruth was crying silently by then, and I didn't want to upset her more. But I wanted to be honest with them, not to tell any more lies.

"On the ship, we couldn't tell how fast it was happening. There was an awful noise from the funnels, but otherwise, everything seemed normal. People were still standing around drinking; there was music playing. But as the lifeboat was rowed away, I turned back and the front of the ship was already sliding under the water. So I think the lower decks, where the cabins were, must have been flooded even then, and she took a wrong turn and was trapped."

I looked at Ruth. Tears were coursing down her face now, and Per took her hand.

"I'm sorry," I said. "I know she would have had a good life here with you."

"But you had it instead. So, go on . . . what did you say your real name was?"

"Elinor."

"So go on, *Elinor.*" She said my name as though it was poison in her mouth. "When did you decide that you would come here and pretend to be Molly?"

This would be the hardest part to explain. I still found it unbelievable myself.

"It was because of what I'd seen."

And what I'd heard. But I couldn't bring myself to describe those awful screams in the night.

"In that cabin, on the *Carpathia*, I thought of all the people on the ship, who were coming here, like Molly was, for a new life. They couldn't have that life, she couldn't have that life, and there was nothing I could do about that. But us surviving, it was like a second chance, for me and Teddy, and I couldn't waste it. I'm not saying this to give myself an excuse. I did wrong, lying to you, taking Molly's place. But that's why I did it."

There was silence around the table. Ruth was staring down at her hands, but then she raised her head and it was as though she was looking at someone she'd never seen before.

"How do we even know this story is true? Because to me it sounds ridiculous! Lord and Lady—what did you call them, Stornton? And your father a millionaire? It's like a ten-cent novel. It's nonsense."

I was about to remind them about the photograph in the newspaper, the day after I arrived, but then Anna said, "Of course it's true. Don't you remember her hands when she came here? Soft and white. Strange for a servant's hands, ladies' maid or no."

I should have known those shrewd blue eyes had seen more than she let on.

"She couldn't even slice a potato. You didn't see it, but I did."

Ruth's mouth dropped open. Both she and Per stared at Anna.

"You suspected her all along?" said Ruth. "But you didn't think to say anything to us?"

"She was a young woman with a child, in a foreign land, like I was when we came from Sweden. And her journey here was a terrifying one. Would you have turned her out into the street?"

"No, but—"

"Well then."

"That's not the point! We had a stranger here and we didn't even know. What were you thinking?"

"Molly was also a stranger," said Anna.

"She was family!"

"All the same, we didn't know her. So I would have watched her, to see what kind of person she was. And I watched . . . this one." She waved a hand at me. "She wasn't stealing from us; she worked hard and paid her way from the start. So, tell me, where was the harm in letting her stay?"

"She lied to us!"

Anna shrugged. "I believed she must have a good reason for that, and now we know she did."

Ruth threw up her hands. "How can you defend her?" She turned to me. "I can't believe how you sat here and told me lie after lie. Were you laughing at us, for being taken in so easily?"

"No, of course not, I—"

Per held up a hand to interrupt me. "What I'm wondering is, why are you telling us this now?"

"Because we have to leave New York. And I couldn't go without being honest with you. You were so kind to us when we had nothing. I know you only did it because you thought I was Molly. But you feel like our family now, and I can't tell you how many times I've wished you were."

Ruth gave a tight little laugh. "Feel like your family? We don't even know you."

Per said, "Let her explain. What do you mean, you have to leave?"

I told them about seeing Lissy and about the private detective asking after me.

"I didn't think she'd recognized me, but she must have. And now my husband's dead, they're legally Teddy's guardians. They made the arrangements when Teddy was a baby. And if they find us, they'll take him from me."

"But you're his mother," said Anna.

"It doesn't make any difference. They've got the law on their side, and they'll use it. Teddy's the heir to the estate and the title, and that means more to them than anything. So we have to go. We've got no choice."

Per frowned. "Where would you go?"

"I haven't had time to think about it. But somewhere far away, where they won't think to look for us. If you'll just let us stay tonight, we'll go tomorrow, take the first train we can get."

Anna shook her head. "Go where you'll know no one? This is a crazy idea."

"Do you have a better idea, Mama?" snapped Ruth. "Because she can't stay here, not now."

Up until then, I'd kept alive a tiny, tiny hope that Ruth might forgive me. But it died then. Of course she wouldn't, and I didn't deserve for her to.

"If you have to go," said Anna, "you must go to Minnesota, to the Anderssons."

"She can go where she likes," said Ruth. "It's nothing to do with us, and we've no reason to help."

Per put his hand on hers. "I know you're angry. I am too. But we can't just abandon a woman with a child." He turned to me. "You should have been straight with us, a long time ago. I can't believe how you lied and lied. Even to the children! But what's done is done. The Anderssons are the family we came over from Sweden with—Mama's right, if they'll take you, you should go to them."

"I'll write to them, ask them to help you find somewhere to live, and some work," said Anna. "And no one will think to look for you in a little town full of Swedes."

I shook my head. "I think it's better if I go tomorrow. I should have told you all the truth long ago and gone then."

Ruth slapped her hand on the table, making us all jump.

"Yes, you should have! But Per's right, you can't just take off into nowhere, on your own." She rubbed her eyes, wiping away the last of the tears. "We'll hide you here, until we know you have somewhere to go."

"Thank you," I said. "I know I've—"

"Oh, don't thank me, *Elinor*. This isn't for you. It's for Teddy, who's innocent in all this, and doesn't deserve to be out on the streets because his mother is a liar and a fraud. So you can stay till we hear from the Anderssons. And then you can leave and never come back."

CHAPTER 55

I was already awake when Per tiptoed out to work the next morning, but I pretended to be asleep, ashamed to face him. He'd said nothing more the night before, but he didn't need to. He was disgusted with me, and why wouldn't he be?

We'd agreed to say nothing to the children about what was happening, so breakfast was a peculiar affair—the three of them chattering on as usual, the three of us barely speaking at all. Ruth wouldn't even look at me; from the minute she got up, she'd acted as though I wasn't there. But when I started gathering up the breakfast dishes to take them out to the sink, she said, "This place must look like a hovel to you."

What could I say to that? I took a deep breath.

"I promised I wouldn't lie to you again, and I won't. It was a shock, when I first got here, how small the apartment was and, well, the outhouse. But I could see that you'd made it a home. And I don't suppose you'll believe me, but I've felt more at home here than I ever did at Winterton Hall."

She turned away from me, muttering "Winterton Hall" as if it were the most ridiculous thing she'd ever heard, and

snapped at Micke and Lena to hurry up and not be late for
school.

When they'd gone, Anna sat down to write to the Anderssons, saying I was a friend who needed a refuge from some
family problems.

"You can decide for yourself what to tell them when you get
there," she said.

"I'll tell them the truth," I said. "I owe them that."

"You owed *us* that," said Ruth as she took her coat down
from the hook behind the door. "But you still lied."

"Ruth," said Anna. "She's said sorry. What more can she
do?"

"Well, words come easily to her, don't they?" She looked at
me. "Why should we believe you're sorry when we can't trust
a word that's come out of your mouth since the day we met you?
How do we know you're even telling the truth about Molly? For
all we know, you sent her back to your cabin to fetch . . . I don't
know, your diamonds. Or your money. And it's your fault she
died!"

Anna laid her hand on Ruth's arm. "I don't believe she lied
about that. And you don't either. You're angry and you're saying things you don't mean."

"I swear," I said. "I would never have got into the lifeboat if
I'd thought Molly was going to be left behind."

Ruth looked me in the eye. "Well, we'll never know, will
we?"

She left and slammed the door.

Anna took the letter to be posted and came back saying it
would take two days to get there, and at least two days for the
reply to come.

"We can't stay here for four days," I said.

"Ruth will calm down. In time."

"She's got every right not to. You all have."

"Well, you already know my point of view. I don't say it was a good thing you did, but you were in a desperate situation. But it's different for me than for them. Molly was just a name to me, but she was much more to Ruth. And when you hurt Ruth, you hurt Per. So it's hard for them." She shrugged. "It's not going to be a pleasant four days. But you don't have a choice, if this detective is out there looking, do you? So let us keep you safe until then."

As Anna sat at her machine and started stitching, Teddy was already grizzling and grousing about not being able to go out. I managed to settle him with a picture book, but I couldn't just sit there, so I swept the floor, polished the stove, and scrubbed the table. And all the time, my ears were pricked for footsteps on the stairs, and I kept going to the front window to look down at the street and check for suspicious-looking strangers. It made my skin crawl to think there was someone out there, looking for us, maybe rubbing his hands at the money he'd earn when he found us. He wouldn't know the real story; he'd have been told I was a mad woman who'd kidnapped her own child. And perhaps he wouldn't care either way, as long as he was paid.

Anna sewed all morning, just as she used to when all three of us were working for Mr. Klein: head down, no talking, just occasionally humming to herself a little. In the middle of the day, she stopped for a while, and we ate bread and cheese together.

"A long time since we used to do this every day," she said. "You were a good worker, for a woman who's had servants all her life."

"When did you know? That I wasn't Molly?"

"Your hands, like I said, I noticed straight away. But I said to myself, it can't be—why would the woman whose life gave her those hands want to come here? Then when I saw that you didn't even know how to slice a potato, I thought, yes, it's true."

"Did you never think of telling Ruth and Per?"

"No. Because I knew you must have a good reason to leave that life for this one."

When she went back to her machine, I fetched a pair of Micke's trousers that I remembered Ruth saying needed patching on the knees. Teddy put aside his book and came and watched me.

"Is Micke coming home soon?" he asked.

"Micke's at school, you know that. He'll be home later."

"Will we get the cart soon?"

"No, I told you we're not going out with the cart today. We're staying at home. Be a good boy and read your book."

He sat back down, thank goodness, and I eked out my task for as long as I could. Just as I finished it, Anna stood up, pulling a face as she stretched her back.

"Let me finish your shirtwaists," I said. "I can't sit here doing nothing."

She nodded. "All right. But take it slowly. This fabric is the devil to stitch."

She was right. It was a very slippery imitation silk, and on top of that, I was out of practice. I had to finish the first one more slowly than I used to, but I got it done. I was just about to start on the second, hoping I could finish two before Ruth got back, when Teddy came over and pawed at my leg, saying, "Mama, when is Micke coming home?"

"I told you, after school. And you know not to come near the sewing machine. Go and sit down!"

His face fell and he started to cry, but he didn't move. I gave him a little push and turned round to get started on the first seam. It was just the side seam, completely straight, very easy, so I sped up, and just as I did, Teddy's tears became a wail. I turned my head and the needle jabbed right through my fingernail, pinning my finger to the machine.

I screamed and Anna shouted, "Keep still, keep still!"

She jumped up and carefully used the wheel to lift the needle; the pain was so bad I felt sick. Teddy was bawling at the top of his voice now, frightened by my scream. And then I saw that I'd bled onto the fabric. The piece would be useless now.

The door crashed open and Ruth appeared, out of breath. "What's happened? I heard screaming—"

"Molly's had an accident," said Anna.

"I'm sorry," I said. "I'll pay for the one that's ruined."

I looked down at the hole in my fingernail as a bead of dark red blood bubbled up, and suddenly there was a rushing in my ears. I seemed to be looking through a gray tunnel and it was closing in.

"Sit down," said Ruth, pulling out a chair. "Put your head between your legs. Take deep breaths."

I did as she said, while she crouched down next to Teddy and rubbed his back, saying, "Come on, Teddy, Mama just hurt her finger. She's fine now, no need to cry. You don't want Micke to think you're a baby, do you?"

His wails subsided into sobs, and eventually to hiccups. Anna brought me a cup of water, and I sat up slowly and sipped from it.

"I'm sorry," I said again.

"You just felt faint," said Ruth briskly. "Happened to me once, when Per cut the tip of his finger off with a chisel."

"No, I mean I'm sorry about the fabric. I'll pay you whatever Mr. Klein takes from your wages."

"We'll worry about that later. Let's have a look at your finger."

She crouched in front of me and I held it out, my hand trembling.

"Nasty," she said. "But it didn't go in too far, by the looks of it."

Anna fetched the dark brown bottle of disinfectant we used on the outhouse and cleaned my finger. It stung like someone had shoved my hand into a flame, and with that coming on top of the fear and the worry, I had to bite my lip hard not to cry.

As Ruth bandaged it up with a strip of cotton from my scraps box, she said, without looking at me, "Had a bit of a slow day on the cart, and I couldn't concentrate, so I packed up and came home. When I heard you scream from downstairs, I thought someone had come for you and Teddy. Is it really true that they could just take him away from you?"

"Yes. Everything I told you yesterday is true, I swear it. I know you've got no reason to believe me, but I've got no reason to lie, not now."

She sighed. "I don't know how to think about this, Moll— It's ridiculous, I don't even know what to call you!"

"Well, she's Molly to me," said Anna. "What difference does it make what her real name is?"

"But she's not Molly, that's just it," said Ruth. "If you'd just made up a name, that would be one thing, but Molly was Mary's daughter, and she lost her mother so young. I wasn't there to take care of her then, but I thought I was taking care of her now."

She ran a hand over her hair. "And that's another thing I don't understand—how could you do this to your own mother and father?"

In my rush to tell them the story of that night, I hadn't even said that my father was there.

"My father was on the *Titanic* with us. My mother died when I was fifteen."

"So," said Anna. "You're taking care of another woman's daughter. Is that so bad?"

Ruth bit her lip. "You talked about Mary—Molly's mother—as though you knew her," she said. "How could you?"

"I didn't know, in the beginning, how close you were to Mary. Molly told me she'd never met you, so I thought you were just offering a relative a place to stay. And I didn't intend to be here long, just till we found our feet, so I thought there'd be no harm done. And then later, when I knew, I told myself that perhaps it was better that you didn't know Molly was dead."

"Oh, you were doing us a *favor*?"

She looked at me as though she hated me, and suddenly I just felt tired and beaten and it all came spilling out.

"Ruth, I'm just being honest with you. It was wrong, what I did, coming here, but I did it four days after I'd lost my father and my husband, and I'd watched a ship with more than a thousand people on it sink. I sat in a lifeboat and heard people, hundreds of people, cry out to be rescued. And then the cries faded away because those people had died knowing no one was coming for them."

I had to stop and take a breath to hold back tears, before I went on: "So if you're imagining that I sat there and coldly and calmly planned all this, you're wrong. I'd just lived through a nightmare, and I was frightened about what was ahead of me, and Teddy, if we went back. I wasn't thinking straight, and you think my old life was wonderful, but it wasn't, it was miserable and lonely, and it was going to get worse, for me and for him."

Tears were falling now; I couldn't stop them.

"I saw a chance to escape and I took it. And do you know what? If you'd been me, you might have done the same."

Ruth looked at me for a long moment. "And if this hadn't happened, that woman seeing you here, would you ever have told us the truth?"

I wiped my eyes, sniffed hard to stop the tears. "Honestly, I don't know. I wanted to, but the longer it went on, the more lies I told, the harder it was to see a way out. In the beginning, I was just afraid that if I told you, you'd throw us out and we'd have nowhere to go. But then I got to know you all, and I wasn't lying when I said you feel like my family now. So if you couldn't forgive me, I had a lot more than a roof over our heads to lose."

"I don't think I can forgive you. I'm not even sure I can forgive *you*"—she turned to Anna—"for not telling us."

Anna shrugged. "Forgiveness is for God," she said. "So you can leave that to him. Your Molly died. It's a terrible thing, but it's not this Molly's fault. She needed our help, and I'm not sorry we gave it to her. But you're right; I should have spoken up. It would have been better if you had learned the truth earlier."

"Yes, it would," said Ruth. And then, to me: "I'm not heartless. If you'd explained, right at the start, and told us the truth about Molly, of course I wouldn't have thrown you out. Per wouldn't either. For goodness' sake, we're not even throwing you out now! But every time I look at you, I'm angry. I just can't help it."

"I know. And if it was just me, I'd go now, and not put you to any more trouble. But for Teddy's sake, I can't afford to turn down your help with finding us a place to go. So perhaps we should find a cheap hotel, for the next few days."

Ruth shook her head. "Don't be ridiculous, you'll need your savings. We said we'd keep you safe till you leave New York, and we will. But don't tell me again that you think of us as your family. Every time you say that, I think of Molly. *She* was family. You're just a stranger we're sheltering, and that's all."

CHAPTER 56

Once, when I was very young, I heard a cuckoo in our garden at Cleriston. My mother was with me, and she told me all about them, how they laid their eggs in other birds' nests, and then the cuckoo chick hatched out there and demanded to be fed. She laughed when I said how horrible it must be to be a cuckoo chick and know you were where you weren't supposed to be, and nobody wanted you in the nest.

Now I was that cuckoo chick, and if it had been difficult sharing the tiny space before, that was nothing to how it was now. Because I knew how Ruth felt. After I learned about Lissy and Frederick, I went over and over conversations I'd had with her. Wondering what was going through her mind when she said the things she said, whether she was laughing at my naïveté, thinking what a gullible idiot I was to be so easily fooled. Whether there was any part of her that really was my friend and liked me for my own sake. And over the next few days, trapped there in the apartment, I'd glance up and see Ruth looking at me, and know she was asking herself the same questions. And when she spoke to me, it was exactly as she'd said, as though she were talking to a stranger. But I couldn't blame her for any of it. I just wished with all my heart that I'd had the courage to confess earlier.

The four days seemed endless, and the nights were worse; I couldn't sleep and I lay there in the dark, telling myself that no one would be out looking for us in the middle of the night, but still jumping at the slightest sound. So when the reply from the Anderssons came, I could have sobbed with relief.

I hadn't seen Anna's letter to them, but tears came to my eyes when I read theirs and realized what she must have said about me.

> *Molly and her son are welcome to stay with us while we find them somewhere of their own to live, and there are good opportunities here in Taylors Falls for a hardworking and smart young woman such as you describe. Since you say how much you'll miss her, when she's settled in, please come for a visit, Anna—it's been too long since we've seen you.*

Per went to the station to check about trains and reported back that there was one the next day with tickets that wouldn't make too big a hole in my savings. It was a slow one, but that didn't matter to me. Once we were on it, we'd be safe, and grateful as I was for the Anderssons taking us in, I wasn't going anywhere I wanted to be.

That night, I tossed and turned on my featherbed on the floor, listening to Anna's snores, with memories drifting through my head: making that first shirtwaist, when I was sure I couldn't; Mr. Klein counting my first wages into my hand; dinners eaten crammed, all seven of us, round that little table; all those conversations with Ruth when the others had gone to bed. Hot nights sleeping up on the roof, cold days out with the cart. Coney Island, the trip to the moon, and Ruth holding my hand as we waded into the water. And now it was over. Now it was just me and Teddy, starting again.

My eyes refused to close and, eventually, I got up, got myself some water and sat at the table. As I did, the door to Per and Ruth's bedroom opened, and she came out.

"Sorry," I said. "I didn't mean to wake you."

She shook her head. "I couldn't sleep either."

To my surprise, she sat down opposite me.

"All the times we sat here," she said, "and I thought you were her. I told you things I'd never told anyone else, and now I feel like such a fool."

Perhaps it was the quiet, and the darkness, with just the glow from the streetlamps spilling round the curtains, but it felt a little bit like those times, and not like the past few days when anything that came out of my mouth seemed to make things worse.

So I took a chance and said, "I told you things I'd never told anyone else too. What I said about Teddy's father, about him not loving me, about me deceiving myself that he did . . . it was all the truth. I tried not to lie to you more than I had to."

"But you talk about this naïve, downtrodden girl I'm supposed to believe you were, and yet you were bold enough to take another woman's name, and to come here, to strangers, and pretend to be her."

"And I was terrified, from the moment I gave her name as mine. But the only way I can explain it is, I was more terrified of going back."

"To this Winterton Hall?"

"Yes. It was awful before, but it was going to be so much worse. They didn't want me there in the first place. They only wanted my father's money. Frederick didn't love me, but being his wife gave me some sort of place there, and that was gone. But most of all, it was about Teddy."

We both glanced at the door of the bedroom where Teddy would be sleeping soundly, curled up against Micke. They were going to miss each other so much.

"I know we moan sometimes when the children are noisy, but, Ruth, can you imagine only being allowed to see Micke and Lena for twenty minutes a day? Being told not to comfort them when they were upset? And then sending them away to school when they were seven, to get trained for a life that meant putting buildings and land and a title over everything, absolutely everything else, and marrying someone they didn't love just to keep the whole stupid nonsense going for another generation? I saw a chance for him—and for me—to escape that life, and I took it."

She sighed. "All right, that part I can try to understand. But how you pretended, for so long . . . is it true you'd never even peeled a potato?"

"I'd never done any of the things Molly would have known how to do. I only knew what she'd have done as a ladies' maid, because I'd always had one. Those first few months, I was sure I'd give myself away."

"Well, you did, to Anna. I can't believe she realized, and I noticed nothing at all. Do you remember, at the dock, when I said how much like Mary you looked? What a fool I was."

"You weren't a fool. You were expecting Molly, and I said I was Molly. And actually, we weren't unalike. She was about my height and build, and we had the same coloring."

"I wish I'd met her."

"You'd have liked her. I thought she was marvelous, right from that moment on the docks at Southampton. She saw an opportunity, and she just grabbed it. Then when I heard about her predicament, and how she'd picked herself up and dared to leave and find a better life for her and her child, I envied her, and I wished I could be like her. When I was scared, when we first came, I used to say to myself, you're Molly now, and Molly would be brave."

Ruth looked down at the table, tracing circles with her finger, the way I'd seen her do so often. "You'll write and let us know you're all settled, won't you?"

"If you want me to."

She rolled her eyes. "Of course I do. I know I've said some horrible things to you, these past few days—"

"You had every right to."

"Yes, I did. But I've been thinking, about what you said. And you were right. In your place, I might have done the same, if I'd been brave enough."

"It was Molly who made me brave enough. Like I said, I borrowed her courage as well as her name."

She gave a quiet little laugh. "Well, you won't need to do that now."

"What do you mean?"

"You're not Molly. You never were. And yet you made this mad idea work and you made a life for yourself and Teddy here. Yes, we helped you out in the beginning, but you learned to make those blasted shirtwaists even though you'd never lifted a finger in your life, and then getting the cart and making it work, that was all you. And you made yourself a part of this family, who—" Her voice wobbled. "Who we all came to love. You, not Molly. And I'm going to miss you so much."

We had a little cry together, the tears wiped away with a laugh when Ruth said, "Swedish women would never cry like babies," and then she went back to bed. I was about to lie down and try to sleep too, but instead I took out the newspaper again and looked at the photo of Lissy. She stood there, her lovely face framed by a pretty straw hat trimmed with rosebuds—perhaps the very one they were shopping for at Macy's that day—smiling at the photographer as if she didn't have a care in the world. And here was I, trapped like a fly in a spider's web. Jumping at every footstep on the stairs, terrified that at any moment, my son would be taken from me. Frightened and powerless, just like I'd been at Winterton Hall.

But Ruth was right: it wasn't Molly who took a risk to find a new life for myself and my son; it was me. It was me who did things and learned things that I never expected to. It was me who worked hard to build that new life for us, a life I loved, and Teddy loved too. And now I had a choice. I could run away and let it all be taken away from us, like the girl I used to be, or I could take a risk, and fight back.

I read the newspaper story again. The ball was in two days' time. Quite likely she'd be sailing back to England straight afterward. If I was going to fight back, I couldn't afford to wait.

CHAPTER 57

The Biltmore Hotel was vast, stretching across an entire block and eleven stories up into the sky. I walked toward the entrance, in an outfit borrowed from Erin downstairs, though I'd stuck with my own shoes, just in case I had to run. Shoppers were strolling along Broadway, carefree as mayflies, but my stomach was churning and my legs felt weak. Even when the plan came to me in the small hours of the night, it had plainly been risky, but now, out in the morning sunshine, it looked very close to crazy. I'd spent four days in hiding, terrified of every footstep on the stairs, longing for the moment when we could escape, and now here I was, about to walk into the hotel where Lissy was staying and confront her.

Right now, she couldn't know for sure that I was alive. She couldn't possibly have been certain, in that split second, that it was me she saw, and if she wasn't certain, Lord and Lady Storton couldn't be either. Their detective had been sniffing around, but he hadn't found me yet, and until he did, it was just as likely—more likely, really—that Lissy had only glimpsed someone who looked like me. But once I walked into that hotel and showed myself, there'd be no going back, and if it went wrong . . .

My footsteps slowed. Was I really going to take the risk? There was still time to run. Stick to the original plan, get on that train to Minnesota. We had a place to stay there; I'd have work. Couldn't that be enough?

No. No, it could not! Teddy was happy and loved here, and so was I. If there was a chance we could stay, I had to take it. I'd let them beat me once before, but I'd worked too hard and learned too much to let them do it again without putting up a fight. I reminded myself of Anna's words at Coney Island, words she'd repeated to me before I left the apartment that morning.

You are a strong young woman; you don't run from things that frighten you.

Squaring my shoulders, I walked up the steps, giving the doorman a nod as if I breezed in and out of the city's grandest hotels all the time. At the reception desk, I left the anonymous note I'd brought with me, saying I had information about the whereabouts of Elinor Coombes, and asked for it to be delivered to Alicia Harcourt's room. The concierge glanced at cubbyholes full of keys behind him before he handed the note to a lobby boy to take. She was in, then. In a few minutes' time, she'd know she'd been right about seeing me. I'd set the thing in motion now, and there was no going back.

Affecting a casual attitude as if I was meeting a friend for coffee, I strolled into the ladies' lounge, where I'd said in the note I'd be waiting. Heart hammering, I chose a table tucked away to one side, where I could see the door but not immediately be seen. She'd come when she read the note, I was certain of that, but I needed her to come alone. If Lady Harcourt was with her, the whole plan would fall apart, and I'd have to get myself out of there without them seeing me. Then run.

As I hoped, most of the tables were taken: mothers and

daughters sipping coffee, a group of well-dressed ladies chatting, a handful of women on their own, reading or writing letters, the hum of conversation and spoons tinkling on porcelain just loud enough to make our conversation inaudible to anyone else. I quickly mapped out an exit route—turn my back to the entrance, thread through the tables as if I'd spotted an acquaintance, and out the door—then sat perched on the edge of the chair, ready to move if I saw two women and not one. My eyes kept flicking to the ornate gilt clock on the wall as I waited, my face tight with the effort of looking calm and unconcerned. For goodness' sake, how long could it take her to read a two-sentence note and come downstairs?

Then there she was, in the doorway. She must have left the room in a hurry; a lock of copper hair was hanging down at the back, a hairpin dangling from it. As she looked around, I went to stand and say her name, but stopped myself just in time. She wasn't alone.

I didn't recognize the woman beside her, but whoever she was, I couldn't risk two people seeing me. It was all over, and I had to get out of there right now. Head down, I stood and turned to sidle out using the route I'd plotted, but as I did, a waiter passed in front of me with a tray of coffee cups and stopped beside the next table, blocking my way. Panicked, I tried to dodge past him but one of the women at the table had her chair pulled too far out, and I couldn't get through.

"Excuse me," I said. "Can I just get past you?"

She huffed and puffed and moved her chair a tiny bit.

"Please," I said. "Can you move? I'm in a hurry."

She tutted and moved a fraction more. I squeezed past, head down.

Get out now, before she sees you.

Too late.

"Elinor?"

It's so automatic, turning when someone calls your name,

and in my panic, I did. And what I saw was that she was alone. The other woman was hurrying across the room, waving to someone in the far corner. They hadn't been together at all; they'd just walked in at the same time. The plan was still on.

I took a deep breath and said, "Hello, Lissy."

She gasped, her hand at her mouth. "Elinor! It *was* you! . . ." She stepped forward, her arms open. "Oh my goodness, we thought you were dead."

I took a step back and forced my voice to sound calm. "Well, as you can see, I'm not."

"I can't take this in . . . What happened? Where have you been?"

"I've been here, in New York."

"What are you talking about? Where? How?"

"Let's sit down, and I'll tell you."

We sat opposite each other, just as we used to in the tea room at Fortnum's when we went shopping together. It felt like another lifetime, that. She glanced at my hat and coat. They might be the latest style, but Lissy would spot in a second that I wasn't being dressed by French designers anymore.

"What on earth is going on?" she said. "Why were you listed as missing? Is Teddy—?"

"He's alive, yes. I gave a false name when we left the ship, so we could stay in America. I had a chance to make a different life for us, and I took it."

She stared at me for a moment, and then shook her head as though she wasn't sure she'd heard right. "You can't mean . . . I thought perhaps you'd lost your memory—one reads about that happening—or you were ill again, in your mind. You're not saying you deliberately let everyone think you and Teddy were dead?"

"Yes, I am."

"Why? Why on earth would you do that?"

"You wouldn't understand if I told you, and I haven't come here to explain myself to you. I've come because I need you to do something for me." Her eyes widened as I went on. "Elinor Coombes is dead. So you're going to tell Lord and Lady Storton that you didn't see her after all. You saw someone you thought looked a bit like her, but you've seen that woman again, and you realize now that you were mistaken."

Complete incomprehension on her face; I could have been speaking Greek. "What on earth are you talking about? I can't pretend I haven't seen you!"

"Yes, you can. Because if you don't, they'll come after me and they'll take Teddy away."

Look them in the eye and smile when you name your price.

"And if they do that, I will come back to England, and I'll tell everyone about you and Frederick."

I'd wondered, back then, if she'd ever suspected that I knew. But the shock in her eyes told its own story.

"Elinor, I—"

"Please don't insult me by denying it. I was gullible back then, but I'm not now. I know all about your affair, and if Teddy is taken from me, I'll make sure everyone else knows too. I'll even go to the press if I have to. The gossip columnists will lap it up."

"You can't mean that." She reached for my hand on the table, but I pulled it away. "Look," she said, "I understand you being angry with me. But Teddy is the heir to Winterton. That's where he belongs. You can't seriously expect me not to tell Lord and Lady Storton that he's alive?"

"That's exactly what I expect. And I've just given you a reason not to."

"They've been through hell. We had a funeral for you, all three of you. There's a gravestone in the churchyard with your names on it. The press were like ghouls, writing about it."

Hold your nerve once the bargaining starts.

"I'm sorry that I put them through that. But I'm not sorry we stayed, and we're not going back."

"Have you actually gone mad?" She spoke slowly, as if to an idiot. "Without Teddy, when Lord Storton dies, the title disappears. Six hundred years of history, gone forever. That alone has broken their hearts, and then there's the estate—Lord Storton's had to make a will leaving it to Kitty, and if she inherits, it wouldn't be Coombes land anymore. But if Teddy's alive, that changes everything."

She leaned forward. "Look, we can say you were ill, or something, but you've got to come back. You can't possibly imagine I'm going to let them carry on thinking Teddy's dead. It's unthinkable."

I recognized that tone. They all had it, her and George and all Frederick's family. It was the one Frederick used to tell me that we'd have to make the best of the marriage he'd tricked me into, and the one Lady Storton always employed to say that a conversation was over and nothing I had to say mattered. Here I was, threatening to expose their affair to the world, and with that unshakeable confidence they all seemed to have been born with, Lissy was blithely assuming that I wouldn't do it. Just like Frederick did on the ship. Certain that I'd see that their way was the only way, and give Teddy back to them. And if I couldn't convince her, I'd lost. They'd find us and take Teddy and then what use was it to me to ruin her?

As if she'd read my mind, she said, "I know you don't mean these silly threats. We'll forget all about them, I promise. Let's go and fetch Teddy now, and then we'll get you a room here till we go home."

She stood and looked at me, expectantly. "Elinor?"

There had to be something else I could say. Something that would frighten her like she was frightening me. I looked up at her, and I thought, *What would be the worst thing I could say to you? What's more important to you—to all of you—than anything else?*

"You told me once," I said, "that we had a responsibility to future generations to keep the line going. Well, here's why you need to do what I'm asking you to. I won't only be telling everyone about your affair. I'll tell them that Frederick might very well have fathered your sons."

It was a bluff, of course. I knew she'd promised George that she'd stay out of Frederick's bed until they had an heir. I was counting on her realizing that even the suspicion that she hadn't would be enough to cause a scandal she'd never recover from. But as what I thought was a lie came out of my mouth, the color drained from her face. And for once, that face told the truth.

How I hid my shock, I'll never know, but in that moment I must have, because she sat back down and said, very quietly, "How did you know? Freddie swore he'd never tell anyone."

I smiled. I couldn't help it.

Don't miss the moment when you've got them where you want them.

"I didn't know. But I do now. And I'll use it if I have to. You know, George told me he was too embarrassed to call off the wedding and let the world know the truth about you—"

Her hand flew to her mouth.

". . . but if he, and his family, were to find out that the boys might not be his, we both know it would be a different story. He'd have no difficulty getting a divorce."

"George wouldn't divorce me!"

I shrugged. "Maybe not. But can you be sure? And you know, even if he didn't, I don't think that nice life you have at Bellingham Hall will be quite so nice once they all know the truth, do you? So it really is best all round if you do what I'm asking you to, and tell Lord and Lady Storton that it wasn't me you saw. And then go home and get on with that nice life."

She looked down at her hands, twisting her engagement

ring from side to side. Then she sighed, looked up, and said, "I don't need to tell them that."

"Yes, you do, because if you don't—"

"I don't need to tell them, because they don't know yet that I saw you."

"But they sent a private detective to find me."

"*I* engaged him. It seemed so impossible that I'd seen you, that you were still alive, and I didn't want to get their hopes up without being certain."

I have to admit that was a relief. I'd no love for Lord and Lady Storton, but I wasn't heartless. I'd had to steel myself to go ahead with the plan knowing how they'd feel when their hopes came to nothing.

"Well, that makes it easier, then, doesn't it?" I said.

"But you're doing wrong by Teddy, keeping him from his birthright! He's Frederick's son. His rightful place is at Winterton Hall."

"His rightful place is with me. He's happy here, and he'll be able to make a decent life for himself when he grows up. All I'm keeping him from is a family who put buildings and land and titles before everything else. I don't want him to end up like his father, loving someone he couldn't marry and marrying someone he couldn't love. And not caring who got hurt in the process."

"Frederick never meant to hurt you. And nor did I."

"Well, you both did a good job of it anyway. And if anything, you hurt me more than he did. I learned early on that Frederick didn't love me—he told me that himself—but you pretended to be my friend right to the end."

"I wasn't pretending, Elinor. I loved you like a sister!"

Same old Lissy, convinced her charm would work, even after all we'd just said.

"I've never had a sister, Lissy, but I've learned what a good friend looks like. And you were not a friend to me."

She opened her mouth to reply, but shrugged, like a petulant child. And then, very softly, she said, "Do you know what it was like for me to stand in that church and watch him marry you? To know it would be you who had his name, when I loved him so much? And even when he died, I couldn't mourn him properly. I'd lost the love of my life, and I had to pretend he was just a family friend."

I could have said a lot of things in answer to that, none of them kind. But I remembered that last night on the ship, and the sadness in Frederick's voice when he talked about her. The whole horrible mess hadn't made anyone happy.

"On the night he died," I said, "he spoke about you. He said he'd loved you for as long as he could remember, and he always would."

Her eyes filled with tears. She pulled out a handkerchief, releasing the smell of roses in full bloom.

"Thank you," she said, dabbing delicately at that beautiful face. "I know you didn't have to tell me that."

"Consider it a parting gift," I said. "And just so we understand each other—you keep my secret and I'll keep yours. But if you don't, I'll create such a scandal that you will never be able to show your face in polite society again."

A waiter came over, a silver tray balanced on his hand. "May I get you anything, ladies?"

"No, thank you," I said. "I'm just leaving."

I stood up. "So, are we agreed? That Elinor Coombes is dead?"

She nodded.

"Good," I said. "Goodbye, Lissy."

I looked up at the clock in the lobby as I left. Less than an hour had passed since I arrived, but everything had changed. We were free. We could stay in New York, keep the life we'd made. I'd been so frightened, seeing Lissy step out of the cab that day, but if I hadn't, I'd still be lying to the people I'd come to think of as my family. Still running the risk that if they found out who I really was, my new life would collapse around my ears. Now all that was behind me. Behind us.

How ironic that what really saved us was Lissy's own broken promise to George. From the look on her face when I said it, she must be fairly sure that Frederick was the twins' father, even if she couldn't know for certain. And I was surprised to find that I was glad for her, that in the boys, she still had something of Frederick. She really had loved him, and he her. What a waste.

It wasn't far to Grand Central Terminal, but I ran anyway. And there they were, under the clock, Ruth holding Teddy by the hand. Waiting by the platform for the train to Taylors Falls, as we'd agreed that morning. Just in case I hadn't won and we needed to run.

I picked him up and hugged him to me.

"You did it," said Ruth, wrapping her arms round both of us. "You did it!"

Teddy said, "Are we going on the train now, Mama?"

"No," I said. "We're going home."

CHAPTER 58

For a long time, I avoided the *Titanic* memorial, the one that had been paid for by millionaires' checks and schoolchildren's pocket money. But on the fifth anniversary of the sinking, I went to see it. It was a lighthouse, set on top of the Seamen's Church Institute, a red-brick building thirteen stories high and looking out over the harbor. I stood in the street, as people rushed past, and looked up at it, remembering that night. Five years, and my memories were as clear as ever.

I thought of Frederick, who should have married Lissy and been happy and never set foot on that ship. I thought of Molly, who would have loved New York. And I thought of my father, who'd given me so much more of himself than he would ever know. I took one last look up and said a silent goodbye to all of them.

Then I walked back across the bridge to Brooklyn, to the apartment building we'd moved to the year before, across the hall from Ruth, Per, Anna, and the children. Our apartments were still small, but Teddy and I each had a bedroom now—and beds! No more stinking outhouse either: we had running water and shared a bathroom. Very luxurious, after our Sunday trips to the bathhouse, and it was only occasionally, on a cold winter morning, that I had a wistful memory of soaking in the hot, scented baths Rose used to run for me while my towel warmed on a big iron radiator.

Now and then, I wondered how Kitty was getting on with running the estate. Now that she was in line to inherit it, I'd no doubt she and Mr. Bannerman would have moved back to Winterton, and she'd be working alongside Lord Storton already. Very likely making a better job of it than her father and brother ever did. I hoped Lord and Lady Storton were at peace with the situation. Perhaps Kitty had a son of her own by now, and surely then they'd see that the estate was still in the family, even if the name was different? I doubted they'd ever come to terms with losing the title, but when I thought of them making the guardianship agreement over my head, I couldn't drum up too much sympathy over that.

But mostly, I didn't think about my old life. I was too busy: a small shop had become vacant nearby, and we'd worked out that if I could negotiate the rent down a little, Ruth and I could afford to retire the carts and take it on. I hadn't told her that some of the money for the stock we were buying had come, eighteen months earlier, in an envelope postmarked from a town in Nebraska. Double the amount that I'd given Tommy Jenkins, with a note saying:

Returned with interest. Thank you.

Back across the bridge, I stopped at the bookshop on the corner to buy a book for myself and one for Teddy. The owner was unpacking boxes in the back, and waved a hello as I came in. I went into the shop so often that he knew my name and would sometimes keep aside a new book he thought I'd like, and he'd been right every time. When I called in the previous week,

Ruth was with me, and by the time I'd chosen a book from the shelves, she'd managed to ascertain that he was a widower with a daughter a year older than Teddy.

"And he's got a twinkle in his eye for you," she said as we walked home.

I laughed it off, but it surprised me to find I didn't mind the idea. Time would tell if she was right, or if he was just being nice because I was a good customer; when we moved to Brooklyn, Per built me a set of bookshelves for the new apartment, and I'd been steadily replacing all my old favorites. *Jane Eyre* was there, *Great Expectations*, *Under the Greenwood Tree*, *Middlemarch*, *North and South*, all the Jane Austens, even *Lady Susan*. But alongside them stood lots of new books. New stories that didn't always have a wedding on the last page. Because I'd learned, by then, that there's more than one kind of happy ending.

Advertisement from the *New York Sentinel*, March 13, 1951

OPENING TODAY:
MORTIMER'S ON SIXTH AVENUE

New York city's newest department store, with three floors
of merchandise, "Anna's café" serving coffee and cake, and
an extensive lending library in the basement. Owner Teddy
Mortimer promises to continue the personal service, quality
goods, and reasonable prices that have long brought loyal
shoppers to his six clothing stores across the city.
Don't miss the opening-day offers!

ACKNOWLEDGMENTS

When you write historical fiction, there's always a lot of re-search to do, and no matter how many books you read and websites you comb, every book throws out some little extra questions that need expert help. Twitter (I will never call it X, what a stupid name!) has saved me many times before, helping me find just the right person to ask, and it was kind to me again with this one. Thank you to Timothy Clarke, for information on how entails work, and whether the arrangements I wanted to give the Winterton estate were feasible; to @Ipsedixitissim, for helping me work out Elinor/Molly's travel arrangements to Minnesota; and to Lucy Jane Santos, for information on early radium treatment for cancer, which I ended up not needing when the plot changed between drafts, but was so interesting that I might well keep it for another book. Any mistakes or slight tweaks to reality for plot purposes are, of course, mine.

Thank you to my longtime writing buddies, Kate Clarke and Lucy Barker, who, despite very busy lives, are always generous with their time and their ideas, and have dug me out of many a plot hole. Thanks too to my friends in the D20 Authors, a group of writers who, like me, survived the weird experience of hav-ing their first books published when bookshops were closed during the Covid lockdowns. They've been an amazing source of support, inspiration, and advice ever since. Special thanks this time to D20's Caroline Bishop, for helping me figure out the ending; to Louise Fein, for a lightbulb moment that changed *everything*; to Charlotte Levin, for a last minute injection of suspense; to Matson Taylor, for suggesting the biography of Mary Quant that gave me the idea for Elinor/Molly's pushcart merchandise; and most of all to Nicola Gill, for plot clinics, pep talks, and believing in this book from start to finish. Not forgetting Polly Crosby, Zoe Somerville, and Louise Fein again, for great company and brilliant brainstorming on the writers' retreat in Norfolk where the last few chapters were written.

As always, thank you to my inspirational agent, Alice Lutyens, for good advice, great ideas, and for being the sort of perfect cross between a cheerleader and a Rottweiler that any author is lucky to have. Thanks of course to my super-talented U.K. editor, Clare Hey, who with one sentence summed up what was wrong with the first draft and how to fix it. (The sentence was "Reverse the arc," if you were wondering, and it was genius.) Thanks too to the team at Simon & Schuster, especially Judith Long, Jess Barratt, and Rich Hawton.

This is the first of my books to be published in America, and I've loved working with the team at Ballantine Books, getting childishly excited when emails arrived at weird hours because of the time difference, and picturing the daytime buzz of New York City while we in Brighton were getting ready for bed. Thanks go especially to my sharp-eyed and wise U.S. editor, Susanna Porter, and her assistant, Anusha Khan, for all their help with preparing the U.S. edition; Belina Huey, for the beautiful cover; and Elizabeth Eno, for the page design.

One of the very best things about having your books published is hearing from readers who've enjoyed them. Thank you so much to all the readers who've said lovely things about my first two books, *The Smallest Man* and *That Bonesetter Woman*, on Twitter, Instagram, and Facebook. So often one of those messages would pop up just when I was wrestling with some tricky bit of this book, and it was just what I needed that day to help me crack on. Sometimes people tell me they don't know if it's silly to contact an author to say they like their book—it never is! We're praise junkies, so if you've liked a book (not just mine), do let the author know—you might just turn a bad writing day into a good one. You can find me on Twitter, Instagram, or Facebook.

Last but never least, thanks to my husband, Mike Jeffree, and the cats, Nalle, Siggi, and Freya, for their patience while we shared our home with yet another set of imaginary people.

FRANCES QUINN grew up in London and studied English at King's College, Cambridge. She became a journalist, writing for magazines including *Prima*, *Good Housekeeping*, *She*, *Woman's Weekly*, and *Ideal Home*, and later branched out into copywriting. Upon winning a place on the Curtis Brown Creative novel writing course, she started work on her first novel, *The Smallest Man*. Her second novel is *That Bonesetter Woman*, and *The Lost Passenger* is her third. She lives in Brighton, England, with her husband and three Tonkinese cats.

X: @franquinn
IG: @franquinn21
Facebook.com/AuthorFrancesQuinn